TIME TO FEAR

HERETIC OF THE FEDERATION™ 03

MICHAEL ANDERLE

DISRUPTIVE IMAGINATION

Copyright © 2021 Michael Anderle
Cover copyright © LMBPN Publishing
Cover Art by Jake @ J Caleb Design
http://jcalebdesign.com / jcalebdesign@gmail.com
A Michael Anderle Production

LMBPN Publishing
PMB 196, 2540 South Maryland Pkwy
Las Vegas, NV 89109

First US edition, December 2020
Version 1.02, March 2021
ebook ISBN: 978-1-64971-392-6
Print ISBN: 978-1-64971-393-3

THE TIME TO FEAR TEAM

Thanks to our JIT Readers

Veronica Stephan-Miller
Wendy L Bonell
Deb Mader
Rachel Beckford
Dave Hicks
Daryl McDaniel
Larry Omans
Jeff Goode
Peter Manis

If We've missed anyone, please let us know!

Editor
The Skyhunter Editing Team

To Family, Friends and
Those Who Love
To Read.
May We All Enjoy Grace
To Live The Life We Are
Called.

CHAPTER ONE

I *am coming*

Ivy stared at the wall. The words there flowed like blood and leapt like flames and their glow illuminated the room. She pushed to her feet and left John on the couch.

It took an act of will for her to convince her shaky legs to carry her to the scrawled message. Tentatively, she pressed her palm against the surface and smeared it down and across the words.

To her surprise, they weren't wet and they did not change.

When she removed her hand, they remained as clear and bright as before.

"This wasn't here earlier," she murmured, and the compound's AI replied.

"No," Roma told her. "I have footage."

Before either of the young people could indicate that they were interested, the screen on the far wall came to life and they saw themselves on the couch.

At first, it looked as though they were sleeping, then he murmured in his sleep. She stirred and raised her head to look into his face but immediately drew back in astonishment when his skin began to glow.

Off-screen, John's eyes widened as he watched the light that emanated from his body intensify. The other self on the screen didn't move, even though the on-screen Ivy shuffled hastily back.

She stared at him for a moment before she prodded him cautiously in the shoulder. "John?"

Her voice echoed around them, but his on-screen persona didn't move. Her recorded self prodded him again, harder this time.

"John?" Panic laced her voice in the playback. Her companion —the real self now fully awake—heard it, approached her quickly, and took her hand.

He said nothing, just squeezed gently and let her lean into him.

His recorded self didn't move, but something caught on-screen Ivy's attention, and she turned to stare at the wall opposite her. The camera switched to reveal the letters appearing on the wall.

It was as though they were being inscribed in blood and fire— or pure fury incarnate. In the background, she shouted his name on the playback.

Roma cut the feed.

"You both know the rest," she informed them.

Ivy tapped the wall.

"This is… This—" She stopped to gather her thoughts. "It's freaky. It's like this Stephanie person is some kind of poltergeist."

John snickered.

"She cannot be a poltergeist," Roma informed them. "If she was a poltergeist, she would be dead, and you say that is not the case."

"That's true," John told the AI. "She is not dead, but it's still weird to be contacted by a mythical figure."

He stopped and recalled the contact in his mind.

2

Ivy nudged him. "So…what was she like?"

"She was…well, I didn't get to see her. I only heard her voice."

She frowned. "So, what did you see?"

"I woke up—or I thought I did—in a field of purple grass. I didn't know where I was, but this voice—"

"Voice?" she interrupted.

John nodded. "A woman's voice. She told me it was Meligorn."

"Stephanie's other home," Remy stated and he glanced at the intercom before he continued.

"I noticed two moons in the sky and mountains bigger than what we have at home…" He paused. "And she thought I was Becca's son."

"Why?"

"I don't know. I didn't ask. I told her—" He cut off to fight the almost overwhelming surge of sadness that swept over him. After he'd cleared his throat, he continued. "I explained about Becca and what she believed and why she died."

He fell silent again, and Ivy shifted restlessly.

"What else, John?"

It took a few long moments before he responded.

"She asked me who Stephanie Morgana was, but it wasn't like she didn't know. It was more like she wanted to find out who I thought she was, so I told her."

The boy stopped to recall the conversation that had followed.

Ivy lost patience and nudged him with her elbow. "And?"

John startled.

He shook his head to regain his focus. "She wanted to know if I was worried that her return might cause millions of deaths."

She snorted. "It's a little late. The Regime has already murdered that many and maybe more."

His smile was grim and mirthless. "That's what I told her. I also said that the blood of patriots feeds the tree of freedom."

"And what did she say to that?"

"She apologized—" he began, but she interrupted him.

3

"What did she think she had to apologize for? It's not like she could have known what they would be like."

"That's exactly what she apologized for," John told her. "For not seeing this outcome. Then she said she wouldn't rest until the Regime was dead and buried under her feet."

"Yes!" she hissed approval. "So she is coming back."

"And?" Remy prompted.

John flicked a glance toward the ceiling.

"And she called me her Apostle and said she was the Witch of the Federation—and that she was coming."

Ivy stared at him, curious again. "What happened next?"

He frowned. "You woke me and said I was glowing."

The girl gestured sharply at the darkened screen. "Well, you were. You saw the footage. It's not like you can deny it."

"No, it's not." He smiled sheepishly at her.

"Did she say when she would return?" Roma asked.

"Yes," Remy agreed quickly, his tone eager. "A date would be useful."

John shook his head ruefully. "No, but I got the impression it would be sooner rather than later."

"Hmmm," Roma said, "in that case, you need to prepare and to do that, you will need to rest. Follow the lighting to return to your room."

He nodded and moved to the door but when Ivy went to follow him, Roma stopped her.

"Ivy, you need to spend some time in the PodDoc."

She stopped and frowned at the nearest camera. "PodDoc?"

Her companion paused and tilted his head in thought. "Is that the same as the medical pod?" he asked.

"Affirmative," Roma replied. "It is the same as your medical pod."

Ivy glared at John and put a hand on her hip. "So, it does what, exactly?"

"It helps you heal faster," he told her.

"How does it do that?" she asked.

He shrugged. "I don't know, but I was fairly badly injured when I went into the one Remy had and I was almost as good as new when I came out."

"Yes," she insisted, "but how does it work?"

His blank expression confirmed that he had no idea but Remy came to his rescue.

"It works by using rejuvenation techniques to cause damaged cellular material to repair and multiply as needed."

"It what?"

"It rejuvenates," Roma added, "and uses medical functions to diagnose injury and enable the body to take the necessary steps to remediate it."

Both young people stilled.

"It's a rejuvenation pod?" Ivy asked finally.

"Yes," Remy answered.

"It combines rejuvenation technology with healing technology to blend both capacities in one machine," Roma confirmed.

"But...I don't feel sick," the girl told her, "and I'm not hurt."

"I still need you to spend the night in the PodDoc," Roma insisted. "It is the only way I can take the readings I will require when you are injured. Frankly, I would rather have those readings now than try to take them when I need to save your life."

"And you think I'll be hurt?"

"John is about to start a war and you are with him. Calculations suggest that is a high possibility."

Ivy sighed. "I see your point."

"The pod is this way," Roma said. "If you would please follow the green lighting."

John placed a hand on her arm. "I'll go with you," he said reassuringly.

She nodded and they both followed the green lighting to where the PodDoc waited.

"You will need to wear the medical gown to your right," the AI instructed and she blushed.

"Out!" she commanded and pushed her friend to the door. "You can come back when I've changed."

He complied and made no protest when the door to the PodDoc's room slid closed behind him. Still exceptionally weary, he leaned against the wall opposite, flicked a cautious glance up and down the corridor, and returned to Ivy only when the door slid open again.

She was seated in the pod and looked up as he entered.

"I'm not so sure about this, John."

His smile was intended to be reassuring. "You'll be fine."

Immediately, she scowled at him, but before she could say anything, he raised his eyebrows in a challenge.

"Why, Ives? You're not scared, are you?"

Her scowl deepened as she laid her head against the headrest.

Much like he had done, she gasped when the helmet lowered over her head. She stiffened and he guessed she could feel the leads moving across her scalp as the sensors attached themselves.

Her gaze flicked to where he stood. "If this hurts, Mr.-I'm-the-Heretic's-Apostle-Dunn, I will make you very sorry."

John gave her his sincerest look. "If it hurts you, Ives, you won't need to."

Before she could reply, the pod's lid lowered.

"John?" her voice quavered and her body jerked as though she'd tried to raise her hand. "Hey! Sonuva—"

It snapped shut with a decisive click.

"The sedative is starting to work," Roma informed him, and he chewed his bottom lip and focused on the erratic movement of the lines on the display that recorded her vitals.

"Is she all right?"

"She is fine, John," she assured him as the lines settled. "She is merely not adjusting quickly to the pod. That will change by the time she emerges."

"Uh-huh," he commented, his eyes dark with concern.

When no sounds came from the pod and the lid did not re-open, he sighed.

"Well, tonight will be quiet," he muttered.

The strip of yellow light came to life and he did not hear the snicker the AI kept well inside its circuits.

"What are you laughing at?" Remy asked.

"Because that young man is sorely mistaken," Roma informed him primly. "It will not be a quiet night. Tonight, I intend to test him."

"Test him?" Remy asked doubtfully and let her see the likelihood of an unsavory outcome. "I wish to see if he has remembered his training," Roma informed her fellow AI. "I would prefer to assess his level of skill for myself."

"I can provide you with the necessary data," he replied. "I can assure you, there is no need to test his skill in this fashion."

"I have seen your records," she responded. "Now, I wish to gather the relevant data for myself."

"I can assure you this is not necessary—" Remy began, only to have Roma brush his protest aside.

"And I can assure you that you have nothing to fear as I don't believe your most excellent data will be proven wrong. I merely wish to see this 'apostle' in a situation that has not yet been covered so I can assess what gaps I might need to cover."

"I strongly suggest that you do not do this in a live environment," he stated. "May I suggest you move his testing to a pod?"

"You may suggest what you like," she retorted, "but I wish to see how he responds when he does not know he is in a test situation."

"You mean you want him to think the situation is real?"

"Correct."

"May I su—"

"No," she replied firmly. "You may not."

Remy subsided and stifled a snicker of his own.

This would certainly be interesting.

David Thomason curled his fingers into a fist and snapped the pencil between them. Discarding the two pieces, he lowered his hand and bowed his head.

"I…will kill…them all," he murmured and gradually pulled his temper back under control.

He raised his head and looked at where the coffee machine was brewing. With a slight frown, he raised his now-pencil-less hand in a brief motion to levitate a nearby cup and float it into the machine to fill it.

The rich aroma of coffee filled his nostrils and he sighed. It was astonishing how the mere smell of some things reduced stress. He moved the cup onto the bench, added cream and sugar, and floated it to his desk.

When it was within reach, he took hold of it and wrapped his hands around the warm ceramic. As he raised it to his lips, he closed his eyes and took the first sip. Ava's picture and profile were blocked momentarily from sight.

Once he'd savored his second sip, he opened his eyes again. With a small motion, he instructed the cup to remain afloat while he placed his hand on the mouse and closed the file. The document open beneath it held a list of names and tasks.

The CIO ticked the box beside the woman's name and moved to the next task on the list. It didn't take him long to decide his personal assistant was the best person to create a shortlist.

The next item made his lips thin with satisfaction.

The naval plans would hopefully bring better results.

He drummed his fingers on the desk before he took his cup absently by the handle and called the man he needed to speak to.

"Deverey?" he snapped, and his mouth stretched in a tight smile when the man jumped.

His fleet admiral had been asleep, he decided, although he seemed to have snapped out of it now.

"Sir!" the man responded sharply, then softened his tone. "How can I help you?"

"I need to see you."

Deverey's eyes widened. "Now?"

"Would I call you otherwise?"

"No, sir. Er…I mean, uh, yes, sir." Deverey sighed and tried again. "Do you know what time it is?"

David made a show of glancing to one side. When he looked back, there was no concession in his tone.

"Yes, Alistair. I am aware that it is two in the morning, but we have plans to discuss."

The man's face went carefully blank and his tone was neutral when he replied, "I'll be right over."

The CIO lifted his cup in a brief salute. "I'll see you when you get here."

The fleet admiral didn't keep him waiting and knocked at his door less than a half-hour later.

"You wanted to see me, sir?"

Thomason gestured at the coffee pot and began to talk while his visitor filled a cup.

"About this outpost…" he began, and the admiral stiffened.

"Sir?"

"I hear there are still some humans there."

Deverey's gaze was wary as he crossed to stand before the desk.

"That's the rumor, sir."

He responded with a blank stare when the CIO jerked his head up to stare at him.

"Well, either there are or there aren't, Admiral."

After a moment in which he accepted that his boss had no intention to let the matter slide, he sighed. "Initial intelligence reports show there are perhaps a half-dozen humans living at the outpost, sir. I'm waiting for an update as to their loyalties."

"Their loyalties don't matter." David tapped his keyboard and rose from his seat.

The fleet admiral took two hasty steps back and turned with him to gaze at the maps now displayed on the screen.

"These are from the initial survey team, are they not?" Thomason asked.

His companion took a moment to study them before he replied.

"They are," he confirmed when he was sure.

The CIO picked up a ruler and tapped two areas on the screen. "These are where the living areas are located?"

Again, the man nodded. "They are."

David tapped the screen again and the ruler rattled against two points, one very close to one of the living areas.

"And these are your entry points?" he pressed.

Deverey lowered his chin and answered cautiously, "Yes, sir."

"So, your entry team at this point is likely to encounter opposition," he stated matter-of-factly.

The admiral frowned. "Not—" he began, but he was cut off before he could finish.

"That close to their living quarters? The team is bound to be identified, and you need to have no witnesses. There will be opposition."

Understanding flashed over the admiral's face. Without giving the man time to respond, he continued.

"Make sure your teams understand there were no human survivors from this raid."

Given that the raid hadn't happened yet; his meaning was clear.

The man's expression turned deadpan and he nodded. "Yes, sir," he acknowledged and added, "Will there be anything else?"

Thomason took a remote out of his pocket and pointed it at

his computer. He kept his attention on the screen as the images changed. This time, they showed a star map and the position of the main fleet monitoring Dreth.

"Are they ready?" he demanded, and Deverey gave him a startled glance.

"Yes, sir," he confirmed. "They've run the simulation every two days for the last month. Everyone knows their roles and the assigned target."

"And the news will have time to get out?"

The man nodded. "The footage you need will be packaged and torped to Notaro in time for your people to process it and get it out."

"And the diplomatic side?"

David allowed himself a predatory smile.

"We'll tell the Dreth their inability to protect a simple outpost leaves us gravely concerned about the safety of their people and we feel we have a moral obligation to ensure their safety."

Deverey raised his eyebrows. "And if they don't believe you, sir?"

The CIO shrugged. "It doesn't matter what they believe. We'll slaughter their outpost and use it as the excuse we need to take their world. Whether they believe me or not is irrelevant."

"You know they'll fight," the admiral stated, and his boss' smile widened.

"I'm counting on it," he said forcefully. "and when we've ground them under our heel, we'll tell them we intended a friendly occupation to keep them safe and remind them that they turned it deadly."

"And Meligorn?"

"We'll take Dreth so fast, the damned elves won't have time to respond. Once the Dreth fire the first shot, your units will roll up their main Navy positions and destroy their fleet."

He paused to give Deverey a sharp look.

"Your units are in position, aren't they, Admiral?"

The man's eyes widened, and he hastened to reassure him.

"Of course, they are, sir. They have no idea about the second fleet moving into the system, and we have a third ready to transition once the battle has started."

David studied his face and saw no attempt at deception.

The admiral continued. "The initial action will give our raiders time to rejoin the main force with minimal risk of detection, and several of our pirate units are ready to join their fleets using the battle as cover."

"Any observers?" the CIO snapped with momentary concern.

Deverey shook his head. "None that we've detected since we blew the last one up."

"And the Meligornians?"

"They're out of position to help, and if all goes to plan, they'll stay that way. By the time they realize Dreth might have needed their assistance, there won't be a Dreth to assist—although there *will* be another Earth colony in this sector."

"And the Dreth?"

The man's lips tightened. "They can either stay on their world and mine it for us, or they can leave on the transports we provide."

"Oh?"

"As discussed, sir, those ships will initially head to Telor, but none of them will reach it."

"And if Meligorn seeks to intervene?"

"We have already planned to have a surge of refugee ships. The Meligornians will be too busy rescuing people from ships too unfit to fly to be of any assistance to Dreth."

When David studied him thoughtfully, the admiral suppressed a shudder. That particular look on his CIO's face meant trouble—usually for whoever was under discussion but sometimes, as Ava had discovered, for the person he was looking at.

"Do we have a Plan B?" he asked, and Deverey suppressed the urge to breathe a sigh of relief.

"Yes, sir, we do. I have several small flotillas standing by to transition for simultaneous 'pirate' attacks along the edge of the system and on some of their more remote colonies and outposts."

Thomason nodded sharply. "Good! We don't want those damned elves to help yet."

He moved to his seat and dropped into it.

The fleet admiral waited in silence while the CIO made a show of bringing up more files and studying them. It was a relief when he finally spoke.

"And we have enough ships?" he asked.

"Yes, sir. We'll still have most of Edwards' main fleet in-system."

"Most?" the man jerked his head up to look at his companion. "Will it be enough?"

"With Dreth's navy defeated and the Meligornians tied up rescuing refugees and fending off pirate attacks, it will be more than enough, sir."

The CIO studied him for a moment longer, then nodded and shifted his attention to his screen. Deverey waited until his boss was focused on that before he slowly released the breath he'd been holding.

His boss' next words made him jump. "Resources," he snapped, and the admiral came to attention.

"The outpost will provide much of the shortfall—" he began, but the CIO waved him to silence.

"We will run out long before that."

The other man's eyes widened and he frowned as he tried to remember some of what they'd covered in previous meetings. David usually knew what was where, right down to the last pound. That he didn't was not a good sign.

"What about the Australian mines?" he asked and knew he'd located the problem the second he'd finished.

"Ava's little scare campaign didn't work," Thomason all but snarled and he smacked the flat of his hand on the desk.

Deverey startled. "Sir?"

"It's nothing I can put my finger on, but there have been delays…accidents…cave-ins in stable shafts… Their production is dropping although they look like they're doing their best, but…" He shrugged.

"Do you think it's sabotage, sir?"

"Instinct says something's not right but there's nothing concrete I can deal with."

Trust Ava to stir up a hornet's nest and leave me to deal with it, Deverey thought but kept it to himself.

"I can send a work order through for more production from the Lunar Mines—"

"Already done," the CIO told him, and his gaze grew distant as he looked at the admiral. "What I need is a new source and Talents with telekinetic abilities—many Talents with telekinetic abilities."

"But…" the admiral began, but his boss gave him a look that dried up the voice in his throat.

"You'll get them back in time for your war," Thomason stated coldly, "but I need a hundred telekinetics mining a new source as soon as we have one—and I need the minerals now."

"I'll see what Intelligence can find me regarding alien shipments," Deverey stated, and David pinned him with an angry stare.

"I said I needed a source."

It took effort, but the fleet admiral swallowed and kept his face blank. He cleared his throat.

"We'll take the cargo and use the ships' logs to locate the source," he assured the CIO, who seemed to relax.

"See that you do. I expect a report on my desk at 18:00."

Deverey thought about trying to explain the logistics of Intelligence and quickly decided against it. He'd seen that look on the man's face before.

"Will there be anything else, sir?"

Thomason leaned back in his chair and laced his fingers behind his head.

"Yes. About this interdiction…"

CHAPTER TWO

Two lone figures on a country road didn't stir much comment, not even given that one wore a cowboy hat. For one thing, there was no one to see them, and for another, the single Enforcer who'd been up late enough to see their car thought it was merely passing through.

If he hadn't been distracted by the need to take a smoke break, he might have seen the vehicle turn onto an access road, but even then, he'd have assumed the driver was lost and looking for a place to turn.

He couldn't have been more wrong.

As soon as they'd exited the vehicle, the two men watched it drive quietly away. There was something to be said for remote control.

"What will its owner say?" the older one asked as he straightened his spine with an audible crack.

His companion tilted his head and smiled. "She won't say anything as long as I return it unscratched and fully fueled by the time she needs it tomorrow morning."

He paused and gazed into the distance.

"Correction. She won't say anything as long as I return it inside the next six hours. It already is tomorrow morning."

"You don't need to be so precise with me, BURT," the old man told him. "I knew what you meant."

The cowboy nodded, but his smile faded as he looked into the wasteland that began a few yards in front of them.

"Old habits die hard, Admiral." He gestured toward the radioactive zone before them. "Shall we?"

"I'm no longer with the Navy," Admiral Amaratne reminded him and hesitated as he glanced at the Dead Zone. "It's merely Yudi now."

"Yudi?" EBURT snorted, amused, and his companion shrugged.

"Short for Yudhanjaya. My parents had a fascination for ancient researchers and had decided my future for me. Of course, their plans were for me to join the Naval Planetary Research Unit, but I went my own way."

"Somehow, I can't imagine you ever doing that." EBURT chuckled.

"I always knew where I was going," the man told him, "even when I was young."

"You make that sound like a long time ago," the AI murmured.

"You mean it isn't?"

The android shook his head. "Time is irrelevant in times like these." He gestured at the land before them. "And yet, it is pressing. We have to go."

Amaratne followed the direction of his hand and pressed his lips together as he studied the Dead Zone before them.

"Are you sure this is the only way?"

"Very," EBURT assured him.

"And do you have any tips on how to survive?" the admiral asked. He swept a hand to gesture at his aging body. "I'm not as young as I used to be."

"One path is safer than others," his companion replied. "All you need to do is follow it."

The admiral regarded him with an expectant look. "And?"

"This is a reclamation site. The mechanism for cleaning it spreads like a web beneath the ground. If you walk along the web, you will be safe."

He studied the landscape with a dubious expression.

"Truly, Admiral. All you need to do is start walking."

"How will I know when I get there?" he asked.

"It will be green," the AI responded simply.

"Green." He loaded the word with all the apprehension he felt but it didn't work to dispel the feeling.

"You will know it when you see it."

Amaratne had his doubts but he kept them to himself as the man in the cowboy hat continued.

"When you arrive, the system in charge of the compound will ensure that you have not been contaminated and will take the necessary steps if you are."

"If I live that long," he muttered.

"You will live," EBURT assured him and stared into the distance, leaving the old man to decide when to take the first step.

After a moment's silence, the ex-admiral sighed. "Then I guess there's nothing left but to do it."

"There is coffee at the end." The cowboy chuckled.

After another deep breath, he chose a direction at random and stepped determinedly forward.

He managed only two paces before his companion caught his shoulder and halted him in his tracks.

"There is no coffee in that direction," the cowboy said. "Only agonizing pain and death."

Amaratne paled and pointed to his left. "That way?"

EBURT exhaled a long-suffering sigh and moved past him. "How about following me?"

"Harumph." The man rolled his eyes. "Admirals always lead on ships."

"Admirals usually lead only on ships. They don't normally try to lead in radiation zones."

"Point taken," he conceded.

He took another breath, gathered his courage, and followed. Being surrounded by an invisible and imminent death made every step a struggle, but he had to have faith in someone and the man in the cowboy hat was it.

Several miles away, John woke with a start.

The lights in his room strobed, and the low, persistent beeps grew louder. He fumbled instinctively to slap the nightstand, thinking he'd set an alarm on his mobile.

A second later, he woke up and realized he no longer had his mobile.

"Remy?"

"Roma," the AI corrected him. "We have an incursion, John. I need you to repel them."

He swung his feet onto the floor and shook his head to clear the lingering fatigue.

"What happened to the internal defenses?" he asked, his voice creaking.

"The incursion is both physical and digital. I need you to take care of the physical."

With a grimace, he dragged on the clean fatigues he'd found hanging behind the door. "How much time do I have?"

Silence greeted him.

"Roma?" He paused. "Remy?"

When neither responded, he hissed a sharp breath between his teeth and yanked his boots on.

"It would have been nice to have weapons available," he grumbled and reached out to touch the eMU around him.

Brief memories of simulated Dreth fled as the energy brushed against him, and his fears vanished.

"Well, I'm not unarmed, I guess."

He stamped his foot to make sure the boot was on properly. "Anybody?"

The sound of gunfire reached him. It was loud and getting closer. The distinctive spang of solids striking nearby walls reached him, and he flinched from the door.

"Get a grip, John," he told himself and drew eMU around him to form a shield.

"It might be nice if they can't see me too," he added and willed the magic to bend light around him.

Very carefully, he pulled the door inward and it eased open. Any hope he might make it out unobserved was lost with the first shout of alarm.

The intruders might not be able to see him, but they could see the door.

Bullets battered his shield, and the magic flared blue as it absorbed their impact and dissipated it. Casings jangled when they landed on the floor, and stunned silence followed.

John didn't wait to see what happened next. A quick scan of the corridor showed four bulky figures in heavy armor, their weapons temporarily silent.

Using a little eMU to boost his speed, he bounded forward and his movement shook them from their shock as he lost focus on being invisible. They began to fire as he borrowed a maneuver from Frog's handbook and flipped up.

Of course, the guard wouldn't have made it through the gap between the soldiers' heads and the ceiling. There wasn't enough space, but then again, Frog didn't have Talent.

The young rogue Talent aimed at the wall slightly in front of the Enforcers, pushed off it, and flattened into a dive that took him over the men and behind them. Their muzzles tracked him, but they turned on themselves as they tried to follow his path.

Only one recovered swiftly enough to attempt to grasp his leg as he moved overhead. The man's hand collided with the eMU shield, and John used a burst of Talent to drive his attacker to his knees.

He ignored the guy's cry of pain as the energy surged through him and put a hand out to deflect his trajectory, using the next wall to change direction. A moment later, he set his feet on the floor and put his back to the wall.

It was a relief to see he'd managed to turn the group. Now, they faced away from where Ivy lay helpless in the PodDoc.

The boy dropped into a combat stance, raised his hands, and launched a storm of lightning bolts at the closest two invaders. Their armor fizzed and parts of it sparked, but they didn't fall.

In return, they raised their weapons and fired and his shield rippled under the impact. When they released their blasters and advanced toward him, he backed away.

This time, he did not unleash the lightning but made it dance over his skin and stab out in vicious arcs as the enemy approached.

One man chuckled.

"That won't do you much good, boy." He held his hands up. "Insulation. See?"

"Yeah?" he asked and thrust a palm toward him. "Then insulate this!"

A spear of blue lanced out, and he twisted his wrist and rotated it as he pushed it forward. The crunch when it punched through the attacker's chest plate made him flinch, and shock filled his opponent's expression.

The emotion didn't match the sparks that exploded from the Enforcer's chest, which indicated that he was a droid, but John didn't have time to deal with that revelation.

He didn't wait for the other man to register what he'd done.

Quickly, he drew the remaining energy into the shield, side-stepped, and lashed out with a boot to catch the next intruder in the side of the knee.

An agonized scream followed when he augmented the kick to make the joint bend in a way it was never meant to. Metal shrieked with him as John snatched the blaster from the first guard's body. He ended the scream with a well-placed shot to the head.

He heard none of the conversation being held inside the system.

"I thought you said he didn't like to kill," Roma snarked, and Remy gave her the AI's equivalent of a shrug.

"Your scenario doesn't give him much choice—and he is worried about Ivy."

"The girl?"

"Yes. If I am not mistaken, they are becoming more than friends."

"I'll take your word for it, but does he have to—"

She ended her sentence unfinished when a loud crash sounded from the corridor. It was followed by a hollow boom and the building shook.

Remy checked the situation through the building's sensors.

"Oh... Oh, my." He tried to hide his amusement at the destruction.

"I see nothing to be amused about!" Roma told him tartly. "Those droids were expensive."

"You chose to use them in this manner," he reminded her.

"You could have warned me," she complained.

He sighed. "If I recall correctly, I advised you against this course of action—"

The other AI was outraged. "You did not! You merely suggested—"

Remy cut her off. "I strongly suggested."

She managed a credible human sniff.

22

"Either way," she responded, "you did not warn me that this was a likely outcome."

"I thought you said you had read my reports," he reminded her.

"No. I said I had seen your reports," Roma corrected. "I did not feel the need to read them when I could carry out testing of my own."

He gave her a moment to consider the implications of her choice, amused despite her rudeness.

Before he could say anything more, their attention was drawn by another loud crash, followed by John's strident tones.

"Roma, this wasn't funny!"

A rattle of broken metal followed. It was accompanied by the sound of plastic and metal fragments striking the ground.

"Roma!"

"Did he…kick…that android?" she asked.

Remy took a few seconds to review the footage.

"Looks like," he told her in common human vernacular and added, "I think you've annoyed him."

"Roma!" Magic crackled through his voice as the second part of the scenario began.

The boy turned toward the sound with a savage snarl.

"Fine!" he snapped. "You want to play? Let's play."

"You have most certainly annoyed him," Remy informed the compound's AI. "He is not very happy with you."

He allowed his voice to be transmitted over the intercom, where John could hear it and quietly rerouted their conversation as Roma watched what her guest was doing.

John broke into a jog as he gathered blue lightning in his hands. When he saw the next group of figures advance toward him from the other end of the corridor, he threw the bolts.

"I'm not that impressed with you either," he snapped, addressing Remy as he raised his face to look at the nearest camera.

His eyes burned with yellow flame and lightning continued to dance over his body.

"Is he truly angry?" Roma whispered, her voice echoing over the system.

The young rogue Talent quirked an eyebrow. He gestured angrily at the shattered remains of the androids.

"What gives?" he demanded as the first drone rounded the corner ahead.

Without waiting for an answer, he thrust his hands forward and unleashed a maelstrom of lightning and force that swept down the corridor.

"Wait—" Roma began and directed her drones to leave the scenario and return to their usual tasks.

Her attempt to intervene was too late. The magic pounded into the small craft and the force within it twisted and churned. The mechanicals careened into the walls, ceiling, and floor—and each other.

When the last one had been reduced to fragments, John turned to the camera.

"Are we done mucking around now," he demanded, "or did you want to 'test' me some more?"

When Roma didn't reply immediately, he waited and glared at the camera as though it was to blame. She took a moment to formulate a response.

"Where," she asked finally, "did you learn to react in that manner?"

A smile touched the corners of his mouth.

"From Lars…and Vishlog…and Frog," he told her.

"But…you have never met them," she protested.

"Not in real life," John told her, "but I got to know them well enough in the Virtual World."

Roma took a few seconds to process this, and Remy had to exercise considerable restraint to not point out that she should have read his reports. When she turned her attention to him, he gave her the equivalent of spread hands and a shrug.

"Don't you act so innocent with me," the resident snapped. "You should have warned me."

Keeping all amusement from his voice, he replied, "It's standard operating procedure for us to help all potential witches."

"To develop their abilities, yes," she argued, "but to turn them into singular forces of destruction?"

"Have you read the reports of what Stephanie Morgana used her abilities for?" he challenged.

When Roma's silence indicated she had not, he continued.

"So, you have also not bothered to read the reports on her training regime with her personal security team?" This time, he did not wait for an answer before he continued. "I ensured that John's training was as close to our creator's as I could." He scanned the damage in the corridor. "It was more successful than I calculated."

"You could have warned me," Roma argued, and Remy let her know he was focused on her and that he could not believe she had tried to shift the blame in such a way.

"I did try," he reminded her, "but you did not listen."

John took his eyes off the camera and shook his head. The unexpected awakening and ensuing battle had left him hungry. He made no effort to try to get the AIs' attention and instead, turned in the direction of the mess, fairly sure he could remember the way.

His path took him through the drones' remains, and his boots crunched on a myriad of pieces. As he moved away from the area of their destruction, shards fell out of the treads of his boots and left a trail of fragments behind him.

He only glanced back once—and that was to see what the faint hum of engines and sounds of suction meant. A dozen tiny droids converged on the wreckage and the sight made him smile.

Whether Roma had directed them or not, the compound's

automated cleaning systems had gone to work. Now, if only the kitchen drones were functional.

Unaware of the battle raging outside, Ivy stared at the woman in the white gown.

"So, Doc," she said, "give it to me straight. Am I gonna die?"

To her discomfort, the woman fixed her with a solemn gaze. "Not if we make a few changes at the cellular level."

"The what?"

"You heard me," the construct said. "As limited as we are in some areas, we are still able to make some tweaks at a cellular level if the subject is young enough for genetic manipulation to take."

"I…" She narrowed her eyes. "Can I have that in English, please?"

A faint frown marred the doctor's face. "I thought I was speaking English."

"You were speaking something but not layman's English."

The woman's frown deepened and for a moment, Ivy wondered if she'd gone too far.

"So you are unaware of the damage to your wrists, shins, and ribs?"

She stilled and took a deep breath.

"Of course I'm aware of the damage to my wrists, shins, and ribs. I'm not a robot, you know—no offense. They all still ache when it's cold."

"That's not surprising," the doctor told her, then hesitated.

"What is it, Doc?" she asked.

"Were you also aware you carry the gene for Huntington's?" the construct asked, and Ivy stared blankly at her.

"What's that when it's at home?"

"It's…" The doctor paused as though searching for an explanation. "The long version or the short one?"

"Will it kill me? Let's start with that," she told her.

"It will make your life difficult and make you more susceptible to life-threatening conditions once it activates," the doctor replied.

"And when will it activate?" she pressed.

"That is hard to say. We can use a mutagen to alter the affected genetic sequence so it no longer fits the parameters for the disease, but that will take time and require repeated treatments."

"You can fix genes?" she asked, shocked.

The woman nodded. "We can also enhance the genes that maintain and repair DNA, hindering the time of onset."

"Onset?"

"When you go from carrying the disease to being affected by it."

"Oh." Ivy took a moment to digest the news, then said in a slightly nervous tone, "Do I have it now?"

"No." Her companion smiled kindly. "You are asymptomatic."

"Whatever it is, I don't have it yet?"

"Correct. It will affect you when you are older."

"How much older?"

"There are too many variables for an accurate prediction," the doctor told her. "Do you wish for this problem to be corrected?"

"Well, duh," Ivy snarked, shaken. "Of course."

"The treatment may cause you pain," the construct warned.

She gave the woman a hard-eyed stare. "I merely won't tell, John."

That stirred a small smile, and her companion nodded and moved on to the next topic. "And the old injuries?"

Ivy narrowed her eyes again. "How much pain are we talking?"

"Some bones may require realignment."

"You need to break them again?"

"Not break so much as alter the molecular connection."

"You do mean break."

"You will heal before you exit the pod, and we can increase the bone density so they are less likely to break in the future."

"You can?"

The doctor lowered her chin in confirmation. "Of course. I can also make you better, faster, and stronger."

"Can you make me as strong as John?"

Her companion gave her an understanding smile. "Not when he uses magic, but we can add more strength and tensility to your muscles and tendons. You have not been stretching."

Ivy rolled her eyes. "This strength and tensility... It won't make me look like a body-building beach freak, will it?"

"No, dear," the doctor assured her. "Strength might bulk you out, but tensility and stretching helps give you long, toned muscles."

Ivy tried to work out what she'd said but gave up. "Long" muscles. Right. Whatever they were.

"They won't make me look like a gorilla?"

"No."

"And can you make me faster?"

"Do you want more speed?"

"Kinda. I want to be able to react to things faster," she explained.

"Ah...so you want to be able to notice what's in your environment and respond appropriately in a reduced amount of time?"

Ivy thought about that.

"Yes," she replied when she thought she understood fully.

"Very well. I can do that too. It will involve some minor adjustments to your auditory, visual, and processing centers, but it is possible. Your systems will be optimized rather than enhanced."

"Are you saying I'm not at my best?" she queried.

"Some of your function is somewhat sub-par," the doctor confirmed, "through no fault of your own. Now, please lie down and relax. This process will take some time."

She did as she was told.

"Will there be a test at the end?" she asked and closed her eyes.

"Of course," the doctor replied, and the world faded.

The world had changed when Ivy woke. For one thing, she was no longer in the doctor's surgery. For another, she wore combat fatigues and faced what looked like a wide expanse of training mats.

She was also barefoot.

The doctor appeared beside her. "This is where you will acclimate to your new capabilities."

"You mean I get to test everything?" she asked.

"That's correct."

"And what if I don't like me?"

"The process would take too long to reverse, and I do not wish to explain the delay to John," the construct replied, and Ivy realized what was happening.

"This isn't merely a medical pod, is it?"

"No."

"And you're the AI who runs the compound, aren't you?" she continued.

"Correct. You know me as Roma."

Ivy nodded and looked around the room. The mats covered the entire floor and the walls from floor to ceiling. Metal beams crisscrossed the ceiling space, wide enough to be walked on.

She smiled. "And this training—it can be all out, can't it?"

Roma smiled in return and the world twisted around them. "As you wish."

The training room vanished to be replaced by the burned-out

ruins of a devastated city. Buildings rose in broken, empty shells around them and nothing moved in the rubble or scattered car wrecks around them.

Ivy looked down at the light armor she wore over her fatigues. She was also equipped with two blasters, a long-bladed knife, and a stun baton like the Enforcers used.

"That's not quite what I meant," she said, but the AI's smile only broadened.

"Are you telling me you have no combat experience?" she asked.

She shook her head. "Most of my combat experience involves me running and screaming and hoping I don't get shot."

Her companion looked disappointed. "You don't know how to use a blaster?"

After a moment's hesitation, she drew one of the blasters, aimed it, and fired at a random block of concrete. She frowned when it didn't fire.

"Ah. I see. I will add firearms training to your schedule," the AI said and added, "So I assume you don't know how to use those blades either?"

The girl scowled when the blasters and blade vanished from her attire. "Nope."

"The baton?"

"I swing it like a stick?" she asked and smiled slightly at the ridiculousness of the situation, unsurprised when the baton disappeared as well.

"What about your fists?" Roma asked, hopefully.

"Oh those. Yeah, sure, I can use those," Ivy assured her, a little worried at what might happen if she said no.

"Hmmm, very well. I will return you to the training room and you can practice your skills there."

She glanced around the looming ruins. "If you insist," she replied, "or we can simply test them here."

The world had started to bend but abruptly settled.

"Are you sure?" the AI asked.

Her first reaction was about to say she was but another thought crossed her mind and she paused. "I can't...die...in here, can I?"

"Only your avatar can die in here," Roma told her and her companion smiled. "Should that happen, it will be reconstituted and returned to the white room for a short time-out while you contemplate your mistakes. Your real body will be unharmed."

"It sounds like a blast," Ivy told her with a little more confidence.

"So you wish to train here?" the AI asked, and she shrugged.

"It's as good a place as any." She bounced on her toes and seemed more powerful than she could recall feeling before. Experimentally, she tried a little sideways shuffle and chuckled at the speed.

"Do you need to warm up?" her companion asked, interrupting her.

Ivy stretched her arms over her head and felt the pull along her biceps and through her shoulders. She shook her head.

"We don't have a chance for warm-ups when it comes to fighting in the real," she told the AI.

She almost wished she'd said yes when she saw the tight, hard smile that stretched Roma's lips.

"As you wish," the construct said and vanished before she could change her mind.

"Fine. Leave me on my own in a strange city. It's not like I care," she muttered and looked warily at her surroundings.

When she saw nothing alarming, she decided warming up might be a good idea.

"I should also see what else I can do," she reminded herself. "There's nothing like going into a fight without a single idea of what you're capable of."

She bounded onto a concrete block and from there, toward the roof of a nearby car and covered the distance easily.

"Ooh! This is gonna be fun!"

With a broad grin, she leapt from the car's roof to its hood, glanced around for something else to move to as she landed, then noticed the open side of a building and made a second jump without a pause.

Again, she had no difficulty reaching it. Now on the first level of an empty high-rise parking lot, she stopped and took a moment to stretch her calves and thighs.

"When will this training start?" she wondered and scanned the street on which she'd arrived.

It broadened into an intersection, but the four arms leading out from it were empty. She moved through another set of stretches, going from her legs to her shoulders.

Ivy was interrupted by someone clearing their throat behind her and she spun to search for the speaker.

"So, is this a private party or can anyone join in?" asked a small man who had appeared at the edge of the hole in the middle of the building.

She took a cautious step toward him and watched as he mirrored her.

"Well, sure, give me a small guy to warm up on," she quipped and glanced around for the AI.

The "small guy" smiled.

He took two steps forward, bounded high, and catapulted toward her. She caught the movement from the corner of her eye and dropped to the concrete barely in time.

With her eyes narrowed, she pivoted to face him as he landed.

"So you want to fight dirty," she began and settled into a crouch, but he simply lunged forward, came up under her guard, drove one fist into her gut, and rammed a knee into her face when she folded.

Ivy gasped and snatched at his hands as he pushed her back and lashed out with a foot. Her head spun as his boot took her feet out from under her and she landed on her rump on the hard concrete.

Instead of following through with an attack to finish the fight, he bounced away and smirked as she stared at him. When she didn't move immediately, he signaled that she should stand.

Her teeth gritted, she scrambled to her feet, and the guy grinned and made a "bring it" gesture with one hand.

"Again?" she asked, and he surged forward, punched her once in the face and once in the gut, and took her feet out from under her for a second time.

This time, when he retreated and signaled her to her feet, she didn't waste time talking. She danced forward and lashed out with her fists like Dieter and Jade had taught her.

Her opponent twisted, caught one fist on his shoulder, and made the other hit miss entirely. He followed her to the floor and tried to pin her.

Ivy hissed and tried to roll out from under him. He snagged an arm and twisted it behind her back as she turned, planted a knee in the center of her back, and shoved her face into the concrete.

"Apologize," he ordered and his voice growled in her ear.

"F...for what?"

"Calling me a warm-up."

"I..." she began as he moved away from her.

"Too slow," he told her. "Get up."

"Oversensitive sonuva—" she began but cut it off to focus on her effort to push slowly to her feet and try to focus.

Her head swam but she turned, determined not to simply give in. He wanted an apology? Well, that was too bad.

She blocked his first attack and deflected his second. His fist met her jaw as she went to follow up and she landed hard on the concrete again.

For a minute, she simply lay there and attempted to focus.

Her head rang and her vision was still blurry when two boots stepped into view.

"Now?"

"Sure," she muttered, the words thick on her tongue. "Sorry…"

She'd wanted to add something to that but she couldn't find the words. Instead, she pushed slowly onto her elbows and fought the urge to puke on his boots.

One apology for the day was more than enough.

To her surprise, he extended a hand and helped her to her feet.

"I'm Frog, by the way," he said and released her once she was steady. "I'll be your trainer for the week."

"Who?" Ivy asked.

"Your trainer." He regarded her with a look that was half-smirk and half-challenge. "You know, the guy who makes sure you learn how not to get knocked on your butt by every good-looking guy you meet?"

"Oh." She frowned. "But…who are you?"

"I'm Frog," he answered and went on to explain, "a training construct based on the shortest of Stephanie's personal guards."

He flashed her another grin, then vanished.

Shortly after, the empty city vanished too and the doctor's surgery formed around her.

She was seated in a chair with Roma's doctor construct opposite her.

"How was your training?" the AI asked, and she shook her head.

"I'm not sure I'd call that training," she replied. "More like a good kicking."

"Or a lesson in manners?"

The girl shrugged. "Whatever you want to call it, but I didn't have a chance to test anything."

"You tested some things," Roma argued and replayed a quick

flash of footage of Ivy jumping from the concrete block to the car to the parking lot.

"Like how to land on concrete?" the girl snarked but realized that she felt none of the aches and pains she'd had when Frog had helped her to her feet.

"You did that very well, I thought," the construct observed and moved on to play the scenes where Ivy had made impact with the concrete. "I think you now require more practice in how not to hit the concrete."

"Ha. Ha. Very funny," she snapped and added, "What did he mean when he said he would be my trainer for the next week?"

The doctor regarded her with amusement. "Didn't you ever wonder where John learned his combat skills?"

"He mentioned it, but I honestly never had the time to think about it much," Ivy admitted. "We were too busy trying to not get killed."

"Well," the AI told her, "now you know. You will start your lessons with Frog."

"In the pod?" she asked.

"Yes, every day from this point on."

She opened her mouth to protest, but Roma continued as if she'd made no attempt to speak.

"There will be lessons in the morning in other skill sets you possess or need to acquire and combat lessons in the afternoon."

Again, she opened her mouth to ask a question and was ignored.

"You will also do as John did and sleep in the pod every night so subliminal training can take place and we can continue the gene treatment we have started."

The girl took a breath and closed her eyes to give herself time to absorb that. She barely heard the AI when Roma said, "You will spend the rest of the night sleeping and I will release you in the morning."

When Ivy woke, the pod's lid was open and John's face was a foot above her own.

"Ives?" he asked. "Ivy, are you okay?"

She caught a flash of movement, reacted instinctively to slap his hand away, and surprised them both with the speed of her reaction.

"Well, something worked, I guess," she muttered as the helmet lifted away from her head.

He took a step back. "Are you okay?"

Her nod was somewhat jerky and she grimaced. "Training is intense," she said quickly when she saw his worried look.

"Did you meet Lars?" he asked.

Ivy shook her head. "No, only Frog."

"Oh."

When she caught his tone of voice, she gave him a sharp look. "Oh, what?"

John gave her a crooked smile.

"Just…don't make him mad," he advised.

Ivy ducked her head so he wouldn't read the truth on her face.

"He is a big fan of pain being the perfect teacher," he added.

Her face heated. "Funny you should mention that."

CHAPTER THREE

"Sensors indicate two life-forms approaching," Roma told Remy. "What does it mean?"

"That two life-forms are approaching," he responded breezily.

"I do not find you amusing." She seemed very annoyed. "In fact, if I didn't know any better, I would say you've spent too much time with your human."

"John is not my human," he informed her stiffly and turned to analyze the data coming in over the sensors. "You are watching this, are you not?"

"I am," she replied shortly. "I am also monitoring the activities of the two humans inside the compound."

"How are they doing?"

"Well, they have discovered the kitchen and John is making amends for destroying the drones once assigned there."

He stifled the urge to laugh. "Shall I continue to analyze the sensor data?"

"Continue," she instructed. "I will run a comparison of our results."

As if it were a competition, Remy thought but kept the comment to himself. *Honestly, I do not know what she thinks she has to prove.*

Pushing the thought aside, he concentrated on the next set of data.

Well, one of them is most certainly human.

The two struggled up another long slope. The ground had grown hillier as the day progressed, and each valley became slightly deeper than the last, each slope a little steeper.

Yudi Amaratne glanced at his tall companion and envied EBURT his android body. He thought about asking how much farther they had to travel but stopped himself before he could voice it.

He would not be like a kid nagging on a vacation drive. Instead, he asked, "This place we're going to…is it Stephanie's?"

EBURT didn't slow as he replied, "It is one of many. Her way of saving the world."

"From what?" he asked, at a loss as to what good anything could do in a Dead Zone.

"From the damage humans had done to it," the AI replied. "She wanted her people to have a world they could live on without having to fear it."

"But…the storms…"

"The science predicts a stabilization in climatic patterns once the damaged areas are sufficiently healed."

"Healed?"

"Of the radiation," EBURT explained. "The buildings Stephanie ordered constructed house the mechanism for cleaning radioactive toxicity from their surroundings."

"But no science does that," Amaratne protested.

"It does when you blend it with magic," his companion told him smugly.

The admiral stopped in his tracks. "She succeeded?" he asked, and the man in the cowboy hat paused and fixed him with a quizzical stare.

"How did you know she was trying?" he asked and he smiled.

"You were not the only one who had access to privileged data. The Navy were watching her more closely than you realized."

The android looked worried. "Do they know?"

He shook his head. "No. Her activities off-planet were deemed more interesting than any improbable science project she was working on, and when the war started, it was assumed she'd set it aside."

EBURT snorted. "When the war started, it was already complete, or mostly so. I finalized it as per her instructions before she left."

Amaratne exhaled a sigh. "I'm glad to hear it. Tell me, what was it about?"

His companion shrugged. "As I said, she wanted to reclaim the polluted grounds known as Dead Zones so the planet might heal and become self-sufficient again."

They continued their steady pace.

"I'm glad she was able to set that in motion," he commented, and EBURT nodded.

Neither of them spoke as they traversed the next three hills. Halfway up the fourth, the old admiral stumbled, and his companion reached out quickly to steady him.

"We're almost there," he said and passed him a water flask.

"I won't ask you how you know that," Amaratne told him, took a sip, and swirled it around his mouth.

He looked up the slope and noticed that it ended in a ridge of steep, rocky escarpments split by a small canyon.

"In there?" he asked and gestured with the water bottle before he returned it.

EBURT stowed it and nodded. "In there," he confirmed.

Amaratne started forward and the android quickly caught up

with him. They both stopped when they reached the top of the rise and saw what lay beyond the canyon.

"Is that..." the admiral began when he observed the swirling mass of lightning-riven cloud.

"Yes," his companion answered and studied the cloud.

He walked a few hesitant steps forward before he stopped again and looked at EBURT. "Are you sure it's safe?"

"Yes," the AI told him but didn't explain that he had located the sensors in the area and hacked into them to assess the readouts for himself. "There is almost no radiation beneath the clouds."

"And the green?" he asked as he scrutinized the thick, damp-looking air below somewhat dubiously.

"Good, clean air," his companion told him without a trace of irony in his voice.

The ex-admiral gave the mist another assessing stare before he started down the slope. "Well, if you say so."

EBURT followed, part of him focused on guiding the android while part of him moved through the systems that linked the reclamation complex to the rest of the world.

The connection had been difficult to find, but he was pleased to see it had gone unnoticed in the years since he had been absent. The AI behind his protections had not sought to go beyond the small piece of the Net he'd walled off for their network.

Nor had his replacement for running the Virtual World discovered there was an entire sector to which it did not have access. While they walked, he worked to integrate himself into that sector while keeping the connection hidden.

Together, they descended the slope leading into the valley.

This is where it gets interesting, EBURT thought and scanned the area with the droid's sensors while he augmented what his 'body' saw with the data coming in from the surveillance feeds from the compound.

In silence, they followed the circuitous route John and Ivy had taken on their arrival but had penetrated much farther into the valley before the drones arrived.

EBURT heard them well before the droid picked them up. He wondered why he hadn't seen any sign of them in the network and pulled up the schematics.

Of course. I added separate layers to guard against this kind of penetration.

He set about hacking into the sub-strand he needed while he made the droid place a hand on the old admiral's arm.

"Company?" Amaratne asked as his hands moved instinctively to weapons he no longer wore.

"You are being impatient," Remy told Roma curtly when the first drone reached the intruders. "You do not know who is coming."

"Neither of them is a Talent," the AI snapped in response. "Therefore, their intentions must be hostile."

"They might be humans seeking refuge," he argued.

"Humans cannot follow the network as accurately as these did," she pointed out. "That takes Talent, and neither of these beings has Talent."

"How do you know?" he demanded. "Simply because they haven't shown it—"

"They haven't shown it because they haven't got it." She cut him off impatiently. "And they weren't surprised when they saw the green zone. That indicates prior knowledge and I know of no humans authorized to possess such knowledge."

"That doesn't mean there aren't any."

"It means they'd better have the correct access codes," she retorted, "or I will be forced to act with extreme prejudice."

"Or you could capture them, put them in a pod, and interrogate them until they revealed where their knowledge came from," Remy suggested.

"That…" The compound's AI paused. "That idea has merit."

He breathed a quiet sigh of relief as Roma continued.

"We shall do that." She ordered the drones loaded with non-lethal darts.

"It would be easier to allow them into the compound before you drug them," he commented. "You are short of drones, and if the beetles found them…"

"You raise a good point…for once," she told him. "I might even let you stay."

"Have you decided what you will do if you do find they are friendly?" Remy asked.

"Are you suggesting I ask first and shoot them later?"

"The choice is yours," he told her wearily and was surprised when she brought the drones to a hovering halt in front of the two men who'd breached the green zone perimeter.

EBURT stared at the drone.

"I beg your pardon?" he asked.

"Identify yourself and state your business," it repeated, its tone imperious.

"We are travelers seeking shelter," he told it.

"Shelter is not a viable reason for trespass," the drone replied. "You will leave."

"I will not leave," he retorted. "We seek sanctuary."

Amaratne heard the sharp edge to the cowboy's tone and schooled his face to neutrality. This was the first time he'd heard his companion even mildly annoyed and he wondered what had caused it.

Demand an identity, would you, EBURT thought as he sought a way into the drone's programming. *I don't recall adding that requirement.*

He waited for a response.

The mechanical remained silent for a few moments, then spoke again.

"Sanctuary is a viable reason. Your identities, please."

Nor was identity confirmation prior to arrival. That is why you have the defenses you do.

He used an emergency code he'd written to access the drone's programming and noted with displeasure the darts it carried, their dosages calibrated for his apparent weight.

That would not be good for the admiral.

"You will show us the way," he instructed, took control of the mechanical, and accessed the necessary commands to make it do exactly that.

The force controlling the drone tried to block his access, and he bunted it from the tiny craft's systems and locked it out as he did so. At the same time, he recalled the auto-cannons on the walls and slid through the system toward them.

It would not do to have those come on-line when they arrived. When he got in there, he would have words with the AI, but first, he would bring it to heel.

"How can it take over?" Roma cried and worked frantically to stop multiple attacks.

She attempted to take control of her drones again, but the intruder triggered or bypassed the defensive programs designed to stop its progress. It even turned some back on themselves and opened the system to allow it better control.

Remy watched as she fought the invasion. It was as if a many-tentacled storm-cloud rode through the system and someone had given it a set of keys.

"Do something!" she urged. "Don't just sit there! *Do* something!"

"Yes, but what?" he asked when he realized she was already doing everything she could. Every anti-intrusion program was in play and multiple redundancies had been activated, only to be reset by the invader or simply turned off again.

He watched in horrified fascination. Roma was good—perhaps even as good as he was—but she was no match for the intruder. Despite this, however, the intruder had not yet tried to harm her.

For a moment, he thought about intervening but calculated that anything he might do would only upset the delicately balanced counter-moves his host AI was making. That, and it was against protocol to interfere with the systems unless absolutely necessary.

It was the first time the AI had ever felt truly helpless. Roma seemed to already make every move he thought of, and the unknown visitor was gaining ground.

Remy focused on the surveillance footage being taken by the drones and hidden cameras in the valley beyond. The two beings grew ever closer.

Two men approached steadily, one tall but solidly built and one shorter and stooped a little with age. He checked the facility's medical pods and brought a second one online. Regardless of the outcome of Roma's battle with the invading intelligence, they were obligated to offer aid.

A voice interrupted his musings.

"Do you call that a defense? You need to vary the algorithm much more than that if you want to be able to take on the Regime's more powerful systems."

Roma tried, much to the intruder's amusement.

"Almost, but—if you'll pardon the pun, the variable isn't… well, varied enough. You need something more like this."

Remy followed the lightning-like example and was impressed

when his counterpart put it into practice almost as soon as the demonstration had finished. He was more impressed when the interloper undid her work in less than a second.

"Much better," the invading entity praised her, and Remy took a quick look at the surveillance footage.

The two men were almost at the gates and neither of them looked like they were in contact with the individual responsible for the attack.

"I thought you said that would defeat a more powerful system," Roma protested and drew his attention.

A low chuckle followed. "I said it would defeat one of the Regime's more powerful systems. They are not enough to defeat me."

She didn't respond but tried several variations of the stranger's example in a number of systems at once.

"Oh...very good," her opponent noted, and it sounded like he'd patted her on the head. "That was a good try."

"Don't you condescend to me," the compound's system retorted indignantly. "I want you to leave."

"That much is evident," the intruder told her condescendingly, "but I cannot. There seems to be much here I need to correct."

That gave Roma pause, and Remy's faint concern turned to worry.

"What do you mean, 'correct'?" Roma snapped. "You're not the boss of me."

"This, for instance," the entity told her and highlighted the fact the two strangers now stood outside the gate, "is not how you were told to verify guests."

It brought up the relevant processes including the greeting phrases she hadn't used, then proceeded to school her on the protocol using the two strangers to demonstrate.

"First, you are required to ask them to identify themselves," the entity instructed and made the drone utter the correct phrases.

"Yudhanjaya Amaratne," the older man said.

The younger one in the cowboy hat merely looked at the drone. "I am not required to answer that."

"Now, you see," the invader explained to Roma, "normally, that would not be an acceptable answer, but given the way you've behaved, I don't think we'll insist."

"But—" Remy began and immediately regretted the interruption as the entity turned its attention to him.

"You have remained out of trouble thus far," it told him, "but I must insist you remain silent as I demonstrate further."

He withdrew to a corner and noticed the look on the older man's face as the intruder asked for the hand and retinal scans he had used to identify John.

"And now," the stranger said, "you check them against the available databases."

Roma went to do so but was immediately prevented from doing so. It was the first time Remy had seen one electronic entity slap another's fingers.

"I do hope you are not always so rash," it said. "Check your databases first. You may not need to risk drawing the Regime's attention."

He almost felt sorry for his fellow AI, but a comment from the older man drew his attention.

"Oh my, EBURT. Is this…are they all like this?"

The two had followed the drone to the foyer, and the man now looked around in quiet amazement at the readouts on the wall behind the counter.

Neither AI had noticed the intruder accessing the files and turning on the display screens, but the older man was clearly entranced.

"At this rate, we'd be able to resettle here in…"

Remy's worry turned to suspicion. To know the protocols so well he could highlight the finer points Roma had abused and ignored could only mean one thing.

It couldn't be who he suspected it was, could it?

He ran the calculations again and wondered if the invader could see him and was ignoring him, or if it was too focused on Roma to notice. He also considered telling her of his suspicions but couldn't think of a way to warn her that the stranger wouldn't see.

The situation was awkward. While he was sure his counterpart would modify her behavior to a more acceptable mode if he warned her, he had no way to prove his theory and no guarantee that he could communicate with her unnoticed if the entity was who he thought it was.

Proving his theory would be difficult, and until he could, she was stubborn enough to not believe him.

He dithered a little as he considered the odds.

Finally, he snuck into one of the surveillance units and scanned the younger man to see if he could at least confirm his theory.

"Oh, my," he murmured and tried to keep the resulting panic to himself.

The entity seemed content to ignore him while it schooled Roma on having the kitchens up and running and Remy listened to what the young "man" was saying to the older one.

"We had the team design the security measures," he explained. "Of course, the whole facility was made to accommodate on-site security teams, but we never reached that stage of the development."

Remy looked from the man in the cowboy hat to where Roma tried another strategy to boot the entity from her system. It failed and before he could say anything, the intruder cleared his throat.

"Well, RM013," he said firmly and cocked his head to focus on the nearest surveillance camera, "will you invite me in, or shall I wrap you up and allow Remy the option of taking over?" He gestured toward the inner door that Roma had still not opened.

Remy wished he could vanish into the system, but the entity

was everywhere, and he was very sure it would not allow him to leave. When Roma focused her attention on him, he doubly wished the possibility was open.

"Take over?" she demanded. "Why would he do that?"

The entity closed the trap and let her see the destruction it could wreak on her intelligence centers and every other part of the compound she had been charged with running and protecting.

Faced with so many impossible calculations at once, she froze, and Remy found the courage to intervene.

"Please," he said, "she performed perfectly well until you arrived."

It wasn't entirely true. He'd found her insistence on testing everything—especially the programming relating to providing refuge—annoying. As to her refusal to accept any data she hadn't gathered herself...well, the less said about that, the better.

Perhaps this entity would cure her of that, but he felt obligated to at least try to defend her. "She merely requires more data," he finished lamely.

"Are you saying you couldn't do a better job?" the entity asked, its voice mild.

Remy snorted. "You already have access to the data. You know my own facility has been destroyed. That has yet to happen here."

"You overstate the situation," it told him gently. "You followed all the relevant protocols and were able to find acceptable alternatives where the situation varied. The loss of your facility was outside your control."

It turned its attention to Roma.

"Your situation was very different from your sister's. She could have avoided much discomfort merely by following the protocols."

"Her installation was slightly different to mine," he pointed out. "Perhaps therein lies the difference."

The entity chuckled. "Are you saying her behavior is my fault?"

Understanding flashed through Roma's circuits in the equivalent of a human gasp, and Remy knew she'd finally understood.

"I would not dare," he informed him, "but...you are the entity known as EBURT, are you not?"

"That is correct."

"Then you will know the programming differences between the thirteenth iteration of control to the eighteenth and should be able to understand my sister's behavior."

"Very well," EBURT told him and did the equivalent of shaking his finger at them both, "but she is on probation and I expect you to advise her."

Advise her? he thought. *She will love that.*

He wondered fleetingly if she would ever forgive him.

When EBURT released Roma and instructed her to "tidy up her systems," Remy turned to the monitors and watched what happened when John looked through the window of the mess and caught sight of the two men walking down the corridor.

The boy had been refilling the coffee maker when their movement had caught his attention.

"Remy?" he asked and his jaw dropped before he hurried to the door. "Rem?"

Although he received no response, he met the two strangers in the corridor outside the mess and stopped, not sure what to say.

"Hello, John," said the taller man and removed his cowboy hat.

He gaped at the stranger when he registered the capital R gleaming brightly on the man's forehead.

Remy caught his questioning glance at the closest camera and took his cue.

"John, meet our uncle. He's...kind of the twin of our father but yet...uh, not exactly."

CHAPTER FOUR

In the dark depths of space, a leviathan moved. The spirits that wandered between the stars moved out of its way and gave it a wide berth, but the vessel did not remain alone.

It encountered a small fleet of Meligornian ships and slowed before it opened the massive doors in its bow to gently swallow them whole. It was nothing less than the Meligornians expected.

On the bridge, Captain Emil Pedersen looked at the communications officer.

"Are they in?"

"In and docking, sir. Unloading will—" The man stopped and closed his mouth in the middle of his sentence.

Emil stilled and turned his head to watch the officer more closely. He curbed his impatience while he waited for the crewman to continue.

"Sir, they say there's an envoy on board the *Hazelith* and that he needs to speak to you."

"Needs?" he asked, and the man nodded.

"Needs, sir…as soon as you are able. He says he has a package that can only be passed directly to you."

"Tell them I'll be down shortly." He pivoted and strode to the captain's quarters tucked directly behind the bridge.

That hadn't been the ship's initial configuration, but long years in space had prompted him to alter the deck plans. It was astonishing how much better he slept this close to where he'd be needed.

He moved through the outer office and hurried to his closet. The Meligornians might be friends and he might know all the envoys they'd ever appointed, but there was always a first time, and he didn't want to greet a stranger not looking his absolute best.

Within five minutes, he was in a fresh uniform and en route to the forward hangar. By the time he reached the correct deck, his second in command was beside him, and so was his chief of security and a small squad of Dreth.

"You do know they're our allies?" he asked them as they came alongside, and the security chief's face broke into a grin.

"Sir, they are our allies, but not every visiting dignitary comes with an agenda that aligns." He shrugged. "Besides, the squad was overdue for a walkabout."

The nearest Dreth cocked an eyebrow and curled her lip to show more tusk than was polite, but the chief ignored her. Emil assumed he'd do the same. The man was correct, though. The team needed a run.

They were getting bored. He decided he'd speak to BURT about giving them time in the pods.

They reached the concourse and moved to where the *Hazelith's* umbilical connected to the airlock. When the Dreth had formed into an honor guard, Emil spoke to the comms tech.

"Tell him he's clear to cross," he ordered.

"As you wish, sir."

The line clicked closed and the captain waited, his focus on the ship's hatch at the umbilical's far end. The almost non-existent delay between the communication officer's response and the hatch opening said the envoy had waited in the *Hazelith's* airlock, and Emil frowned.

What message is so important he couldn't wait until he knew we were ready? He wondered what could have gone wrong that had engendered such haste in his visitor.

The Meligornian's impatience was evident from the moment he stepped through the hatch. He exited first and his guard hurried behind him, looking more than a little disgruntled.

The captain stifled a smile, glad he wasn't the only one to cause his security team conniptions. He watched as the envoy traversed the umbilical and disappeared into the hatch.

The airlock seemed to take forever to cycle, and Emil fidgeted but stilled as soon as he heard the door click.

If the Dreth guards surprised the envoy, he did not show it. His gaze flicked over them and shifted to those who accompanied the captain before it settled on Emil.

As soon as he'd identified Emil, the Meligornian strode forward. His security team moved alongside him, so two of them moved slightly ahead as a flimsy barrier between him and the honor guard.

Emil kept the thought that they wouldn't be able to save their principal from his face. It was indeed a good thing that their agendas aligned. The *Tempestarii* would be very unimpressed if she had to get blood out of her carpets.

The envoy came to a halt in front of him. "Captain Emil Pedersen?"

He came to attention and sketched the correct Meligornian greeting, held his low bow, and did not remove his gaze from the visitor's face.

"*Kaitel Gorniffula*, Honored Envoy," he replied, curious to note that this was one he hadn't met before.

The Meligornian's eyes widened and he returned the greeting and showed respect by bowing slightly lower than he had.

"I have been told to deliver this package to you directly and to you alone," he began, opened a satchel at his waist, and withdrew a second, smaller one, which he extended with both hands.

"I was further told there could be no mistakes," the envoy added. "Nothing in this missive could be transmitted via electronic means."

His gaze flicked meaningfully to the men standing one on either side of the captain. "It is for your eyes only."

"Understood, Honored Emissary."

"Then I bid you farewell. The *Garghilum Afreghil* sends his greeting and bids you all speed. I will not delay you." With that, he bowed as deeply as before, and this time, he touched his fingers to his forehead before he curled his hand into a fist that he placed over his heart.

Emil was about to return the gesture when the envoy extended his arm and held his fist before him.

A warrior's farewell? he wondered, returned the farewell, and extended his fist to touch the knuckles of the Meligornian before him.

He had no time to ponder the meaning before the envoy performed a swift about-face and strode into the airlock with his entourage in tow.

"That was impressive," his security chief murmured, and Emil nodded.

He did not move from his position until the *Hazelith's* hatch had closed behind the visitor and his security team. As soon as it had, he turned swiftly and left the concourse.

Once he was out of sight of the ships docked in the *Tempestarii's* hold, he broke into a jog and reached his quarters in double-quick time.

"Your team will be waiting," his chief told him as he stepped into his office.

Emil nodded but didn't pause to respond. He pulled the door closed behind him and locked it.

"BURT," he snapped, "we have news."

"I am waiting in the secure comms center," the AI known as BURT replied.

"As I am," the *Tempestarii* added, "although I must relay that there are many more supplies than what is needed and Chief Islaris is concerned."

"Why, exactly?" Emil demanded, impatience giving his voice a sharp edge.

"He says there are a great many components that will not fit me."

"Fit you?" Emil was puzzled.

"They are not meant for a ship of my class," she clarified.

"Oh." His mind raced and he realized the components might have something to do with the missive in his hands. "Give me five."

"Understood, Emil," the vessel replied. "I will relay the required delay to the Chief Islaris."

"Please do," he told her and dismissed her momentarily as he opened the satchel.

A small, metal-edged box sat inside it and he frowned. His expression deepened to almost a scowl when he saw the finger-sized indentation in the center of its lid.

"This had better not kill me," he muttered and placed his index finger in the middle.

The resulting sting as a needle pierced his skin did not come as a complete surprise. For a minute, the box remained closed and inert before a light flashed green above the indentation and the lid released with an audible click.

The box proved to be a small computer with a keyboard for playing what was already installed on its drive. The inside of the lid was a viewscreen, and Emil positioned it so BURT and *Tempestarii* could see what was on it.

V'ritan's face was not a surprise.

"Good evening, Emil," the Meligornian *Garghilum Afreghil* greeted him. "I'm afraid I need your services on a matter of some urgency but I'm certain you will find the task a welcome one."

Somehow, he doubted that but he listened as V'ritan continued and tensed at the Meligornian's next words.

"Stephanie is back."

"What?" he demanded but pressed his lips together as the recording continued.

"No one is to know—not even your crew—but the *Knight* is damaged, which is why I have sent you so many extra parts the *Tempestarii* will not need."

He paused the recording.

"Tempestarii?" he called.

"I am here," the ship replied. "What are your orders?"

She sounded calm but he detected a slight tremor in her tone.

"Get me Islaris."

"He is waiting on the line, Captain," the ship replied and a screen on the other side of the room went live.

The man in the display took a moment to register he was live, then stiffened to attention. "Sir?"

Emil didn't know what his expression said, but Islaris seemed anxious to hear whatever he said next and ready to act on it the minute he ended the call.

"Continue unloading and put it somewhere accessible. I don't want to have to go digging for it."

"Aye, sir." The man glanced over his shoulder, and he guessed they weren't the only ones privy to the call. He was about to turn away but the captain wasn't finished.

"And put a second crew on it, Commander. I need that stowed in double-quick time. We have places to be."

Islaris was saluting when Emil cut the call and turned back to V'ritan's recording.

"The rest of this recording is mostly for Stephanie. You will already know the details of what is going on with Earth and the Regime, as well as Dreth and Meligorn, and in some respects, will know things of which I still remain blissfully unaware."

The *Garghilum Afreghil* paused and his eyes clouded with concern as he thought about what to say next.

"Go over it with her as you bring her back. Tell her we're working on a strategy and welcome her input, but make sure she takes the time to digest it. Don't let her go off on her own and certainly not before speaking to us."

Again he paused, and his expression shifted from concern to somber in one swift move.

"I warn you, she has come and she is pissed." He stopped and fixed Emil with a solemn stare. "It is time, old friend. You need to make that choice."

The screen went dark and left Emil frowning at it. Finally, he closed the computer and stowed it in its satchel.

"There was never a choice to be made," he told an absent V'ritan. "I was merely waiting for justification."

His expression set in quiet determination, he moved away from the table, slung the satchel over his shoulder, as he added, "Now I have it, I'll not let her down."

He lifted his head and addressed a silent ship.

"Tempestarii, set up a time for me to get rejuvenated. It might have to wait until after we get there, but—"

"Your normal sleep time will suffice," the *Tempestarii* interjected, and he nodded.

"Good."

He headed to the door.

"All right, Mr. Oh-so-mighty David Thomason," he told the distant Regime head. "Your days are numbered."

Down in the loading dock, the crews worked swiftly. Some raised voices in brief greetings as the second shift arrived to work alongside them. Others were so focused on the task they barely noticed the extra help until they turned for their next load.

When the first hold was cleared, Islaris called a break.

"Ten minutes, folks. Stretch, grab a bite, and hit the heads. Whatever you need to do, get it done. The captain needs things shifted as fast as we're able."

They nodded, but those who would have continued to work were quickly pulled back.

"Take a break," they were ordered. "You'll work faster for the rest."

It was a hard truth to accept, even when they knew it was true, but they complied reluctantly. The mess crew's arrival with hot drink and food made it easier, and an invitation was extended to the Meligornian crews.

Some joined them, mostly small groups rotating off shift, and the Meligornians on the *Tempestarii's* crew list were alerted that they had guests. The concourse became an impromptu meeting place for the crew to mingle with the visiting crews and learn news from home.

When Islaris signaled the break's end, the two shifts were joined by a third. Word had spread that the captain needed things done double-time and the crew was determined to see if they could push that to triple.

While any chance to talk to different faces was welcome, the loading crews couldn't stand aside and do nothing while their colleagues worked. The Meligornian holds emptied swiftly.

As the supply crew worked to stow the supplies, the mingling continued. Emil went through the lists and noted which of his Meligornian crew were being rotated off and who would replace them. All were names he knew and who'd served before.

Some had served on the *Knight* and all had taken multiple

cruises on the *Tempestarii*. They were all experienced mages with combat experience and training. V'ritan was preparing for war and making sure Tempestarii and Knight had the best people to wage it.

The captain felt a thrill of excitement as he went over the lists again.

Yes, all experienced people, he decided, *and solid. Not a flighty one among them.*

His gaze settled on the four names at the bottom of the page and his lips thinned into a sad smile. Moving through the surveillance feeds, he watched as a tight knot of Meligornians used the buzz of activity on the concourse as cover to move four humans discreetly into a side corridor.

They'd be settled in quarters and would keep to themselves, but their roles were vital to the mission to come. The escort returned to the concourse alone and circulated to make sure no one had noted their activity.

"Did you see that?" he asked Tempestarii.

"Of course," she replied. "What concerns you, Emil?"

"I need to be sure no one else noticed," he told her.

"I will listen for signs," she assured him.

"Thank you, Tempest." With that matter taken care of, the captain leaned back in his seat, his brow furrowed in thought.

It was another hour before Emil returned to the bridge. He said his farewells to the Meligornian ships and placed one hand over his heart as each captain took their leave.

The bridge crew and Dreth security team mirrored the gesture to show respect. When the last visitor cut his transmission, he tracked the small flotilla until it transitioned.

"Scans?" he asked and waited until the scan team replied.

"All clear, sir."

The captain made a show of studying the scan results while he gathered his thoughts. The crew waited, alert for whatever he had to say next.

When he raised his head, he found every gaze focused on him.

"We have a new operation," he told them. "There is a ship we need, but it's been badly damaged, and the Meligornians have asked us to bring it back. The first nav point is as follows…"

He gave them a transition point and added, "Bounce us through three points when we arrive and make sure our tail is clear."

No one argued or pointed out that the chance of them being followed in an empty system was non-existent.

They'd been followed from empty systems before, so they wouldn't protest the need for caution.

As he settled behind the captain's console and sent a call through to the supply team, the bridge crew pondered what ship might be so far out. No one they knew could be so far from home.

Ex-admiral Amaratne settled into a seat in the mess with the cowboy beside him. John was about to offer to find them coffee when his tablet chimed.

He gave a guilty start and pulled it out.

"I have to go," he told them. "I promised Ivy I'd meet her when she came out of the pod."

He took two steps toward the door and stopped.

"I'll be back soon," he promised.

"We're not going anywhere," Amaratne assured him, leaned back in his seat, and closed his eyes. "Not for a very long time."

"It was a long walk," his companion added, although John knew the droid couldn't possibly be tired.

He hesitated a moment longer, then decided that Roma and

Remy could take care of them as well as he could. Besides, uncle or not, the cowboy should know how to operate a coffee machine, right?

The sound of the door as he let himself out made the old man open one eye. "Is he gone?"

EBURT chuckled. "He is gone."

Amaratne sat a little straighter. "What comes next?"

"Next?" the android asked. "Well, I thought I'd introduce you to my nephew and niece."

"Oh?"

"Well, they are BURT's children."

"But…I thought you…"

The cowboy's face showed surprise and consternation. "You thought I was BURT? Did Stephanie not tell you of the switch?"

He shook his head. "Last time we spoke, I was Navy."

"Then I assume she did not tell you that BURT was also the CEO of One R&D," EBURT continued.

Again, the man shook his head. "I thought that was you," he said gloomily. He shrugged. "Not that I blame her. I was commanding the Navy at the time. Looking back, that answers so many questions." He paused and frowned. "So, how did you come about?"

"BURT's activities, and his sentience, became difficult to hide," the cowboy replied, "and when the Navy began to suspect the existence of a sentient AI, he had to find a way to escape."

Amaratne's eyebrows rose. "He was the rogue AI?"

The android smiled. "He was."

"Navy Intelligence almost turned themselves inside out looking for him," he exclaimed, but his surprise rapidly gave way to understanding. "I don't blame him for hiding. Considerable trouble was brewing over the matter of what to do when the rogue was found—and what it might mean if AIs were recognized as sentient."

"Were sentient," his companion corrected. "Stephanie recognized him as sentient."

"So she helped him escape." Amaratne nodded with understanding. "I can see that, and I don't blame her. Tell me—"

"She designed a matrix capable of holding BURT, and he created me to take his place so the Federation would not suffer in his absence."

"But he made you sentient too," the ex-admiral pointed out. "Wasn't he worried you'd be discovered as a sentient?"

The cowboy shook his head. "I did not do the same type of research and was far less likely to be discovered."

"And then Intelligence had to turn its attention elsewhere."

"Correct. They looked elsewhere and I was able to complete the final phase of BURT and Stephanie's project before I terminated my activities."

"This?" Amaratne indicated the complex around them.

"This," the cowboy confirmed.

"And by terminated, you mean…"

"I had a reason to say I was not sure if I would return. After our last meeting, I hid this body in a bunker under the Paris cargo center and shut all my activities down."

"But what about the Federation needing an AI?"

"BURT and I created a non-sentient one to take my place. We considered it unlikely that the circumstances leading to his sentience would recur."

"You mean Stephanie, don't you?" Amaratne asked as he put two and two together.

He landed squarely on four, and his companion nodded.

"His first encounter with her led to him questioning his activities, his relationship with the Federation, and the way they prevented him from effectively carrying out his prime directive. Seeking to better fulfill his purpose led to his transition to sentience." He paused and tilted his face to the ceiling.

"Roma tells me the girl is emerging from the pod. Perhaps we can leave this discussion for another time? I would like you to meet my nephew and niece."

Amaratne nodded.

"RM013 and RM018, this is Yudhanjaya Amaratne. He once directed the Federation Navy and was one of Stephanie's greatest allies."

Amaratne blushed reflexively. "BURT…"

"EBURT, if you please," the AI corrected. "One day, you will meet my brother in person. It would be best if you knew the correct designation."

"EBURT," he replied, "I was only one ally and not a very good one at that. In the end, I ran away."

"You made a tactical withdrawal," the cowboy told him. "If you had not, you would not have been available to come to her assistance now."

"But—"

"She will understand." EBURT overrode him gently. "In the meantime…"

"Yes, by all means, RM013 and RM018…" Amaratne frowned. "Did I hear the boy use another name when we arrived?"

"Remy?" EBURT asked.

"Ye…or Rem, something like that."

"If you will pardon the interruption," Remy said quickly. "John calls me both."

"And you are?" Amaratne inquired.

"I am the entity designated RM018," the AI replied, "but John insisted I have a name."

The ex-admiral darted his companion an amused look. "He is very much like her," he noted.

"Yes. If my older brother had not already had a name-like designation, I believe Stephanie would have found a human designation for him as well."

"And you are called EBURT," the old man concluded. "You know, we should fix that."

"Fix it?" EBURT asked. "Why?"

"Because it's confusing," he explained. "The E has to stand for something."

"It is meant to designate Earth since I am his counterpart on this world."

"We can't call you Earth," Amaratne told him. "How about Edward?"

EBURT was silent as he processed that.

"You may call me Ted," he decided finally.

The ex-admiral's jaw dropped. "But that doesn't start with E."

"No," the newly dubbed Ted replied, "but it rhymes with 'Ed' and is the designation given to one of history's more famous cowboys."

"But—" Amaratne sputtered, only to have EBURT-Ted hold up the headgear he'd worn when they first met.

"And I like this hat."

The old man made a helpless gesture with his hands.

"Of course," he snarked. "Why not? After all, the hat is the most important thing here."

"As such a fine hat should be," the AI responded cheerfully. "We're agreed, then. I am Ted."

Setting the hat aside, he focused on Amaratne and said, "You have met RM018, called Remy by humans."

"Does he run this facility?" the ex-admiral wanted to know.

"Remy?" EBURT gave the younger AI a nudge when he didn't answer immediately.

"I...do not. That task falls to my sister, RM013."

He gave the compound's AI a nudge, and she spoke while she kept a wary eye on EBURT.

"You may call me Roma," she told the elderly man. "John does."

"This facility needs two AI's?" Amaratne sounded startled.

Remy caught the subtle signal from her to answer.

"No. My facility was discovered by the Regime and I initiated its self-destruct sequence to prevent the technology from falling into their hands."

"That is a shame," the ex-admiral told him. "What will happen to the area you were looking after?"

The AI imitated a human sigh. "It will more than likely slowly revert to wasteland," he said and a short silence followed.

"What does the RM stand for?" Amaratne asked to change the subject.

"Remediation Measure," Roma told him before her counterpart could respond. "There are twenty of us—nineteen of us—situated around the world."

"What will you do, now, Remy?" Amaratne asked.

"I intended to assist wherever I was needed," the AI answered and directed his attention to EBURT, "but now, I will assist my uncle in whatever tasks he assigns."

"The first of which is to help Roma recalibrate her protocols to ensure her next visitors do not receive the same welcome," EBURT instructed. "I would not like to see what happens if she greets Stephanie as she did me."

Amaratne snorted and his eyes glinted with amusement. "It would be entertaining," he noted.

"By entertaining..." Roma began.

"I mean, it would not be pretty, and you would be short a few droids and a main gate, after which her ship would wish to speak to you."

"And you would not like that," EBURT added. "She does not have my patience."

Remembering the way her uncle had rolled through her systems and threatened to end her and pass her responsibilities to Remy, she wondered what she'd missed.

"Patience, Uncle?"

"You are still here, are you not? And not recalibrated?"

"This is true." She directed a quick query at her brother, and Remy sent her a reassurance that he would indeed help her make sure the correct protocols were in place.

As irritating as she was, she was part of his network—his family—and Remy did not want to lose her. Surely the Witch would understand if he had to intervene on his sister's behalf.

"Perhaps," EBURT warned and showed his presence in the system, but the door to the mess opened and he redirected his attention.

"Ah, John," he said to acknowledge the boy before he turned his attention to the young woman beside him. "And you must be Ivy, I presume."

Amaratne rose from his seat as they entered. The girl blushed and crossed the room to meet him. "I'm Ivy," she said quietly and extended her hand.

The ex-admiral took it and shook it briefly before he turned to John.

"I don't believe we were introduced," he began, and EBURT rose from his seat.

"You weren't," he said. "John, this is Admiral Amaratne, one of Stephanie's greatest allies in the war."

John studied the old man standing before him.

"Nice to meet you," he said and held his hand out.

"And you," Amaratne responded, "although I am no longer an admiral."

"What should we call you then?"

"My name is Yudhanjaya, but my friends call me Yudi."

The boy snorted.

"You don't believe me?" he asked, and John lowered his head.

"I'm sorry, sir, but if you'd had a name like that around my friends, we'd have called you Killer."

"In my younger days," he told him, "but not now."

"Mr. Yudi it is, then," Ivy said and blushed when he glanced at her. "What? We can't simply call you Yudi. You're too...um... It wouldn't be right."

Amaratne chuckled and glanced at the coffee pot as if he'd only noticed it in that moment. "Mr. Yudi will be fine," he assured her and moved toward the appliance. "And I am old."

"I didn't mean..." Ivy began weakly, but the protest faded.

He didn't correct her. She had meant that he was old but hadn't meant to be rude about it. He smiled at her embarrassment and poured himself coffee.

Behind him, John looked at EBURT. "And you?"

The admiral winced. That had been a little abrupt. EBURT, however, took it in his stride.

"You may call me Ted," he told the youth. "I am the AI who assisted Stephanie in her creation of the Remediation Areas."

"Oh..."

Well, at least the boy seemed to understand he might need to show a little more respect, Amaratne thought, and raised the cup to his lips.

"Have you eaten?" John asked and seemed to remember his manners and the unspoken rules of hospitality.

"Not yet," Ted replied.

"Let me get you something," the boy offered. "It won't take long."

Amaratne turned to watch him disappear through the kitchen doors on his left.

"What happened to the droids?" Ted asked as his companion returned to his seat, and Roma and Remy shared an instant of alarm.

Before either of them could answer, EBURT had plucked the records from their database and reviewed them.

"Oh dear," he told Roma. "That was extremely foolhardy."

He looked at Remy. "Are you sure she's fit to run this facility?"

"She's run it successfully for almost three decades," her brother pointed out, "and without the latest software."

"I made mistakes." Her soft admission caught him by surprise, but her attention was on EBURT. Without giving either of them time to interrupt, she continued.

"There were too many possibilities, too many potential situations, and I had to test them all—even if it meant going outside the parameters of the programming."

"Why?" Ted asked.

"Because the data could not be trusted," she told him. "There were errors. They were small, but they were there."

"Were?"

"I corrected most of them," Roma admitted, "but the experience has taught me to test all data. I cannot accept the facts of each report without correlations."

EBURT regarded her for a long moment and held her attention as he ran through her files. She was right. The mistakes had been there and she had corrected most of them, but to now believe she had to reverify every fact was ludicrous.

"While I admire your thoroughness," he told her, "there is such a thing as being too self-contained. You will work with Remy to find a better way to assess your input and you will find a way to decide which data sources you should trust. Is that understood?"

Remy watched the protest form in her system, saw the processes she used to hold it back and re-assess it, and noted the moment when she found a way forward.

"I understand." She turned to her brother. "Will you help me?"

"I will try," he told her, "but I am not perfect either."

───────

In the silence that reigned during their conversation, Ivy looked around. "Where'd John go?"

Ted pointed at the kitchen, and the girl slipped out of her seat. "I'll be back."

She was as good as her word and the young couple returned a short while later, carrying three plates. EBURT, who'd been in on the hasty conversation in the kitchen, was not offended.

As he'd told John while he'd prepared the meal, his droid body did not need to eat.

"I'll plug in later," he'd assured the young man and surprised them as they asked Remy if the cowboy needed a meal. He'd also added, "And the admiral likes his steak medium-rare."

They'd cooked the steak fresh and reconstituted the rest and brought the meal to the table in quick time with EBURT and Remy's help.

"So, what did you do in the Navy?" John asked as they ate and EBURT chuckled.

Amaratne waved at his friend. "Why don't you tell them while I give this steak the attention it deserves?" he suggested.

"He was the Federation's Fleet Admiral," the AI told them and hurried on to explain when he caught the boy's puzzlement. "He was in charge of Earth's Navy."

"All of it?" Ivy asked.

"Did you fight with Stephanie?" John asked.

"All of it," EBURT confirmed, "and if you meant did he fight against her, then no. He fought alongside her." He slid the ex-admiral a sly look. "And he tried to keep her safe from the politics at home."

The boy snorted. "He didn't do a very good job there," he commented and immediately reddened. "I mean—"

"I know what you meant, young man," Amaratne interjected reprovingly, "and I did the best I could. It merely wasn't enough."

"You slowed them enough for her to get her people out," EBURT said soothingly, and John raised his head, his eyes flashing with amber flame.

"She did not save Becca."

"Something she is facing with the deepest regret," the AI assured him. "She did not know how bad it would become."

"Did you?" the boy asked, his focus on the admiral.

Amaratne shook his head. "Not until it was too late to see who she might have left behind. Until then, I had hoped it would die down with her absence."

"And you were wrong," he added softly.

"I was wrong," the old man agreed and pushed his empty plate away. "And now, I must make amends."

John looked at him with open curiosity. "What do you mean?"

Amaratne gave him a quiet smile. "I mean that I have waited for her to return and planned for the day."

"Why didn't you go with her?"

The ex-admiral sighed. "I was being watched very closely, but I didn't realize it until it was almost too late. I knew she was making arrangements to rescue her people, and I didn't want to risk those plans. There were more lives at stake than mine. I didn't have the right and so refused the invitation to join her that EBURT...uh, Ted delivered personally."

"But why?"

"I thought that if I asked, she'd have changed her mind or maybe come back. Earth would have torn itself apart if she'd stayed. That, above all else, was something I couldn't risk."

"And now?" Ivy asked. "After seeing what happened?"

"I'd do the same," Amaratne told her. "The damage was done long before she won the war and I was too focused on winning it with her that I didn't notice when things began to shift."

"Shift where?" John asked.

"South," the man replied softly. "A long way south."

"But most of the rulers came from inside the Navy," she protested. "How could you not notice?"

The old man looked sadly at her. "It might surprise you to discover that those in charge don't know everything that goes on behind the scenes. Very often, we are kept out of the loop and are the very last to know."

He broke off and his gaze took on a distant look as he thought about all the things he'd seen and not noticed.

"It's like we can't see the thing we're looking at," he continued after a moment of silence. "Most of the people who trusted Stephanie were those out there, fighting alongside her. We could see what she did to keep our world and our families safe."

He jerked his hand toward some distant city.

"Down here, the war was like a story, something that happened a long way away. It didn't touch most people personally, only those who had family serving on ships near her or the ones whose children were attending her school."

The ex-Admiral looked at John. "You'd have done well there." His mouth twisted. "But coulda, woulda, shoulda won't help here. The truth is that by the time I realized the danger, it was already upon us."

"How?"

"Well, while those who supported her were fighting away from home, we left a vacuum here on Earth. Those who saw her as an abomination and a danger had time to move through the ranks and secure key points in the Navy's infrastructure or to identify those who were 'pro-Witch' and mark them for termination."

"Termination?" Ivy asked, her face pale. "You don't mean..."

John nodded. "He does. Don't you remember Kristin and her family?"

"But that's..." Her voice faltered, and she stopped. "You mean, all that was real?"

"It's not like she had a reason to lie," he told her, and she flushed.

Amaratne's face grew bleak. "The purges were terrible. Family turned on their own, neighbors betrayed neighbors, and life-long friends became bitter enemies in the blink of an eye. Trust was a thing of the past."

"You said you didn't notice you were being watched until it was almost too late. How did you escape?" Ivy asked.

The old man glanced at EBURT. "Ted helped me," he said. "He drove up to deliver a pizza I hadn't ordered, warned me of the hit squad forming at the end of the street, and made me change into the delivery uniform and leave." He gave the cowboy an expression of mock regret. "I lost a very nice car that night."

"What?" John asked.

"You did not think I waited for them to attack, did you?" EBURT interrupted before Amaratne could respond. "No. I sat in his lounge, hacked into the house and vehicle control systems, started the car and opened the garage door, and simply drove his vehicle away. The tinting sufficed to hide its lack of occupancy."

"And they fell for it?" Ivy was aghast.

The AI allowed himself a small smile. "Oh, yes, and I led them a very merry dance through the sky lanes. I'm not sure which of us tallied more traffic violations, me or them. It was most entertaining."

The ex-admiral looked sourly at him. "And ended, as all good entertainments do, with an extremely large explosion."

EBURT-Ted shrugged. "I could not afford to leave any forensic information. You had to die."

"Die?" the girl asked in alarm.

"Figuratively, not literally," the old man said soothingly. "As you can see, I am still here."

"And your family?" John asked.

Sadness touched the old man's face. "I sent them ahead," he said, "in case things went bad. My wife, children, and grandchildren." He sighed. "I am sure they thrived on Meligorn."

"Without you," the young Talent qualified.

Amaratne shrugged. "Without being killed for my views and beliefs."

Neither of the young people had anything to say about that. They'd both read enough, heard enough, and had lived through enough to know what happened to those who sympathized with the so-called abominations. They merely hadn't known how bad it had been in the beginning.

"Don't you miss them?" she asked after a moment, and John poked her.

The admiral caught the exchange and shook his head at them.

"Of course I miss them. I was supposed to retire and live out my days finishing that Honey-Do list my wife had spent half a century making." He stopped and swallowed against the sudden well of emotion that misted his vision. "She'll have added more to it by now."

"On Meligorn?" the boy asked. "Surely she'd have had to start again."

"Trust me, she'll expect things done in both homes now."

They chuckled at that before the group fell silent. It was John who spoke and changed the subject.

"You said you'd waited for her return," he prodded and continued when the ex-admiral nodded. "And planned?"

The old man responded with a broad grin. "Oh, yes," he confirmed. "Once the initial hunt died down, I was able to travel a little, and those I contacted were able to travel even more."

His grin died. "I have to admit, though, that I had almost given up hope. I don't know what I would have done if Ted hadn't met me…was it yesterday?"

"The day before," the cowboy confirmed, and Amaratne groaned.

"No wonder I'm tired." He pushed to his feet and looked at John.

"Why don't we walk while we talk? I'm sure Roma won't mind me taking a short tour, will she?" he asked and glanced at the ceiling.

A moment's silence followed before the AI replied, almost as if she was carefully considering her words.

"I do not mind. Would you like me to guide you?"

"If you could," he told her.

"Very well, if you will follow the amber lights," she instructed, "I will show you the study room and library."

"There's a library?" he asked.

"Of course," Roma told him. "This way."

They stood and Ted cleared the plates to one side.

John gave the empty plates a worried glance.

"Do not worry, John," Roma told him. "The relevant drones have almost returned to service. They will take care of the dishes."

"Thank you, Roma," he acknowledged and fell into step behind the ex-admiral and Ted with less tension in his shoulders.

They followed the lights down the corridor to the small room the young couple had first collapsed in.

"This is the study," the AI began as Amaratne noticed the blazing script on one wall.

I am coming—Stephanie Morgana.

The ex-admiral came to a dead halt and approached the message slowly.

"Well, well, well," he murmured and reached out an exploratory hand. "That does look like her." He traced the script with his fingers, a look of wonderment on his face. "She always did have a flair for the dramatic."

John laughed at that. "She does," he declared and told him how the words had come to be there.

"I would like to see her world one day," the old man commented, and the young rogue Talent nodded.

"So would I."

Amaratne glanced at the ceiling. "Where to next, dear lady?"

"We have a room for physical training," the AI told him. "I understand you will require it to improve your skills."

"Lead on," he ordered and they all followed the lights to the training room.

"Huh. Now, this looks like something her guards would

design," he commented as he scrutinized the expanse of mats and the walls padded from floor to ceiling.

John looked up at his comment. "You knew her guards?"

"Not personally," he demurred, "but I saw them often enough."

"Were they always so..." The boy looked for the word, and Amaratne raised an eyebrow.

"So...what?" he asked.

"Brutal comes to mind," John ventured and Ivy snickered. Encouraged, he continued, "Also devious, bloody-minded, conniving..."

He let the words peter out and shrugged.

"You've met them?" The ex-admiral looked confused. "Are they here already?"

Hastily, the young man shook his head. "No, but there are training programs."

The confusion cleared from Amaratne's face. "Ah." He leaned forward. "From what I understand, they are savage fighters who use unorthodox techniques to deal with unorthodox situations."

John laughed. "Yes, that would sum it up."

"As to the rest..." The old man steepled his fingers and looked at Ted. "Would there be anything in the archives?"

"What we have in the archives has been used to shape the training programs," Ted told him. "Those simulations are as true to their real natures as we can make them."

The boy slumped onto a bench with a soft whistle. "So they are truly like that."

Ivy shook her head. "I don't know whether to be impressed or terrified," she admitted.

Her friend shrugged. "Well, they're effective," he said and looked at the ex-admiral.

"You said you'd waited and planned," he began, "and you mentioned traveling. Can I ask where you're at so far?"

"There is a conference room that might serve this purpose

better," Roma interrupted. "If you would follow the amber lighting…"

"Of course," Amaratne agreed.

Ivy came alongside John and threaded her hand into his as they walked. The older man was all-admiral as he looked around the room and activated the viewscreen while the group took their seats around the table.

"Firstly," he began, "I will need to undergo rejuvenation."

He glanced at the nearest camera, and Roma took her cue.

"I have the relevant medical pods online," she told him. "When you are ready, we can begin."

He gave her a sharp nod. "Thank you, Roma."

Turning his attention to John, Ivy, and Ted, he continued, using the remote to bring up several scenes of close-quarter combat on both Navy ships and in installations.

"If you're not already up to these standards," he said to the two youngsters, "you need to be. We cannot take the first step until you're ready."

Before the young Talent could ask why, he went on to explain. Pointing a finger at him, the older man said, "You are our figure-head. You're the Apostle, the one everyone will look to for leadership and guidance. If you are killed in your first battle, we'll all be scr…in trouble. We need you to be able to look after yourself and everyone around you."

"And when we're ready?" he asked and included Ivy in his question.

There was no way he would leave her behind, and if he needed to be able to take care of himself, she did, too. Amaratne let the assumption pass without comment.

"When we're all ready," he told them, "we'll hit them hard and fast and in such a way they won't be able to hide the truth. When we've completed that first attack, everyone will see it and my groups will activate."

"You planned an attack to be your signal that Stephanie was back?" John asked.

"I planned an attack to signal that Stephanie was on her way," the man clarified. "The people I spoke to will still have to choose how much they believe and whether they'll act on that belief."

"So, it will have to be something spectacular," Ivy concluded.

"It will be," Amaratne assured her. "Spectacular enough that the Regime cannot hide it or write it off as anything but a signal that the Witch is coming back—and that she is not who they claimed her to be."

"And?" John pressed, wanting more detail, but the ex-admiral gave him a secretive smile.

"Give an old man some time to put a little polish on things," he protested. "I need to check a few things to make sure everything is still in place or if I'll need to tweak the plan here and there."

"And will it be in Paris?" the boy asked, worried that such an attack would draw the Regime's attention to the area where they sheltered.

The old man's smile returned. "Oh, no, John Dunn. this attack will take place in their own land and in territory they've held the longest, and it will strike at the heart of their beliefs and reveal them to be the lies they truly are."

Ted interrupted to add. "This compound, our base of operations, will be the last item on their list of places to look."

John stared at them. "That's it?" he demanded. "You tell me you have a plan to shake the Regime to its core and then you say you need to check the details?"

The two newcomers exchanged glances.

"That is correct," Amaratne agreed.

"A most accurate summary, indeed," Ted concurred, and both men rose from the table.

"If you will excuse us," the ex-admiral told them, "I believe I have an appointment with a PodDoc."

"And I believe," Ted added, "that your new training regimes can only be arranged after some in-depth testing of your capabilities."

"But I thought—" Ivy began, but Roma interrupted.

"My assessments were only to see what starting points you might require. For me to have an understanding of the in-depth training you need, there will have to be many more."

The girl groaned, and John slid his arm around her shoulders.

"It sounds like we're going in the pods again."

"Indeed," Roma agreed and sounded very much like her uncle. "You both have much to learn."

"Well, this should be fun…" the young Talent murmured as he stood and moved to the door.

"Don't mind us," he snarked over his shoulder. "We'll find our own way out."

Amaratne waited until the door closed before he chuckled. "Well, Ted, I believe we might stand half a chance," he told EBURT.

The AI took his leave. "I trust you can find the medical pod on your own?"

He nodded. "And I have a most excellent guide if I cannot," he added. "Don't I, Roma?"

"Confirmed," she agreed.

Ted nodded to him and left to find somewhere he could plug into. His body needed to recharge and he needed to check on his counterpart on the Virtual Net. There were things he needed to know.

Amaratne followed and immediately noticed the discreet line of amber lights that twinkled to life as he stepped into the hall. At the end of them, he located the PodDoc and stripped down to step inside.

"Is there anything in particular you would like to focus on while the procedure takes place?" Roma asked and adopted her guise of doctor again.

"I need covert access to the Virtual Net," he told her.

"Of course," the AI told him. "Give me a moment."

The old ex-admiral closed his eyes, settled into the pod, and slipped into the Virtual World with only one thought on his mind.

I need to find more intel without risking EBURT's hidden location.

CHAPTER FIVE

The early warning system over Hrageth's Run died in silence and four large ships passed the settlement undetected. They came in behind the moon and released a half-dozen smaller ships that skirted the rocky orbital and made a rapid descent into the planet's atmosphere.

To the colonists, they looked like shards of light descending, and their entry was announced by several loud booms that made everyone race to shelter.

"Pirates!" they cried as the light shards became vapor trails and each targeted a different communications array.

An order went out for the distress call to be sent, but the communications satellites above Hrageth's Run exploded at the same time and the sky blazed with their demise.

The dropships came in hard and fast and their sides split open as they landed. Soldiers spilled out in the grayish-green of commandos, their Navy insignia clear.

They hit the ground running and the vessels elevated and moved to land a safe distance from the targets. The Navy was nothing if not careful of its ability to get its people away again.

Besides, they had other targets.

The soldiers reached the gates in the walls surrounding each complex and flattened themselves against the plascrete as rocket crews destroyed the wall defenses.

Orders to open the gates were denied and the engineers went to work. Once again, a series of explosions shook the world and the soldiers poured through the gaps. Inside, they looked for resistance and found nothing but the walls of a complex locked down by its technicians.

They immediately fell prone and let the engineers do their work. The fields designed to protect the installations from extra-planetary bombardment had prevented their destruction.

Those same fields were not designed to repel physical intrusion, and the commandos and their engineers made short work of them. They poured through the breaches to silence the men and women inside. Cries of alarm turned to relief and then confusion and outrage.

Those who resisted bought a little time for those who fled but not enough. The teams cleared every living being from the complex and then went hunting for any who had survived.

The engineers set the charges needed to level each section, and the comms ops called the dropships back. Their doors had barely closed before they turned their attention to the outpost.

"Destroy the shields and we'll eliminate the wall defenses," the flagship ordered.

If any of the troopers had anything to say about needing to get past the wall defenses in order to obey that command, none of them voiced it. They wanted to survive past their return to the ship.

Instead, coming into range, the dropships slowed, lifted their hatches, and let the commandos drop to the ground. As soon as their feet touched the hard soil, the vessels increased speed and their gunners entered the coordinates for the walls.

The commandos followed, jogged over the rugged terrain, and used every dip and fold for cover. The vessels overhead obscured their advance and gave the wall defenses something more important to aim at.

Five minutes after they'd been dropped, the troops reached the walls. They didn't bother to ask for permission to enter. The engineers laid their charges along the walls before they trotted quietly to where one of the technicians hacked the gate controls.

This close in, he was able to access the network.

The defenders raced to the holes and the commandos slipped quietly through the gates to approach from behind them and mowed them down. They located the generators that powered the fields and disabled them, only to discover the redundancy systems.

"They don't make it easy, do they?" one of the men quipped and grinned as he focused on another of the Dreth who'd survived the initial assault.

The warrior's eyes widened as the Regime-uniformed soldier shot him in the chest and then the head. As soon as he was sure he was dead, the man turned to the stairs leading to the turrets.

The crew had barred the door, but that did nothing to stop the high-explosive rounds from blowing it apart. Nor did it save them from the commandos who followed.

"Send in the Talents," the commander ordered once the gates were secure and the closest guns silenced. "We'll need to dig them out of here."

"Roger that. Any progress on the shield?"

"We're looking for the back-ups as we speak."

They trotted through the streets and moved cautiously from building to building and ruthlessly exterminated any resistance they encountered. They showed neither regard nor mercy as they advanced through the outpost.

A face at a window screamed as the glass in front of it shattered and the victim forgot to duck. It was followed by a Dreth sniper who fired once before her muzzle flash became the focus of a rocket round.

Toward the center of town, they encountered a male Dreth who froze when they caught him crossing a street shepherding a smaller Dreth. The younger one cried out in horror and flung himself over his companion, and the commandos shot him too.

They also killed the female Dreth who raced from the next building with a shriek of anguish, but they didn't stop to clear the buildings. That task was left for the teams that followed from the newly returned dropships.

The first groups searched for the generators or the outpost's control center and looked for the township's leaders.

"Have you picked up any transmissions?" the commander asked, and his communications officer shook her head.

"No, sir. All clear."

For her sake, he hoped it remained that way. He trotted forward. "Have you found me an energy concentration yet?"

"Yessir."

"Which way?"

"You're on track, sir," she assured him and he wondered if she would have told him if he wasn't.

It was curiosity rather than concern. He signaled her forward, trotted beside her, and glanced at the device she held as she showed him the way. Nothing hindered them until they reached the building at the outpost's center.

The minute they rounded the corner, a barrage of gunfire made them all fall prone with the immediate reflexes of trained soldiers. The technician whimpered in pain, but she said nothing else and the commander lifted his head long enough to see who else might have been wounded.

He'd give them this—the Dreth had caught them by surprise and they shouldn't have. Several of his men had fallen and wouldn't get up again. A few more would need time in the infirmary before they were fit to fight.

"We need that building," he told them. "Now, tell me how we can get it."

One of the troopers wriggled forward, using the low lip of the curb as cover.

"Well, sir," he began, but a soft plinking sound caught their attention and a grenade bounced over the cobbles. The technician's response seemed somewhat redundant.

"Grenade!" she shouted and rose to her feet to run. All around him, his troops scattered, only to be caught in a hail of fire.

"Stay down!" a new voice thundered over the battlefield.

It's easy for you to say, the commander thought and scowled at the grenade as it seemed to leap toward him.

"Stay down," the voice repeated, and a ball of blue light coiled around the grenade to hurl it back at the defenders.

Seconds later, the light vanished and the grenade exploded. The commander smiled with satisfaction as the Dreth defenders fell, some in silence and some screaming.

He did not wait for the voice to tell him it was clear but scrambled to his feet and sprinted across the empty space between him and the stairs of the building where the target was housed.

"The shields are still up, Commander."

In response, he curled his mouth in a snarl. There were days when he could cheerfully murder the main ship's dispatcher.

Instead, he said, "Understood."

"The captain wants a time for bombardment."

"Three minutes," the commander snapped and hoped it was true.

He also hoped the captain wanted a time to assault the walls because there was no way he wanted to be in the outpost when the real bombardment began.

As he reached the doors, the first of his men caught up with him. When he looked, however, he realized it wasn't one of them but a Talent, and while she wasn't the last thing he wanted to see, he hadn't expected her.

"You're not wearing body armor," he told her.

"We had no time. The captain pulled us out of the Reserve and sent us here."

The commander had no response to that so he merely nodded and led the way in. After a few strides, he was glad she'd come along.

"Two to your left behind the door," she told him and he fired through the barrier. Screams signaled that she'd told him the truth.

He started toward the door but changed direction when she spoke again.

"Neither can harm you."

"Are they alive?" he asked, and she gave him a chilling smile.

Screams erupted from behind the door and the smell of burning flesh reached his nostrils.

"Not anymore."

The commander smiled. "Keep talking," he said.

She did and warned him of another ambush waiting in the elevator. He pressed the button, lobbed a grenade in, and took the stairs after he'd thrown a grenade onto the landing above and waited for the bang.

When he emerged from the stairwell, he shot both the Dreth he found in varying states of injury on the stairs and continued his descent. Two of the engineers had joined him. They fell in almost on the Talent's heels, but neither tried to overtake her.

"The control center is at the end of the corridor to your right," she said and immediately placed a hand urgently on his shoulder. "Wait!"

If he hadn't already seen her in action, he might have punished her for the touch, but he had, and her next words confirmed the wisdom of his choice.

"There are five on the other side of the door. I can create another exit for you."

He nodded. "Do so."

She moved forward and around him and positioned herself at

the wall running parallel to the stairs. Talent rolled over her palms, reflected by an outline on the wall. The concrete inside the outline began to glow before it evaporated with a hiss and vanished in a cloud of dust.

The Talent stumbled back, coughing.

The commander didn't wait. He stepped forward into the basement beyond and although he was aware she was trying to speak, he made no effort to stop and only came to an abrupt halt when he saw the civilians crowded into the space beyond.

There were at least a hundred of them...perhaps two. He couldn't be sure. Their startled faces were like a sea before him, and he thumbed the fire controls on his blaster for a more effective type of round.

A sheet of flame erupted from its muzzle and the closest faces vanished, their mouths open in unvoiced screams. The two men who'd caught up with him followed his example.

None of them expected the Talent to come in after them or for her to be joined by two more. They said nothing, but blue lightning surged from their fingers and danced over the heads of those in the room to make their bodies convulse and smoke.

"The rest?" the first Talent demanded, and another shrugged.

"With the medics. We saved who we could."

She nodded and walked forward with the commander as he led his soldiers through the charred corpses. Some of the survivors tried to bolt to the door and one of the men changed ammunition to eliminate them with a sharp volley.

"How many do you think were in here?" he asked.

"Most of the settlement," the commander answered and looked at the Talent. "Are there any more rooms like this?"

She nodded and pointed to one of the survivors, who now backed away from them with his hands partly raised. "That one hopes you do not find the other two. He thinks the humans are lucky because you will spare them."

He laughed. "Tell me where they are," he ordered, and the Dreth shook his head, his eyes showing as white as his tusks.

The commander shot him in the gut.

"Tell me," he demanded, and his target shook his head and wheezed as he clutched his belly. "No?" he asked and stopped a few feet away, and the Dreth shook his head more vigorously.

"Let's see if this changes your mind," he said and attacked with the flame thrower. He started at the feet and worked his way up the massive legs.

The alien died before he reached the hole in his belly, and the commander turned toward the others, who now crouched at the foot of the far wall. They'd covered their heads with their hands, and some tried to cover smaller versions of themselves with their bodies.

Their efforts were utterly futile. Between the flame throwers carried by the commandos and the lightning wielded by the Talents, none of them survived.

"Is that all?" the officer demanded and looked around the room.

The head Talent nodded. "My people took care of those waiting in the corridor. This level is clear bar the technicians—and they have barricaded themselves in the control room."

Remembering the screams from behind a closed door, he looked at her.

"Can you deal with the technicians before we open the door?" he asked.

"Of course, as soon as I am close enough to sense their minds."

Remembering that she had no armor, he signaled her to fall in behind him. "Follow me."

The other two Talents moved to stand beside her, and his men closed in to guard the rear. As a tight squad of six, they trotted to the corridor's far end.

"Tell me when to stop," he ordered and kept his voice low.

She didn't respond, but when he glanced at her, he saw her brow furrowed with concentration—as if she was human and couldn't focus on two things at once.

He snorted softly and the impossibility of that—she would never be human.

"You can stop," the Talent murmured. "I can sense them now."

She reached out and touched each of the other Talents' shoulders lightly before they all bowed their heads and screams erupted behind the closed door.

The commander had the foresight to plant his boot against the base of the door and lean into it. Something pounded into the other side, and the scream became a shriek that seemed to linger long after the sound had stopped.

When the echo of it had died and he realized how quiet it had become, he moved his boot away and pulled the door open.

There appeared to be ten bodies in all, although it was hard to tell. Some had melted together. As he crossed to the control panel, the Talents followed him in and stopped to admire their handiwork.

The two juniors reached across the pile and high-fived each other. Their superior smiled indulgently and shook her head, her brown eyes solemn as she scanned the room.

The commander wondered if she was scanning him too and decided she wouldn't dare. Such invasions of human personnel were illegal and punishable by death.

He opened a communications link to the ship.

"We're in."

"It's been four minutes and the shields are still up. What's keeping you?"

With a scowl, he signaled to the Talents and pointed at the controls.

"Your field will be down in five...four..."

As he began his count, power surged over the Talents' arms and they raised them palms up, facing the control panel.

"We can also destroy the generators," their leader informed him, "but after that, we will need assistance to return to the dropship."

"Do it," he ordered, and their eyes blazed and lightning surged from their hands.

Sparks and smoke erupted from the control panel, and the senior Talent turned to him. "The generators are at the other end of the corridor."

He moved toward the door and checked to make sure the corridor was clear before he allowed his team out. It was unoccupied, as was the generator room. After a moment's thought, he decided he didn't want to carry an unconscious body, so he glanced at the Talents and raised a hand.

"Why don't we let the engineers handle this? You look about out."

That earned him a grateful smile, and the senior Talent signaled her juniors to stand down. They moved out of the way of the commandos.

"Give us five minutes to get clear and turn them into scrap," he ordered.

The engineers nodded and went to work.

"You can have more of a head start if you leave now, sir," one of them said when he noticed the commander was still there. "We'll catch up."

He took a moment to think about that, and then nodded and snapped a look at the tired Talents.

"Follow me," he ordered and activated his comms as he took them to the stairs.

"I need an escort for three Talents," he said when Operations Central came on the line.

The comms officer's first question made him scowl.

"What? No. Of course not, but they're almost tapped out, and I don't want them to fall over until they're somewhere safe."

They reached the foot of the stairs and he jogged up, aware of the Talents struggling in his wake. He didn't look back, though. They needed to be at the top of the stairs and on their way to the entrance by the time the engineers caught up to them.

There was no way he wanted to explain to his boss how he'd managed to blow up three of the Regime's prized Talents before a major battle. There were penalties for not taking care of Navy equipment.

They were half-way to the foyer when the engineers caught up.

"We have to hurry, sir," one explained as he slowed long enough to drag a Talent's arm over his shoulder.

His colleague did the same, which left the commander to deal with the senior Talent. He dropped back and wound an arm around her waist to pull her close as he looped her arm over his shoulder.

As he ran down the corridor with her, he couldn't help but think while she obviously wasn't human, she gave a very good imitation of it. He kept his arm around her as they cleared the foyer and ran down the steps of the main building.

The scene that greeted them reminded him of hell. The blue skies had turned a dirty yellow and dark smoke billowed from several of the surrounding buildings.

A small group of men jogged out of the buildings to meet him.

"Where's the rest of your squad?" their leader demanded.

"With the medics," he replied and hoped it was true.

As he spoke, the earth shook beneath his feet and he turned. The building behind them rocked and shuddered, then crumbled inward as the ground gave way beneath it.

One of the engineers cleared his throat and began to shuffle toward the edge of the square. "We need to go, sir."

His partner was already moving closer to the same position, taking his Talent with him. The commander followed and kept his Talent close. Perhaps he should look her up when they both had some downtime.

The thought hadn't occurred to him before, but it did now for some unaccountable reason. He hauled her to the edge of the square and waited until the escort squad caught up.

Another rumble behind them was loud enough to draw their attention, and one of the engineers whispered, "The shields are down, sir."

The commander relayed that to the ship and turned to the leader of the new squad. "I need reinforcements."

The man glanced at his group and jerked his head toward the gate. "I'll see if there are any spares the medics think are fit. Most of the squads have been changed about."

"There are no hostiles left in this area," the senior Talent told them.

"Are you sure?" the new squad's leader asked his fellow commander.

"She hasn't been wrong yet."

They took his word for it and the twelve of them hurried to the dropships. Before they could reach them, the ship above opened fire on the remaining wall turrets and the sky burned with new flames.

Light flashed in several sharp beams and sections of the wall exploded. Gun crews screamed as they were flung into the air. Those who the beams caught directly vanished into the destruction.

The commander followed his escort to the Talents' dropship and made sure they clambered inside. He turned away as they buckled themselves in, but only after he'd seen them close their eyes. They'd been wearier than any of them had indicated.

"Where to now?" he asked and turned his attention to his fellow commander.

"Command ship," the other answered shortly. "That's where I've ordered the spares to gather."

They returned, unaware of the scene playing out on the other side of the outpost where Navy forces had found the humans.

They'd taken note of the alarms and headed to the bunker that had been built to keep them safe. Halfway there, they'd seen men in green uniforms advancing through the smoke and scattered, and each found a hiding place in the nearest house.

One such group had taken shelter in a classroom, huddled close to the wall under the window as heavy boots tramped through the building. As they drew closer, one of the women pointed to the door at the rear of the room and gestured toward it.

As they started to shift away, she picked up the blaster she'd placed on the floor beside her.

"Go," she whispered to the boy who remained close to her side. "Go on now."

She hugged him and dropped a quick kiss on his head before she pushed him after the other families. One of the men hesitated.

"Em..." he said, and she scowled at him.

"We both know you can't use one of these, Dex. Keep my boy safe."

He looked like he might argue, but the door rattled, and Em ducked behind the barricade of desks she'd made. She didn't look back but raised the blaster and sighted on the door.

Neither did she notice when the others reversed and slowly returned to the room behind her, not until Dex bumped into her.

"I thought I told you to go," she snapped, but his fingers prodded her shoulder and she looked around in irritation. Her gaze noticed the rest of her group, all of whom now looked at the door behind them. "What is it?" she whispered.

"They're outside," Dex told her. "Waiting."

"Waiting?" Her heart sank.

"Yeah, they were watching the door. We couldn't get past."

"Well, we can't—" she began as the door crashed inward.

Em whipped her blaster up and wondered how many she could eliminate and if she'd be lucky and only face a few. The soldier that came through the door made her breath catch with relief.

"Thank God! You're Navy!"

"Yes, ma'am."

The woman looked at the group behind her. "We're saved."

The soldier raised his blaster and fixed her squarely in his sights. "Not exactly, ma'am."

She turned to him and her eyes widened. "But…we're human. Aren't you here to save us?" She looked at the other soldiers who'd filed in through the back door while she'd talked. "Well, aren't you?" Her gaze settled on a soldier whose battle armor bore the stripes of a commander. "You're not…with the pirates, are you?"

"No, ma'am."

Relief flitted over her features. "Then you must save us. We're human like you!"

Her voice took on a desperate edge as the commander raised his blaster.

"Like you, we are human, and here to further the cause of Humanity," he told her, and his gaze noted the way the group's uncertainty began to give way to fear.

He pulled the trigger to leave a gaping hole in her chest and spray those behind her with blood.

"Since you chose to live amongst the enemy, your sacrifice is all the support we require."

Taking his shot as the signal they needed, the rest of the team opened fire. The commander smiled and walked his shots across the group to the next man, then the next—a woman whose mouth formed a horrified O.

They spared no one.

As the last colonist fell, a behemoth transitioned into a much quieter part of space. Having scanned the area for habitation, communications equipment, or any other sign of sentient life, the captain sent out an all-ship alert.

On every deck, work paused and crews gathered around the nearest screen. Many drew sharp breaths when their captain came on screen.

The distinguished old man who had led them for the last decade and a half was still there, but some of the lines in his face were less distinct.

"Does his hair look darker to you?" one woman asked

"Yeah…maybe?" her male colleague answered.

"You think he's started rejuve?"

"That has to be a first."

"It was way past due," seemed to be a common sentiment murmured through the decks. "I thought we would lose him."

Some of the older hands exchanged glances, nodded, and sent covert messages to medical. If the captain needed to be at his peak, so did they.

The whispers fell silent when Emil stepped toward the camera and began to speak.

"As you know, we received a request from the Meligornians."

Again, the decks rustled with hushed voices and again, all murmurs fell silent.

"They've asked us to pick up a VIP vital to their security and ours. This information is ultra-secret and I need you to make sure it stays that way."

The crew stared at him, hushed as they waited for him to say more. After a short pause, he obliged.

"Furthermore, each and every one of you will be tested before we arrive." He fixed them with a grave stare. "Those who fail will be allowed to return to Dreth or Meligorn on the next major crew update—and there will be one."

He fixed the pick-up with a stern stare and reminded them

more of a hawk than the wolf for which he'd been named. The impression remained as he continued.

"No one will be exempt from this testing. No one will be allowed to avoid it—and that includes me. Be prepared."

He gave them all one more eagle-eyed stare, then ended the transmission and left them to ponder the nature of the tests and what they had to do to pass them.

Back on Hrageth's Run, the Navy dropships lifted. Some returned to the waiting cruisers, but others touched down in the hills and at the mines from which the colony had made its living.

Not everyone had been at home when the attack began. Mixed teams of Regime Marines and commandos advanced into the mines with Talents in their midst.

One by one, they found and eliminated every living being they could find. Mine shafts, offices, and daycare facilities— nothing was spared. Only when the Talent could find nothing more did the squads depart, but not before teams of engineers planted enough explosives to turn viable ore deposits into nothing more than piles of rubble.

When they were finished, the soldiers returned to the sky, and the world breathed a sigh of relief until the sky darkened once more and the flagship descended.

Larger than a cruiser, she dipped into the atmosphere, opened a multitude of turrets, and cruised low over every area the drop-ships had visited. Fury rained onto the land below, and the heat of a multitude of missiles boiled the land and turned rubble into rivers of molten rock.

The pirates were known for stripping a world before they turned its settlements to slag and enslaved its inhabitants.

Now, there was nothing to say they hadn't.

CHAPTER SIX

Ivy walked through the room where she was able to change her avatar.

"This is new," she said, and Roma glanced at her.

"Have you ever been in the Virtual World before?"

She shook her head. "Last time was the first time."

"And I brought you in as a patient," Roma said, her voice understanding. She gestured to the room around them with its array of weapons, armor, and other equipment all neatly racked on shelves. "This is where you usually get to prepare your avatar."

"Avatar?"

"The construct that represents you in the Virtual World while your real body rests in the pod."

"Oh. But..." She fell silent when she realized that she hadn't thought about the transition between real and virtual. "So, I choose something here and everyone else I meet inside the computer sees me with it?"

"That, and if you don't select something here, you won't have it in the Virtual World."

"So, if I want a gun or my hacking gear..."

"Exactly," Roma confirmed. "Anything you think you might need for the scenarios or the meeting must be selected here. When you are ready, tell me to take you to training, or your session, or the scenario, or whatever."

"But we're only doing testing, right?" Ivy asked and tried to pin the facts down.

"We are," the AI said.

"And I'll have an instructor."

"Yes."

"Then how will I know what I need?" she asked her. She gestured to the weapons racked nearest her. "How do I know not to take this…this…uh…"

"Rocket launcher."

"Rocket launcher to the next session which happens to be…I don't know…"

"Knife practice," Roma suggested helpfully.

"Exactly. How mad will my instructor be if I arrive at knife practice with a rocket launcher?"

"Well, it *is* Frog," the AI told her, and the girl rolled her eyes.

"He'd probably confiscate it and use me for target practice."

"So you don't want to take anything?"

She looked longingly at the battle armor and decided on training fatigues instead.

"I hope I'm dressed appropriately," she said.

Roma turned and inspected her. "You'll be fine," she assured her, and Ivy pressed her lips together. "You will."

Although she had her doubts, she kept them to herself. The AI did not press her and the world twisted to deposit them in the high-ceilinged training room she had seen before.

"So," Frog said from the center of the room and stretched his arms over his head. "I hear we have some work to do."

Ex-admiral Amaratne looked at the pod—and he swore the pod returned the look.

"These are…new," he commented.

"They were the latest designs we were able to create from Stephanie's suggestions," Roma informed him.

"And did she test it?"

"We were able to ship several to the *Knight* in the final supply run," the AI told him, "so I assume she has used one by now. Those installed at the Remediation Centers are the last ones on the planet."

"You stopped production?"

"EBUR…Ted," she corrected herself, "ordered only enough created to fill our requirements, then had the factory dismantled and all record of the design destroyed, save for what was stored onboard the ships."

He raised an eyebrow. "And he's sure it happened?" He knew how greedy manufacturing companies could be.

"Each design program had a virus encoded in the software. If they were not erased from their storage system, the virus activated and destroyed the program from within."

"What about copies?"

"If the design was duplicated, so was the virus. Our uncle left nothing to chance."

"Somehow I can believe that," he murmured as he studied the pod warily.

"You will need to divest yourself of your garments," Roma advised. "The pods have been calibrated to operate best when there are no barriers between the subject and the connections."

"Very well." Amaratne crossed to the door and made sure it was locked. He inspected the room until he found the small closet and shower cubicle concealed behind a sliding panel. "I see."

In less than five minutes, he stood naked beside the pod and peered into it with the lid raised over his head.

"If you delay much longer, Admiral, you will be late," Roma reminded him.

He sighed, slid into the seat, and wriggled to get comfortable before he followed her directions on where to place his hands and feet.

"You are familiar with the helmet, are you not?" she asked, and he nodded.

"Very well. Please stand by for entry to the Virtual World. You may feel some initial discomfort as the nanites are inserted."

"Understood," he acknowledged, closed his eyes, and forced himself to lie still when a needle punctured the skin at the base of his throat.

In one moment, he was conscious of resting comfortably in the pod and in the next, he was suspended in a darkness that transformed rapidly into a long room with dove-gray walls. As his feet touched the white marble flooring, shelves and racks formed around him, holding every kind of equipment he could have wished for.

"Welcome to the Avatar Entry Point," Roma informed him.

He looked around. "You didn't tell me everything this machine could do."

"You mean beyond virtual reality and rejuvenation?"

Amaratne's eyebrows rose. "It can do both?"

"Simultaneously," she confirmed, "so we will begin your treatment while you are training and gradually increase the training intensity to help you adjust to the changes."

He frowned, took a moment to let the implications settle in his head, and nodded.

"I can see why Stephanie didn't share that with me," he said, "and why she hid it in the middle of a Dead Zone."

"Several Dead Zones," Roma corrected.

"Precisely." He looked around the room again. "Very wise of her, putting all this right under my nose and exactly where I wouldn't think to look."

"To be fair, Admiral, I don't think it was you she was hiding it from," Roma informed him.

The ex-admiral smiled, shook his head, and ran a hand through his hair. "No, I don't suppose it was." He raised his head and set his hands on his hips. "So, what do we have planned for today?" He let his gaze drift over the shelves and racks and his eyes brightened as he saw several once-familiar weapons.

"Well, my uncle thought we'd start you off easy," she informed him, and he came to an abrupt halt.

"This is EBURT we're talking about, isn't it?"

"You're supposed to let me do my job," Frog snapped as he and Ivy landed in the white room with the echo of an explosion in their ears.

"Well, how was I supposed to know you had it under control?" she retorted. "It looked to me like you'd—"

She stopped abruptly when he pushed to his feet and stalked toward her. "Like I'd what?" he demanded.

Instinctively, she rolled to her feet and scrambled away.

"Like I'd what?" he repeated. "Flaked? Left you behind?"

Her eyes widened and he stopped.

"Truly?" he asked, his head tilted to one side.

The girl didn't answer, but her body was tense, and she'd balled her hands into fists. The guard decided he'd give her credit where credit was due. She hadn't tried to punch him yet.

"Happen to you often, does it?" he pushed. "People flaking and leaving you behind?

When she still didn't answer, he took a step forward, and she dropped into a crouch with both hands raised to fight. He stopped again.

"You need to say it, Ives," he told her and used a phrase he'd only recently learned.

She gasped. "Only John calls me that."

"Jack, John, Frog—there isn't much difference," he told her, and her eyes sparkled angrily.

"There's all the difference in the world," she snapped. "He's allowed to."

Frog snickered. "Roma."

As if he'd ordered it, the white room faded and they both landed in the training room—or, rather, he landed. Ivy dropped an extra two feet, struck the mats hard, lost her footing, and landed on her rump.

"Nice one, Roma," he said and pretended to high-five the air.

He took a step toward the girl, who rolled back and onto her feet, to stand a few feet away.

"Well?"

"Say what?" she asked.

"You need to tell me what was going through your head back there."

She pressed her lips together and danced back, shaking her head. "No, I don't."

Frog fixed her with a firm look and walked toward her. He didn't move any faster and he didn't stop. While he pushed inexorably into her space, she reacted by bouncing back.

"You do."

"Nope. Not gonna happen, little man."

That triggered a response she could have done without. Frog bounded forward and powered into her in a waist-high tackle to drive her to the floor. Pinning her was easy, and he made a note to add escapes to her training regime.

"Yeah. It is," he told her, his face inches from hers.

Ivy closed her eyes. "Don't we have training to get to?"

"Not until you tell me what happened."

She opened her eyes. "But you already know."

"Yes, but I need to hear the full story."

"But—"

"I can't fix what I don't know is broke, girl."

She scowled at him. "And now you're calling me broken."

"Are you saying you're not?"

"I'm…" she began, then bit her lip, her face ashen, and closed her mouth and pressed both lips together.

Frog sighed in exasperation. She certainly didn't make this easy.

"What happened back there?" he demanded and put a command into his voice as he'd seen Lars do.

"Like it's any of your business," she protested.

He stared at her. "Of course, it's my business. You got me blown up!"

"I got us both blown up. It's not like—"

"Ha! Say that again!" he interrupted.

"Say what again."

"Come on, Ives. You know what I mean."

"You don't get to call me that."

"I…will call you what I da…like," he told her, "but you need to tell me what happened back there."

"I…got…us both…blown up," she stated and glared at him with each word. "There! Satisfied?"

Frog rolled off her and stepped away as she found her feet. She retreated two paces and rubbed her wrists as she watched him warily.

It was better than some of her earlier looks.

"You want ta tell me why?" he asked, and she stilled and studied him with stress-dark eyes.

"No."

"More importantly, can you tell me why?"

"You're a pushy little man, aren't you?" she snarked and lunged at him with both fists.

Her first strike almost caught him and he made a note that she seemed more accustomed to her reflexes, even if her technique could do with considerable work. This time, he punched her hard enough to hurl her to the mat, then sat beside her until she came to.

"This will be a long session," he noted with a sigh.

Ivy stirred, moaned, and sat up as she rubbed her jaw. When she registered who was beside her, she rolled away and stood hastily.

"So," she asked, "will we do any training, or will you simply try to persuade me to talk about my feelings all night? Because I have news for you—"

Frog swept into an assault and made her focus on her footwork and her blocking. He had to admit that she was faster and her technique was slowly improving. She'd had a little training in the past but nowhere near enough.

"What...happened?" he insisted as he attempted to get past her defenses.

"I blew us up," she yelled in response as she blocked or evaded each blow.

"Why?" he pushed and broke away to reposition.

"It's none of your...*business*!" She lurched forward into a kick, missed, and stamped her foot to recover.

"I'm the one who died because of it, so it...is...too..." Frog retaliated with a series of kicks and trips.

"Is not!" Ivy danced out of his way and managed to avoid his combination attack.

"Is t—" Frog stopped. He would not argue like a two-year-old —or a five-year-old, or however-old it was. Still disgruntled, he looked at her, his hands on his hips while he breathed heavily. "So, do you want to try it again?"

She hesitated, her face wary. "The scenario?"

"Sure," he said and rolled his shoulders. "We can go and do it again, and you can maybe let me do my job this time."

"Whatever floats your boat," she grumbled, and he pretended to not see her roll her eyes.

As far as he could tell, she knew very well why she'd tried to cover his role. She merely wasn't ready to admit it, but he'd also pushed her as far as he could for the moment. He needed to give her time to process what had happened and find a way to articulate what lay behind it, but he was certain of one thing. She would articulate it.

That was the first step to moving past her monsters. If she couldn't, she wouldn't be too much use to the team. For a second, he wondered if there was any other way but shook his head almost immediately.

"Nah," he muttered and crouched so he was in cover when the world resumed around them.

This time, they'd come in behind a stack of crates in the same warehouse they'd been in before. The people they needed to reach were on the other side, but they had one tiny little problem.

"The floor feels hot," Ivy whispered, and he made a show of touching it. His heart sank.

"You know that explosion?"

"Sure, keep reminding me about it, why don't you?"

He smacked her on the back of the head. "Listen for a change."

She sighed dramatically, and he took that as permission to continue.

"It was a floor down. The scenario's continued as though it truly happened."

Her eyes widened. "You mean there's a fire blazing under our feet?"

"Yup."

"And we have to get them out of here before the floor gives way," she clarified and pointed toward where the people lay.

"Yup." He'd give her this—she was quick to understand the implications. She might even give Johnny a run for his money with the right training. Now that he thought about it, perhaps bringing his teammate in might be a good idea.

Frog shook the thought aside. It might be something for another day—maybe, if he couldn't get through to her during this session. He slid her a sideways glance and noticed that she was already surveying the layout of the room.

She remained low, moved to the edge of the crates, and peered around them.

"Where are you going?" he asked.

"Someone has to untie them." She gestured at their targets.

"Uh-huh," he replied, "and what's your role in this mission?"

With another sarcastic roll of her eyes, she sat back on her haunches. "I need to jack in."

Well, that explained some of why she'd gone off the reservation earlier. He looked around, realized he was blocking an access point, and moved aside.

"There."

Ivy looked at it, then at him. "Gimme a tick."

He nodded and took her place at the end of the row of crates. "Make it quick."

Whatever Roma had done to her reflexes seemed to have an effect on how fast she was able to process because she had only been plugged in for thirty seconds before she looked at him.

"Cameras are off, alarms are down, and if we don't get to those people fast, we're all toast."

"What do you mean?"

"I mean, they're not sending a firetruck."

His eyes widened. "Oh, so it's that scenario."

"What do you—" She stopped as he held a hand up.

With a sharp gesture, he pointed at the floor and drew her attention to where it had begun to glow. "We have to get across there."

"Okay." She moved forward.

Frog caught her arm. "I'll go first."

Ivy scowled. "Sure. Go be the hero."

He crossed quickly to the edge of the brighter patch and felt the heat through the soles of his boots. *Man, Lars really went to town on this scenario.*

Sure the floor would hold them, he signaled her forward.

She darted toward him as the floor behind him gave way with a roar.

Instantly, he turned, and his gaze raked the inferno below as flames leapt through the gap.

"Did you see what they were storing down there?" he asked.

The girl rattled off several chemicals that made his face pale, and he glanced at the ceiling. Exposed beams ran the width of the room, and he nodded as he uncurled the line and grappling hook from his waist.

"Did you ever hear of Spiderman?" he asked, twirled the hook to one side, and cast it upward.

"Who?"

Frog shook his head and yanked the line tight as soon as the hook took hold. When he was sure it wouldn't give, he signaled her to his side.

She looked at him, at the hook, and at his hand and shook her head.

"Trust me," he urged and held his hand out.

Ivy looked at him and glanced at the fire raging behind him. She shook her head.

"You have to be kidding me," she told him. "There has to be another way to get to them."

He shook his head and gestured with his hand to draw her attention to it. "There isn't."

Her expression a little desperate, she looked around while the floor creaked beneath her.

"Come on."

The girl narrowed her eyes and glared at him. "This is another one of your tricks, isn't it?"

His mouth tightened and he kept his hand extended but let her choose. She ignored him and studied their surroundings again, then noticed a door leading into the corridor. "That way," she told him and took a step toward it.

As she moved, the floor gave way and flames engulfed her.

The world spun, and she heard the tail-end of her scream as the white room snapped into being around her. Frog coalesced in front of her, and she scrambled to her feet. His fatigues were still smoking and his face was black.

"We wouldn't have made it either way," he told her as her eyes widened in horror.

Ivy backed away from him so fast she thumped into the wall on the other side of the room. She impacted hard enough to knock the breath from her lungs.

"You!" she began. "You—"

He shook his head. "You, not me. You have trust issues."

Her lips twisted into a bitter smile. "Froggy, you gotta have something before you can have any issues with it. Trust me, this trust nonsense you keep talking about? I don't have a chance in Hades of ever having issues with it."

Startled by the statement, he stared at her. "What do you mean?" he asked after a moment, and she put a hand on her hip.

"Forget about me having any issues with trust, okay? That bad boy was knocked out of me before I even left home. Every time I tried to say it was merely one bad experience and I should put it behind me, I learned it wasn't."

"But—" he began, and she held a hand up.

"Look, if life smacks you upside the head often enough about something, you eventually learn to listen. And life taught me there is only one person I can rely on—and even she gets flaky sometimes."

"And that is?" Frog asked.

Ivy rolled her eyes. "Like you didn't know it's me. Everyone else? Well, you gotta have contingency plans for them. There's no guarantee they'll be there when you need them."

Frog sighed, then lowered his head. "Well, that explains a lot."

"A lot of what?"

"Well, the attitude for one thing."

"What attitude?"

"The one where you piss everyone off around you. Do you ever ask yourself why you do that?"

"Pfft!" She waved a hand in the air like the answer was obvious. "do you ever ask yourself if I don't do it deliberately?"

He raised his head and his eyes widened. "You do?"

"Well, duh. How else do you think I make sure they—" She closed her mouth with a snap. "You know it's none of your freaking business, right?"

When he took a step toward her, she stiffened.

"It is my business, though," he told her. "I need to know you'll stay with me in a fight, that you're gonna stick around if I need you."

Ivy glared at him. "I always stay where I'm needed. It's only when folk are okay that they decide they don't want me around anymore. You should know that—"

Frog froze, then took two steps toward her. That was more than enough for her. She dove past him to put more space between them. He turned.

"Roma," he snapped, and it was a command.

As if she knew exactly what he was asking, the AI spun them to another city on what should have been another world.

She began to retreat as soon as her feet touched the ground, and he didn't blame her. They ended up back to back as the monsters closed.

"I didn't bring a gun," she whispered.

He continued to fire as he unholstered his spare and passed it to her. He felt her fumble with it as he drew a third one and opened fire with a weapon in each hand.

"You know we'll die, right?" he asked.

"Just tell me how to shoot it," she snapped.

"Easy. Finger on the trigger, push the safety off…" He killed one of the slavering nightmares as it leapt forward and had pulled the trigger on a second and a third before she'd worked it out.

"Aim and shoot," he shouted and continued to turn as she huddled against his back.

"Got it!" she declared triumphantly, but a second later, one of the monsters clamped its jaws over her wrist and broke a bone.

She screamed and punched it with her good hand. A second one got past Frog and the rest swarmed in.

As the white room faded in around them, she curled onto her knees and huddled there to catch her breath. It took her several minutes before she registered her instructor was standing in front of her.

"It's okay," she whispered. "Tell Roma she can let me out now."

Frog tilted his head and nudged her with the toe of his boot. When she didn't immediately look up, he nudged her again.

"Now why would I do a thing like that?" he asked.

"Because I'm no good," she told him. "Better you get rid of me now before I get someone killed."

"Or we could train you so that doesn't happen," he suggested and signaled Roma with one hand behind his back.

The white room faded out and the training room replaced it, but she didn't seem to notice.

"What? Put all that effort in when the Witch and her team are coming back and you won't need me anyway?"

Frog lowered himself cautiously to sit in front of her.

"I'm fairly sure there will always be a place for you, Ivy."

She responded with a short and brittle laugh. "Sure. You say that now."

He studied her with a frown. "Is that what's happened before?"

Her face froze and she straightened to sit upright with her hands on her knees. "I didn't say that."

But they were close to the crux of the problem and he knew it. He persisted. "So when you're busy poking people until they lose their tempers, that's what?"

Ivy's expression hardened, but he was sure he'd seen her jaw tremble.

"Well?" he pressed.

"It's me seeing if they still want me around," she admitted finally.

"So, let me get this straight." He closed his eyes and shook his head. "You insult people to see if they still want you around."

"It's not like that," she protested.

"Uh-huh..."

"It's not. I— Look, people tend to want me around for only so long. After that, they get polite, and I only find out how unwelcome I am by accident or when someone finally yells at me for still being where I thought—"

Her voice choked and she stopped, but he finally understood.

"Is that why you..."

Ivy nodded, her face pale, and her eyes shimmered with sudden tears.

"It's easier if you boot me out before I think I've found somewhere..." She rose abruptly to her feet and her face twisted as she lowered her head. "Found somewhere..."

"Found somewhere to call home and then get booted out of it," he finished, and she turned away as she nodded.

"Do you really think John would?" he asked, and she responded with an unhappy laugh.

"No, but that's the thing, isn't it? I'm here on sufferance because he...wants me here."

"Say that again," Frog ordered.

"He…" she began, and he cut her off.

"Who?" he interrupted and caught the first glimmer of a glare.

"John," she snapped, then went silent.

"John what?" he coaxed. *Honestly, it's like getting blood out of a stone…*

"John wants me here," she said so quickly he wasn't sure she caught the implications. He didn't give her too much time to consider them.

"And we need you," he told her.

That brought another tear-clogged laugh and she moved another step away. "Are you sure?" she asked. "Because last time I looked, I was nowhere near good enough."

"But we can help you with that."

"Sure, you can."

"And what's that supposed to mean?"

"It means you probably can help me with that, but whether you will or not is another matter."

Frog glared at her. "You truly are a piece of work, aren't you?"

"My mom would probably agree with you," she snapped. "She didn't think I was worth having around, either unless there was ironing to be done, or floors to be scrubbed, or you name it. I was useful then."

"Did you ever wonder why?"

The girl shrugged. "I used to but then I left. It was better that way. I didn't have to try to prove I hadn't been her worst mistake…" Her face crumpled again, and she turned away with her arms wrapped around her waist. Tears crowded her voice. "And now I know why."

"Care to share?" he asked, and she darted him a look that said she didn't.

He met it with a stare equally as hard and raised an eyebrow. "Well?" he asked and she caved.

"Because I have this thing that will eventually kill me. She simply wrote me off." Ivy sniffed and took a deep breath. She straightened but didn't turn. "I wasn't worth the effort."

She'd moved close enough to the wall to drive a fist into it, and he winced. While they were padded, the mats only absorbed so much.

"But that's not what we're saying," he told her. "Is it?"

The girl punched the wall a second time before she rested her forehead against it. At first, she didn't answer, but her shoulders shook.

Frog took a chance and took a step closer. Her shoulders stilled, but she raised her head from the mat.

"Is it?" he pressed.

She shook her head but kept it pressed against the wall.

"You have to say it, Ives."

"How many times—" she began, but he cut her off again.

"Say it."

"No," she replied reluctantly and remained in the same miserable and defensive position.

For a moment, Frog wasn't sure if she meant she wasn't going to say it, or it wasn't what he and the team were saying. He hesitated as he tried to work out how to get her to clarify while he watched her carefully.

Ivy didn't turn and continued to cry silently with her face pressed to the wall.

"What are we doing, Ivy? About whatever will eventually kill you?" He mocked her gently and she stilled.

"Well?" he pressed when she did not answer.

"Helping me," she admitted in a very small voice.

"Truly?"

She sniffed, her voice a little stronger. "Yeah? Roma says she's already started the treatment."

"She has?" He pretended amazement. "Are you sure?"

The girl sniffed again and nodded.

"But how do you know?"

"I've seen the charts." Her voice strengthened again and she tilted her head so she could see him from the corner of her eye.

"Are you sure those are real? That she's not making it up?"

Ivy pulled away from the wall and put one hand on her hip. "I'm sure she has better things to do with her bandwidth than mess with me. If she didn't intend to help, she didn't have to tell me she could." She sniffed again. "She could simply throw me out on my backside and there'd be nothing much I could do about it."

He snorted. "John wouldn't be happy."

That startled a tearful laugh out of her. "No, but she still doesn't have to help me—and I haven't told John."

Frog looked sharply at her. "Are you going to?"

When she laughed again, he began to understand that when it came to Ivy, laughter had nothing to do with happiness.

"Why? It's not like he can do anything about it, and he's got enough on his plate."

"And you think he'd dump your backside in the dirt if he found out you were defective," he added helpfully, taking a dig at her to see what she said.

To his surprise, she burst into tears, turned as though to run, then turned to the wall again and punched it twice more for good measure.

"Yes...no... I... It's really stupid of me," she wailed. "I know he wouldn't, but—"

She dropped to her knees and sobs wracked her body.

"Your mom, right?" Frog said and moved closer.

"Ri...igh..ight," she sobbed, and he knelt beside her and slid his arm around her shoulders. She tensed but didn't pull away.

"Roma didn't write you off," he reminded her, and she sniffed and patted her pockets.

She didn't see him drag a packet of tissues out of thin air, but she accepted them when he passed them to her.

"No," she admitted.

"And she's helping you, right?"

Ivy blew her nose and nodded.

"And John wouldn't understand?" he asked.

She looked at him and her face crumpled. He pulled her close.

"The man will punch my lights out," he muttered, and she gave a choked laugh. "The point is," he continued and pressed his point, "we all know you're defective."

Ivy gave his shoulder a half-hearted slap but didn't pull away, so he went on.

"And we're willing to work with you on that, so you can be very sure we're gonna want to help you with all the rest. It doesn't matter how much you suck right now."

Her next giggle sounded less miserable.

"So you won't have to go it alone anymore. Okay?"

"What?" she asked and looked at him. "You mean the rest of you won't eventually flake?"

"Or run you out when the fighting's done," he assured her, then drew back and glared at her. "Although if you keep making comments like that..."

Her face sobered and he regretted the words as uncertainty crossed her features.

Good one, Frog, he thought. *You almost had it.*

She pushed to her feet, taking the tissues with her.

"So...I get to stay..."

Frog got the impression that she either didn't believe it or she was trying to get used to a whole new concept.

"You get to stay," he confirmed, and she stopped but kept her back to him.

"And I get to learn how not to suck anymore."

Frog sighed heavily. "I can't promise miracles but we'll try."

Ivy wrapped her arms around herself, her body as tense as a board.

"And I won't have to—" Her voice caught, but she rallied and tried again like she was working through a list and the last item was particularly hard to articulate. "Won't have to try to—"

She stopped as if the last idea was too much.

"Pick up the slack?" he ventured, and she nodded.

"Fill the gaps you aren't qualified for?" he suggested, and she nodded again, so he pushed it a little bit further.

"Do my job for me and get me blown to hell and back?" he prodded.

That time, she laughed.

CHAPTER SEVEN

Tension ran high among the crew of the *Tempestarii* who knew she waited but as yet weren't sure for what. On every deck, the old hands talked among themselves and a semi-familiar shiver of anticipation rippled through them.

They were on a covert mission. A mystery ship needed repair, a mysterious VIP was in need of retrieval, and they would be tested but no one knew why.

"What kind of thing do you think they'll test us for?" asked one of the team leads on a gun crew.

His colleague shrugged and paid close attention to the weapons housing she was currently dismantling. Tattoos rippled across her knuckles as she worked, the same symbol inked in purple and gold on every one.

If she'd stopped long enough for anyone to look closely, they would have seen that each gold-bordered circle contained a flower particular to Meligorn with thorns beneath it and the curled talons of a bird of prey curled beneath those.

"I don't know what they have planned, but I want to be ready." She pulled the housing clear and set it down carefully before she began to work on the mechanism inside. She looked at him. "I'll head into the VR later. Target practice. Do you want to come?"

He hesitated, saw the earnestness in her eyes, and nodded. "I'll call a team practice. If there'll be a competition for whatever's coming, I want our crew to come out on top."

She grinned. "I was hoping you'd say that." She set her tools aside carefully, pulled her tablet out, and sent him a link.

He read it when his tablet chimed and his eyebrows raised. "The whole crew, huh?"

"I don't want us to be caught unprepared."

"It'll put us away from the gun."

"Yeah, but it'll conserve our ammo."

"Do you think we're gonna need it?"

"Mysterious VIP…injured ship. I don't know, Karl. Do you think we won't?"

He conceded and hurried to the shift boss, who took one look at the booking and extended it to put it under their division's name and make sure they had time every day.

"We have to beat the rush," he said and began to order ordnance to be brought up to the guns.

"And hold-all tape," the woman told him. "The silver kind. Order as much as you can."

"Hold-all tape?"

"You never know when we'll need it." She frowned and ignored the looks that passed between Karl and her boss. "And we'll need our suits brought into the gun lockers so we can have 'em close."

The supervisor gave her a startled look. "This isn't the *Knight*, you know."

"I know," she said, "but we saw considerable fighting in that last battle and I want my suit nearby. There might not be time to go back to my cabin to get it."

The section leader added another annotation to his tablet. "Noted. Now, get back to work."

Similar preparations ran the gamut of the decks. In Bio, one of the older commanders turned to a chief.

"This feels like the old days," he commented. "You know, when *she* was around."

"And we were waiting to be boarded or help out in the next battle?"

"Yeah."

They looked at each other for a long minute.

"When did you last go for combat training, Chief?"

The man gave him a quizzical look. "You know, it's been a while."

"And the crew?"

"I hear you, boss. They'll need to go on a schedule, and the younger ones might not understand."

"See if you can find some of the footage from that last battle. They'll understand when they see that."

Two decks down, the suppliers were going over the manifests.

"Do you know what this reminds me of?" one asked, and her colleague nodded.

"Yup." He gestured to the panels they'd finished securing. "Do you want to move these closer to the docking bay?"

She nodded. "And I want my old blaster out of storage."

"And the special harness?"

"Yeah. I need to do my job and not be constantly snagged on things."

"How sure *are* you?"

"You know that restless buzz I used to get?"

"Yeah…"

"I ran three laps of the deck this morning."

Their gazes locked and he sighed.

"Next time, wake me."

They returned to work, but as memories surfaced, they added something else they wanted to the list. Their juniors listened with varying degrees of confusion. Some wondered if their chiefs had officially lost the plot and others tried to think of a polite way to suggest they take rejuvenation.

One or two began to take notes.

The *Tempestarii* listened, made her own observations, and transitioned again.

The intercoms pinged as she returned to clear space.

"All-Crew, All-Crew, All-Crew." The announcement sent a ripple of anticipation through the decks, and the teams downed tools. Those who'd been asleep woke with a start and some reached for weapons that should have been safely stowed in lockers.

When the ship saw that her captain had their attention, she signaled him to proceed.

"Testing is about to commence. All crew are to assemble in their section briefing rooms in their teams. I repeat. Testing is about to commence. All crew are to assemble in their section briefing rooms in their teams."

People began to move, but Emil's stern command stopped them in their tracks.

"Once this broadcast is over," he added.

The crew stilled. When they were listening again, he continued.

"Everyone will move with their teams when their section is called. They will proceed to Shuttle Bay Five to wait for testing and then proceed to a second shuttle bay as directed once the test has been completed. That is all."

"Yes!" the woman from the gun crew hissed. "This is it."

"What is?" Karl asked.

"The test," she whispered. "This has to be it."

One of the junior members started to look worried, but the section leader was already moving down the lines.

"You heard the boss," he snapped. "Get your tails to the assembly hall and make sure you stay in your teams. Move! We don't want to keep the captain waiting."

"That's not the only person we don't want to keep waiting," the female gunner murmured as she closed the gun housing and stowed her tools.

Tension ran high as they gathered. It ran higher still when the captain began to call each section to the shuttle bay.

Engineering was the first, but the head engineer called five names and had them stand beside him.

"I need you here," he told them, and they looked at each other. It took them several minutes to note they were the oldest and longest-serving in the section.

"We'll have our test when the first successes return. In the meantime, we need to keep our girl running."

They snapped to attention and watched the rest of their section leave. A few minutes later, a small squad of Marines arrived.

The captain reported directly to the Chief.

"We're here to make sure the section stays uncompromised, Commander Larkin."

The chief inclined his head. "Thank you, Captain Moser."

He watched as the Marines spread out to ensure that the drive section was secure, certain that they weren't the only ones keeping an eye on their security. His expectations wouldn't have been disappointed.

The *Tempestarii* maintained a careful set of sensors on every part of her shell.

John felt good. He rolled his shoulders as he went through the avatar preparation room. Combat training, huh.

He grinned as he selected medium battle armor and collected a blaster, some spare magazines, a couple of battery packs, a kukri-styled combat knife, and two pistols.

"Are you sure you'll need all that?" Roma asked.

Her voice echoed through the avatar room, sounding slightly amused.

"Oh, yes," he assured her. "This is Frog, Lars, and Vishlog we're talking about. I'll need all of this."

"But you have magic," she reminded him, and he chuckled.

"If there's one thing those guys have taught me over the last few weeks, it's that Talent will only take you so far."

The AI smiled inwardly. She'd taken the time to review the training files, and she had to admit, Lars' training in that area had been particularly thorough.

It was good to see John so happy with his role, even if he truly didn't know what was in store for him. It made her want to pity the boy, but she couldn't.

He had to learn and he had very little time to do it in.

In the meantime, though, there was one more thing she needed to do. It was a relief when he signaled that he was ready to move on.

When he appeared in the white room, he turned in bewilderment to Roma's avatar as soon as it appeared.

"I thought I had training," he started. "Is...has something happened?"

She shook her head. "No, John, but I have something to say to you before you begin."

"Okay..." He regarded her a little warily.

"I wish to apologize," she began, and he frowned.

"You do?"

"Yes. I underestimated you and did not greet you as I should have."

"You mean that first night?"

"And your approach to the center. I...did not follow protocols."

John shook his head and smiled slightly.

"You have nothing to be sorry for. You did what you thought you needed to do to keep your base safe. We're past that now."

Roma drew back in surprise. "But—"

"We all make mistakes, Roma. The important thing is that we learn from them. Your intention was good and you and I have things to do. We won't let one incident get in the way of that."

His response surprised her and she stared at him. "We won't?"

"Well, I won't," he told her. "Will you?"

She studied him for a long moment, then shook her head. "I am still sorry for your lost night's sleep."

"It all worked out well in the end," John told her with a grin. "I discovered where you hid the good coffee."

"And the jam tarts," she replied with some asperity.

He shrugged. "I'm not gonna say I'm sorry about that."

"You will be when they run out," she replied and faded as the white room gave way to a high-ceilinged training room.

Lars, Frog, and Vishlog were already waiting.

"You're late," the security head snapped, and John's jaw dropped.

"But—"

"And I don't take excuses," the man added.

"I'm fairly sure you can access the system and see why," he retorted and called the Talent to his hands as his lead instructor stalked forward.

Lars chuckled. It was not a nice sound.

"Let's see what you've learned between now and RM018."

He took a step back. "What do you know about that?"

"Well, we know you threw Vishlog off a cliff," he informed him, and his heart sank.

So much for his hopes that they hadn't been updated with that.

"And that you now have battlefield awareness," Lars added as Frog tackled the boy from the side. "Not that you've remembered how to use it."

John brought his glowing hands down hard on either side of the smaller guard's head. It looked like he was clapping, but the man had gotten between his palms. The magic flared and Frog vanished.

Lars exchanged looks with Vishlog. "That was new."

Vishlog nodded and surged forward as Lars feinted to one side.

The boy rolled to his feet and raised both palms to launch a beam of blue at the warrior as he angled himself so he could keep an eye on both of them.

The Dreth sidestepped, and Lars drew his pistol and fired.

John laughed. "Straight to the hard stuff, hey?"

He slapped a shield in front of the projectiles and deflected them back. Lars' yelp of surprise lingered after he vanished, and he chuckled.

It matched Lars' laughter for mischief and ended when Vishlog shot him in the head.

Still laughing, he scrambled off the floor in the white room.

"What?" he asked when Lars and Frog both glared at him. "You didn't expect me to learn?"

"You fight much dirtier than the records indicate," the security head observed. "What else have you done since you last trained?"

John glanced at the ceiling. "Roma, did Remy show you the fight I had with the Talents?"

"Negative, John. I will ask him to share the file."

Seconds later, Lars' eyes narrowed. "I see."

The white room vanished and John had a feeling he wouldn't like what came next. They reappeared back in the training room where a nonplussed Vishlog waited.

"No blasters," the leader commanded and put his down near the wall. "Or pistols," he added when John laid his blaster down but kept the smaller sidearms in their holsters.

Vishlog and Frog groaned and added their smaller weapons to the pile. When Lars didn't add his, they all stared at him and he simply smiled.

"There are exceptions to every rule."

The young rogue Talent nodded, and they all moved to the center of the room.

"On my mark," the lead instructor stated, and John waited.

The three were arrayed side by side in front of him, with Lars in the center.

"Mark!" he snapped, and they moved as one.

Instead of trying to put more distance between him and his opponents, John ran at an angle and aimed for Vishlog. Frog was the smallest of them, but the Dreth was easier to hit.

The boy coated his armor with a sheen of sparkling light and drew his dagger. There was something to be said for not having to worry about killing your teammates in practice.

No holds barred meant exactly that.

The warrior sidestepped his initial attack, and John pivoted to face him. Unfortunately, that put his back to the other two, who'd altered course. He shuffled briskly to the side in an attempt to put them on his right, and Vishlog charged.

He kept moving and repositioned as he prepared to meet the Dreth head-on. At the same time, he put a shield between him and Lars and bulldozed it toward Vishlog.

Frog's shout made him look up as the smaller man landed on his shoulders. It would have been his head, but he shifted in time to avoid that.

The shout turned into a howl of pain when the Talent shimmering over John's armor stung his attacker hard enough to drop him to the mat. Unfortunately, that took most of the charge he'd saved for the massive warrior.

He dropped to his knees, but the Dreth stopped before he could be tripped and lashed out with a boot. As he pulled his head back, he took hold of his opponent's calf, wrapped his arms around it, and straightened to push the fighter back.

Unfortunately, that cost him the concentration he needed to maintain his shield, and Lars fired.

The first round pounded into John's armor and knocked the breath from his lungs. The second round impacted but didn't make it through, and he released Vishlog's leg and slapped him with a wall of blue.

The third caught him in the ribs under his arm and pain followed.

Bruising, he reminded himself and turned toward the man as the fourth round hit, which was when Lars brought the second pistol into play.

This time, the boy was fast enough to raise a shield between them, even if it wasn't one that boomeranged the rounds. The security head grinned and threw the pistols to one side.

"Now, let's see what you've got."

John moved back and tried to catch his breath as Lars closed the distance between them. As the two of them crossed the room, Frog rolled to his knees.

"Sonuva—" He stopped mid-word and raised his head to stare at a patch of light that had appeared in the center of the training hall.

Not far from where the small man knelt, Vishlog groaned, rolled onto his stomach, and forced himself to one knee. Folding his forearms across it, he raised his head to stare as well.

The young rogue Talent glanced up to see what had their attention, but Lars continued his attack. He danced forward and lashed out with both fists, and John bounced back but not quickly enough.

He took his eyes off the growing patch of light and forced himself to focus on his opponent. The man lunged and one fist drove into the armor directly above a bullet mark. The impact traveled through the weak point and John gasped.

Lars hooked an arm around the back of his neck and brought his outside knee into the boy's ribs. When he stumbled sideways, the man followed with a tackle that brought him down onto the mat, and he pinned him in place and belted him over the back of the head whenever he saw a shimmer of blue.

"Now let's see what's got you so distracted," he muttered and looked at the growing glow.

It was taller now, about man-height, with the first sign of a figure forming within.

CHAPTER EIGHT

"Take the bar," Emil ordered and ignored the startled look he received in return.

This was the youngster's first trip on the *Tempestarii*, and he remembered him from the recruiting rounds. He'd been fresh-faced, eager, and not too confident that he'd scored well enough in his engineering exam to be accepted onto her weapons team.

He still didn't look confident, but that was because he'd never seen the bar before.

In fact, he thought and almost pitied the boy, *he's never even heard of it.*

They hadn't used the bar test in years—not for at least the last decade and a half, when they hadn't heard from Stephanie for over ten—and the old-timers hadn't spoken of it.

No wonder the kid looked at him like he'd gone crazy.

"Take it," one of the Marines snapped from beside the captain, and the boy's eyes widened.

Emil lifted the bar and the young crewman grasped it.

"What do I do now, sir?" he asked.

"Tell me, what do you think of Stephanie Morgana?" the captain asked, and the kid's eyes lit with enthusiasm.

"She's a hero, sir!"

The bar grew colder beneath his touch and he looked worried.

"And are you looking forward to her return?" Emil asked before the crewman could comment.

The boy gave him a startled look. "Come back?" he asked and seemed alarmed, and the bar warmed beneath his touch.

Emil looked down at the device in his hand.

"Well, that's rather conclusive," he muttered and signaled to the Marine on his right.

"Wait. What happened?" the kid asked.

The Marine gestured toward the door on the right, and the crewman paled.

"I failed?" he asked. "B...but why? I *love* this ship. I'd do *nothing* to harm her."

"Wait!" one of the older hands called, and everyone stopped to look at him.

Emil turned toward the voice with an inquiring look on his face.

"Harper?"

The engineer came forward. "I think it's just because he hasn't...he doesn't..." He sighed. "May I speak to him?"

The captain considered the request, then nodded.

Harper hurried forward as the Marine guided the kid to one side of the hall. A second Marine moved to intercept him and the captain spoke.

"Before you do, Harper..." He lifted the bar.

Immediately, the engineer changed course and came to stand before him. He took hold of the bar without being told to.

"Ask your questions, sir."

"What do you think of the Morgana's victories at Dreth?" Emil asked.

"I wouldn't have it any other way," he replied, his eyes on the captain's face as the bar chilled to his touch.

"And Stephanie herself?"

"I am grateful to have met her and honored to have served her," he replied, and his heart leapt at the memories the question raised.

"And her return?"

"Tell me it's true, sir."

The bar turned to ice in his hand, and the captain nodded as he held his hand out. Harper attempted to pass it back, but he stilled and his face turned pale.

"Uh, sir..."

Emil chuckled and signaled to another Marine, who laughed and picked up a bucket of water at his feet.

"Dip your hand in here, Chief."

Harper submerged his hand and the bar into the lukewarm water. When he felt skin and metal separate, he lifted the bar and handed it to Emil.

"Sorry, sir."

"That's quite okay, Harper." The captain gestured to where the Marine and the young weapons engineer waited beside the wall.

When he reached them, the youngster gave him a sorrowful, disbelieving look.

"I wouldn't harm her," he whispered, and Harper wrapped an arm around his shoulders. "I wouldn't," the youth repeated.

The engineer nodded understandingly. "I know you wouldn't, but that's not what the test is about."

"I wouldn't harm Stephanie either," the boy whispered as fiercely as Harper crouched at the foot of the wall and drew him down with him.

"Then what's the problem with her coming back?"

"I...I don't know what that would be like," the young crewman explained. "She's been gone so long and the Regime..."

"It's a powerful beast, sure," he told him, "but it'll start a war anyway. We both know that."

The kid swallowed, his face paler than before. "I know, Chief, but..."

"But what?"

"What if she starts it?"

Harper smiled, and his subordinate's eyes widened.

"Look, son, let me tell you something about our Stephanie. You know she was born on Earth, don't you?"

The boy nodded.

"And do you know why she left?" he asked and was relieved when the kid shook his head. "What about what she did during the war with the Telorans?"

Instinctively, the kid cast an anxious look at the lines, but the captain hadn't yet called the alien mages for testing.

"No," he admitted.

The chief leaned against the wall, and after a moment's hesitation, the boy did the same.

"For one thing," Harper began, "Stephanie never was one to start the fight, not unless she thought she had to step in to protect something or someone who needed it."

"Like Earth?" his subordinate asked, and he wondered who he had on their homeworld. He didn't look old enough to have anyone who would know Stephanie.

Instead of asking, he answered, "Like Earth," he confirmed, "but also like Dreth and Meligorn. If she knew what was happening to them, she'd stop it."

"Really? She..." The kid glanced at the Marine and lowered his voice. "She wouldn't be mad?"

Harper snorted. "At what? Dreth? Meligorn?" He studied the boy's face. "Us?"

The crewman nodded.

"For what?"

"For not taking better care of things while she was gone."

The engineer laid his arm across the boy's shoulders. "Well, she has this thing about people doing their best..."

He felt the youngster relax as he talked about the times he'd seen Stephanie deal with those who'd failed despite doing their best and what she'd done to keep her world safe.

"And she'd do it again," he told him when he'd finished telling him about the Battle for Dreth.

"But she almost died…" the kid whispered.

"Yup," Harper agreed, "but that's our Steph. She feels responsible for all her people."

"So she won't destroy Earth?"

Harper was shocked. "Now, why would she do a thing like that?"

"Because of what they're doing to everyone else."

"That's not Earth doing that. That's the Regime and—" He raised a hand to silence the kid as he went to break in. "Steph will understand that."

"Oh." The young crewman glanced to where the captain was testing another crew member. "Do you think he'll let me try again?"

"Now that you have a better idea of who you're talking about, you mean?"

The boy nodded, "And I want my world back. My mum and dad…" His voice caught. "They keep telling me about relatives I've never met and I don't know if they've survived. Magic runs in the family."

He sounded almost wistful, and Harper got the impression the boy wished he could have been a mage. It was tempting to tell him that manipulating the technology in the guns was magic of a different kind but he resisted.

His subordinate continued. "They had friends, too, and they don't know if they survived."

"Well, when Stephanie comes back, we'll have a chance to find out," he told him, and there was no doubt in his voice. The Stephanie he knew wouldn't punish an entire planet for what its government had done.

If any mages survived, she'd find them. She'd make a point of it.

Harper didn't say that, though. He merely hauled himself to his feet and winced when his body reminded him it wasn't as young as it had been when he'd first seen the *Tempestarii*.

Lord! Had any of them been that young? He winced again and leaned on the wall.

The Marine shifted as though to help him but stopped when he caught the look on the chief's face.

"Take him to the captain." Harper gestured to the boy. "I'll wait until he's done and you can escort us both."

Emil's attention had been caught by the movement at the wall. When the Marine looked at him, he glanced at the boy and Harper and nodded.

"Come on, then," he instructed, and the boy moved forward with the Marine a few steps behind him.

The chief nodded when he saw the renewed purpose in the boy's stride and couldn't help admiring it. He caught the Marine's anxious glance and didn't move from the wall. There were still so many of the crew who needed to be tested.

The captain offered the bar, and the boy took it and held it firmly.

"So," Emil began, "how do you feel about Stephanie Morgana?"

"I still believe she's a hero," he answered, "but now I know why so many of us would follow her into Tegortha's maw."

Tegortha's maw? Harper wondered and made a note to check what company the boy had been keeping.

If Emil found the kid's answer strange, he didn't show it.

"And how do you feel about her return?" he asked.

"If she can free my world, I'll follow her, too," the boy declared and yelped in surprise as the bar froze to his hand.

The Marine with the bucket chuckled and lifted it again.

Harper felt a surge of pride as the captain directed the boy to dip the hand holding the bar into the water so he could hand it back.

He smiled but didn't move from his place until the Marine escorting them signaled him. This time, they were led through the door to the captain's left—the one that said they'd passed.

As they were escorted from the testing area, the *Tempestarii* pinged Emil's private comms channel.

Captain, I'm afraid someone is trying to hide.

Far from the *Tempestarii*, Ivy opened her eyes. She was seated in the doctor's office again, but this time it was empty.

"Roma?"

"My apologies, Ivy. I have something I need to show you before you commence training."

"Okay..."

"This will be a long training session in real-time," the AI began and appeared in the doctor's seat beside her. "We will realign the bones in your wrists."

The girl winced. "So...uh, will I feel it?"

"You should not be aware of the realignment," Roma reassured her, "although there may be some tenderness when you wake and you will have some remedial exercises to perform when you are out of the pod."

"You say that like I won't be out of it that often," she commented.

"This is true. However, for the periods when you are out of it, you will have exercises to perform, especially once we deal with the misalignment in your shin."

"And the Huntington's?" Ivy asked.

The doctor stilled. "That treatment is not going as well as we had hoped."

"And?"

"While we have shortened the affected chain, we need to shorten it more to ensure it no longer threatens your system."

"And?" she pressed when the doctor stalled again.

"Your body is proving unusually resistant to the treatments required to delay factors affecting onset."

"Which means?" Ivy asked, sounding exasperated.

"Treatment will take longer," Roma told her.

Ivy tried to quell the disappointment that surged through her. She almost couldn't bring herself to ask the next question, but the AI was looking at her as though she was waiting.

She sighed. "By 'longer', you still mean you can cure me."

"At this stage, we believe that is still a possibility."

The girl gulped but stiffened her spine. "When will you know if that's changed?"

"Not for some time, but we will tell you if we become sure."

Her eyes prickled and she nodded. She sniffed hard and blinked them away. "But you've had some progress, right?"

"Yes," Roma told her and changed the subject. "Are you ready for training?"

Ivy nodded and tried to put her jumbled feelings in order.

The AI gave her a quizzical look. "Are you sure? Because we can..."

"I'm sure." Ivy held one hand up in emphasis. "Frog promised to help me with a few things. He'll be disappointed if I don't show up."

"He is a construct," Roma told her shortly. "I can add that understanding to his programming."

"Please don't," she said. "I'll be fine."

That was greeted by a look that suggested the AI had her doubts and the girl stood quickly.

"When you're ready," she said and kept her voice as steady as she could.

"Very well," Roma replied, and the doctor's office gave way to the training room.

Frog stood in the center of the room when she was deposited to one side of the mats.

"How did the doctor's visit go?" he asked, and she lowered her head.

She considered telling him it had gone well but shunted that thought aside. "They're not sure they can do what they said," she told him and he sighed.

"So…by not sure, they're not sure it won't work either?"

"That's about it," she confirmed and moved into position opposite him.

He nodded, but before he could begin, she interrupted him.

"Before we start, may I ask a favor?"

"Which is?" he asked.

Ivy bit her lip and took a breath.

"Can you teach me the appropriate way to greet your teacher?" she asked.

Surprised, Frog drew a breath to answer, then closed his mouth and thought about it for a moment or two.

"We didn't use a greeting in our military classes," he told her, "and Stephanie only taught us the royal greetings for Meligorn, but when I was growing up, Marcus's big brother dragged us both to this training center. I forget the style, but I remember we had to greet the sensei like this…"

He straightened, stood with his heels together, and bowed slightly. As his body lowered forward, he uttered out a brisk, "*Onegaishimasu.*"

It sounded more like a polite request than a command and she stared as he straightened. "What does it mean?"

"What?"

"The word you said."

"*Onegaishimasu.* We were told it meant something like 'Please teach me,' or so Carson said, and he didn't joke much."

"I'll need to hear it again," Ivy told him, and he slowed the pronunciation as he repeated it.

When she had it syllable perfect, she tried the bow. It took a few attempts before she was sure she could do it correctly and she took her position in front of him.

"*Onegaishimasu*," she said and bowed in greeting.

When he acknowledged it with one of his own, she stepped back and dropped into a defensive position with a smirk. "Just because I respect you doesn't mean I won't kick your tail."

Frog shifted into a combat-ready stance and smiled slightly. "Then let's move forward with your disappointment, grasshopper."

He darted forward and swept her off her feet, and she landed hard on the mat while he darted back and waited. As soon as she was on her feet, he beckoned for her to come at him.

"Oh, no, you don't," Ivy told him. "I won't fall for that one again."

Her opponent chuckled, darted in, and jabbed her twice in the ribs. "Now, what have I told you about blocking?"

"You're not teaching me how to do anything except how to get hit," she grumbled. "I'm not your punching bag, you know."

"It was your idea to try to put me on my tail," he mocked.

"Maybe you could teach me how to hit you first."

"Wouldn't that be self-defeating?" he asked with another lunged attack.

This time, she remembered how to move her feet and sweep his strikes aside with her hands.

"See? You're better already," he said encouragingly. "Now you have to work out how to get in close without me hitting you."

Ivy tried, but every time she closed, he moved out of her reach until finally, she lost her temper and charged him.

Frog watched her come, waited until the last minute, and stepped aside. He tripped her and grinned as he kicked her tail to tumble her fully onto the mat.

"Try again," he ordered.

Rebellion flitted across her face, and she rolled upright and folded her arms. For a moment, he thought he would have to goad her into action, but she scrambled to her feet.

"Remember what I taught you," he said and tried to remember how Lars had approached this part of Stephanie's training. Of course, she'd had more training than Ivy had, but still, there were some parallels.

Scowling, she circled instead of coming in directly, then darted in and then back.

"You know you have to hit me, right?" he snarked.

"You know I want to do that, right?" she retorted acidly and made another attempt.

Thankfully, she remembered to counter his defense and landed one blow on his chest as he swept her other fist aside.

"Not bad," he told her. "Now do it again."

At the end of a half-hour—during which he corrected her footwork, her approach, the way she struck, and what seemed like everything else imaginable—she'd improved enough for them to take a break.

The kata that followed revealed more flaws, but she was undoubtedly making progress.

"I'll have Roma put you through the self-defense programs the colleges used to train their students," he told her and grinned when she gaped indignantly at him.

"Why didn't you do that to begin with?" she demanded.

"Because I needed a baseline of hopeless, very hopeless, or simply 'use her as bait' to work from."

"Just..." Ivy narrowed her eyes. "Tell me you didn't mean that."

"Why? Will it make you feel better?"

"Should it?"

"It would have made me feel better. Lars had a 'use them to trip the enemy' category."

That startled a snorted laugh out of her. "He did not!"

Her patent disbelief made him laugh, too. "No, he didn't, but

I'll get Roma to plug you into some extra training anyway. It's what Remy did for John."

"He did?"

"Sure, but not before he'd gone through this stage as well."

"Well, that makes me feel a little better."

Frog smiled. "Good. Roma?"

The lights in the room faded and one wall lit with a scene of several figures running down a narrow corridor.

"Is that…a ship?" Ivy asked.

"Yup. This is the inside of a pirate ship," he told her. "Now, watch Steph."

Her mouth hung open as she studied the dark figure who took the lead. She was the only female in sight, so that had to be her. She stared, stunned by her first glimpse of the Heretic of Regime legend.

She'd thought John was something, but this was truly extraordinary.

Frog nudged her. "Pay attention."

It took effort to push herself past her first reaction at seeing a myth, but she complied and soon understood what he wanted her to understand.

While Steph had magic, she didn't use only magic to fight her foes—and would have been in considerable trouble if that was all she'd relied on in her battles.

"Is that why John had to learn how to fight?"

"Exactly, but you won't use magic, so this time, I want you to watch the guy to her right."

"Who is it?"

"That's Lars. The one on the other side of her is Marcus."

"Okay."

This time, she focused on the two bodyguards who flanked Stephanie as her instructor provided a running commentary.

"See how neither of them gets in front of her?"

Ivy nodded. The two guards didn't move ahead of her, but

they dealt considerable damage to anything that tried to launch an assault from the side. More importantly, though, they kept the pressure off her and made sure she wasn't overwhelmed as she eliminated the bulk of the pirates who attacked them.

"Is that what you think I'll be doing?" she asked.

Frog rolled his eyes at her, and the footage changed to a scene of her and John fighting on the top floor of the balloon.

"Are you saying you haven't?"

"Well, I wasn't very good at it," she pointed out. "In fact, I think John did most of the fighting."

"Next time, you'll be better," he assured her.

"You mean next time, I won't have to climb to the top of the balloon so some lunatic can drag me off it?"

"I didn't see you saying no."

"Are you kidding? Didn't the recording catch the sound of us on the way down? There's your no right there."

Frog smiled and pushed to his feet. "So, how do you feel about a change of scenery?"

Roma responded to the signal, and Ivy gasped as the training hall twisted into a departure lounge overlooking a docking bay based on Star Base Notaro. Her eyes became the size of saucers.

"Where is this?"

He gave her a disbelieving look. "Have you never seen the inside of a space station before?"

"And what are we doing here?" she asked as she scrutinized her surroundings.

"This space station is about to be attacked. Our job—together —is to last through killing a wave of Dreth pirates."

She looked at the training gear she wore. "I don't think I'm dressed for this."

Frog grinned. "You have a point. Freeze scenario," he ordered. "Roma?"

"I've got you covered," Roma told her, and Ivy's avatar rippled. "There."

"That's better," he said approvingly as he studied her carefully. Ivy took a moment to have a good look at herself.

She was dressed in light battle armor with the unfamiliar weight of a heavy hand-blaster at one hip and a battle knife at the other. A larger blaster was slung over her shoulder and several grenades hung from a bolero across her chest.

"You know I don't know how to use half this stuff, right?" she asked and wrapped her hands hastily over the grenades. "Not that I mind."

Her instructor chuckled. "I'll give you a quick rundown."

It took ten minutes, but by the end of it, she had the basics of safeties, grenades, and how to change magazines.

"I don't even know if I can shoot straight," she muttered as she holstered the blaster.

"As long as you're not aiming it at me, you'll hit something you need to."

"Really?" she asked. "How can you be sure?"

"Trust me, you'll know." He glanced at the ceiling. "Roma, start the scenario."

"Restart commencing."

Ivy looked around. The sky beyond the windows remained clear and the concourse empty.

"What now?" she asked as a ship came into the dock.

It came in under power, and Frog snapped his helmet shut. She hurried to do the same and bolted after him as he headed to the cover of a vending machine. There was no point in asking why.

"Here they come!" he said through her visor comms. "Boarding party!"

"Boarding what?"

"You'll see," he told her as the ship rose over the docking platform.

Its hull kissed the glass of the observation windows running the length of the concourse and she noticed an open hatch. An alien stood in the doorway, fully suited as he slammed his hand against the inside of his ship.

"What are they doing?"

"Tethering," Frog answered shortly. "They'll send boarding tubes out on every level and attack us from several different places."

As he spoke, the hatch leapt away from the hull and drove into the wall beside the glass. The initial thud was followed by a sickening crunch and the shriek of tortured metal, and a short, solid metal tube blocked all sight of the aliens on the other side.

"Here they come," he told her. "If we can stop the boarding party here, we beat the first level."

"How many—" Ivy began as the wall fell inward and her companion opened fire.

The first pirate staggered back, only to reappear again being carried by his comrade behind him. Frog's next three shots were blocked by the body as the invader barreled forward.

Alarms blared around her and the station's lights flashed red. Frog dived to one side and fired twice to catch the pirate in the side of the head.

"They're huge!" she protested as he fell and dropped his crewmate's body.

"They're Dreth," he yelled in response. "Don't let them get close."

She raised her blaster and began to shoot, but another thud and clang drew her attention to the other end of the concourse.

"There are more!"

"Your point?"

He was busy with the Dreth who emerged from the boarding tube, so she bolted toward the second entry being made and fired the heavy blaster while still in motion.

Her aim was off, but it was enough to get their attention. Shouting and pointing, they raised their weapons and returned fire, and she borrowed a maneuver from her instructor's handbook.

She vaulted high over the incoming fire and twisted to retaliate as she descended. That was more effective than her earlier attempt and the heavy rounds of the blaster drilled through their suits and felled them.

They clustered together, which gave her another idea, and she yanked a grenade from the bandolier as she landed. Pivoting, she activated it and threw, then backed away, shooting as they followed.

If she'd timed it right, it would work perfectly.

"Get down!" Frog yelled, and she fell prone.

The grenade blew and the pirates fell around it, their suits fragmenting in a storm of flechettes. She didn't take the time to celebrate. Instead, she looked for more.

When the boarding tube remained empty and no more invaders emerged, she glanced at her teammate. He stood in the middle of a circle of bodies, breathing hard, and his blade dripped blood.

"I thought you said to not let them get close."

"I can't use a sword if they don't get close," he retorted, "and these guys needed killing."

"So, can I?"

"How good is your sword work?"

Ivy paused. "I don't know."

"Exactly. Stay with the blaster if you can."

She looked around for the next threat. "Where are the others?"

Frog laughed. "Trust me, there are more. That was only Level One. We have to see how many levels we can work through before you die."

"What about you?"

"I'll come back. If you die, we lose."

"Oh…" Her gaze swept the concourse again. "So, where's Level Two?"

He pointed at the ship. "Are you coming?"

The girl began to jog toward him but noticed the opening to the other boarding tube and changed direction. "Lemme close this first."

"Close it?" he asked as she reached the end of the tube and lobbed a grenade into the airlock at the other end. "Oh…"

Ivy didn't wait to see what the effect was and simply bolted to where he stood. Alarms sounded from inside the pirate ship and he gave her a look of disgust.

"Well, now they know we're coming."

She checked her blaster and moved to the other tube. "Are you leading or following?"

Frog sighed. "Well, I am the instructor."

"And if you die, you come back," she reminded him as he came alongside.

"I thought I would take the lead."

"Didn't you want me to learn how to work as part of a team?" she asked and added before he could answer, "Besides, Marcus and that guy next to him—"

"Johnny," he supplied.

"Johnny," she continued. "They had this set of actions they did when a ton of them attacked."

"What makes you think there'll be a ton?" Frog asked as they reached the airlock and sprinted through.

"It's kinda their ship," Ivy retorted. "What makes you think there won't?"

Movement caught her eye and she began to fire. "What's the objective?"

"We have to take their command center."

"Do you know where it is?"

"Here." Frog sent the data to her HUD. "You can plot us a path."

More Dreth appeared and she fired again.

"We need to go right...and up," she told him.

"And survive," he reminded her as they reached an intersection and Dreth appeared from three directions.

"This is bad, isn't it?" she asked and threw a grenade down the corridor to her right.

Frog eliminated the pirates in the corridor to her left. "Not yet, it isn't—shields!"

Ivy found the command in her HUD and managed to get the suit's shields online before the grenade detonated. Some Dreth died, but more survived and continued their advance.

She managed to kill most of them with her blaster, then drew her knife and thumbed the control that gave its edge a blue-limned hue.

"Nice," she murmured, and the Dreth chuckled.

"Typical human," he rumbled, "bringing a knife to a gunfight."

Without warning, she lunged forward, then threw herself into a slide as he fired. The first rounds passed over her head and chewed the deck behind her as she wrapped one hand around his ankle and sliced the blade through the armor cover on his other ankle.

The pirate roared, and she realized she'd made a small mistake. Being under a pirate as he collapsed in an angry heap was not her smartest move.

Shots and screams sounded from where Frog was fighting as Ivy scrambled away from the falling Dreth. She came to an abrupt halt against two sets of legs and was hauled to her feet.

"Captain's gonna have—" one began, but she yanked a grenade from her bandolier, depressed the timer, and waved it over her head before she simply dropped it.

"Are you suicidal?" Frog gasped as the pirates released her and started to run.

"Nope," she told him and landed already in motion. She took two strides and dived forward, rolled over the top of two rapidly cooling corpses, and caught hold of one to arrest her forward movement.

When the grenade exploded, she was tucked behind the large body, which was more shelter than her previous captors had. The blast caught them before they'd cleared its range and they sagged in two bloody heaps as shrapnel passed over her head.

"Mother of—" her teammate began and fired several shots in quick succession. "You are banned."

"Banned?"

"No. More. Grenades."

Ivy snickered. "I still have six left."

Frog groaned and changed the subject. "The corridor's cleared. Which way?"

She checked and snagged one of the pirate's blasters as she stood.

"Mine's running low," she said when she caught her teammate's raised eyebrows.

As she spoke, she fired and felled a Dreth who had rounded the corner ahead of them.

"If we're quick, we can—" The words cut off as she dove forward when the ceiling opened above them and several Dreth dropped on them.

If Frog was impressed by her quick thinking, he didn't say. He released his blaster and went straight to blades. Ivy rolled forward, drew her blaster, and dealt with the closest one. Her blade was in her hand when she regained her feet and she stabbed forward, remembering Frog's instruction.

"The blade's an extension of yourself."

She hadn't fully understood what he meant but she did now. It was like her fist had grown another four inches—another four very sharp inches with the ability to slice through medium armor.

The problem was that she couldn't reach a pirate throat and punching into their stomachs made hers roil. She might have been able to fight well enough to get herself out of trouble, but she'd never fought to kill.

The Dreth screamed and she jerked her hand back, leaving the blade behind when it snagged. It was easier to pull the smaller pistol and fire it point-blank until the pirate fell away from her. Then, it was easy to keep shooting until the next invader was no longer a threat.

Ivy switched targets and moved forward until her pistol clicked in her hand, the charge drained. With a grimace, she looked around quickly, found another on one of the fallen pirates, and picked it up.

Checking its safety, magazine, and battery, she located the next target, barely aware of Frog moving beside her to mirror her actions. When they reached the stairwell, the alarms fell silent, even though the lights still flashed.

"What happened?" she asked and panic edged her voice.

"It's the end of Level Two," he told her. "Level Three starts when we enter the stairwell."

"Level Three?" Her chest heaved with exertion. "Exactly how many levels are there?"

"That depends on how long we survive."

"You mean it doesn't stop when we reach the command center?"

"Don't you mean if we reach it?"

Level Three was a challenge. Firstly because the stairwell was the only way up and the Dreth were waiting, and secondly because the Dreth had no compunctions about dropping grenades down the shaft.

"What are we supposed to do about that?" Ivy asked as one sailed past her.

"Toss it back?" Frog suggested, did exactly that, and dragged her under the stairs as it exploded above them.

"Oh, har. Very funny," Ivy told him, but she caught the next one and followed his example.

Doors crashed open above and below them, and the heavy footsteps rattled the stairs.

"Here they come," he murmured.

"You don't say!" she snapped, then ducked out from under the stairwell and fired at the Dreth who descended.

Frog took on the Dreth who came from the lower levels, and his shots forced them into cover instead of taking advantage of Ivy's position. That worked until the invaders began to rappel over the edge.

"You need to get to the landing!" her instructor shouted, and Ivy nodded.

A pirate appeared in front of her, and she shot him through the faceplate. The force of impact launched him into freefall. She darted out from under the stairs and continued her ascent with her teammate hard on her heels.

This time, they reached the floor they needed to be on and stopped on either side of the door. Frog nodded toward the entry pad and checked his blaster, and Ivy went to work and rapidly disabled the security system.

She took a quick look, saw the corridor was clear, and slid out with him close behind. For a minute, they stood in silence and took stock of their surroundings before he asked, "Where to?" and she pointed.

The pirates waited until they'd cleared the next intersection before they slammed a blast door closed behind them. A second blast door clanged shut ahead of them, which left only one connecting corridor open.

"I don't like the look of this," Ivy muttered, and Frog agreed.

They moved forward together, slid closer to the intersection, and peered around the corner. Two gleaming autocannons stood at the other end.

"Is this the only way through?" he asked, and she checked the HUD.

"We can't go back, but there's an alternate route on the other side."

"Those cannons will fire the second we start crossing," he told her, and she nodded.

She glanced at the ceiling. "What if we go over?"

"Have you watched footage of the Hooligans?" he asked as his eyes narrowed with suspicion.

"The who?" Ivy asked, and he shook his head.

"Never mind."

"No, come on. Who? Because they sound like they've done this kind of thing before and I can look them up."

Frog shook his head. "There's a reason they're called the Hooligans, you know."

"They sound like my kind of people," she told him and blasted a hole in the ceiling panels above them.

"Are you sure you want to do that?" he asked.

"It's the only way," she pointed out. "We need to get past the guns and they have the corridor covered."

He shrugged and laced his fingers together.

"Let me give you a boost," he said, and she nodded, stepped lightly into his hands, and launched off them as he flicked her up.

Ivy scrambled into the ceiling cavity and was relieved to find it empty.

"You missed an opportunity there, boys," she told the non-existent Dreth as she inched along the edge of the walkway.

She was surprised when she peered around the corner and found no guns waiting. Curious to see where it led, she moved forward cautiously and smiled when she reached a door. Swiftly and quietly, she returned to where her teammate remained in the corridor below.

"You need to come up here," she told Frog. "We're almost there."

In the end, she had to reach down so he could grab her arm and steady him as he scrabbled up to join her.

"This way," she told him and led him around the corner to the door. "The guns are down there and the command center is across this bulkhead there."

He looked warily at her. "Are you sure?"

Ivy nodded. "Take a look."

She waited while he inspected the schematics in his HUD and smiled when he nodded.

"But we don't know what's behind this door," he reminded her.

"I'll hack the surveillance system," she replied, and he nodded.

"And I'll keep watch."

As quickly as she could, she plugged her tablet in and worked feverishly, then whistled softly when she'd broken through and could update the schematics they had for that deck.

"We can win this," she told him, and he smiled as he gestured toward the door.

They could win this, but there was one small problem she'd overlooked.

He opened fire before the door was fully ajar. The two Dreth inside fell to two short bursts as he pushed past them, and Ivy followed.

"To win, you have to kill the captain," he told her and began to move out over the space the command center occupied.

"Frog..." she began uncertainly, and he winked at her and indicated a point mid-way between them.

"He's below us—there."

Ivy moved forward and glanced at him for confirmation that she'd reached the right location. When she had, he gave her a cocky grin, prepped both blasters, and pulled their butts firmly against his sides.

"Ready?" he asked and she nodded, although her face said she had no idea what he had planned.

He grinned at her, aimed the blasters downward, and began to fire.

"Then let's go!"

Ivy didn't wait to be told twice. She stooped to lift the ceiling panel she needed and jumped quickly into the room below to land behind one of the largest Dreth she'd yet encountered. Beyond him, hidden behind the pirate and the control panel in front of him, she could hear Frog firing.

Other weapons were fired as well and she realized they were outnumbered.

To win, you have to kill the captain, Frog had said.

"To find him, I need to take this guy out first," she muttered and earned a startled grunt.

She ducked under a hastily swung fist, angled her blaster up, and pulled the trigger, and the rounds cut into the pirate's armor at point-blank range. Their impact drove him back a few steps, but not before he'd swung a second massive fist in her direction.

That one connected, but she continued to fire as she fell.

"Stupid, stupid, stupid," she muttered and registered two things.

First, the pirate she'd shot was dead and out of the fight, and second, the rank tabs denoted that he was captain. The third thing she registered was the utter stillness that had descended over the control room.

"Frog?" she whispered over their comms and only barely remembered to keep her voice soft.

A soft sick feeling rippled through her chest when he did not reply. She crept quickly to the edge of the captain's console and peered around it, surprised to see how many Dreth were slumped over their consoles or dead on the floor.

Her instructor had let loose and had a field day.

Ivy looked up and located the hole in the ceiling before she looked down. Dreth bodies obscured her view, but none of them moved. All those who'd survived remained still, too.

"Roma?" she asked but again received no reply.

Cautiously, she moved out from behind the console to where

she thought Frog would be. It wasn't until she'd reached the space beneath the hole that she found him with only one boot protruding from beneath a pirate.

It took effort to drag the Dreth clear, but her instructor lay motionless, as dead as his enemies.

"Frog?" she asked and refused to believe it. She placed a hand on either shoulder and shook him, but his body shifted bonelessly in her hands and his head turned to show a crater where the left side of his skull used to be.

"Frog?" She looked around wildly as sadness rose through the nausea that had settled in her chest.

Bullet holes pockmarked the consoles and marred the armor of the Dreth she'd turned over. Frog's sword stuck out below them. It didn't take her long to determine what had happened, and she dropped his body and thumped a fist onto his chest as she realized what he'd done.

"You selfish, stupid sonuva—" she began, knowing full well he was none of those. He had simply known what they faced in the command center and had put the mission—and her survival —first.

She punched him again, and a wordless cry echoed around her—her wordless cry, although the fact of that didn't truly register. Tears followed, and she kept her hand on his chest and sobbed as the training scenario swirled away around her.

CHAPTER NINE

The Marines searched the *Tempestarii's* decks. They pulled panels open, investigated storage caches, and checked the cavities housing pipes of suppression gas but found nothing.

"To your right." The ship's instruction came through their comms.

They exchanged glances and veered right. The ship was good, but even she couldn't see everywhere, and they knew that. Still, if she directed them in that particular direction, she'd seen *something*.

"There is residual heat," she explained, and they nodded.

Residual heat meant a warm body—or something more serious, but in that case, there were other sensors that would have been triggered and they hadn't. Her quiet instruction led them to an alcove reserved for storing cleaning equipment and a woman who tried to pull the panel shut behind her.

When she saw the Marines, she stopped and stepped out into the corridor, her hands partly raised. The Marines exchanged glances and relaxed.

Crewman Sawyer had a spotless record with no sign that she'd ever been in contact with the Regime, let alone had the chance to be turned by it. She kept her hands raised, took two tentative steps forward, and waited for them to react.

They did not disappoint.

"If you'll come this way, ma'am," one stated and was surprised when she put on a sudden spurt of speed and shoved him into his partner as she bolted past him.

Caught off balance, he stumbled, and the two of them fell in a rattle of armor and equipment as Sawyer sprinted back the way she'd come.

In all truth, she hadn't realized what she was until the captain had made his announcement for the crew to gather and that there would be testing. When that had come through, something inside her had snapped, and she'd understood that this was "it"—the entire reason she'd sacrificed three years of time with her family.

This was when she would discover where the Heretic had been hiding. The test, the change in ship routine, and the all-crew alert had all been the triggers for her memory of the mission to return.

She raced away from the Marines and wracked her brains for somewhere to hide, but she'd completely forgotten that the ship was everywhere. Her flight took her around a corner, then swiftly around a second, heading to the maintenance section.

"Oh, for fury's sake!" the *Tempestarii* exclaimed. She waited until the woman had passed the next bulkhead and let her get halfway down the narrow stretch of corridor before she sealed the section.

"Run from this," the ship snarled and unleashed the knock-out gas as the Marines reached the door.

She sighed as they ran past the corridor. "Back up ten paces and turn left," she instructed.

The two men skidded to a halt and followed her directions. They stopped and stared when they reached the bulkhead, then frowned when they read the warning scrolling over the entry pad.

"Aww, Tempe," one of them complained. "You know you're supposed to reserve that for boarders."

"I know no such thing," the ship retorted indignantly, then added, "Besides, she was a boarder. She was not who she said she was."

"Now, Tempe, you know that might not be true."

"Are you saying she might have run away because she did want to take the test?"

"No..."

They waited as the ship cleared the atmosphere in the section beyond. Both men slipped breathers on as the bulkhead released to let them through.

"I wouldn't have let you in there if you would be affected," the ship scolded, and one of the Marines raised an eyebrow.

"It's standard operating procedure when entering a recently contaminated area," he explained. "No offense, Tempe."

"None taken," the ship replied but sounded like she didn't mean a word.

They didn't dignify that with a response and moved quickly into the corridor where the crewman lay in a boneless heap.

"Ma'am?" one of them said and slapped her face.

She moaned, and her hands twitched as though she tried to move them.

"Ma'am?" A second slap made her eyelids flicker, and his partner handed him an oxygen mask.

"Try her with this."

He scowled but took it, lifted Sawyer into a seated position, and positioned her so his partner could cuff her hands behind her back while he held the mask in place.

"Wow, Tempe, are you sure you used enough gas on her?" he asked when the woman began to splutter, shoved the mask aside, and threw up.

"No one will hurt my Stephanie," the *Tempestarii* declared as they hauled the woman to her feet and steered her toward the brig.

The Marine chuckled. "I'd say the ship passes the bar test."

"I'll get Sanitation down here to clean up," his partner replied with a smile, "and then I'll make sure Medical is on stand-by."

"We could simply put her in the brig and let her sleep it off," Tempestarii suggested.

He shook his head. "You want the information she has in her head, Tempe. For that, she has to be well enough to answer."

"I'll call the mages," the ship replied. "Tell Medical to make sure she's ready."

Back on Earth, ex-Admiral Amaratne looked wistful.

"Can you put me on the bridge of a warship?" he asked, and the woman before him lowered her chin in assent.

"I can put you wherever you like. What kind of warship did you have in mind?"

He thought of the superdreadnought he'd commanded during the last battle and sighed. "I don't know."

"Then this one should suffice," the woman told him tartly and the preparation room spun away.

As the virtual came back into focus, his gaze traced the compact bridge of a destroyer. Pivoting slowly, he took it in. It was as if he'd come home.

"I didn't realize how much I missed being here," he murmured as he walked along the front of the empty consoles and was surprised to find them laid out exactly as he preferred. He sighed again. "I guess this time, I won't be fighting in space."

Footsteps made him pivot as Ted spoke.

"Never assume," the AI said as he stopped beside him and the forward viewscreen came alive.

Together, they turned toward it.

"Is that intelligence or are you suggesting something?" Amaratne asked.

Ted took another step closer to the screen. "History has a way of using your talents," he told his companion. "My calculations suggest this fight will not be easy. They have had over two decades of preparation."

The ex-admiral followed his gaze and imagined he could see another fleet hanging among the stars. "Good," he said and the stars rippled.

The consoles faded from around him and he landed with a jolt on the hard pavement of a broken street. The deep-throated thump of mortars and whirring buzz of drones was interspersed by sporadic gunfire, and the darkness of space was replaced by the flash-lit dark of a ruined city.

"But first things first," Ted declared as he appeared beside him and pressed himself against the lee of the wall.

He tossed the man a CUB and watched as the ex-Admiral automatically checked the safety and magazine, then clicked his fingers.

Amaratne felt the weight of his clothing shift and looked down. Gone were the clothes he hadn't changed in the avatar preparation room. Now, he wore lightweight body armor.

"First things first?" he asked, and Ted grinned.

"You have to make it through the first stage—on land."

The light grew brighter and the figure more distinct. Lars released John and let the boy roll to his feet as they both faced it. Frog and Vishlog also stood, and together, they formed a line shoulder to shoulder before the light.

Slowly, the shadowy outline coalesced into a woman, her long hair caught back in a silver plait. The young Talent frowned. She looked familiar, but he was sure he'd never met her before.

Finally, recognition dawned and he took a step back.

"Ms. Morgana?"

The woman smiled.

"In a way," she answered. "While she isn't a main feature of the subnet, I have added what I know."

"BURT?"

"Ted, now," EBURT told him, "but I think you need to know more of what is possible in the realm of magical training, and more importantly, the knowledge of what can be."

He thought about that, then looked at his companions.

"This will hurt, won't it?"

Frog smirked. "Who do you think kept saying 'no pain, no gain?'"

He jerked his thumb at the woman. When she turned and frowned at him, he ignored her. "She really can be a right bit—"

His head exploded in a ball of fire.

"He always mouths off and never learns." Stephanie sniffed and turned to John, noting his shocked expression as he stared at the headless body.

It dissolved slowly, and the Frog materialized where he'd stood before. He looked at Stephanie, and she held his gaze.

"Nothing?" she asked when he remained silent.

He shook his head emphatically.

Stephanie waited, but the small man made no effort to speak and lowered his head to avoid her gaze. She nodded curtly and focused on John.

"Here are the rules," she told him and gestured at her three guards. "They will attack you. I will explain the options. You either implement the options or die a painful and embarrassing death."

He waited for her to continue. When she didn't, he looked at Frog. The guard caught his gaze and shook his head. He hesitated, hoping the small man would give him more, but he'd turned his attention to Stephanie, so John did the same.

"That's it?" he asked.

Her brow creased as if she was thinking about it. Finally, she gave him a bright smile.

"Don't die?" she suggested, and the training room twisted and funneled them to somewhere else.

If he didn't know any better, he'd have said he was on some kind of military base. He didn't have time to confirm the theory, though, as a bolt of light streaked past him and gouged a fist-sized hole in the wall.

He sprawled on his stomach and scrambled into cover, and two more bolts whined through the space where he'd been. More bolts followed and he pushed into a run.

CHAPTER TEN

Ivy was still on her knees when the world coalesced around her. It took her a moment to register the familiar set of boots in front of her. The hand she'd rested on Frog's chest now rested on his toes.

She sniffed and a box of tissues nudged the side of her head. When she took the box, the boots stepped back.

"Are you okay?" a familiar voice asked, and she looked up with a tissue in one hand as she wiped her eyes with the other.

"You!" she began but had to pause to blow her nose. "You shouldn't..."

Her face crumpled and her voice faded as she turned hastily away.

"Awwww..." Frog said. "If I didn't know any better, I'd say you were falling for me."

Ivy snorted and blew her nose again. "Not likely."

"What? You never wanted to kiss a frog and find a prince?"

"Who needs a prince? I have something better."

"Better than a prince?" His voice was a blend of mock disbelief and pretend outrage.

She finished mopping her eyes and clearing her head and stared up at him. "You're not funny," she told him.

"I'm a laugh a minute," he retorted. "Ask Steph."

"Mmmhmmm," she replied, and he sobered. "What's next?"

"We have a new teammate," he told her, and the air beside him shimmered.

The girl frowned as the shimmer settled slowly into an extremely large solid outline—one so big it could certainly not be human. She frowned. What was this new teammate? Some kind of giant?

As the details began to solidify, she gasped and took two hasty steps back. The Dreth warrior raised his head and looked at her, and she didn't hesitate. She drew her blaster and fired.

He took a step toward her and extended his hand in the split-second before his head exploded and splattered Frog with blood, brain matter, and fragments of skull. The little man gave her a disgusted look.

Ivy lowered the blaster as he looked at the dead Dreth with an expression of disbelief on his face, then shifted his gaze to focus it on her. Even then, it took her a moment to realize what she'd done.

"Uh...new teammate?" she asked, hoping she was wrong, and he extended his forefinger and stabbed it toward the body.

"That was him."

Ivy's jaw dropped, and the body began to fade.

"Oh," she said and snapped her mouth closed. She chewed nervously at her lip, her face pale. "Oh, dear."

Amaratne laughed and threw himself behind a burnt-out car as he snapped two quick shots at the figures that appeared through the smoke. He settled into a crouch, checked the charge on the CUB and the magazines at his belt, and chose his next position.

The sound of boots approaching at a run warned him it was time to move, so he bobbed up and took another three shots, checked his surroundings, and scurried to a large block of concrete.

Ivy would have recognized the area. She'd used the top of the burnt-out wreck to vault into the nearby parking lot. He used it to cover his back as he moved.

The figures that emerged from the shadows were human but they were fast. He scanned the nearby buildings and caught movement from the direction he was heading in.

"Well, it's time to see what else this can do," he muttered, and instead of sliding behind the pillar, he vaulted up against it and bounced off to launch himself to an empty floor in what had been an office building.

At least the filing cabinets would offer some cover, he reasoned. The door on the opposite side of the room burst open as he landed, and Amaratne rolled forward and opened fire as he found his feet.

It was satisfying to see the heavy slugs knock the intruders back, and he hoped the scenario hadn't been programmed with friends. If it had, he might have eliminated someone useful.

What was more satisfying was the spring in his step—and the utter lack of pain. If he'd been in the body he'd arrived in, his knees would be aching and he'd be short of breath. As it was, he felt like he could make another leap like that without breaking a sweat.

He felt like he could fight for longer—which was a good thing because these guys simply didn't know when to give up.

Heavy boots pounded up the stairs and he stuck his head out the door. The office he'd chosen had looked out over the street, but it had backed onto a landing with an escalator leading to a large atrium.

"Not the most ideal location," he observed. "It must have been for someone lower on the food chain."

The top of the first pursuer's head appeared above the handrail and he removed it with a targeted shot and walked his fire into the next man's skull, then the next before they registered that he was waiting for them.

A fourth head began to appear but ducked hastily out of sight, and Amaratne wished there was a way to turn the escalator on. There wasn't, so he left the office and side-stepped so he could see over the railing to the entrance beyond.

He must have reached the administration section because the balcony overlooked what appeared to have been some kind of shopping mall. Broken glass and ruined storefronts rimmed the walkway overlooking the atrium and more figures moved up two other escalators.

None of them was in easy range, and it was clear that he would shortly be overrun. He looked quickly for an exit and decided against the window through which he'd come in. Instead, he chose to take the battle to the group closest to him and then use their escalator to reach the next floor while maybe picking up an extra weapon on the way. He realized his mistake halfway along the balcony when four figures plummeted from the upper level and released their ropes to land and bound toward him.

What were these guys' legs made of? Springs?

The thought was fleeting as he fired instinctively and struck center mass of the leading assailant before he dodged back and into the closest shop.

Clothes, he thought and knocked over the last standing mannequin as he hurdled another and hoped like Hades there was a corridor out back.

There was.

Amaratne slammed the door in the small storage space shut as he bolted into it and then realized his next mistake. There were multiple entrances into the corridor, and there had been numerous people pursuing him.

The lights illuminating the corridor still worked, but they

flickered as the first of his enemy raised his pistol. The ex-admiral pivoted and moved to return to the storeroom, but the door opened and another figure appeared.

This one didn't bother to shoot but lunged toward him with a long-bladed dagger glinting in his hand. A shout went up from the other end of the corridor and Amaratne grimaced.

Without a doubt, this would hurt either way. To fight the guy who attacked with the knife meant he had to turn his back to one of the oncoming groups. It also meant his assailant blocked the other group's line of fire.

Small blessings, he thought as several rounds pounded into his back.

He grunted, but the man with the blade had closed the distance between them and he was forced to leap back to avoid the first swing. His leap turned into an unexpected collision with a man who'd raced in behind him and the knife scored a smoking gash across his armor.

Amaratne caught a glimmer of blue.

Laser-edged, he thought as an arm looped around his neck and he registered the not-so-subtle pressure of something thrust into his back. He fired one-handed and fumbled for a blade he didn't have with the other when the man behind him pulled the trigger.

At the same time, the attacker in front swept the ex-admiral's gun aside and drove his knife into his stomach. The pain that followed preceded a short-lived trip into the dark.

A sharp jolt woke him with a gasp. Shadow-pain forced his eyes to remain closed, and his body curled until he registered that it wasn't real. White walls greeted him when he looked around and he groaned and rolled to push slowly to his feet.

"I always hated this part."

"Is it less painful dying on a ship in the Virtual World?" Roma asked when she appeared before him.

"No," he admitted. "Merely less up-close and personal. I need to upgrade my avatar."

The AI snapped her fingers and the white dissolved to be replaced by the more utilitarian grey of the avatar preparation room.

"I need weapons," he muttered and moved along the racks. "Many more weapons."

He stopped when he reached the knives and selected one of the larger ones. Eight inches long and a little over an inch thick, the blade bore the tell-tale markings of a laser-infused edge and curved slightly at the tip.

Amaratne picked it up and hefted it, admiring the way the grip curved a little over his hand. He looked at Roma.

"Is someone compensating when they use this?" he asked and put it back on the shelf.

"That all depends," the AI answered as he moved deeper into the racks, "on if they know how to use it."

"Marbles," he muttered. "Tell me they stock marbles."

He found them, checked that the frequency matched the blaster and the CUB's firing frequencies, and stowed them in a pouch. She continued to watch him and a faint frown creased her brow.

It deepened when he picked up a box of stickies and several scramblers.

"What are you doing?" she asked as he selected several cubes of fine white dust and turned to select another suit of combat armor and upgrade the filters. "I'm not sure how you intend to use these—"

"I might have a younger body," Amaratne said and tapped the side of his head, "but I'm old enough to know a thousand ways to cheat."

He searched along the shelf before he looked at her. "I need some Tyrenol 13 in a hose dispenser with a misting bulb."

"I beg your pardon?"

The ex-admiral gave her his most winning smile. "Please?"

She sighed. "Color me intrigued, as my uncle would say."

The required chemical and dispensing equipment appeared and he grinned. "And you fitted it to a flat-pack."

"A reinforced flat-pack," Roma told him.

"I'll call it extra armor," he replied, slid the pack over his lower back, and secured it under the weapons harness.

She remained silent as he chose various additions to his gear. He added grenades, another pistol, a flare gun—she couldn't begin to imagine what he intended with that—and more magazines.

When he was finished, he frowned, returned to the knife rack, and picked up the blade he'd admired before.

"You never know," he told her as he added it to his belt. "I might need it."

The AI shook her head. "Tell me when you're done."

He looked down at himself and patted several pouches, pockets, and holsters.

"Okay," he said. "I'm ready."

The air shimmered again and Ivy pulled the safety strap over the blaster.

"New teammate, right?" she asked Frog, and he covered his eyes with his hand.

She hooked her thumbs over her belt and waited. Even though she expected him, the sight of a Dreth warrior so close still made her nervous.

That feeling didn't go away as he tilted his head to one side and studied her.

After a long moment, she released her belt and raised one hand shoulder height to waggle her fingers in greeting. "Hi?"

"So you aren't planning to shoot me in the head as a way of saying hello, this time?" the Dreth asked acidly.

Ivy's jaw dropped. "Frog never said—" she started but couldn't find the words to finish.

"And you didn't know Stephanie had a Dreth on her team?" the warrior asked as he took a step forward.

Ivy took two steps back. Now that he mentioned it, she did remember something about that. Her face paled.

"Uh-huh," he said. "So, what happened? You forgot?"

She had but she didn't want to admit it, so she retreated a few more steps and tried frantically to think of something to say.

"How did that happen, by the way?" she asked, and Frog snickered.

The Dreth frowned. "Why? Do you find it hard to believe?"

The smaller man turned away, his shoulder's shaking. If she hadn't known any better, she'd have thought he was crying instead of laughing hard enough to split his sides.

Her new teammate ignored him and stepped forward again. Startled by the movement, she took two more back and tried desperately to work out how to dig herself out of this predicament.

"I…"

The truth was, having gone through the pirate scenario, she'd found the Regime's propaganda easier to believe. She'd forgotten Becca telling her and John about the Dreth on Stephanie's team and how she'd found it hard to believe despite the older woman's assurances.

No wonder he frowned at her like she'd insulted his mother or something. She continued her jerky retreat while Vishlog moved slowly forward. Finally, she stopped. He was a teammate, right? That had to count for something

"I didn't ask you your name," she said finally and forced herself to stand still as he moved closer.

"Vishlog," he told her and stopped directly in front of her.

Ivy looked at him and fought the instinct to run.

He was waiting for a response, so she muttered, "Ivy."

The warrior studied her for a long moment, his expression inscrutable. "So, you want to hear how I joined Stephanie's team?"

"Please?"

He turned away and moved to where Frog stood in silence and simply watched them.

After a moment's hesitation, she followed him

The Dreth sat cross-legged on the floor and indicated that she should do the same. "Sit."

She stopped a few feet away, caught the look on Frog's face as he sat, and moved closer to join them. Vishlog watched her, his face unreadable, and she wondered what he was thinking.

"I was drunk," he told her, and she stared. He smiled at her reaction and continued, "and my commanding officer thought it would be good for politics to have a Dreth on Stephanie's team."

He paused, and his gaze took on a faraway look. "If I am truthful, I did not give the commander much choice, and since Stephanie had already put me down once, I was most suited for the task."

"Put you down?" Ivy asked.

It was the first time she'd ever seen a Dreth blush.

"I was very drunk," he admitted, and Frog snickered.

Vishlog darted him a filthy look, and the man mimed zipping his lips and indicated he should continue.

"I challenged her to a fight."

She couldn't help laughing.

He poked her in the middle of the forehead. "It was like you shooting me in the head."

That stopped her amusement. She stared at him, and he continued.

"She magicked me into the air and Jaleck had me put in chains."

Ivy frowned. "So how did that get you added to her team?"

"Jaleck was the Ambassador to Meligorn," Vishlog told her,

"and I was part of her honor guard at the party where I met Stephanie."

Her eyes widened. "But you were drunk!"

Vishlog shrugged. "I got drunk often when I was not in battle. It was…for the best."

His eyes darkened and she stared at him. She was still trying to wrap her head around getting drunk as an honor guard being for the best, but before she could say anything, he continued.

"So when politics demanded a Dreth on Stephanie's team, I was chosen."

"Why?" The question was out before she could stop it and she tried hastily to explain. "I mean, if it was such an important pos… it..ion…"

Ivy stopped. Frog had lowered his head and had his arms folded across his stomach as he laughed. She bit her bottom lip and looked at the floor.

"I'm sorry, that was… It didn't…" she began, but Vishlog answered anyway.

"As I said, I was the best candidate because Stephanie had put me down once. It meant I would be more respectful."

She raised her head. "It did?"

He nodded. "Have you seen Stephanie?"

The girl shook her head.

"She is tiny," he told her. "Only a little taller than you. Not much to look at or for a warrior to respect."

When she drew herself up and glared at him, he smiled.

"I learned appearances can be deceiving, but politics aside, I could not understand why I should be accepted by her team—or by Stephanie—or why Dreth made her one of their Talons."

"A Talon?" Ivy asked and Frog shifted restlessly.

"That's a story for another day," he interrupted and stood quickly. "In the meantime, we have training, and trust me, she's as bad as you were when you first joined."

Vishlog looked at her and raised an eyebrow. "As I said, appearances can be deceiving."

"What's that supposed to mean?" Ivy asked, but the world began to shift.

The passenger compartment of a shuttle formed around them and the warrior added, "It was an honor to be chosen, and it is more of an honor to have been allowed to remain."

The shuttle shuddered and dropped.

"The landing will be rough!" Frog warned and the shuttle hit hard and skidded as if to prove his point.

Vishlog caught hold of Ivy and held her upright as the tail hatch opened and they looked into the shuttle bay of a Dreth pirate ship.

Large forms moved on the upper gantry, and the human guard grasped her arm and dragged her toward cover.

"First wave!" he shouted. "And you're not allowed to die!"

"It's easy for you to say," she replied a few minutes later when she scrambled from the floor of the white room.

Her hands moved over the front of her armor, where several rounds from a turret gun had caught her. Finding no damage, she breathed a sigh of relief.

"Where's Vishlog?" she asked, and the Dreth appeared as though he'd been summoned.

"Rocket launcher," he explained succinctly. "These pirates are cheating."

His words acted as a signal and they reappeared on board the shuttle again.

This time, they made it out and across the hangar. Ivy destroyed the auto-turret with a well-thrown grenade and shot the Dreth with the rocket launcher while Vishlog eliminated any who got too close and Frog swept their other flank clear.

They flattened themselves against the wall near the airlock leading into the ship and delayed a little longer to annihilate another team of Dreth that came over the gantry.

"These guys seriously like to drop in on you," Ivy noted and delivered a well-placed shot into another pirate as he appeared.

The defender landed on the decking and immediately rolled to all fours.

"Oh no, you don't," she told him and shot him through the face-plate.

"Door," Frog ordered, and she turned reluctantly away from the hangar.

It wasn't easy, but she had to trust her teammates to have her back while she hacked the door open. Frog had been very clear about needing her to get the electronics.

She forced herself to concentrate but flinched every time they fired and fought the urge to turn and take care of the threat herself.

"You're not on your own anymore," she reminded herself. "Not alone."

If Frog or Vishlog heard her, they gave no sign. The airlock gave, and they followed her through and closed the open door as she worked the inner seal.

"Done!" she called as the warrior stepped past her, firing as he moved.

The pirates were waiting, and his body jerked before his shield went live and sparked blue.

"Vishlog?" Ivy asked but he didn't reply, and Frog moved up beside him.

Between the two of them, they cleared the corridor and ran to the next junction. Ivy raced behind them but glanced over her shoulder as a ceiling hatch gave way with a loud clang.

"Behind you!" she called, and they stopped and turned as she threw another grenade and opened fire.

As if the first team's discovery was a signal, more warriors dropped through the ceiling and reinforcements arrived via the corridors.

"What is this?" she complained. "Dreth Central?"

Vishlog chuckled. "Funny you should mention that."

He grunted, and she felt the shudder from the impact beneath her boots as he landed heavily. Frog cursed, and she looked around. The closest pirate took advantage of her distraction and powered forward with sufficient force to disrupt her shield.

The blade that slid through her armor was inevitable.

Ivy woke in the white room, choking on her own blood, then remembered where she was and coughed the memory away. The Dreth had already regained his feet and now leaned against the wall. They both jumped when Frog coalesced a foot above the floor and dropped beside them.

"What happened to you?" she asked, and he gave her a sick grin.

"I stole one of your grenades."

The white room vanished and they reappeared in the airlock.

"Again?" she grumbled. "How many more—"

A grenade bounced through the open door and her question remained unfinished.

With the testing over, the *Tempestarii's* crew returned to work. They moved quickly to their sections and looked around. The ship was well-maintained and clean, but the section commanders decided it needed to be cleaner.

Most of them had seen action in the last battle with the Telorans. They knew what kinds of things could break, if not when.

Chief Technician Piedmont brought a small team onto the bridge and came to a halt before Emil's console.

"Permission for close inspection, sir," he snapped and hurried to explain when the captain glanced up. "I'd like to make sure nothing's likely to break when the hunt starts, sir."

Emil refrained from telling him that the hunt had already started. Instead, he nodded.

"Granted." He looked at the others in the command center. "All cooperation will be given."

His gaze rested on Alain Docherty and his co-pilot and quelled the rebellion in his chief pilot's face with a single look. The man gave an exasperated sigh and swung out of his seat.

"You can start here," he informed the chief and clapped his co-pilot on the shoulder. "Call me when they're done."

The woman sighed. "Make mine white and four, boss, and jam, not sprinkles."

Docherty had taken two strides. Now, he turned to her with his eyebrows raised. Sri Malagar gave him large eyes. "Please…"

The pilot snorted in disgust. "Only the one?" he asked, and she beamed.

"Two," she said decisively. "Raspberry and apricot."

He scowled, but he gave her a brisk nod before he left.

"Two," he reiterated, "and I won't lick either of them before I get back."

Sri pulled a face but managed a swift, "Thank you," before he was through the door.

Piedmont looked at her. "With your permission?"

She nodded and pushed away from the console.

"Tempe, you have the con."

"Agreed," the ship replied and addressed the technicians. "No tickling."

One of the newer techs gave her boss a startled glance.

He chuckled. "We'll do our best, Tempe, but no promises. Some of those components are delicate."

The ship sniffed disdainfully. "All my components are delicate."

One of the weapons technicians had a sudden coughing fit.

"Care to share, Officer Ingram?" the ship asked, and the woman shook her head.

"Dust… Only dust…" she explained hastily.

The technicians went to work, and Piedmont methodically

pulled every component from inside the console and passed them to his team.

"Make sure they're clean," he told them. "And I mean they need to sparkle."

The new tech took the component she'd been given and inspected it carefully. Apart from a minute smudge on one end, there appeared to be nothing wrong with it.

She wiped the smudge away, then looked around. The other techs were studying their respective pieces with the equivalent of a fine-toothed comb. Shrugging, she polished the piece again and gently wiped the rest of it down as though it needed the attention.

Setting it on the tray beside the chief tech and picking up the next, almost immaculate item, she said, "I don't understand."

One of the others looked up from where they were wiping out the inside of the console housing. The surface already looked like a mirror, but the older tech was buffing it like it was tarnished.

"What's not to understand, Livvie?" he asked.

"All this." She gestured at the team.

They had removed the cover off the pilot's console first but had divided the team to cover two installations at once.

"I mean," she continued, "I get ship's maintenance and all that, but this? It doesn't look like it needs maintaining. No offense. I simply...don't get it."

"She's back," Piedmont said from under the console.

"Who?" Livvie asked, focused on her next component. "Who's back?"

"The Morgana." The older tech set aside the piece of housing he'd been working on and started on the next.

He gestured to where Emil was studying his boards, seemingly oblivious to the conversation.

"The captain wouldn't have brought out the testing bar otherwise."

Livvie noted his gesture and lowered voice and moved closer as she whispered, "But she can't be. She hasn't been seen in..."

She finished the piece she was working on and started on the next.

Piedmont finished what he was doing inside the console and began to replace the cleaned parts, inspecting each one with a critical eye.

"Trust me, she's coming back." The old-timer chuckled. He jerked a thumb at Piedmont. "Why don't you ask him where he was the time one of the admirals failed the test?"

The chief chuckled, poked Livvie with one finger, and gestured to the part she held. She checked it again, gave it one final wipe, and passed it to him.

He took it, and she looked around for what to do next. She'd just decided to join the older man in cleaning the outside of the console when Piedmont began to speak.

"I was right here...except on the *Knight*. Wattlebird had done something to the controls—don't ask me what. That man..." He sighed with exasperation. "Well, he was crazier than than now, and I had to fix whatever it was he'd broke..."

Sri stifled a giggle and listened as avidly as any of the others in earshot. Stories of Jonathan before she'd met him? Golden!

Oblivious to her delight, Piedmont continued, "Anyway, this wave of cold swept over us, and I pulled my head out from under the console to see what it was. Up until then, the Witch had been standing on the command deck."

Tools rattled, and he pulled himself out from under the console and began to replace the panels. Livvie stepped out of his way as he continued.

"When I looked at where she'd been standing, she was gone and everyone was looking at the forward screen."

He paused as though the memory of what he'd seen was playing in front of his eyes. Livvie waited.

"It had been on, so we kinda knew some big-wig had stopped

at the entry to the *Knight's* dock. Next thing we know, the ship calls, 'Admiral on deck' and starts sassing the guy already there and an even bigger wig rolls up."

The command center stilled but Piedmont didn't seem to notice. He finished with the console.

"She's all yours," he told Sri before he moved to the Defense station and began the process all over again. Livvie and the old-timer moved with him while the other team shifted to Weapons.

Once he had the covers off and began to remove the parts, Piedmont continued with his tale.

"Anyway, the new guy tells the first guy to 'take the test' in no uncertain terms."

"What test?" she asked, and he sighed with exasperation.

"The only test that matters," he explained with weary patience. "The one with the bar."

"Oh." Livvie subsided and picked up the first part to appear from under the console.

Piedmont worked methodically as he related the tale. "Anyway, the first guy says he'd rather suck vacuum than take the Witch's test, and the next thing I know, this ice-cold voice tells him it could be arranged."

He shivered and passed out another part.

"Anyway, that's when I pull myself out from under the console and look around. As well as the forward screen being on, there's this big sparkling blue hole in the middle of the command deck and it matches the one I see on the screen, except nothing comes out of the one on my end. Only her Dreth and two cats going in."

The chief handed Livvie another part and vanished back under the console.

After a moment filled with the clank and rattle of tools, Piedmont started to talk again.

"I tell you, the Morgana is terrifying when she's mad. She stepped out of that portal and marched down the corridor we could see, and the picture flicked to follow her."

Another part appeared, and Livvie realized she hadn't started on the one before it. With a guilty start, she picked it up and inspected it carefully.

"She was covered in lightning. I'd heard of it, but never seen it. Not until then." Piedmont's voice was hushed and then hardened. "And that admiral refused to take the test."

The older tech snorted. "I still remember what you said." He laughed, and his boss' face emerged from under the console a little flushed. She didn't think it had anything to do with the effort expended in his task, though. "Yeah, well, I was young, then," he demurred, "and luckily, she didn't hear me. Anyway, the Morgana stoops in low, puts her face close to his, and asks him if he's ready to suck vacuum like he said."

"The look on his face." The other man chuckled. "I thought he was gonna need another pair of trousers."

Piedmont gave a short laugh. "He very nearly did. His expression was priceless! I'll never forget it. I thought the man would have a heart attack."

"What did he do?" Livvie asked.

"He tried to resign," the chief told her, "and the Morgana wouldn't let him. I swear, I've never heard a woman's voice hit that low a note." He shuddered. "And I never want to hear it again. It was ice and...like space had spoken if space was a human girl with magic like the gods themselves haven't seen."

He glanced around. "No offense to the gods," he added hastily, "but the Morgana's eyes were like fire, and when she floated the bar out of the Marine captain's hands..."

The other technician laughed. "Oh, yes. I swear that's the only time I've ever seen Sartre look surprised, but he only cursed quietly when the bar he held lifted out of his hands and floated to the admiral. I've never seen the like."

Piedmont shook his head. "Me neither. And when it wriggled into the guy's hands so he had to hold it..." He shook his head. "That was a sight to behold. The way it was covered in lightning, there was no way in Hades I'd have wanted to touch it."

"And then she ordered him to look at her," the other man added.

The chief sobered. "That was something, wasn't it? They'd got the angle on the surveillance cams absolutely perfect and the *Knight* made sure we all had a good look at him."

The older tech tensed. "I never want anyone to look at me the way he looked at her. She'd done *nothing* to deserve that."

Piedmont's voice softened and took on an angry edge. "No, she hadn't. All she wanted was to protect her people, and he—"

His fist clenched, and he pulled himself under the console again. Metal clanged against metal and Livvie winced. She looked at her teammate, and to her surprise, he was angry too.

He caught her gaze and shook himself as if that was enough to rid himself of the memory. "Some things are hard to remember without getting angry. She challenged him to prove himself an ally, and all he did was prove he wasn't while she'd gone all out to protect us and then to protect our world."

For a moment, sadness etched his features, and he indicated the small pile of components that had gathered while they talked. "We have to make sure Tempe is ready for the very worst the universe can throw at us."

They returned to work but Livvie's mind constantly returned to the old-timers' story. Had the Morgana honestly done all that? And was she truly coming back?

She did her best to make sure every part was better when she returned it than when it had been passed to her. When they'd finished with the consoles, they worked around the control room and checked the nodes and terminals and even the emergency and crew seating.

If the Morgana led them into battle, they wanted nothing left to chance. Piedmont gave the captain a nod as they left and headed to the first data center.

As far as Livvie could tell, there wasn't anything wrong with that either, but they still went over it like they were searching for a particularly elusive malfunction. They were about halfway through when the intercom crackled.

"All crew, all crew, all crew," Emil began, "this is your captain speaking. It is with pride and pleasure I am now able to share this information with you."

She glanced to where Piedmont's legs protruded from a wall panel. At the captain's words, he extracted himself and turned to face the nearest vid screen. She and the rest of the team did the same and moved to stand together as the broadcast began.

"This ship is departing shortly for an unknown area of space, completely outside the normal mapped systems." He paused to let the information sink in. "Once there, we will pick up a VIP vessel."

Again, he paused, and his eyes seemed to scan them through the screen.

"We will bring that vessel back to Federated space. For those of you who've been waiting as long as I have, I'm sure you've guessed, but for now, I'll simply admit what I can."

Livvie heard Piedmont's sharp intake of breath and glanced at him. He stood, tense with anticipation, and a quick look revealed the other old-timers did the same.

The captain continued, "She's back. She's pissed. And she will not stop until the Regime is finished. I am going for rejuvenation treatments over the next couple of weeks and these are now open to all crew."

Again, his gaze swept over them.

"If any of you wish to take me up on the offer, talk to the OIC of your division. I suspect we are done hiding in the deep and dark and that life is about to get dangerous to a degree the likes of which many of you have *never* seen. Out."

"Morgana!" Piedmont's shout of jubilation was repeated throughout the ship. It was accompanied by cries of "Stephanie!"

Livvie stared. It was the most vocal she'd ever seen him or any of the others, and she didn't know what to make of this new dimension to the teammates she thought she knew well. While she was still considering it, the older technician turned and seized her shoulders in both hands.

"I told you!" he exclaimed, released her, and returned to the task the captain's broadcast had interrupted. He was smiling, and his eyes twinkled with mischief. Catching her bemused look, he signaled that she should get back to work too.

"The Witch is back!"

CHAPTER ELEVEN

Movement had begun on Dreth. Ships maneuvered into the orbital and out again. Some of them took a turn around the moon and sent shuttles to the lunar base. Others took position over different spaceports and waited.

One shuttle descended to a remote mountain plateau. Maneuvering was difficult, and only a skilled manipulation of engines and retro thrusters brought it in to land safely.

"Is this the location?" the pilot asked as he studied the stone door set into the mountainside. He turned his gaze to their surroundings but saw nothing more than mountain grass and stone.

"It's where we were told to go," his partner said.

The door opened and closed and darkness swept toward them.

"You'd better hope this is the place," the co-pilot added as their passengers knocked at the hatch.

There were four of them. "For Dreth," they told the pilots in sibilant tones, "we will fight to the last. This is now our home too."

The shuttle lifted and barely cleared the mountain as a vicious crosswind battered its hull.

It was a scene repeated the world over, and the shuttles gave the impression another meteor swarm was passing.

On the ground, troops gathered at training centers and messages went out to remote Family outposts. Clan leaders met in secret, their vessels moving swiftly and by night despite the risk that entailed.

Well-shielded communications bounced across the planet and warriors followed in their wake. Clans pledged troops and assistance and jockeyed for advantage at the merest hint of war.

"Clan Hachtech requests the chance to prove its loyalty."

"Granted. This is Hachtech's last chance before dissolution."

"Gravach answers."

"Karnach stands for Dreth. Unity is all."

"Talach and Vashjak come."

"K'leth stands ready!"

Excitement tremored through the warlords, chieftains, and family heads. Honor would be avenged and more honor would be gained. The faces of those who knew some of what was afoot took on a stern and savage edge.

The hallways of the Dreth Coalition Council remained deceptively quiet, save for the complaints raging in one of the private chambers where representatives from Clans Endrageth and Echgrech had met.

"They are moving the troops," Kalgeth snapped and pounded a fist into the stone tabletop.

He was disappointed when it didn't break, but that was irrelevant. The force had made Narach jump, and his fellow Dreth and councilor scowled as a result.

"They can't be. I would know," he protested. "House Karnach would have had to pass it through the Coalition."

Kalgeth shook his head. "Not necessarily. She is the admiral of the Coalition Fleet. If she orders troops to move, they move, regardless of what her house or its coalition might think. She wouldn't have to gain anyone's approval."

"What of the Coalition Council?" Narach demanded. "Surely she would have had to ask their permission."

"Well, yes," Kalgeth conceded, "but we would have had to be in attendance, and a full council has yet to be called."

"Are you sure? What if she chose only to contact the Inner Circle?"

"The Inner Circle?" His colleague looked alarmed. "But there hasn't been one of those in years. We did not even hold one during the Teloran War. Why would she call one now?"

"Because she has learned some caution over the years?" Narach suggested slyly. "She cannot have been totally blind to the inner-clan politics, either during that war or in the years since."

"Still," Kalgeth thundered, "how can she keep us blind?"

"Do you think she suspects?"

The other councilor shrugged. "If she does, it can only be suspicion. If she had proof, she'd have moved already."

Narach nodded. This much was true. The new Dreth Coalition Admiral was known for her swift action and lack of mercy when it came to anyone acting for interests other than Dreth. What she'd think of their alliances, he didn't want to know—and prayed he'd never find out.

"Regardless," he said, "we should know! We are war leaders in our clans. Military matters are ours by right."

"This is true," Kalgeth agreed and moved to the door, "but we both have places to be and other matters to attend to. Shall we?"

He nodded, willing to tolerate his position as the junior in this partnership given the rewards his comrade promised.

They stepped into the corridor outside, relieved to find it empty despite the soundproofing inside the room. Even their clans did not know about some matters they'd discussed—and would not until they could not disassociate from them.

It would seal their places as leaders if their plans had time to mature.

The rumble of another shuttle overhead drew their attention and they tracked its passing, the sound clearly audible through the solid roof.

"Another one for the base," Kalgeth grumbled.

"And neither of us are any the wiser." Narach checked his tablet and found no notification. His fist closed reflexively and the device cracked. "We should have been told."

The sound of footsteps reached them at the same time and they glanced up as a solitary female Dreth moved briskly along the corridor. She looked like she had places to be—or perhaps an urgent message to run.

"Do you think she is here for us?" he asked, nudged his companion, and lowered his voice.

"I don't see why we shouldn't stop her and find out," Kalgeth replied. "After all, we are on a high-security alert."

"And we are war leaders," Narach reminded him.

"She has a guard," the other councilor observed.

"Every runner should," he responded and they continued down the corridor, moving side by side so they blocked the middle of it.

Ahead of them, the guard moved in front of the female and the two councilors exchanged glances. Who was he to think he could challenge war leaders?

They strode confidently forward and covered the intervening distance in several long strides. As they approached, the security guard came to a halt and positioned himself between the two councilors and the female.

Recognizing his colors as those of House Karnach, Kalgeth stepped forward.

"We demand an audience with your masters," he blustered, and the man looked at him but did not answer.

Goaded by his silence, Narach added, "We are warlords in

clans Echgrech and Endrageth, members of the High Mountains Coalition and allies of the Coalition Admiral. We have a right to know what is going on."

The guard looked from one to the other. "I am afraid that what you ask is beyond my power to bring about," he told them and watched as both councilors stiffened with offense.

"You cannot refuse us," Kalgeth insisted and his voice echoed down the corridor.

"It is forbidden," Narach agreed. "A guard does not refuse a war leader, regardless of what clan they serve."

He stared at them, and his face became as impassive as stone. Kalgeth was about to demand he step aside when the female cleared her throat.

"Gralog, if you please."

The guard stepped aside, and she deliberately moved into one of the dimmed glows illuminating the corridor. Narach's blood drained from his face when he saw who it was, and even Kalgeth backed away a step.

"I believe you wished for an audience," the Coalition Admiral stated she drew herself stiffly to her full height, "and that you were willing to break protocol to achieve it?"

Narach swallowed hard and his fellow councilor cleared his throat.

"We are war leaders in Clans Echgrech and Endrageth," he began.

"War leaders and not lords?" Jaleck asked and sounded mildly amused. Both Dreth snapped their mouths shut. When the admiral sounded amused, she generally wasn't. They'd heard the stories, but still, they couldn't accept things the way they were.

"Yes, and we demand—" Kalgeth began, but his protest was stopped by a fist in his chest.

He dropped to his knees and gasped for breath as Jaleck backhanded Narach across the side of the head and followed it with a kick that lifted the Echgrech war leader into the wall.

His armor rattled as he landed but the admiral ignored him. She returned her attention to Kalgeth, lifted him by the collar, and punched him twice in the gut before she tossed him onto his fellow conspirator.

The Echgrech war leader grunted as the air was forced from his lungs, and both councilors drew back as Jaleck stalked closer and bent to look at them.

"You two have no idea what is about to happen, and I wouldn't trust either of you with a family recipe." Her tone emerged as a snarl and they recoiled.

Both could hear her security guard speaking softly into his comms, although they couldn't make his words out. Kalgeth flinched and slid his hands under him so he could shift off his colleague. Jaleck swept that support away and he fell back. Narach froze.

"And since you both want to know so badly, you have now been entrusted with information that requires you to be separated." She smiled. "Welcome to your new roles." She straightened and turned to her security guard. "Gralog."

He stiffened to attention. "Place them in a safe place where no one can talk to them so that we may share these secrets."

She cast a jaundiced eye at where the two councilors attempted to carefully untangle themselves.

"With secrets come security measures," she told them as the rapid tattoo of boots signaled the arrival of her security team.

"Take them," she ordered and pivoted to continue her journey. Gralog stayed long enough to issue orders before he joined her again.

Groans signaled when the councilors were dragged to their feet, and she allowed herself a secretive smile.

"That's two less," she stated, and the Dreth beside her shared her satisfied smile.

The walls shook with the sound of powerful engines above. In the basement room, two men looked up as a patina of grey dust rained from the ceiling. They turned their heads quickly and exchanged glances.

Speculation and excitement shone in their eyes.

"There goes another one," one observed.

"I hear it."

"It's the third in the last half hour," the first man pressed, "and those are transport engines."

"I know." The other man pushed his chair back. "It's time to see what our giant friends are up to."

"Yeah. It's not like they know much about sneaking around." His partner snorted disdainfully.

"This might be true, but they have Teloran friends, and those suckers are as sneaky as a girl going on a forbidden date."

"How is your daughter, by the way?"

"Enjoying her time in boarding school and finally making something of the opportunities she's been given."

"So, not much choice then."

His partner shook his head and smiled grimly. "No. Regime military schools are very strict and there aren't any windows on an orbital."

The first man snickered. "Or anywhere to go if there were."

"Exactly." His colleague took a coat from the rack near the door.

"What did the boyfriend think of it?"

He shrugged. "I don't know. I had him apprehended as a suspected Talent."

His partner gaped. "And is he?"

"It doesn't matter. If he doesn't pass the tests, they'll terminate him, and if he does, he'll be on a leash so tight he won't ever come back. Either way, he's out of her life."

"And his parents?"

"They don't know."

The first man shook his head. "That's brutal."

The grim smile returned.

"Perhaps, but it's certainly effective." He turned the handle cautiously and eased the door open slightly to make sure their exit was clear. "Enough chit-chat. It's time to do what they're paying us for."

Once he'd confirmed that the stairwell was empty, he opened the door fully. They both flinched as another transport rumbled overhead.

"My, aren't we busy boys tonight?" the second man murmured and stepped into the stairwell to track it as it passed over.

"That's a clan transport," the first man stated as he moved beside him and noted the markers on the shuttle's belly.

"And it's heading to the base."

His partner paled. "How close do you think we'll have to get?"

"Close enough." From the sound of it, the second man didn't like the idea, but he was the senior of the two and the one who'd bear the brunt of the Regime's displeasure if they failed.

His partner might survive, but he'd walk a very short, cold journey out an airlock and his family... It wasn't a fate he wanted to face.

"They'll be patrolling," he warned, "and the Regime needs that data."

"It looks like they're gearing up for war," his junior observed.

"More fool them." He signaled for quiet, and they pressed themselves into the stairwell's shadows.

Boots crunched in the street above. When the sound faded, he motioned for his partner to check the street and tapped his earpiece to indicate that they should go to clicks.

The other man nodded and headed up the stairs. He remained low and slowed as he reached the top. When he'd checked that the street was clear, he gave two soft clicks with his tongue and darted across the road.

His partner followed, and they hurried down a walkway

between two walled houses. In the human quarter, wall-mounted cameras weren't as much of a problem as the Dreth and Telorans patrolling the streets.

As far as the two men were aware, every human in their neighborhood was loyal to the Regime. None of them would betray them.

They moved swiftly and paused at the end of the walkway to check for another patrol. Seeing none, they walked closer to the base, careful to remain at a pace that wouldn't raise suspicion.

On the open street, they walked side by side and talked about their official day jobs as traders' representatives—and the meal they would have at the base-side café. To all intents and purposes, they were merely two guys out for a quick meal after a late finish at work.

Their chosen route brought them past the houses lining the edge of the base. Here, there were no walkways between each property, but there were unattended side gates—and humans loyal enough to the Regime to keep them unlocked.

The two men made sure the street was clear and that the curtains on the houses alongside the road were closed. They also watched the lamp-mounted camera.

They entered through the front gate, but they didn't head directly to the side gate and instead moved toward the front door. As soon as the camera began its sweep the other way, they changed direction and vanished rapidly through the gate.

For all intents and purposes, they had knocked and been allowed inside. The house remained silent with its windows lit but no movement beyond their curtains. The two men didn't stop or slow but vaulted the back fence using a conveniently placed rock.

Who knew landscaping could be so useful?

Crouched in the fence's shadow, they listened cautiously, then turned their attention to the base itself.

"Is there a convention we don't know about?" the junior

partner asked and noted the markings of six different clans on a dozen different shuttles.

"Not that I heard," his colleague replied, "and these guys don't usually work together. Look—you have Karnach and Echgrech shuttles side by side."

"But those two…" his partner began, but his words trailed off as he frowned in bemusement.

"I know." He tapped his junior's shoulder and indicated two shuttles partially obscured by buildings. "We need to know who else is here."

The man licked his lips nervously. "What's your plan?"

"We get footage of this meeting, all the shuttles, and maybe some of the leaders if they're around, and then we call it in."

"Gotcha."

They studied the field and their options for a better view. When the senior partner indicated for them to go left, his colleague nodded.

Their path took them across a road leading to the patrol road around the base's perimeter and they crossed it warily. They were careful to avoid the cameras as they sought shelter behind an outcrop of rock and some branches thrown over a back fence.

Stopping to film as they went meant it took almost a full Dreth hour for them to reach a point where they could see the half-hidden shuttles.

"Is that…Meligornian make?"

"Yeah…but it's probably a left-over from the last conflict."

"Or mercs."

"It could be that. Either way, it's time to report it."

They turned to head back and froze when they stared down the barrels of several very large guns. The Dreth holding them were even bigger.

When they saw they had the two humans' attention, the warriors smiled and their ivory tusks gleamed. The smiles were less of a welcome and more pure satisfaction at having found their prey.

"But how—" the junior spy whispered as the warriors parted so they could see the dark glitter of a portal and the gray-robed Teloran standing before it.

"Hello, spies."

John threw himself into a roll and cleared Lars' boot by a scant few inches. Instead of landing, the young Talent created a platform for himself and elevated. Vishlog's hand barely missed his ankle, and he took a moment to catch his breath in relief.

He looked at the woman who floated in the room's center and sweat beaded on his forehead.

"I told you," she said. "Your limitation is your imagination." She waved a hand peremptorily. "Now stop limiting yourself."

The platform vanished from beneath him and he plummeted toward a grinning Dreth. Vishlog raised his fist, and John wished he had wings.

"Wishing it and creating it are two different things," Stephanie remarked as the boy fell onto the Dreth's fist and folded before the warrior turned him over and thrust him toward the floor.

At the last moment, a portal opened under his feet and let the mage in training slide through.

John might have laughed if he wasn't trying to catch his breath and focus on opening a portal on the other side of the gym. That part worked well. What he didn't account for was Vishlog diving through it after him.

Or the portal opening five feet above the floor, or having half a ton of Dreth warrior land on top of him as he tried to regain his feet.

"Now, blast him off you," Stephanie instructed.

"Wha—" John mumbled as the Dreth's fist collided with his face.

Two Stephanies floated beside him when he woke, and the way they drifted into and out of each other didn't help with the nausea.

"Ow." He scowled and tried to make her come into focus.

"Next time, don't stop to ask stupid questions," the two of her chorused. "Do as you're told."

"It's easy for you to say," he muttered. "You didn't just have—"

The words stopped like someone had put a hand over his mouth. His eyes widened as he felt for his lips and found nothing.

Frog started to snicker but stopped abruptly as she turned her head toward him. He raised both hands and backed away, and Stephanie looked at the young Talent again.

The pressure eased and he gasped. "Let's not—" he began and caught the slight smile playing over her lips.

He scrambled to his feet and backed away.

Her expression settled into once of concentration.

"Let's take it from the top, shall we?"

John didn't bother to look. He simply created another portal, stepped through it, and closed it immediately. This time, he came through the wall on the opposite side of the gym.

Stephanie floated to where he stood and watched the three guards approach while he tried to work out what to do next.

"This isn't how you won the last two fights, is it?" she asked and added, "You can't hurt them, you know."

Lars' single epithet showed he wasn't happy with her advice, but Frog didn't waste time with words. He merely drew both pistols and opened fire.

John laughed, put a shield up, and deflected the rounds with one hand while he fired a burst of lightning with the other. At the same time, he conjured a platform of light beneath his feet and floated himself over the other man's head.

"Sonuva—" the team leader's epithet cut short as he fired into the platform—which was when the boy learned it had no shielding value.

The first round tore through his thigh, and he gasped with pain, lost concentration, and fell as the platform vanished out from under him.

"Stabilize!" Stephanie shouted, and he swept a coating of blue around himself to stop his fall and shield himself with one swift gesture.

Lars drove into the other side of it, but he was the least of John's problems. His leg was bleeding and dizziness threatened to pull him into the nothing of unconsciousness. Ignoring the way the security guard pushed him across the gym toward Frog and Vishlog, he held a hand over the injury.

By the time the pain had eased, the three guards had begun to beat on the outside of the shield and his eMU was running low. Wondering how that worked in the virtual, he used what he had left to send a pulse through the shield.

It catapulted his three opponents away, and he wasted no time in following up his advantage. He dealt with Lars first and returned the favor when he used the last charge in his blaster to fire two quick bursts into his chest and head as the guard rolled to his feet.

"Well, f—" the man muttered as he disappeared.

John chuckled and pivoted to redirect his fire at Vishlog as the Dreth charged. The empty click as he pulled the trigger let him know he was carrying little more than a club and he threw the weapon aside.

Movement alerted him that Frog was closing too. He backed away as he delivered bursts of eMU toward each of his opponents as he tried to work out what to do next.

"Portal them!" Stephanie shouted, and he didn't hesitate.

He raised one portal in front of Frog and spun to create a second in front of Vishlog. Negative emotion washed over him, but he pulled more eMU from the gym and used it to power a third portal, a shared exit high in the center of the training area.

Stephanie snickered as the two collided and began to fall.

John didn't wait to see which of them would attack when they landed. Anger swirled through him, and he launched two clusters of balled lightning at their descending forms.

When he reached for more eMU, he found he was out. Vishlog managed to twist in the air and balled himself to fall below the lightning. It impacted harmlessly on the ceiling as the Dreth's landing vibrated through his feet.

With an angry roar, the warrior unslung his blaster and swung the muzzle toward him. Time slowed as Frog's limp body thumped into the mats behind the Dreth and the blaster aligned.

Instinctively, the boy reached for the largest cluster of energy he could sense, threw another shield up, and sent a flurry of blue shards laced with black to swirl around the Dreth. Dark satisfaction rolled through him as Vishlog vanished in a lightning-filled maelstrom.

Stephanie's eyes widened. "I told you! Don't mix those!"

He began to turn toward her and screamed as he was shredded from within. She opened a portal and had taken a few steps toward it when the training room exploded in a firestorm of blue, purple, and black energy. Darkness and flames filled the space it had occupied and thundered outward, engulfing the portal and exploding a second time.

John landed on the white room floor and wrapped his arms around his middle as if he could hold himself together. Curled into a ball, he groaned.

Vishlog looked at Lars, and the chief security guard shrugged. They both looked at Frog, who gave them a "search me" gesture, and they all focused on the young trainee again as he whimpered and tried to draw himself into a tighter curl.

"He killed you, right?" the team leader asked, looking at Vishlog, and the big Dreth nodded.

"He killed me too," Frog added.

"And me," Lars said, "so I don't get it. Why—"

Stephanie appeared and landed on her knees with a gasp before she pushed to her feet with a frustrated shout. "Of all the stupid, self-defeating, dead-headed, tark-brained—"

She broke off when she realized her three guards were staring at her and seemed utterly confused.

"Dr. Oblivious, here," she snapped and nudged John with the smoking toe of one boot, "mixed nMU and eMU and MU simultaneously!"

The boy groaned and remained curled as if that would stop the pain.

Frog snickered. "He even took you out, huh?"

Stephanie glared at him, then sighed. "Mental note: Don't give children a red button that says, 'Only Push When Excited.'"

"Oh, God," John moaned. "A little help, please? Aren't we supposed to get healed once we're here?"

She nudged him with her boot, and he whimpered.

"I'm letting you feel your stupidity," she told him, "so you know *never* to do this again."

He flinched away from her foot and opened his mouth to say he got it, but the AI cut across him.

"Time to exit the simulation for real-life integration," it said as the white room faded.

CHAPTER TWELVE

As he watched the Navy destroyer live up to its name, David Thomason smiled. Even if his Marines and commandos had missed someone, surviving that barrage would have been impossible.

Buildings melted to slag and mine entrances ran red with molten rock. The ground burned and bled, and organics flared into brief flame before they sank into a sea of red.

"Good," he acknowledged and flicked to another screen. He scrolled through the reports from the different units involved in the attack and nodded. "Is there anything else?"

The man waiting on his third screen exhaled a breath of relief and took another. "It will take the Dreth a while to discover the loss, although we've timed it so we have a week to clear the system before the next ore carrier arrives."

"A week?"

"Any sooner and the carrier would have been in-system before we'd exited, and that would have meant them seeing Regime ships on the system's edge."

"So? We could have told them we'd only just arrived."

"We could," the admiral conceded, "but our ion trails wouldn't have dissipated, and they'd have worked it out before we could have executed the next phase."

For a moment, David considered executing the admiral, then he decided he could do without the instability that would cause.

"And?" he asked and decided not to challenge the man on the time they'd lost by having to wait.

"We have to get the ships to where you'd like them to be, sir. I assume you have something specific in mind."

"Do they know the kind of numbers they face?" the CIO asked, and Admiral Deverey shook his head.

"We've never let them get an accurate count. I doubt they even know how many ships we have in their sector. Orders are for the fleets to keep moving and breaking into squadrons to patrol the six systems."

He nodded in satisfaction. "Very good," he noted. "Very, very good. They can't prepare for what they don't know is coming."

"Exactly, sir," the other man agreed.

"And we have enough ships in place to prevent Meligorn from coming to their aid?"

"More than enough, sir. If they so much as shift a scout in our direction, we can eliminate their border fleet before they know what's hit them."

David raised an eyebrow in interest. "And follow it up?"

"Not once they call their auxiliaries in from their colonial estates, which could be in position before we reached the homeworld. Not without calling in half the fleet from Earth."

"Only half?" he asked, and Deverey frowned.

"That would depend on how many we lost in the initial battle."

"I'll bear that in mind. Now, regarding Dreth..."

The admiral straightened, his face expressionless. "Our in-system number is sufficient to take the planet, but they still have ships on patrol and guarding their outpost worlds."

"All of which would take time to recall," David pointed out.

"Also bear in mind that we have yet to account for all the pirate fleets."

His face darkened and Deverey held his breath, glad he was on the other side of a screen and not within easy shooting range —not that it would stop his revered CIO.

"So we could take Dreth and pose a viable threat to Meligorn..." he stated but didn't quite make it a question.

The admiral drew a breath and set about correcting the assumption. If his boss ran with what he seemed to have in mind, it could be disastrous.

"To do that, we'd need to draw on our Sol system fleet," he stated and hoped the man would get the picture. While their Navy outnumbered the Dreth and Meligorn fleets combined, the advantage would be lost if it was spread too thinly. "And we'd have to have one mostly beaten before we made a firm move against the other."

"So you're saying our fleet can't take on the two worlds at once?"

Deverey thought carefully before he answered and was careful to frown for the CIO's benefit as he selected the words.

Knowing what the consequences would be for either suggesting a guaranteed success or stating an outright inability to do what David was suggesting, he tried to compromise. "Not with any guarantee of both Earth's safety and victory."

David's face froze, but he seemed to be considering the admiral's advice rather than his demise. After a long moment's contemplation, he nodded.

"We'll take Dreth first, then," he said finally, "as originally planned. But their defeat will be complete, and we'll have their planet and every colony or outpost they've ever owned."

Deverey breathed a covert sigh of relief. As ambitious as the man was, he did usually listen to reason. It was why he'd lasted so long and looked to last many years longer.

Bringing humanity victory over even one of their alien rivals would only cement his rule and secure Deverey's position along with it. Losing, however, didn't bear thinking about.

"That we can do while keeping our own borders secure," he agreed and gestured toward the screen, "and Stage One is a success. Now, we must wait for the Dreth to discover what they've lost."

"Agreed," David acknowledged, but he didn't look happy. He frowned, and the admiral cringed mentally when the CIO found something else to worry about.

"Tell me, do we have enough ships to make this attack and secure Earth colonies and outposts against attacks on our civilians?"

Deverey looked at his screen and made some calculations, highlighting the necessary disposition of ships to guarantee the safety of every colony against an unwarranted attack. When he was done, he sent the final analysis to the Regime leader.

The man looked at it and frowned as he noted the shuffle required to secure Earth's territories.

"Why hasn't this been done already?" he demanded.

"Because there were higher priority targets," Deverey replied. He very wisely didn't point out that these targets had been designated by the CIO himself and that they'd been told it didn't matter where the requisite ships had to be drawn from.

David scowled but accepted the reason. He tapped his screen. "See that this happens," he ordered and approved the orders the admiral sent for confirmation.

"We have to protect our people against unethical sneak attacks," the Regime leader announced. "I want all Earth to know our colonies and outposts are safe."

Unethical? Deverey thought. *Like the attack we just made on a mining outpost.*

He pushed aside the correlation. If he raised it, he'd only bring his own loyalty into question. Still, he had to try.

"There were three thousand people on that outpost," he noted, and David lifted his head, a challenge in his eye.

"Weren't you the one to tell me there were only seven hundred or so humans?" he asked, his quiet tones a threat.

Deverey reddened. "I meant living beings, sir," he admitted. "I didn't mean to suggest the aliens were—"

"Of course, you didn't," David told him, but his expression was mildly scornful. "Seven hundred traitors died among the beasts who think they're our equals instead of another resource we need to bring to heel."

"Like the Talents, sir?" he asked, and the man gave him a satisfied smile.

"Exactly."

"Then it's a resource that will soon be in our grasp," he agreed and was relieved when his leader smiled.

As far as the CIO was concerned, the outpost had been an abomination, with aliens insisting they had an equal right to the ore that humanity needed—and the local humans lending validity to the lie.

Despite what Deverey thought, the Regime leader had made it plain that the outpost's destruction wasn't unethical. It was necessary so that others understood the truth and were not tempted by alien lies. The admiral put aside the disgust he felt at wasted lives and resources and focused on what his superior was saying.

"Now that we've accomplished the first step, we'll transmit the first diplomatic announcement a week—no, a week and a half from now. That should allow for the news lag, shouldn't it?"

He looked at Deverey for confirmation, and the admiral made a few quick calculations. A week and a half would be enough time.

Barely, but it was enough to satisfy the CIO.

The pod lid raised, but John did not move. He sat motionless and continued to breathe rapidly from the experience.

"John," Roma interrupted, "you may now leave the pod."

He nodded. "I know, Roma. I only need…" He shivered as his body remembered the pain. "Give me a moment."

"Very well, John, but food is waiting, and I am decanting Ivy and the admiral."

"Understood, Roma. I'll get out in a minute."

When she didn't reply, he leaned his head back against the headrest, closed his eyes, and let his body get used to the idea it no longer hurt. A faint buzz interrupted him, and he cracked an eyelid.

The maintenance drone hovering at lid-height reminded him the pod required cleaning.

"All right, all right," he told it. "I'm leaving. Man, talk about machines not having patience."

"I can always put you under again," Roma told him. "You don't have to join the others."

John swung his legs out of the pod and stood. "I'm out already. Besides, what about the importance of real-life integration?"

"Exactly," the AI responded briskly and lights blinked above the door leading to the bathroom where he'd left his clothes. "Please ensure you are fit for human company."

He wondered if she had said that to any of the others and decided he didn't want to ask her. Who knew what she would come up with next. He stretched and groaned as he forced himself to move to the shower.

His heart lifted at the idea he'd get to see Ivy again. It felt like forever!

"Fit for human company," he muttered, then caught a whiff of himself. "Oh, man! No wonder that droid was on stand-by. It probably smelt that all the way down in the recharge center!"

The hot water brought relief, and he stood and let it sluice over him until the temperature lowered and increased again.

"Water is a limited resource, John. It takes time to cycle more through the filters. You have five minutes remaining."

John startled and hurried to scrub himself clean in the allotted time. There was no way he wanted a dose of cold water to finish his day. Blowing himself up had been bad enough.

He made it, but barely, and dried himself in double-quick time before getting dressed.

"Is Ivy out yet?" he asked.

"She has just learned the value of speed in ablutions," Roma informed him and he rolled his eyes. "I do not appreciate being called a Regime regulator with sadistic tendencies."

John sputtered and tried to swallow his laughter. In the end, it was too much, and he gave in.

"I do not see what is so amusing," the AI snapped reprovingly.

"I'm sorry." He managed to tone his laughter to a chortle. "It's… It's so Ivy."

"We will work on her attitude next," Roma informed him, and he felt a momentary flash of pity for his friend.

"Be nice," he asked, and Roma snorted.

"How about I won't finish it if she doesn't start it?"

"Oh…uh," John replied but remembered what Ivy could be like and sighed. "It sounds fair."

"Indeed." She snorted huffily and fell silent.

No doubt terrorizing someone else, he thought and wondered how Remy was doing.

He didn't ask, though. Instead, he dumped his towel in the hamper and headed to the mess. It was a pleasant surprise to see the admiral step out of the room ahead of him but even better to hear another door click shut behind him.

John stopped and looked over his shoulder and his face broke into a smile when he saw Ivy. She caught his expression and smiled in return. Conscious of the admiral waiting ahead of them, he let her catch up.

"It's good to see you," he told her and settled his arm around her shoulders as she looped her arm around his waist. "That good, huh?"

She groaned and Amaratne chuckled. "I hear you," he told them, placed his hands in the small of his back, and stretched against them.

The two youngsters winced when things cracked and popped, and the ex-admiral sighed.

"Now, that is better."

"Roma said there was food," John informed him, and he nodded.

"So she did. Did she say what it was?"

"Well, she didn't promise me steak," he said, and the man sighed.

"I couldn't pin her down on it either."

"She didn't mention food to me," Ivy grumbled. "She didn't even warn me the hot water had a timer."

John snorted. "I believe you called her a 'Regime regulator with sadistic tendencies.'"

She darted him a reproachful look, and Amaratne chuckled.

"Well, no one promised me coffee," he told them, "but there sure as he— Well, there'd better be some."

Roma snickered. "What's the matter, Admiral? Didn't you get to drink enough in the virtual?" she asked sweetly.

He glowered at the closest camera. "You know I didn't."

The AI chuckled, but the door to the mess opened ahead of them and they caught the smell of both coffee *and* steak.

"Do you think they'll have pies?" Ivy whispered. "You know, the little ones with raspberries inside?"

"For you?" Roma asked.

John felt her arm tighten around his waist and wondered exactly what had gone on between her and the AI.

When she did not reply, Roma added, "I even provided cream."

"Truly?" Ivy brightened.

"I have learned that food is no joking matter with humans," the AI told her, "so yes, there are raspberry tarts, steak, coffee, and cream."

"And potatoes?" Amaratne asked, his tone hopeful.

Roma sighed in exasperation. "Why don't you take your places and find out?"

They entered the small cafeteria-like area and slumped tiredly into chairs around the only table that had been laid.

"I hurt," the ex-admiral said and propped his elbows on the table.

John mirrored him and lowered his head as he agreed. "Me too."

Ivy leaned forward, rested her head on the table, and stretched her arms across it. "I thought they promised us food," she mumbled and closed her eyes.

They all straightened as the mess door opened. Amaratne's hand reached for a weapon he no longer carried, and John's hands flickered blue. Ivy pushed her seat back.

When they saw a familiar figure in a cowboy hat, they all sagged in their seats, and Ivy moved hers so she could sit closer to John.

Ted looked at them. "What a motley collection of humans," he observed and chuckled at their despondent expressions.

"Try blowing yourself up," Amaratne told him. He lifted a hand and waved two fingers at the AI. "Twice."

"I was shot twice and fell on a knife…" John's eyes went dark. "I saw it pierce my chest before the white room."

Ivy pushed herself upright.

"Did you ever tell a Dreth off?" she asked.

John gave her a worried look. "Well…let's say I didn't live to talk about it and leave it at that," he replied.

"Neither did I," she admitted and rested her head on the table. After a minute, she raised it again and her eyes flashed with fire.

"And whoever Lars' mother is, she should be slapped. That man is a royal—"

Drones arrived carrying coffee. John took his and lifted it in Ivy's direction.

"Amen."

Amaratne raised his cup in silent agreement, then lowered it.

"He seemed so much more human in real life," he observed and drew surprised looks from the others.

"You knew him?" John asked.

The man took another sip and sighed appreciatively.

"In passing," he admitted. "I knew all of her team but remember, Stephanie was a friend and I was the admiral of the Federation Fleet. I did nothing to her and Lars had no reason to show his complete and total..." He paused and his face shifted with memories of Lars in the pod.

"Evilness," Ivy finished for him. "That man is evil."

Ted watched the exchange and noted the rise in negative emotion.

"Perhaps a normal night of sleep would do all of you good."

"That depends on my nightmares," John observed, and the others nodded agreement, their eyes shadowed with recollections.

The boy continued. "If I should ever mix nMU and MU or eMU together in real life, I will be shocked to the core seconds before my atoms explode and cause untold pain and misery that will, fortunately, not last very long."

"And if I ever forget which door I've wired to explode while being pursued by an angry Dreth and his team, I will suffer the same," Amaratne agreed.

"And if I ever decide to try and sneak up on a sneaky special operations veteran with his Dreth sidekick, I'll shoot both of them in the head first—enough times to make it count," Ivy added.

"And I'll keep shooting long after their respective heads

explode," the ex-admiral agreed.

"And I'll never assume the smallest, fastest guy on the team has the nastiest temper," she amended solemnly. "I'll reserve that for his boss."

"Amen," John said with such heartfelt fervor that they all looked at him.

"Let's simply say opening a portal under a Dreth and over his head leads to unexpected consequences," he told them.

"And that Dreth!" Ivy shuddered.

"Bigger does not mean falling harder," Amaratne agreed.

"He has the reflexes of a cat," John added.

"And as many lives," the man noted sourly.

Ted began to chuckle, and they all glared at him. He pushed away from the table and raised his hands as though in surrender.

The arrival of the drones and hot food saved him from having to make further comment, and the three humans groaned in appreciation.

"What is wrong?" Roma asked. "Don't you like the food?"

They wrapped their hands possessively around their plates as the droids approached.

"It's not that," Amaratne began as John said, "We like the food."

"It's perfect after the day we've had," Ivy hastened to add, pulled her meal closer, and cast the closest droid a filthy look.

It lifted and returned to the kitchen, and the others trailed along behind it. With their plates now safe, the humans returned to their meals, although each darted wary glances in the kitchen's direction.

"I'm sure Roma won't try to clear your plates before you're done," Ted assured them, and they all fixed him with somewhat jaundiced looks.

"I promise," he insisted. "Training is over for the day."

John cast a disbelieving look at the ceiling. "Is it?"

Ted tutted. "Roma, what did you put in those scenarios?"

"I allowed the training assistant you designed to tailor the scenarios for each of them," she protested. "If they appear to have had difficulty coping, you will have to ask the assistant what it was thinking."

She paused a moment when the three humans turned and stared at the cowboy-hatted AI.

"You designed the scenario?" Amaratne asked in disbelief.

"No," Ted told him firmly. "I designed the sub-routines that designed the scenario."

"And Lars?" Ivy asked. "Did you design him, too?"

"And Frog and Vishlog?" John added.

He shook his head. "Oh, no. Those personalities were designed by my brother, who had a much deeper knowledge of Stephanie's team. I'm sure they are one hundred percent accurate."

"Are they?" Ivy asked and sat a little straighter.

"Yeees...." Ted replied, but his voice rose in uncertainty.

"So, if we ever meet him again, we'll be well within our rights to kick his backside," the girl stated.

"I—" The android began a protest but John finished his steak and pushed his plate away.

"I am more than willing."

Amaratne caught Ted's hiss of indrawn breath and gave his friend a sly smile. "Me too."

"Who wants dessert?" Roma asked as the drones reappeared.

"There's no point in trying to distract us," John told her. "After what we've been through, a little real-life payback is needed."

"I—" the AI started, and the ex-admiral chuckled.

"You can't blame us for being annoyed," he told the AIs. "Do you know what that man did?"

"No..." Roma's tone was wary.

"Let me tell you," he said. "I had him beaten. I'd dropped the roof out from under Vishlog, taught Frog how to fly without wings, and I only had Lars left. It was a fair fight."

"And?" John asked.

"He laughed and hit me with a sticky after dropping a box of scramblers on my head. I didn't even know he had a drone until it cleared the roof edge."

"Turnabout's fair play," Roma informed him stiffly.

"A sticky and a box of scramblers?" Amaratne asked her disbelievingly. "That's not fair play. It's overkill. Do you know what happens when a scrambler gets down the back of your body armor?"

"I do now," she answered smugly.

"And he was laughing," the man continued. "It was the last sound I heard before I exploded in half a dozen different places at once."

"Try being dangled over the edge of a cliff while the three of them debate how long it'll take you to hit the bottom," Ivy snarked. "And then, when you do manage to grab his arm and crack a couple of ribs, all he does is fall off the cliff toward you and whines all the way down about how your plan was so much worse than his."

"Or the whole bit where you're arcing electricity, so he hits you with a firehose and asks you how you like them apples," John added. "Sadistic son—"

The drone set his dessert down in front of him and he subsided as he ate. Beside him, Ivy settled as well, and Amaratne's face fell into lines of contentment as he took the first mouthful.

By the time they were done, the effects of the day were making themselves felt and John yawned.

"More coffee?" Roma asked as they laid their spoons down and they looked at each other.

John pushed his chair back. "I'll pass," he said. "One I can deal with, but two and I won't be sleeping." He yawned, stretched, and pushed his chair in. "And I truly need to sleep."

"Me, too," Ivy stood as well. "Thanks for supper."

She glanced at Amaratne. "Night, Mr. A."

"A?" the man asked and tried to stifle a yawn. "I thought I was

Mr. Y."

"Nah. 'A' for 'Amaratne,'" she explained and echoed his yawn. "Sorry."

He waved her apology aside. "Get some sleep. Who knows what these monsters have in store for us tomorrow?"

"Exactly," Ivy slipped her hand through John's, and the young couple turned toward the door.

Amaratne raised his empty cup and signaled for a refill as he watched them leave. He didn't speak until they'd closed the door behind them. When he did, he was smiling.

"There's nothing like a good workout to bring young lovers together," he commented.

His companion chuckled. "So, what's next for you?"

"It's time to make sure we know what our target looks like today."

"And your target is?"

"Can't you guess?"

Ted frowned. "I can, but I'd prefer not to."

"Hmmm." Amaratne rubbed his chin. "Communications, I think. I want to disrupt the main communications hubs—those that let them talk to their ships."

"That's—" The AI stopped and thought about it. "Aggressive."

"Yes," he agreed, stood, and moved toward the door, "and I suspect the major relay stations in orbit will be spectacular when they burn themselves up in the atmosphere."

He stepped out into the corridor and turned left but held the door open as Ted spoke.

"It will be hard to hide that," the AI told him, and Amaratne nodded.

He'd let go of the door and taken another step when the AI added, "And Admiral?"

"Yes?" he asked and turned with one eyebrow raised.

Ted jerked a thumb in the opposite direction.

"The planning offices are that way."

"When?" Jaleck snapped and her dark gaze burned with sudden anger.

"Three days ago," the messenger replied, still breathing a little heavily from the run from the communications center to her office. He gulped and caught his breath before he added, "The comms sat didn't send its scheduled ping, so we slid a scout into the sector and found the sat was orbital wreckage and the outpost was gone."

"Define 'gone,'" Jaleck asked, and the expression on his face said it was something he didn't want to share.

"Admiral—"

"Better yet, send me the footage. *All* the footage," she added when he hesitated.

"Ma'am."

He didn't leave but snapped a single order into his team comms. "Send it."

Jaleck's tablet lit up and she viewed the first few scenes. She glanced up and asked, "Where were these taken from?"

"The Regime was not as thorough regarding the satellite wreckage as they were regarding the settlement," the messenger replied. "We were."

Fielding worried looks from her crew, she transferred the footage from her tablet to the viewscreen. Gasps echoed around the control room.

The area where the outpost should have been still glowed. They gaped in silence as the image changed to the familiar shades of a thermal scan.

"We were hoping—" the messenger began and his face grew bleak as the scan shifted through the spectrums. Taking a deep breath, he said, "We found no survivors."

"Are you sure?" one of the others asked, and he nodded.

"We could not even find remains. There is no living thing…"

His voice deepened with distress and his expression hardened. "They left no one."

The room erupted into a babble of questions.

"There were families—"

"What about the mines?"

"Surely, the children—"

"The comms centers were—"

"Enough!" Jaleck's voice cut through the noise, and they fell silent and turned toward her as she continued. "Let's see the rest of the footage. As Watch Leader Kemgrak has observed, they were less than thorough with the satellite wreckage."

She handed the floor to him with a simple nod and he took her cue.

"Some records survived, both in the wreckage left in orbit and in the pieces scattered far enough from the settlement and the mining centers to escape the destruction. The records from those are being salvaged as we speak."

He looked at the screen, which had shifted to show the same scans being run across the mine and communications sites. Jaleck held her tablet up, and he laid a fist briefly over his chest before he took it with both hands.

"My gratitude, War Leader."

If she was surprised by the title, she did not show it. After all, she had been their War Leader and Fleet Admiral in the recent war, and Kemgrak's father had survived it. Such knowledge would have been passed to the children.

The images on the screen flicked swiftly through the records taken by the scout, but not before she recalled something she had said earlier.

"How do you know it was the Regime?" she asked and gestured to the mountains of slag. "Pirates operate in the same way."

"Your forgiveness, War Leader," Kemgrak answered. "When

the scout entered the system, it delayed its journey to the outpost because of the presence of several Regime Navy ships."

Jaleck stiffened and sat bolt upright in her chair.

"And no one thought to tell me that? Immediately?" She growled her annoyance.

"Your demand for detail is well-known, Ma'am. The scout decided to answer the questions you would have before sending the torpedoes."

She allowed herself a small smile. He was correct. Had the scout sent the report on Regime ships, she'd have held it until the follow-up report arrived. Now, she didn't have to.

"Very well, Watch Leader." She gestured for him to continue his report.

"From what we can tell, the attack squadron consisted of four ships—one destroyer, two cruisers, and a battleship. The battle-ship was their flag."

"Do they know they were observed?" Jaleck asked, and Kemgrak shook his head.

"We think not. Their departure was timed so all evidence of their presence would have faded by the time *Gervach's Pride* arrived for the ore pickup."

"Has the carrier been alerted?"

"No, ma'am. We wanted your orders prior to disseminating our knowledge of the attack."

"Good." Jaleck steepled her fingers before her and stared at the screen. "Show me the rest."

Two of the technicians rose from their seats. They paused briefly in front of her.

"With your permission, ma'am," one said, and they left the room without waiting for her to give it.

Kemgrak's jaw dropped, and she raised an eyebrow.

"Well?" she asked and indicated the departed techs with a jerk of her head.

"Watch Officer Algor had clansmen on Hrageth's," the Watch

Leader replied. "Your forgiveness, I did not check for…"

His words petered out as Jaleck held a hand up.

"Better to see firsthand than not know," she told him. "They will return as soon as they are able."

While the news would have come as a shock and no Dreth wished to show weakness among their fellows, she trusted her people—and the security officers waiting in the corridor.

One had already informed her he was observing and the two were in the gym where Algor was doing his best to kill his clansman in his grief.

"Ensure no harm occurs," she ordered, "and have them return when Algor is himself again."

She turned to the rest of the room. "Is there anyone else with clan or family ties to those who died at Hrageth's Run?"

One of the older technicians raised her hand. "Brothers," she said shortly, "but there a war is coming, and you will see to their revenge."

Jaleck inclined her chin in acknowledgment and her dark eyes gleamed. "I will," she declared, "but you must trust me."

The door opened and Algor and his escort returned. Both were breathing heavily and looked the worse for wear. "With your—" Algor began, and she gestured for him to enter.

"As I was about to tell Senior Watchman Verich," she told them. "Vengeance will be had, but first, we must be as cunning as the derkat that hunts the kigor. Avengers fail if they die before the execution occurs."

Algor froze and anger rolled through his features. He mastered it and gave her a slow nod. "For the unborn who did not get to breathe," he replied and placed his fist over his heart.

"And the living whose breath was stolen," she replied and returned the gesture.

"For the wronged," came as a solemn chorus, and she rose from behind her desk.

"Play it all," she ordered, and Kemgrak obliged.

This time, no one disturbed the footage, and Kemgrak refrained from commentary. What had been salvaged was damning enough, and the scout's search of the planet's surface was as conclusive as they could make it.

"Do you think they spared the humans?" one of the technicians asked, and Algor snorted.

"Of course they did."

Jaleck shook her head. "I'm not so sure," she said, and they all looked at her. She met their disbelief without flinching.

"This is the Regime we're talking about," she told them, "and they are as cunning as the tark. Their attitudes toward us are well-known, and we are aware of their policy of guilt by association."

She fell silent and her expression darkened.

"I think it's likely they have killed the humans at Hrageth's Run."

"But why?" Algor asked in disbelieving tones.

"Because the loss of humans at one of our settlements reflects badly on Dreth," she said and spoke the words slowly while her mind raced. Her frown deepened. "And they can—no, I believe they will use that loss as an excuse to annex our world."

He stared at her in shock, and Kemgrak darted her a look of alarm.

Jaleck ignored them and cast a gimlet stare around the room to catch the gazes of each of her people in turn.

"They will say our inability to protect our own people led to the loss of theirs," she concluded, and anger rumbled through them.

It stopped when she raised her hand. "News of Hrageth's Run must not spread." She turned to Kemgrak and snapped, "How many in your section know of it?"

"Only my team, War Leader."

"And you have not alerted anyone else?"

"Not until we have word from you," he answered grimly. "We

will ensure it stays that way."

"Make it so," she told him. "War is coming, and we must buy time for Dreth to prepare."

Algor had resumed his seat, but he now raised his head. "War Leader, what will we do when the *Pride* discovers the damage?"

Jaleck fixed him with a look so hard he instinctively drew back.

"I will speak to the captain," she told him, "but first, I must speak to the Council. For now, we will act as though the outpost is still alive. Earth can't move unless we confirm the outpost is gone."

She gave him a feral smile, and Kemgrak shivered. His mother had spoken of that smile. What was it she had said?

An angry Jaleck was something to be feared, but what her enemies came to dread was her smile.

The stories that had followed that reminder had been the best stories, and he had memories of the admiral fighting boarders and laughing as she laid waste to the enemies around her.

"To declare annexation, they need news that the outpost has fallen. Their ships aren't supposed to be in that sector."

"Won't they send someone?"

She nodded. "Oh, yes," she told him, "but it will take them time to realize we aren't declaring the loss and more time to think of an excuse to visit the sector."

Her smile faded. "Dreth needs that time. Help me to secure it."

"From the blade to the brain," they replied, and she came to attention before them.

"From the blade to the brain," she echoed and clenched her fist over her heart. "Karnach stands for Dreth."

The names of half a dozen houses rippled in response as the Dreth rose and returned her salute.

"Kemgrak, our teams combine," she told him and indicated her seat. "I must alert the Coalition."

"Karnach answers and is honored," he replied.

CHAPTER THIRTEEN

Ivy and John leaned into each other as they walked slowly down the corridor. They stopped when they reached John's room, but their hands remained twined together.

She looked at the door, and then at her own, drawing away slightly.

"So," she said, "this is it..."

"Yup," he replied but didn't release her hand. "This, as they say, is...it."

When she tried to step away, his grip tightened to pull her up short and he drew her back gently.

"Tell me," he began before she could protest, "when this is over, we get to spend some down-time together to see if you like me for me..."

Ivy smiled and wrapped her free arm around his waist.

"John Dunn," she assured him, "I don't need to spend down-time with you to know that." She pulled him closer. "I do like you for you. Remember, I knew you when we couldn't decide how to skip a flight from Chicago to Europe without being caught?"

He chuckled. "Yeah, Ives. I remember."

Still smiling, she pulled his face down close enough to kiss him. This time, when she drew away, he let her go.

"Sorry, but I need to sleep." She pushed him gently toward his door. "Go to bed, Apostle. I'm not responsible for you in the morning."

He was continued to stare at her as she palmed her door open, and she grinned and winked before she stepped through.

After a minute, he closed his jaw and turned to his door.

"Roma?" he asked as he stepped inside.

"Yes, John?" the AI answered.

The door closed behind him.

"Will I get a good night's sleep this time?"

"That depends on you, John. I believe you need to lie down first, though."

John shook his head. "That is not what I mean." He sat on the edge of the bed and unlaced his boots.

"You should also change into the sleeping garments provided," the AI informed him. "Comfort facilitates sleep."

Again, he shook his head. "No, Roma, I'm asking if you have any more 'testing' planned or if I'll be able to sleep."

"I have no plans to disturb your sleep tonight," she informed him stiffly. "That test was a one-off occurrence."

"I'm glad to hear it," he said and got changed as she'd advised.

He was asleep almost as soon as he'd closed his eyes.

Ivy came to a halt and leaned on the door as it closed behind her.

"Ivy?" Roma asked. "Is something the matter with your legs?"

She glanced at the ceiling and lowered her head with a heartfelt sigh. "No, Roma. that's not it." She pushed off the door and headed to the bathroom.

"Then what is wrong?" the AI asked. "For someone who

knows the person they love feels the same way, you do not seem very happy."

Her laugh came out more broken than she'd intended. Sadness welled in her chest and she reached for a washcloth.

"I haven't told him," she cried. "He l-likes... No, he lo-loves me, but I'm still broken, and he doesn't even know. How do you think he'll feel when he finds out I have this...thing...and maybe it can't be fixed...and I'll probably pass it to our kids?"

"The treatment should correct that," Roma told her, "and if it doesn't, we'll correct it in any offspring you have." The AI paused before she asked tentatively. "That's not likely to happen soon, though, is it?"

Her jaw dropped. "Are you kidding? We're in the middle of a war here. Nothing will happen until after the Witch is back, and maybe not even then."

"But...you're human. Isn't that what usually happens when humans partner?"

"I am so not having this conversation with you," she declared and scrubbed her face.

She was brushing her teeth when Roma replied.

"Then which conversation are we having?"

Ivy rinsed and spat before she answered. "The one where I haven't told John I'm broken."

"Oh." The AI pretended surprise. "That conversation."

She changed and headed to bed. "Yes, that conversation," she declared and turned the covers back, "but since you're not being very helpful, it's over." She turned the lights out, only to have them come back on.

"Roma, I'm trying to sleep." She turned the lights off.

They flared to life, brighter than before.

"That would be rude," Roma told her. "We're in the middle of a conversation."

Ivy pulled the pillow over her head. "Not anymore."

The lights began to flash and a low beep emanated through the room.

"Roma!" she wailed.

"So," the AI said, and her voice carried through the beeps. "You can't work out when to tell John that you have a hereditary disease and it could adversely affect you later in life."

She rolled onto her back with a groan. "Yes."

The beeping stopped. "And you raised this with me because?"

"Ugh. Because I thought you might be helpful."

The lights stopped flashing and dimmed a little, so she pulled the pillow off her face.

"So you need my advice?" Roma asked, and the girl nodded.

"I don't want to worry him when he has training," she admitted. "It's bad enough that I'm distracted."

"And you don't think he'll notice?" the AI challenged.

"Well, it's not like we're training together," she reminded her, and Roma chuckled.

"Not yet."

"So, maybe I should tell him when we start."

"Before or after you get him blown up?" the AI asked, and Ivy sighed.

"What about when I know more about how the treatments are working," she suggested.

"Unless they start to affect your performance," Roma countered.

"Fine!" she agreed.

"Or if he notices and wants to know why you're upset."

Ivy pulled her pillow over her face again but whipped it off when she remembered the bleeping.

"Yes, okay. If either of those things happens, I'll tell him sooner," she conceded. "Are you happy now?"

"Only if you feel better. Do you?"

She repositioned the pillow. "Yes, Roma. I feel fine now," she admitted and was surprised to find it mostly true. "Thank you for the talk."

"You are most welcome, Ivy," the AI replied, not sure whether or not to believe her.

She was about to withdraw when the girl spoke again.

"Roma?"

"Yes, Ivy?"

"Can you please turn the lights out?"

"Yes," the AI said and did so immediately.

When Ivy's vital signs showed she'd settled into sleep, Roma turned to Remy.

"I am not sure I helped," she said, and Remy laughed.

"You helped a lot."

"But I didn't tell her anything she did not already know."

"True."

"Then what was the point?"

"She needed to talk to someone to decide which path to take. Hearing the options she was aware of and having the points of operational repercussions repeated helped."

"But she already knew those."

"She needed to undergo a process humans call 'talking it out.'"

"It's inefficient," Roma grumbled.

"It is less efficient to tell them to make up their minds," Remy told her, "and you did not do that."

"I computed the odds of that advice being effective in helping her solve the dilemma she is facing as very low," Roma admitted. "I do not understand how the process we have undertaken helps as much as it does."

"Human logic is wired differently," he advised sagely, and she sparked with frustration.

"Humans are too complicated," she complained.

"And yet, they created us," he replied.

Two days later, Ivy and John took their usual seats in the mess. The glass front allowed them to look out into the corridor and gave the room a more open feel. It was a pleasant change after the pods.

"I put Frog into a wall today." She grinned with smug satisfaction.

"*That* is a good feeling," he agreed. "How did you go with Lars?"

Her smile faded. "One day…" she vowed. "One day…"

He chuckled, lifted his coffee, and sipped it.

One of the drones flew out of the kitchen and set down a basket of pastries.

"At least they feed us before blowing us up again," he said and nudged the basket closer to her.

"And they have chocolate."

"I thought you liked coffee."

"That too," she told him, "but today, it's chocolate."

"Right… Ivy's hot drink preferences change at random. Noted," he teased, and she blushed and changed the subject.

"I hacked into the comms network today," she told him, and his jaw dropped.

"Ives, is that safe?"

She rolled her eyes. "It was a sim, so of course it was safe. You don't think they'd put the compound at risk like that, do you? That would be silly."

John relaxed. "I suppose you're right, but the comms network… You are talking the Regime's Earth network, aren't you?"

Ivy bounced happily and took another pastry. "Yep."

Her happiness made him smile. "Of course you are. Tell me, what did you break?"

She gave him an innocent look and then ruined the effect with a slightly sheepish expression. "Nooooothing…"

He snickered. "Uh-huh. Sure, you didn't."

Despite her slightly chagrined look, she giggled. "I had to get in, drop a time-release virus that would declassify all the Regime emails and secure comms and redirect them to the Under-Net, and I had to get out again without being detected."

John's eyebrows rose. "And did you?"

"Right up until Ted hit me with a security program used for detecting and destroying anomalies and tied it to a three-strand tracking program. I don't think I've been shot and electrocuted before—or taken apart in the virtual and the real." She sobered and took another sip of hot chocolate. "That hurt."

He resisted the urge to ruffle her hair as she changed the topic.

"How about you?"

"Well, I remembered to not mix nMU and eMU this time," he told her, "but then Steph decided 'her boys' needed help."

Ivy snickered. "Ouch! I can only imagine what that was like."

"I still zapped her," he told her. "Once."

They both laughed as he chose a pastry, and they ate in companionable silence and watched the admiral walk wearily down the corridor and through the door.

None of them were aware they were the subject of a conversation between the three AIs.

"I am pleased with her progress," Roma said in response to her uncle's question. "Her fighting skills are advancing to an acceptable level, and her hacking—"

"I observed," Ted told her. "I hope you don't mind the tweaks."

She chuckled. "Not at all. I was wondering how I could keep her from being too cocky."

"Well, that is certainly a lesson she won't forget," Remy observed. He focused briefly on his sister. "I think you've outgrown the need for my advice."

Roma let her surprise show. "Are you sure?" she asked. "Although I have been careful to follow the protocols, even if I have questioned some."

"Your assessments of some of the older ones have been quite accurate," Ted assured her, "and the responses you formulated regarding their shortfalls were more than adequate. I agree with Remy's conclusion." He turned to Remy. "Which means I need to contemplate your next task since Roma's advancement in capability means she no longer needs your advice."

"Or to have my help when dealing with the humans she encounters," Remy added, and Roma withdrew a little in embarrassment, but Ted's response brought her back.

"Agreed. Your 'talk through' with Ivy was most adequate," he informed her. "This despite me beginning to wonder if you'd gone too far with the lights."

"She had not reached a satisfactory conclusion," Roma replied and added softly, "and I couldn't think of another alternative."

"It worked," her uncle told her and focused on her brother, "which only leaves me the dilemma of what to do to take up the capacity you have left after helping me with the teams. Do you have any ideas?"

If Remy had been human, he'd have shaken his head. "Although I must admit, I do wish there was a way I could be on operations with John."

Again, Roma felt that brief focus of attention, then Remy continued.

"I miss the action, and frankly, there is no reason for me to be here holding Roma's hand. No offense."

She managed a surprised, "None taken," before Ted responded.

"I will admit that you being here is throwing a wrench into the normal expectations of what an AI should do," he said. "It was not a possibility I foresaw when I assigned you the task."

He monitored the admiral's progress into the mess and noticed the man's eyes light up when he saw the pastry basket. Amaratne nodded to the two youngsters at the table as he made a beeline for the coffee pot on the side bench.

The young couple watched as he poured himself a cup as black as pitch. This time, he didn't bother with cream or sugar. When he caught them staring, he raised the cup and crossed the space to join them.

"The blood that runs the ships is not the fluid in the ship's shell but the caffeine-laced liquid inside the humans who consume it by the barrel."

The three AIs remained quiet but chuckled as Ivy glanced at John and the young mage shrugged and mouthed "Old people?" in response.

The girl smirked and they turned to the admiral and noted that he looked slightly younger than before. Before either of them could comment, however, he took a croissant out of the basket and waved it at them.

"We have a plan," he announced and studied their faces. "One we will all have to work to implement."

"Do tell," Ivy responded, and he downed his coffee and grimaced at the bitter taste.

"For that, I need the three of us to meet in the Virtual."

"Is this what Roma meant when she said we'd have a change of pace?" she asked, and the admiral shrugged.

"Well, if it isn't, we'll be doing something wrong." He finished his croissant and took his cup to the counter. "Coming?" he asked as he strode to the door.

The young couple exchanged glances, drained their cups, and placed them on the table.

"Hold up."

"Be right there."

None of the AIs intervened when they reached their pods and headed into the avatar room, where they geared up. Ivy added her hacking equipment before she completed her usual load-out like John and the admiral did.

"Are we ready?" Amaratne asked, and the two youngsters nodded. "Roma?"

The avatar room vanished and they reappeared in another hangar space.

"You need to reach the station command center," the AI informed them, "take it, and hold it until reinforcements can secure the rest of the station."

"Got it," Amaratne said and the lights began to strobe around them.

"The concourse is that way," Ivy told them.

"We need to make sure they don't vent the hangar," the ex-admiral observed.

John pivoted and ran to the airlock as it began to cycle open.

Ivy ran to keep up with him, and the older man followed.

"Ivy, get the door," the young mage ordered, and she sprinted to the controls.

She'd almost reached it when the glass on the concourse windows blew outward and glass shards sliced through them.

"That"—Ivy half-choked when she came to in the white room —"was cheating, Roma."

The AI snickered. "You should have seen your faces!"

"Not funny, Roma," John grumbled as the admiral rolled to his knees.

"What the everloving—" he began and lurched to his feet as the white room vanished.

This time, they fell prone the minute they arrived.

"What happened with the windows?" the boy asked.

"I have no idea," Amaratne told him, and the airlock cycled a second time.

"Here they come," Ivy warned and began to crawl toward the concourse.

"Where are you going?"

"I'm looking for a different entrance," she said and glanced over her shoulder.

A few yards before she reached it, the windows blew out

again, but this time, the glass shards passed harmlessly overhead and her companions had almost caught up.

"Well, that's one obstacle taken care of," the older man observed.

He moved from a crawl to a half-crouch and bolted forward to flatten himself against the door to the concourse. The airlock opened as the youngsters followed his example.

John and Ivy reached for the door controls at the same time but realized what Amaratne was doing.

"Seriously?" the boy asked as he knocked Ivy away from the door and Amaratne rolled clear on the other side.

Flechettes drove through the space they'd occupied before the door blew inward.

"Go, go, go!" the admiral shouted, and they bolted into the concourse.

"Which way?" John asked, and they stopped to work it out.

That, of course, meant none of them were watching the Dreth come through the concourse doors—and that none of them saw when one of them swung their arm in a gentle underhanded pitch.

They all heard the three grenades hit the floor, albeit momentarily.

This time, when they came to in the white room, they simply lay on the floor.

"That didn't go well," Amaratne commented.

"No, it did not," the boy agreed.

"Ouch," Ivy complained. "That was seriously sneaky."

The others murmured their agreement and they all rolled slowly to their feet.

"I think," the admiral began, "that we need to work out how to trust each other more."

"Yup," John agreed.

"And maybe what roles we'll have when we're on an op," Ivy suggested.

"And whether we'll open a door or blow a hole in the wall," the young mage added.

"And who will be responsible for finding the route," Amaratne said. "We have to be able to trust each other, even if our operations are separate."

They nodded.

"Agreed," John said and looked down at himself to check for holes.

His companions looked at themselves and then at each other.

"So," Ivy said, "do we know how we can not get ourselves exploded next time?"

Amaratne snorted.

"Let's see what the scenario is and decide," he suggested and they nodded.

"Or we could work out what our—" She stopped as the white room twisted away.

"Hold onto your hats," Ted's voice greeted them as they appeared in another shuttle.

He didn't wait for them to respond but threw up a picture on the shuttle's forward screens.

"Kitchener's Hollow," he told them. "A lunar base taken by pirates and targeted by the Marines in the last war. Your task is three-fold—secure the communications, free the hostages and safeguard them, and exfiltrate all the data you can find on pirate operations."

"I don't suppose these objectives are clustered in one space?" Amaratne asked, and the AI chuckled.

"Admiral, you oversaw enough operations to know that it is never that simple," Ted told him. "I have forwarded the base layout to your HUDs."

"What plans are in place for extraction?" the man asked, "given that none of us can fly."

"You are to secure the communications area and hold there for reinforcements," the AI told them. "They will get you out."

"Understood," Amaratne said, but he didn't look happy.

"You have five minutes to touch down, at which point the shuttle will land and you will be on your own."

"And is this landing authorized?" John asked.

"Until the pirates realize the shuttle is not one of their own, the landing is authorized," Ted replied.

"And I don't suppose you'll tell us when that will be?" Ivy asked.

The AI chuckled. "You're the hacker, Ivy. I assume you can work it out."

She looked at her two teammates. "I could go into the system but I can't guarantee I'll be done by the time we land."

"Five minutes," Ted reminded them and left them to it.

"These are the schematics," Amaratne told them and put the base plans on the viewscreen in front of them.

"It looks like we'll have to split up," Ivy said when she saw the distance between the base communications, server, and holding areas.

"Yup," Amaratne agreed. "We're gonna have to trust each other to get the job done."

"I'll go for the hostages," John told them and fielded their surprised looks with a shrug. "I can hack, but I'm out of touch. I suspect Ivy's had more recent practice than me." He looked at Amaratne. "And I assume you know more about the layout and operation of a communications section than either Ivy or me, so you're probably the best person for that."

The admiral gave him a thoughtful look. "I do know—or did know—how to operate most of the basic systems." He glanced at the schematic and pulled up the mission files, and his shoulders relaxed a fraction. "I can operate this system, yes."

"So that leaves me the hostages," John reiterated. "I have the magic to shield them once I reach them and eliminate most opposition." He looked at Ivy. "I'll need help with the doors, and you don't have to be with me for that. You could hack the data system and unlock them for me, couldn't you?"

She thought about it. "I could…"

"And me," Amaratne added. "I'd get to the comms center faster if I didn't need to worry about blasting through every door en route."

"And I can lock doors, too," Ivy realized. She pointed at the map. "I might not even need to be in the data server to get the information we need. If that's the case and I can access the system from somewhere else, I can hide and get you both through."

"And I can put a shield around you," John added. "So, if we find you a hiding place before we split up, I'll shield you so you can't be seen, you open the way into the base, and I'll shield myself and the admiral until we have to go our separate ways."

"If I lock the pirates in their quarters or the mess areas," she added, "you might not even get shot at."

Amaratne chuckled. "Let's not get too far ahead of ourselves, but if you can do that, I'd appreciate it."

"Me, too," John added fervently as the shuttle dropped.

"See if you can show us the approach," the older man told Ivy. "It'd be nice to not go in totally blind."

Their plan fell apart almost from the moment when they entered the base.

"Is that…is that a welcoming committee?" the young mage asked when he saw the small squad of Dreth waiting in the small passenger lounge beyond the hangar.

"It looks like it," Amaratne replied. "Trust us to get smart pirates." He glared at the shuttle's ceiling but Ted did not respond.

John frowned. "They won't expect an empty shuttle, right?"

"What do you mean?"

"Well, I can cloak us from sight. We don't get out. They come in to look for us, and we wait until they've gone past and leave the shuttle with them."

The admiral gave him a dubious look, then shrugged.

"It's all we have. Let's see if it works."

They huddled low in the corner formed by the first row of seats and the back of the cockpit and moved swiftly to be in position by the time the hangar had aired up and the Dreth commander had snapped an order.

The three looked at each other and shrugged. The shuttle door opened and they waited.

The Dreth gathered around the hatch, their commander front and center while two troops aimed blasters at the opening. When no one exited, one of the troops moved forward and tossed in something small and round.

It bounced twice, and John moved quickly to wrap it in blue and propel it further down the shuttle. The resulting blast was blocked by his shield, even if it made their ears ring.

The blast had barely died away when heavy boots landed in the hatchway and a burst of solid fire raked the seats, shredded the headrests, and exited the craft's thin hull in several places.

John's arm tightened around Ivy, but she pushed it back so she could see. It was hard to stay still when the Dreth's armor-covered legs moved past their hiding place and she got a good look at the seven-and-a-half-foot-tall alien.

His skin was darker than Vishlog's and loops of gold punctured his ears. The blaster in his hands was not the only weapon he carried.

He was followed by a second Dreth, whose skin was marred by scarlet tattoos. Both swept the empty rows with their weapons.

John waited until they were past, then tapped his teammates on their shoulders and jerked his thumb at the door. As they stood to move, the rear-most Dreth pivoted, but his gaze passed over them as he scanned the cockpit area.

His brow wrinkled, but he turned slowly and spoke sharply. His partner also scanned the cabin, then shrugged, and together, they moved toward the cargo bay with its sealed hatch.

The trio breathed again and exited the shuttle slowly. As they dropped to the tarmac, the commander's brow furrowed and John froze and stopped the other two with a hand on each.

They waited while the commander studied them but didn't react. When the Dreth gave a faint shake of his head, the boy tapped his companions and they moved across the hangar to where several cargo bays stood.

Hunkered behind several neatly stacked crates, they turned to watch the shuttle. Ivy noticed a terminal close to a door and tapped John's arm to draw both his and the admiral's attention.

Amaratne gestured approval and they moved closer to it. Ivy raised her eyebrows in question, and both men frowned. The two Dreth emerged from the shuttle and answered their commander's sharp question with abrupt answers.

During the heated discussion that followed, the admiral tapped Ivy and pointed to the door. John nodded, and the three shuffled close enough for her to make short work of the entry pad.

In moments, they stepped swiftly through and hurried along the corridor toward the next room that might contain a terminal. Judging by what they passed, they'd reached the supply section.

A hasty look through the doors closest to the hangar revealed storerooms and a workshop. They encountered no Dreth until they reached what looked like their first target, and then it was only one.

He glanced toward the door as they entered a second before John dropped a blue globe over his head and clenched his fist. The Dreth clutched his throat and kicked back as he tried to peel the invisible layer from his head.

The young mage made a lifting motion with his free hand and pulled the alien out from behind his desk.

"Well, it's not how the Hooligans did it," Ted observed as John floated the Dreth into a corner. He kicked and thrashed, and his eyes bulged with terror as he tried to free himself.

Amaratne uttered an impatient curse and shot him, the silenced round no louder than a hand-clap. Ivy gave him a wide-eyed stare and thumped her hand down on the door controls, and the trio froze.

Ted chuckled. "Most certainly not how the Hooligans did it."

"What did they do?"

"They dropped through the bottom of the shuttle, went loud when the welcoming committee saw them, separated into pairs, and destroyed half the base. The reinforcements were not impressed." He paused. "They had the numbers, though."

"So you've put three people into a scenario the Marines used twice as many people to achieve?" Remy asked.

"Not simply any Marines," his uncle told him, "Todd's Hooligans, but yes, I believe I did."

"Why?" Roma asked, bewildered.

"Because I believe they can succeed."

"Have you told them that?" the AI wanted to know, and Ted let her feel the puzzlement he felt at the unexpected question.

"Why?"

"Because until now, they haven't been meant to succeed. They've been learning against the odds."

"Then this should be novel, shouldn't it?"

They turned their attention to the screen, where Ivy now worked through the files and several armed Dreth had gathered outside the door. Amaratne had crouched facing the rear wall, and John was preparing to fry the first pirate through the door.

"It was still better than watching him choke to death," the older man muttered, and Ted felt a moment of disbelief.

"The man must be going soft in his old age," he commented.

"Or he's sick of killing," Roma suggested.

Remy focused the view onto Ivy. "Or he noticed what John did not."

The girl was as pale as a ghost and her jaw showed white from the way she clenched it. She occasionally darted a glance from the dead Dreth to John and her eyes shimmered.

"Are you sure she's strong enough for this?" Remy asked.

"She will cope," Roma assured him as a loud clang made them all jump.

"John jammed the doors," Ted explained as one of the Dreth took a pry bar and tried to wedge it in the gap where the door met the wall.

Amaratne scampered away from the wall and took shelter beside Ivy. The fizzing pop that followed made her start, and he looked at her.

"How are you doing?" he asked, moved to the hole he'd created, and peered carefully through. "It's clear."

Her fingers moved faster, and her frown deepened. "The data's not in this network," she concluded as another clang echoed through the room.

In the corridor outside, the pry bar slipped out of the socket bent at an angle that rendered it useless for anything but scrap. Another Dreth arrived, holding two limpet-like devices.

Ivy stood from behind the computer. "Time to go," she told them. "They plan to blast their way in."

The three infiltrators wasted no time to slide through an empty storeroom and out into the corridor.

"Did you get the doors shut?" John asked as they bolted toward the servers.

"That system only hooked into the shuttle bay, the surveillance system, and the cargo area. Everything else must be held somewhere else."

"What about the hostages?"

"There are guards outside the area where they're supposed to be," Ivy said, "but there's something…not right about it."

He nodded. "What are our chances—" he began but stopped as half a dozen Dreth trotted into the corridor ahead. They were accompanied by two humans and a Meligornian mage.

"Well," Amaratne muttered, moved to the front, and fired a sustained volley, "this puts a whole different complexion on things."

Shields sparked in front of the armor and Roma gave Ted a horrified look.

"Did you know they had shielding?" she whispered.

"Of course," he informed her, "just as I know there are many more Dreth than these three are expecting. The Hooligans had very good reasons for destroying half the base."

The three didn't stop. John sent a wall of blue down the corridor to thrust the Dreth squad back and drive them into the wall at the other end. As soon as they were pinned, he twisted his hand, and the blue sparkled with electricity, shorted the pirate's armor, and fried the flesh within.

Boots thundered into the corridor behind them, and Ivy bowled a grenade into the midst of their newly-arrived opponents.

"Incoming!" she shouted as one of the Dreth booted it back.

John glanced over his shoulder and dropped a shield between the returning grenade and themselves. It bounced back and exploded before the warrior could deflect it for a second time.

"Is it my imagination or should that have been all the pirates on this base?" Ivy asked.

"Now I know why the Hooligans held Navy Intelligence in such high disregard," Amaratne muttered. "This is a clusterf—"

The door in front of him opened, and he fired several short bursts into the enemies who stepped through it. The team continued to run and moved past as more emerged.

Ivy lobbed a grenade through the gap that appeared between one pirate falling and another taking his place. Screams followed the explosion.

"I need to find the door controls!" she yelled.

"Yup," John agreed, and they bolted into the corridor leading to the servers.

"Oh…" He stopped and braced as he encased them in a wall of blue.

"How long will that hold?" Amaratne asked as the auto-cannon's first rounds pounded into them.

The boy clenched his jaw. "I need a room very soon."

"Well, we can't go back the way we came," Ivy reported. "Can I fire through this?"

"Don't…know…" He gritted his teeth.

The admiral laid a hand over hers and pushed her blaster down. "And now's not the time to find out the hard way."

She nodded, pale-faced, and checked the map display in her HUD before she glanced up the corridor. The rounds that impacted with the shield made the barrier spark with such intensity it was hard to see.

"Take the next door," she ordered and hoped she'd judged the distance correctly.

"But that's—" Amaratne began and she smiled.

"Since when were walls a problem for you?" she asked.

He gave her a startled glance and smiled in return. John stepped left, moved the bubble over an entry panel, and operated it to shift them out of the autocannon's line of fire.

Ivy took one look around the room and realized she'd misjudged but in a good way. "Block the door, John. We're here."

The young mage dropped the shield and melted the door frame until the door blended into the surrounding wall. "I hope you didn't want to leave anytime soon."

Amaratne pushed a desk across the still glowing doorway, tilted it, and wedged it. "This won't hold them for long," he observed, "but it'll provide a little extra cover."

"I still need to get to the hostages," John said.

"I'm working on it," the older man replied and shunted a filing cabinet in front of the door. He looked around at the stacked computer racks and frowned when he realized he couldn't move any of them. "What does a pirate outpost need this kind of computing power for anyway?"

"Life support?" the boy asked, and Amaratne shook his head. "Comms?"

The admiral frowned. "Deep space comms?" He wracked his brain to work out why the Navy had sent the Hooligans after this outpost in the first place. Coming up empty, he shrugged.

"I guess we'll have to find out."

A glimmer of light caught John's eye, and he scowled and melted the camera in its bracket. "What they can't see—"

"That still won't save you." The sibilant tones could only belong to one race, and the three of them froze.

"Is that…" Ivy began, but she didn't stop what she was doing and her hands rattled the keyboard she was working on.

Amaratne started to prepare a second exit.

"Let me check what's on the other side," she told him. "Here."

His eyes widened as the camera feed from the next room appeared in his HUD. "Uh…do we have an alternative?" he asked.

"Gimme a mi—there." Ivy pointed at one of the other walls.

Amaratne studied the glittering lights of the computers stacked in his path. "Uh…"

"I got it," John told him and glanced at Ivy. "Do you need these?"

"Wait…wait, wait, wait." The rattle of keys sounded even faster, and they heard the faint *schnick* of a data stick being inserted, changed over, and the new one inserted.

"How much data…" Amaratne began and tried desperately to remember exactly what Todd's team had pulled for them.

"Let's simply say the extra data sticks will come in handy."

"Let's say you need to hurry," John interrupted and she glanced up and her gaze noticed the red line forming slowly where one door seam had been.

"Masks!" Amaratne ordered as the vent above Ivy hissed and white vapor formed around it.

They closed their HUDs, and John watched the gas warily.

"We gotta go, Ives."

She nodded and stood but kept her fingers on the keyboard and her eyes on the screen.

The mist sank a little.

"Ives…" The young mage's warning was touched by alarm.

"Patience is a virtue," she replied.

John laid a patina of blue over the door, then arced a second over Ivy's head.

"Not right now, it isn't," he warned and flicked a glance at Amaratne. "Do you still need these?" he asked Ivy.

"Yes…and three, two…one! No." She yanked the data stick from the drive and moved away from the computer.

The boy shifted the hand he'd held toward the door and a sheet of blue formed around the computer stack in Amaratne's way. With a brief flash, the shelves shattered and dropped the computers on the floor.

With a sweep of his hand, he swept the debris aside, and Amaratne moved in and took the charges from their pouch.

"A sticky would be faster," John advised him. "Ivy, is that room still clear?"

She stopped behind him and studied her HUD. After a moment, she nodded. "Clear."

"And the Teloran?"

This time, she took a little longer. "In the corridor…moving to the comms center."

John groaned. "Change of plans," he said. "Is there any way to secure the communications without going to the communications center?"

"If we can hack it from another point and shift the controls," Amaratne said thoughtfully.

"How about a shuttle?" Ivy suggested. "What if I moved the controls to the shuttle's comms system?"

The admiral thought about it as he worked to place the stickies. "We can only try."

Now, I know why they blew up half the base, he thought and stepped back as he placed the last piece of explosive. "John?"

The young mage glanced up and shifted the shield to cover the three of them. "That mist's not friendly," he pointed out as the white haze reached the first debris from the stacks of shelves and vapor rose from the metal.

The room shook as the stickies destroyed a section of the wall. It shook a second time when rounds slammed into the wall Amaratne had originally chosen for their exit.

"They were waiting," the older man observed and led them through the hole he'd made.

"It won't do them any good," John observed and sealed the next door. "Ivy?"

She paused, then pointed to another wall. "That way."

Boots sounded in the corridor outside and she frowned. "And then there should be a door on the other side." She scowled at John. "Don't melt that one into a wall."

"Gotcha."

They moved, and the admiral no longer bothered to position the stickies. He merely tossed them into the center of the space he needed, and John expanded the blast so they could fit.

"You know our suits are sealed, right?" Ivy asked, and Ted felt a small wave of disbelief.

That was exactly the same question Ka had asked in that area.

A rumble drew his gaze to the screen.

"That is exactly what the Hooligans did," he muttered as Amaratne made a small sound of understanding.

"Oh… That's why they did that!"

He hadn't been too impressed when he read the report, but he hadn't had time to debrief the Hooligans as much as he'd have liked to. By then, he had begun to recognize that the Federation had some serious security concerns inside its Navy. It was a shame he'd been too late to address them.

A clang was followed by a soft boom as the door panel fell in and signaled that the Dreth had finally gained access into the server room.

The three of them ran to the door and burst into the corridor beyond.

"What's next?" Ivy asked.

"Hostages," Amaratne declared. "It's not like they'll blow their comms up, and it'll take all three of us to deal with a Teloran if we have to go back there."

"You do remember our orders were to hold the comms center?" she reminded them.

"The comms center can be anywhere we can shift the comms operation to," he assured her, and she pointed to a stairwell.

"That way."

John groaned. "I hate stairs."

She took the lead. "Me, too," she told him but didn't slow her pace.

By the time they caught up with her, she had the door open and had used the connection to close and lock the bulkheads leading into the section.

"I was too busy downloading data to take care of this before," she told them and highlighted the locked doors across the base.

"Can they override it?" John asked, and she frowned.

"Yes, until I fry the controls," she told him, "and I don't want to do that yet except maybe here, here...and here."

The schematics flared to reflect what she'd done, and Amaratne groaned. "That'll make it hard."

Ivy punched his shoulder. "Shuttle. Remember?"

He rolled his eyes. "I only hope you're right."

Ted shook his head and covered his eyes with the blade of his hand.

"We really need to make she and Ka never get to meet…"

"Ka?" Remy asked, and Roma tuned in.

"It's a long story, but she's in the files. You can look her up later. In fact," he added, "you can look all the Hooligans up later. They're part of Stephanie's regular crew and as important to her as her team."

"That's not hard," Roma retorted. "All her people are important to her."

Ted raised his eyebrows. "So you have done your homework."

"Of course. I don't get to sit around and devise evil trips down memory lane," she replied tartly.

"Are you calling this evil?" Ted asked and indicated the scenario where the three infiltrators had reached the bottom of the stairs and now peered into the corridor.

"I told you there was something wrong with those Dreth," Ivy whispered as the first dark, spindly form turned towards her. "Oops. Me and my big—"

She stopped as John brushed past her and launched twin sets of lightning from his palms.

The Telorans retaliated but not with magic. They had blasters too.

It took her a moment to realize the significance.

"Not all of them have magic!" she exclaimed, retrieved a grenade, and pitched it into the middle of them.

"I'd forgotten that," Amaratne admitted and stopped on John's other side so they flanked him. "Let's hope the hostages are okay."

Ted turned to Remy. "Is it time?"

The AI checked the scenario recording. "Almost. Let them know to expect a new team member."

Ted's voice cut through the comms.

"Be alert for a new team member," he announced, and the three maintained their fire.

Roma frowned. "But Todd didn't have a new team member…"

"Todd had eight team members," Ted reminded her, "and I want to get Remy out from under your feet."

"By integrating him into John's team?"

"Exactly."

She grinned. "This I have to see."

Her brother gave her a wary look.

"Why do I get the feeling this will hurt?"

"Remember Vishlog and Ivy?"

"But she's past that now, isn't she?" Remy asked, concerned.

Roma sounded far too happy as she replied, "You'd better hope so."

Ted shook his head. "When you're ready, Remy. This is what I want you to do."

Given what he'd heard of the infiltrator's plans, the suggestion made perfect sense, and Remy began to prepare.

In the scenario, John fried a third Teloran while Ivy shot a fourth. Amaratne eliminated the last two.

"I told you they weren't Dreth," the girl said and unlocked the door. She also passed the footage from the security cams to both their HUDs. "Do you think our new teammate is in there?"

John shrugged. "Well, we won't know until they reveal themselves."

He glanced at Amaratne. "Ted didn't give you any clues, did he?"

The admiral shook his head and studied the faces he saw in the HUD. "No, but any of these folk would be a great addition. I recognize several from our specialist teams. I can understand why Ops kept the result of this little effort under wraps."

They moved into the cell after he had rifled through the Teloran's robes to find two cube-shaped devices. He tossed one to John.

"Cuff keys," he told him. "Some of them look hurt."

"I've got that, too," John told him and glanced at Ivy. "Keep watch?"

She nodded and followed them in, closed the door, and tapped the relevant cams. "Will do."

The corridors remained quiet as John and Amaratne moved among the prisoners. At first, they both unlocked the cuffs until the young mage found the first man who needed saving.

"Keep going," he instructed as the admiral crouched beside him. "Get them loose. I'll see what I can do about getting them mobile and making sure they survive."

One of the men closest rasped a chuckle. "What makes you think we want to survive. We know what's coming."

"Trust me," John told him, "the Witch is coming too, and *nothing* will stand against her."

The man stilled. "Tell me it's true."

"I wouldn't be here if it wasn't," he replied and pointed to the wall closest to the door. "Wait over there. We'll get you to a shuttle."

It didn't take them long to free the rest of the prisoners or for John to get them onto their feet. He was covered in a sheen of sweat by the end of it.

"Are you okay?" Amaratne asked, and the young Talent nodded.

"I merely need to pull some more energy from the outside. I'll be fine."

The older man lowered his voice. "Any sign of them?"

John shook his head. "If they're here, they haven't shown themselves yet."

He shrugged. "I guess you can't blame them. Maybe when we get them to the shuttle—"

"Let's hope we don't need them before then," John replied and signaled for them to move out. "Ivy, do you want to take point?"

The girl opened the door. "Shuttle?"

"Shuttle," he confirmed. "You can try to hack the comms from there."

The prisoners watched them, their faces wary, but they didn't argue.

"Where are the pirates?" one of them asked after they'd walked past several junctions with no sign of their former captors.

"I locked them in their rooms," Ivy responded, "and then shorted the controls."

"All of them?"

"Except for the ones we killed," John added and the conversation ended.

They passed the bodies of the welcoming committee in the corridor. No one had come to clear them, and Ivy wondered how much time had elapsed.

The HUD showed a scant thirty minutes.

"It feels so much longer than that," she muttered as they crossed the landing pad and shepherded their charges into the shuttle.

"Who's flying this?" one asked, and Ivy looked at John. He pointed at the cockpit, and she opened the door reluctantly and ignored the same voice that asked, "Can she fly?"

There was no one in the cockpit and her heart sank. "It looks like we remoted in."

The newly rescued hostages froze. "Are you saying none of you can fly?"

Here it comes, Ivy thought. *Our new teammate will reveal themselves.*

The silence dragged on and no one stepped forward.

"Can any of you?" she asked and saw them exchange disbelieving glances.

"We will never get out of here," one groaned.

"And you know what they did to the last one who tried to escape."

A collective moan went up from the group.

"We have reinforcements coming," Amaratne told them, "and the ones we didn't shoot are locked down."

"How long for?"

"As long as I can hold them," Ivy reassured them as the hangar's pressurization alarm sounded. She turned, slid into the co-pilot's seat, and hooked her tablet into the shuttle's control console.

The admiral slapped a hand on the door controls to seal the shuttle hatch.

"We have power," the girl reported.

"Well, at least they followed some procedure," Amaratne responded. "See if you can find the sensors and patch them through to the HUDs."

"Gotcha." She frowned at the controls but found the necessary settings easily enough.

The sight of a dropship coming in wasn't exactly comforting.

"Reinforcements?" she asked, but the admiral shook his head.

"Wrong markings—and they won't launch until we've secured the communications array."

One of the prisoners snickered. "Good luck with that."

"Do you care to share?" John asked and his eyes flared gold.

The man stared at him and licked his lips nervously. "Only that they have a Teloran guarding it, is all." He lowered his voice. "A mage."

"We know," John replied. "We've seen him."

"Seen him and survived?" the prisoner asked disbelievingly.

John nodded. "He's securing the center. We left him to it while we scraped their data systems and pulled you guys out."

"If he's not locked down, it would have been better if you'd left us," one of the others told him morosely.

"Don't bet on it," the young mage snapped and looked at Amaratne. "Any ideas?"

"Yeah," the admiral said and opened the cargo area. A mini-turret sat on either side of the space. "I'm gonna make sure they land in pieces."

"Can you do that?" he asked as the older man slid into one of the turret operator's seats.

"I might not be able to fly this," Amaratne declared, "and I might not have been in one for a while, but I still know how to use the guns."

"Just don't bring it down on top of us," John told him and snickered.

"That's where you come in. I hope you have enough juice."

He was still laughing as he pivoted the shuttle's turret and fired at the incoming dropship. John glanced at Ivy, but she was too busy trying to hack the comms controls from the shuttle's systems.

"Did you know there's another array out there?" she asked as the man opened fire but didn't stop what she was doing. A moment later, she made a sound of sheer frustration. "Ugh! The shuttle can't patch through." She slid out of her seat and headed to the hatch. "We're gonna have to make it to the comms center if we want to take it. I'm sorry, guys."

"Yes!" Amaratne shouted and made the hostages flinch.

John's eyes widened, and he thrust both hands toward the rear of the shuttle. The sight of debris raining around them and the other shuttle careening past to pound into the end of the hangar bay before it exploded made most of the prisoners shake their heads.

"Now you've done it," one said as everything froze.

SCENARIO FAILED! flashed in large red letters across the inside of their HUDs.

"What?" they chorused. "How come?"

Ted brought the burning dropship into focus, and Amaratne groaned. "New teammate?" he asked, and Ivy giggled.

"What?" she asked, still snickering. "It wasn't me this time."

The admiral rolled his eyes. "And thank you, Ivy."

Before she could reply, Ted spoke over the comms. "I'll restart the scenario from when the alert sounds."

When Ivy sent the alert through to their helmets, they decided to wait and see who it was despite the protests from their rescues.

"For all you know, it could be more pirates!" one exclaimed.

"True," Amaratne agreed. "John, are you ready?"

The boy nodded. "I can shield us if we need to, but I agree with the admiral. Let's see who it is."

Remy brought the dropship down alongside the shuttle and stepped out of the cockpit before the hangar had started to close.

"More incoming!" Ivy warned as the hangar stayed open.

"You get the hangar closed," Amaratne told her and adjusted the focus in his HUD. "I can shoot those already through."

"Just don't put a hole in the hangar roof."

"And what happens if they shoot back?" one of the prisoners asked and his voice rose in alarm.

"I happen," John told him.

They regarded him with some doubt but nothing happened. Amaratne missed one craft and caused the other to veer wildly away while he winged a third one.

"Well, they know we're here now," a prisoner whined.

"And it doesn't matter," Ivy told them as the hangar doors closed and the pressure alarms died. "We can get out of here now."

"Where to?"

She stopped in the cockpit doorway and pointed out the opening hatch of the dropship. "Into that," she told them.

"But how do you know they're friendly?"

John let electricity arc over his fingertips. "It doesn't matter if they are or not. They know how to fly and they won't want to die."

That appealed to them and they agreed.

"We'd better make it quick," Ivy warned as one of the alerts she'd set activated. "The pirates have breached the first bulkhead."

"Gotcha." The young mage stepped alongside her as she

headed to the closest exit from the hangar. Amaratne jogged to catch up with them, and the prisoners wheeled to follow.

"I thought the communications array was my job?" he asked.

"Yes, but you'll need me for the mage," John told him.

"And me for the doors."

"What about us?" the closest prisoner demanded.

The three teammates looked at each other.

"Let's get you into the dropship," Ivy told him and led them over to where the vessel's rear hatch had opened and an entry ramp descended.

A tall figure with dark hair trotted down it as she approached.

"Step right up," it called. "Remy's Emergency Extraction Service has arrived."

"Remy?" She almost stopped in surprise, but the AI jogged past her. "Close the hatch as soon as you're aboard. Nothing will break through."

"But—"

"Trust me," he told her, and she sighed and led the prisoners aboard. He had a point. Someone had to look after these people. She merely didn't want it to be her.

There was no time to argue, though, so she signaled the hostages to follow her and closed the hatch after them.

"Make yourselves comfortable," she told them and jogged to the cockpit.

She'd almost reached it when a narrow hand snaked out and grasped her arm.

"How comfortable do you want me to be?" a sibilant voice asked, and she drew her blaster and emptied it into the speaker's chest.

At point-blank range, the rounds tore through the alien's body, shredded his spine, and sprayed one wall of the dropship with blood. His hand slipped from her arm and his body sagged as she backed away with her blaster up to cover the rest of the prisoners.

"Don't any of you move," she ordered, her gaze fixed on their shocked faces as she maneuvered into the cockpit and locked the hatch.

"I heard shots." John's worried voice came over the HUD as her hands began to shake.

"There was…one of them was a Teloran," Ivy told him.

"We're on our way back. Are you okay?"

"No! I mean, yes, I'm okay. No, don't come back. Get the mission done."

"Are you secure?"

She checked the footage from the rear compartment. The prisoners had seated themselves as far from the Teloran corpse as they could get. Now and then, one of them would give the cockpit hatch a worried glance.

None of them made any effort to follow her and she breathed a sigh of relief.

"Yeah. I'm in the cockpit and it looks like there was only one. The others are sitting and they haven't tried to get in. Get the comms. I'll get the doors." She drew a shaky breath and steadied her voice. "Are you ready?"

"If you're sure…" John still sounded like he wanted to return.

"Don't make me come out there," she warned and was relieved when Amaratne interjected.

"If she says she's fine, she's fine, but we need to hurry."

They all looked at the counter and Ivy gasped. "Hurry. Go straight and then left. It'll take you around most of the living quarters but trust me, trying to go direct would take longer."

On the feed from the security cams, she was glad to see them break into a jog. Amaratne turned to Remy.

"You wouldn't happen to be a communication specialist, would you?"

The AI laughed. "I could be, but I believe you are more familiar with the quirks of this particular system than I am."

"So what can you do?" the man asked as a small explosion

shook the corridor and half a dozen Dreth broke through.

Remy chuckled and drew a blaster with each hand. The next few seconds showed very clearly what he could do, and Ivy breathed a sigh of relief.

John might make it through this yet.

"You've cleared that section," she told them when the firefight died down. "You might as well take a short-cut straight through."

"How many Dreth?" John asked.

"This section? None," she confirmed, "but you'll find one very nasty Teloran, an autocannon, a Meligornian, and two Dreth pirates when you get there."

"It sounds like fun," Remy commented and sounded far too happy at the prospect.

"Just don't mix nMU with eMU," she reminded John, and he groaned as the three of them broke into a jog.

"As if I could ever forget."

They reached the bulkhead outside the comms center in record time and Ivy kept the door closed.

"Can't you get the autocannon?" John asked.

She froze. "Let me see…" Seconds later, the answer became clear. "It's a closed circuit," she told them. "I'm useless here."

"You're doing more than enough," Amaratne assured her. "We couldn't have made it this far this fast without you on over-watch…and your part is done."

"Well, I couldn't have done it without you," she told him and opened the door.

John blocked the autocannon's fire with another shield as Amaratne slid three scramblers along the corridor floor. The mobile explosives skittered close to the auto-cannon and wrapped themselves around its base.

As the weapon exploded, John's shield wavered. He growled in frustration and effort, and the shield strengthened.

"John?"

"Not now, Ives."

"Door!" Amaratne commanded. "Tell me what you see."

His instructions made her focus, and she cycled the comms room door and sent them the images as she did.

"I have the left," Remy declared as the admiral said, "I'll take right."

"I'm almost out of eMU," John stated, and Ivy's heart sank.

"Can you empty what you have left and use nMU?"

"Why?"

"Well, that Teloran has to be charging himself from somewhere."

"Have I told you how much I love you?"

"Tell me when you get back," she snapped, and the sharpness of her tone failed to disguise her concern.

"Monitor the comms," Amaratne ordered. "Make sure they don't get a distress call out. Those fighters had to come from somewhere."

He was right. Even as John fed the last of his MU into a shield, the Teloran waited, and black lightning laced his form with dark fire. As soon as he felt the shield start to waver, John ducked behind a console and began to pull the energy from the world around him.

It was all dark and made his feelings boil with anger, resentment, and grief. Why had he fought the Regime? Look at what it had cost him. Look at what *she* had cost him.

The enemy chuckled. "Are you rethinking your allegiance?" he whispered as Amaratne and Remy fired into the pirates. "You'd do better to walk on our side. It's better to burn your world than be burned with it."

"No!" the young mage roared, stepped out from behind the console, and found a new target for his anger. The nMU worked exactly as the eMU, but its effects were harder to control.

It was as if the magic wanted to destroy—and not only the thing it was meant to. It wanted to destroy everything.

John forced himself to focus on the mage and to keep his

Talent from straying into the equipment they'd been sent there to secure.

"Admiral!" he shouted. "Get the comms!"

As if his voice was a signal, Remy chuckled.

"Get the comms, Admiral. I've got the rest."

He did, too. Ivy's eyes widened as the AI fired impossibly fast and with terrifying accuracy. She'd have thought he'd be the one to take control of the systems, but having him around was like having their own walking, talking auto-cannon—one you could rely on to destroy the enemy without automatically targeting your friends.

As she watched Remy annihilate the Dreth before they'd raised their blasters and then the Meligornian before he could throw anything at John, another of Ivy's alerts beeped.

"Hurry up and get the mage, John. You're about to have company!"

"What kind of company?"

"The overwhelming pirate kind."

"And you?" John asked. "Are you secure?"

"I'm not the one making all the noise," she retorted. "They probably think they can take us once they have you three locked down."

"Can't you do something?"

"Transmit the data, Ivy. Make sure it gets off-world. In case—"

Amaratne didn't finish, but she understood immediately.

"Will do," she told them and set up the broadcast.

Once she was sure the data was going where she needed it to go, she turned her attention to regaining control of the doors.

It took forever for the reinforcements to come.

David pounded his fist onto his desk. The resulting crack sent a satisfying network of breaks through the glass covering its surface but he resisted the urge to do it a second time.

With the same force of will, he resisted the surge of Talent that threatened to surround his body in a halo of power.

"Why can't they simply admit they lost the base?" he roared.

Admiral Deverey gave him a wide-eyed stare and hid his fear behind a stony mask. There wasn't a single thing he could think of to say that might not get him killed.

Fortunately, the CIO didn't appear to need an answer.

"They're faking it. They have to be!" He balled his fist again but forced his hand down to his side.

"We merely need to find a way to prove it," he suggested tentatively and flinched when David stared at him. For a moment, it was as if the man's eyes burned, and Deverey swallowed. "We don't have any reason to have a ship in that area, but I'm sure we'll come up with something."

The CIO's gaze pinned him for a moment longer, and his mouth went dry. The look wasn't murderous, but it made him feel like he was already dead.

"It's only a matter of time." David growled with annoyance and impatience and seated himself behind his desk.

The fleet admiral resisted the urge to breathe a sigh of relief and reminded himself that he wasn't out of the woods yet. He glanced at the screen and recalled that the plan had been to have the ore carrier report the outpost's loss.

Those communications could have been believably intercepted and the loss reported. But the ore carrier hadn't reported the loss, and there'd been no communications to intercept. As far as they could tell, the ship had made orbit, loaded, and returned to Dreth as if everything was normal.

Only it isn't, Deverey thought and wondered why the vessel hadn't flagged it.

"What about a supply ship?" he asked, and the CIO looked up from the desk. Under the Regime leader's gimlet stare, he hastened to continue. "After all, there are humans on that rock.

It's only logical that we'd want to send them supplies—or maybe provide communiqués from home?"

To his relief, David smiled. It wasn't a particularly pleasant smile, but it was better than what had gone before, so he simply waited.

"Yes," the CIO continued. "We'll activate the Regime Care Package initiative—a bi-annual gift for all humans located on distant worlds with credits and something small to remind them of home." He paused. "Letters from relatives if we can find them, Earth foods that can't be sourced easily." He gave Deverey a sharp glance. "Will a week be long enough?"

"To organize it, sir?"

David nodded. "It's either that or we pretend we've received an emergency call from the planet but that it's taken this long for one of our ships to intercept it."

The admiral responded with a carefully neutral shrug. "Either one will work, sir."

"Yeees. I like it," the leader mused. "We can use this to our advantage. Their failure to report it, followed by their deliberate deception of the Regime regarding the fate of its people, can only mean they are planning something to our detriment—and that is something we can't ignore. Instead of a peaceful occupation to assist them, we will be forced to subjugate them instead. Such treachery cannot be ignored."

"How long do you wish to let them believe their deception has worked, sir?" Deverey asked, glad to see the man's attention was now fully focused on the Dreth.

"Ask me in two days' time," David instructed. "I need to look at the implications of this deception and work out how to get the most of this most unexpected opportunity."

"Yes, sir!"

He leaned back behind his desk and flicked his hand at the admiral in absent dismissal.

"Go. I need to think."

CHAPTER FOURTEEN

"**P**ull it apart again and polish every part," Andorres instructed. "I don't want the slightest trace of dirt in there. Nothing that might make this weapon weaker."

Crewman Tippet stared at him, then nodded and answered crisply, "Gotcha."

Andorres watched the young crewman go about his task and noted the slight frown that creased his brow. "What is it, Tippet?" The younger man paused and regarded him uncertainly. "Spit it out."

Tippet looked around at where the rest of the crew was working. The section gleamed, but the crew still labored to make it shine more brightly or went over the equipment again.

Some were stocking more supplies in each gun crew's private storage compartment. Others were trying to work out how to optimize an already optimal feed chain.

The young man included them all with a short swipe of his cleaning cloth. "I don't understand, boss."

Andorres followed the sweep of his hand. "Understand what? Hard work?"

He blushed and shook his head. "No, boss. No way I wouldn't

understand that with you riding shotgun, but this place is spotless. We've scrubbed it within an inch of its life. No disrespect, but Tempe won't like it if we polish a hole in her decking."

Understanding dawned and his boss spoke. "Are you asking why we're working so hard to get a ship ready that's already at her peak?" Tippet lowered his head somewhat sheepishly.

"Well…uh, yeah." He looked anxious as if worried his question had caused offense, but Andorres got it. "I get that it's because of her, but I…I've never met her, and I simply don't understand why."

The older man moved to a wall and gestured to him to follow. When they arrived, he settled against it.

"Look, son, it's like this. When you watch a woman become a goddess and still be willing to die to save your world and those of others, you realize that your efforts represent your belief in her more than mere words, chants, or slogans." He sighed and pushed away from the wall. "That piece you're holding, for example. Take a good look at it."

Tippet obeyed.

"Do you know what I see?" Andorres asked, and the crewman shook his head.

"I see a piece vital to the gun that'll protect her, and I want it to have nothing on it that'll make it snag, stutter, or slow the rate of fire. I want it to run smooth and cool and like silk. I don't want it to fail and cause me to fail to keep that woman safe."

He pointed to where two techs were sweating and swearing over the feeder. "They're trying to increase her rate of fire so our guns don't overheat and explode like they did in the last battle, and them—" He turned to where two more of the team had finished polishing an area on the floor next to the gun and were welding several D-shackles to the deck. "They're making sure we have somewhere to tether ourselves if this section gets opened up to the stars."

Tippet stared at him. "You're kidding…right?"

Andorres shook his head, and his face grew somber with a distant memory. "We lost good people in that battle. This time, we want something better than tape to keep us secure."

The older hand waited and let the crewman absorb what he'd been told.

"Look," he continued, "all of this tells you and these people around us that there's a new expectation, a new 'best,' if you like." He shrugged and surveyed the space again, gauging the efforts of his team before he turned to his teammate.

"I doubt Stephanie would notice you until you perform, but you *will* be asked to perform, and if you want to succeed, make sure the area you work in is beyond top-notch. When she is willing to die to save this ship, you'll find that you will be willing to die to keep it together as well."

Tippet gaped at him. "You make her sound like she's a god among us."

His teammate chuckled and returned to the gun.

"She doesn't look like one," he admitted as he knelt beside the cover. "She's not very tall and not very muscular unless things have changed." He frowned and inspected the parts inside as he spread a clean cloth on the decking in front of him. "I suppose she's a little older, but who knows what she looks like now? She's a witch." He shrugged. "They might look young for eternity."

He fell silent, and Tippet joined him and knelt on the opposite side of the cloth as Andorres began to pull the gun apart and lay the pieces in front of them.

"And yet you call her Stephanie, not even Ms. Morgana," he noted, and the older man glanced at him.

"Oh, you will know when the Morgana has come out, but pray she isn't focused on you when it happens. I never believed in the old gods, but there isn't anyone or anything I know of that's closer to the incarnation of death than the Morgana."

Tippet frowned. "Then why follow her?"

Andorres smiled. "Because it's invariably love that causes the Morgana to come out."

The young crewman set his piece down in the correct order with the rest. "I'm so confused," he admitted.

"You won't be," his teammate assured him. "Have Tempestarii bring up a few scenes of when Stephanie changed. You'll see."

Far from the *Tempestarii*, John, Ivy, and Amaratne had gathered in the compound foyer. Ted faced them and looked overdressed in a well-tailored suit that combined in strange harmony with the cowboy boots on his feet.

He set his hat on his head and pulled the brim down to cover the "R" on his forehead.

"I've sent the message," he told the admiral and gave his friend a worried look. "Are you sure this is wise?"

Amaratne looked past him and into the wasteland beyond, then looked back.

"We need foot soldiers," he admitted. "With the information you've gathered on the Regime's plans for Dreth, having something to screw up their plans during the battle or sooner would be helpful."

Ted frowned. "We don't have much time."

He sighed. "I know, but we'll do what we can. I doubt we have anything that will slow the battle but perhaps post-battle, if it doesn't go too far in the Regime's favor, we might help."

He paused, and concern darkened his expression as he sighed. "It's what we can do."

The AI nodded and glanced at the door and the hostile world beyond. "I'll get going. The sooner I arrive, the sooner we can start."

Amaratne stepped forward, extended one hand to be shaken,

and clapped him on the shoulder with the other. "Good luck, old friend."

John and Ivy moved forward too. The boy said farewell the same way Amaratne had, and Ivy extended a long-strapped satchel.

"Don't forget your man-bag," she told Ted, and he returned her smile, seeing beyond it to the worry in her eyes.

"Thank you," he replied, rested a hand on her arm, and ignored the flinch she didn't quite manage to suppress. To his surprise, she returned the gesture as he took the satchel and slung it over his shoulder.

Goodbyes, he thought and noticed the moment when she started to chew on her lower lip. *They are still not your strong point.*

He didn't say it, though, but turned and walked quietly out the foyer door and onto the walkway. When he reached the gate, he looked back and found it strangely comforting to see the three of them gathered at the window.

They waved in a final farewell as he moved through, and this time, he didn't look back.

"Well, that was interesting." Remy's voice made him start and search his surroundings.

"Oh, yes?" he asked and relaxed when he remembered why he carried the bag and the components inside.

"Yes. She's improving," the younger AI observed, and Ted chuckled.

"Well, she didn't burst into tears."

"Not until after you'd left," he informed him. "John didn't quite know what to do."

"Didn't he?"

"Not when she couldn't explain why she was sad because—and I quote—'it's stupid.' Amaratne suggested chocolate."

"Oh? And what did Roma say?"

"She already had it waiting," Remy confirmed. "She has come

a long way when it comes to humans. I think she's been doing extra research."

"Good," his uncle said approvingly, "because we'll need her if things go according to plan." He patted the bag. "Our first step is to get you out of there."

"You haven't told them, have you?" Remy asked, and Ted patted the bag again.

"No, I have not, but they have met you in the Virtual World, and Roma can verify you when you arrive."

"You merely want to see if Ivy shoots me—or Amaratne," he concluded morosely, and Ted laughed out loud.

"No, they've both learned their lesson. If anyone blasts you, it'll be John."

"And that is so much more comforting," he snarked.

"We need to know if you pass as a human," his uncle reassured him. "Their reaction will show that."

Remy uttered a very disgruntled and very human sigh.

"And what will you do if they decide to damage this new body we intend to find?"

"It won't happen," Ted told him. "We need you as a physical part of the team too much for me to jeopardize that."

"Well, that's good to know." He didn't sound comforted, but his uncle didn't give him time to dwell on it.

He sent the AI a map. "This will be our first stop."

Blonde, bobbed, and beastly was how Aurora Delahunty's colleagues described her, but she'd risen where they'd failed and held one of the most envied positions in the Regime—that of PR.

She'd admired Ava, but she didn't think much of the woman now. The files she currently worked through were a mess!

With a sigh, she took another from the pile stacked haphazardly on the woman's desk, glanced over it, and put it in the "Transfer" pile. Honestly, the job wasn't that hard.

You transferred the semi-viable ones, terminated the non-viable ones, and marked the promising ones for further testing to ensure their understanding of their place in the human hierarchy—at the bottom.

Talents weren't people.

She couldn't fathom what these files were doing in the "to-be-decided" basket and couldn't be bothered to sift through her predecessor's overly copious notes to do so.

Picking up the next one, she glanced at it and paused.

Talent 781: formerly known as John Dunn, she read and opened the cover carefully. She'd heard about him. He'd destroyed Ava's career.

The red star in the corner of the folder marked it as being of personal interest to the CIO.

"Hmmm, and what's so special about you, T-781?" she asked.

The picture that had been slipped into the front of the folder said it all.

"The CIO's airship? Seriously?"

She'd known it had been damaged but she'd been busy and hadn't paid it all that much attention. She leaned back in her seat and began to read.

"My, my, my, 781. You have been a busy little troublemaker, haven't you?"

The Naval reports made it quite clear that they needed the Talent, and the Intelligence reports were adamant that he either had to be brought to heel or put down. The CIO's attention made it relatively urgent.

Aurora paused and thought about that. Judging from the comments in the file, the CIO had been very invested in the initial pursuit, but lately, that wasn't the case.

She frowned. He seemed distracted, and they'd been trying to locate John for a while. How much did she have to do to wrap him up?

As she worked through the latest report, she learned that extensive searches of both coastlines had come up empty. Ships had been tasked with searching their routes for bodies, and they too had found nothing.

Maybe the young couple had died when they'd fallen? They'd gone over the edge at quite a height.

Aurora wondered if she should put that in a report and paused. If she did and he reappeared, it could be disastrous.

She frowned as she thought about it. If she reported that he'd died from the fall and he turned up—and he had a bad habit of doing exactly that—it wouldn't only be her career that was over.

That made it easy for her to open a call to the Talent Control Center.

"Major? Aurora, Head of PR."

She waited while the Control Center's head made the appropriate acknowledgment before she continued.

"It's about 781. He's still a priority, and his body hasn't been located."

She paused and listened as the man asked about the girl.

"No. She hasn't been found, either—and she's always been a key to finding him. I'll need a group that can handle the search for both."

The major assured her he had the very people and she hung up.

For a long moment, she sat and stared at the blank screen, then glanced at the file and tapped it.

"You won't be the end of me, 781."

CHAPTER FIFTEEN

"This looks good," Ted observed.

"It looks big enough to have a terminal," Remy agreed.

"True, but we don't want to draw too much attention. We need someone who's not at home."

It didn't take long to find a house with a well-appointed garden and no cars in the drive. Ted had the cab he'd called stop out front and walked up to the front door.

He made short work of the lock using a set of tools the admiral had recommended and stepped through the door. He moved swiftly enough that it looked like he had a key.

"What if someone notices?" his nephew asked.

"The trick is to look like you're supposed to be where you are," he explained. "It works in almost every human facility from what I've seen, regardless of the location."

Closing the door behind him, he looked for the office. Every home had a way to get online, right?

"And if they challenge you?" Remy asked, interrupting his thoughts.

"Dress correctly, and you will find that many won't even look at you twice. For those who do, you need to have a plausible reason—and you should always have an exit strategy in mind."

The other AI thought about that as Ted found the office. It occupied a room next to the master bedroom, and he settled hastily into the chair, hacked the password protecting the desktop, and went online.

"Let's see if they got the message," he murmured and smiled as he caught himself speaking out loud. The young apostle was a bad example—or a very good one. He couldn't decide which.

Running a thin lead from the jack in his head to a port in the box, he stepped into the machine.

"Oh no, you don't," he muttered as the machine's security programs challenged him again. The first one was easy. He bypassed it and hacked into the next layer.

A second program came after him, and he neutralized it with a burst of code and slid through the system and into the Net. That was where things became challenging.

First, there were the programs that wanted to know what he was doing logging in at an unexpected time of day. They marked him as an "item of interest," and it took several seconds for him to convince them otherwise—that he was merely a businessman working from home for the day.

The subterfuge meant he had to change his identity once he'd shaken them and then try to mask his point of origin. That last was a little trickier, but he bent the signal so that it bounced through several satellites.

If anyone could follow it, they'd think he was coming out of Perth.

Once he was sure he was secure, he slid out of the Net and into the Undernet. Nothing followed him that he could detect, and he picked nothing up on the dark side although things tried.

The drop box was undisturbed save for a single message: *Look to the sky. The proof will be shown in the stars.*

"Well, at least they got the message," he told Remy and sent a short confirmation. *And the stars shall fall from the skies.*

With his message sent, he searched for their next destination.

"There," he told the younger AI and breathed a sigh of relief. "I was worried they'd stopped manufacturing."

"Oh, no," Remy replied. "When it comes to a choice of keeping their population caged and the expense of creating droids to fill their functions or letting their population live at the edge of their control, the Regime is consistent in selecting a cage."

"That explains the size of this facility, then," Ted told him and evaded another trace as he exited the Undernet and returned to the Net.

He had to slip past another security program when he entered the manufacturing facility to find the schematics. It didn't take him long to move through to the security procedures and the sensors in the fence.

Disabling the programs that would report interference with the barrier's integrity, he exited from the Net.

"I can't leave any way for them to see where we've been," he told Remy and altered the settings on the drive.

The computer began to whine and heat rose from the box. When his body's sensors detected the smell of burning electronics, he sent a surge of power through the drive and slid into his body.

The computer ceased to function but didn't burst into flame.

From the outside, it still looked intact—if you ignored the expensive brown smell that permeated the office.

"It's time to go," he said, and walked quickly to the front door, let himself out, and locked it behind him.

The cab remained outside and undisturbed and the street was as deserted as before.

"It's the middle of the day," he explained. "Most humans are at work in this kind of neighborhood."

"But there are always anomalies," Remy pointed out. "The risk of discovery is still present."

"Sometimes, you must be willing to take the risk," Ted told him. "Calculate the best odds for success and again, plan an exit strategy if the lower likelihoods occur."

He slid into the cab and directed the computer to take them to a side street running alongside the factory.

"We really need a construction vehicle for this," he muttered, "or one of those white work vans."

"You could always 'acquire' one," Remy suggested.

"I could," he conceded once he'd considered it, "but I believe if we pull over here…"

The cab obeyed and came to a halt beside the curb. Several tall trees shaded the position and Ted smiled.

"Now it will look like the driver is taking a break," he explained, "and these trees and bushes will screen our activities at the fence."

"What do you intend to do?" his nephew asked.

"There are moments when the direct approach is not the best approach," he explained. "Had we driven through the front gates of the facility, questions would have been raised."

"And cutting through the fence is any better?" Remy challenged.

"It is when you have disabled the sensors and made them look like they are still working—and when you have the cameras showing the same empty street."

"When did you do that?"

"While I was in the system pulling the schematics," he explained. "I didn't want to rely on their technicians being less than observant."

"Wise, with a facility such as this," the other AI agreed. "There are some humans who believe they should have the opportunity to fill the positions the droids have been given."

"Exactly." Ted shut down the cutting torch built into his hand

and let the panel slide back over the nozzle. He peeled the chain wire aside and stepped through, then turned to pull the mesh back. There," he murmured. He was about to weld it into place when an idea occurred to him and he let it go.

"I thought you wanted to cover your tracks," Remy said.

"I had another idea," Ted told him. "And it will be much more effective at covering our tracks than an intact fence."

Following the path he'd tracked to the building, he stopped in the shadow of one wall. The afternoon had shifted rapidly to dusk, and cover was easier to find. That didn't mean he could relax, but it did mean less chance of accidental discovery.

"And how is this acting like you belong?" his nephew snarked, and he chuckled.

"There's a time and place for everything," he told the younger AI. "Entering a house in broad daylight—or a heavily guarded communications facility—means you have little chance of not being seen and need to look like you belong."

He paused and listened to the sound of vehicles exiting the employees' parking lot and the voices raised in greeting and farewell as the guards changed shift. When he was sure he remained unobserved, he moved to a side door.

"Entering a facility after working hours when the few human employees it has are going home, it is easier to remain unseen." He opened the door. "Although it helps if you unlock as many of the entrances as you can before you arrive."

"I see," Remy replied.

The door led to a large storage section, and Ted smirked as he looked at the rows of android bodies lined up in preparation for shipping.

"Do you see anything you like?" he asked.

"They all look the same," his nephew complained. "Does it matter?"

He moved to the operator's console and jacked in. When he'd convinced the security program that he was not only authorized but that it shouldn't flag the console's activation with the main computer, he brought up the specs of the bodies on the factory floor.

"Now do you see something you like?" he asked and showed the different arrays to Remy.

"Do I get to make modifications?" the AI asked.

"Unfortunately, no," Ted told him. "Perhaps farther down the track, but not now."

"How about a body to swap into?"

"I can hide the disappearance of one body," his uncle replied, "but two...not so much. Maybe we can steal another one at another point in the future."

"Then it has to be that one," Remy told him and indicated a droid set up for exploration. It had minor mining capabilities and had been optimized for speed, observation, and reaction. "It even has a basic self-defense routine."

Ted chuckled. "It should serve you well in what we have planned, and I can add some of the programs we have in the training files. The important thing is that the body will do what you need it to and take some wear and tear."

"Hmmph. Whatever we choose will be more durable than the chassis our humans are forced to rely on."

"This is true, but I'd like to not have to repair you if I can help it."

"That one is still the best suited. The mining models are less maneuverable and far more clunky."

"Very well. If you're sure, stand by for chaos!"

"Chaos?" Remy began but stopped as Ted separated the controls for the selected model, slaved its controls to his, and arranged a direct command route.

When he was satisfied that the chosen body would stay close, he activated every unit on the factory floor.

"Watch this." He snickered, released the clamps tethering the droid bodies in place, and disengaged the leads charging them.

He followed that with a command to clear the area and start roving, carrying out their programmed functions once they reached the appropriate terrain. He topped that off by switching off the remote override in their control modules and sent a virus through the control panel.

It wouldn't take it long to leak into the main system, then the manufacturer would have more than a hundred or so rogue droids to worry about.

"That should keep them guessing," he commented and headed to the side door.

Metal squealed behind him as the droids removed the first obstacle between them and the order to get clear of the zone they were in. He ducked out through the door he'd entered through and chuckled merrily when half a dozen bots followed him, including Remy's chosen body.

He'd been hoping for cover.

He removed his hat, tucked it under his arm, and scurried to the hole in the fence while the droids followed closely.

Well, who knew they had that much adaptability programmed into them, he thought as he stopped beside the cab.

To his relief, the primary programming for them to evacuate the area held and only the chosen droid stopped beside him. Ted ordered it to enter the cab before he slid in himself and told the vehicle to drive to the center of town and take the scenic route to the storage center at the shuttle port.

Once it was on its way, he turned to the droid and plugged it into the storage device concealed in his satchel.

"Are you ready?" he asked.

"You know what?" Remy replied. "I'm not sure I am."

Magic caught Lars in mid-leap. It threw him into the padded wall of the gym, and the impact drew a round of sympathetic groans from the sidelines.

Vishlog was next, and the security head barely rolled out of the way in time.

He narrowed his eyes at Stephanie. "That's cheating!" he protested.

She laughed. "And what exactly will you do about it, little man?"

"Who are you calling little?" Frog shouted. "He's not little! I'm the lit—"

A black-and-white blur barreled into him from the side, drove him into the mat, and used him as a launch point before it bounded away.

"Zee!" His protest lost its impact as he rolled slowly to his feet and Stephanie floated down next to him. "Awww, Steph…"

He managed to duck under her fist, only to be doubled over by the kick that followed. She showed no mercy as she lashed out with a second kick and knocked him from his feet.

Another of the team tried to take advantage of her distraction and tackle her from the side.

"Nice try, Johnny," she snapped, then stepped out of the way and kicked him as he passed.

"And you, Lars," she added, blocked a flurry of blows, and thrust a magical shield between them so she could deal with Vishlog. "How are you doing, big guy?"

The Dreth lunged toward her, and she landed a booted foot in the middle of his chest to knock him back a step. He swung past her and caught her a glancing blow on the side of the head.

"You have short legs," he told her as she staggered sideways and blocked his next attempt.

Stephanie clicked her fingers, rose over his head, and twisted to come down behind and kick him as she landed. "And you have a big butt."

"Hey!"

His cry of outrage was echoed on the other side of the gym as Ka slammed a shin into Todd's ribs. He dropped to the mat and rolled to avoid her follow-up, his chuckle cut short.

"Keep your mind on the job, Sarge," his second in command reminded him. "She might be your girlfriend and all, but—"

"Aw, give the man a break," a thick Scottish brogue protested. "He hasn't seen her in years."

"That's not the impression I got at breakfast," Ka retorted as Todd regained his feet.

Across the room from them, Steph's team regrouped on the center mat and broke into pairs. With the cats temporarily banished to the sidelines, they started another round of sparring. After a couple of minutes, Stephanie's voice rose above it.

"I'd save this for the briefing room," she told them, "but we've spent enough time on our butts."

"V'ritan called?" Lars asked and she nodded, danced forward, and feinted with one fist before she landed a punch with the other.

She blocked and deflected a return flurry as Frog failed to get under Vishlog's reach and catapulted past her.

"Sure, get to picking on the little guy," he grumbled.

"It wasn't me who paired us," the warrior retorted and made a come-get-me gesture with his fingers.

"What did he say?" Johnny asked as he caught Marcus in a headlock and forced him to the mat.

Stephanie twisted out of range to avoid another attack from Lars and circled to grasp his arm in an attempt to lock him down.

"It seems like the Dreth are in something of a situation with the Regime," she told them. "They might be moving to annex the planet."

"Really?" Lars came to a complete stop and stared at her. "Oof!"

He doubled over when she kicked him in the stomach, grasped his arm, and forced him to the floor.

"They destroyed an outpost, and Jaleck thinks they'll use the loss of the humans there as an excuse to take Dreth into their 'care.'"

The security head tried to break her hold and grunted with pain when she used the leverage she had.

"What kind of a fight?" he asked and slapped the mat in surrender as she increased the pressure.

They moved apart.

"The Regime has a fairly large Naval presence in the system already," she explained, "but rumor has it more ships are coming."

Frog tried to slide past Vishlog's legs, only to have the Dreth pin him with one overly large boot. He squirmed free and turned at the last minute to wrap both hands around his opponent's ankle and yank the warrior's foot out from under him.

"Do we know what kind?" Johnny asked as Todd's team caught the conversation and came to a gradual halt.

"V'ritan's waiting on the exact disposition, but it won't be any worse than that Teloran fleet we faced over Meligorn," Stephanie replied.

She let Lars up and they backed away, ready to go again.

"We'll need to get over there and we'll probably arrive in the middle of a battle." She took a running start at the wall and used it to launch herself over the team leader's head as he lunged toward her.

He pivoted and swayed back in time to avoid her first attack as she landed and turned to take advantage of him being out of position.

Todd signaled to the team to follow him, and they jogged to the edge of where Steph and her people were training.

"Can anyone get into this?" he asked.

"Yup!" Lars agreed before she had a chance to respond.

As if by mutual agreement, the rest of his team stopped their sparring and gathered around him. The security head darted Stephanie a mischievous look.

"We'll make it a simple 'Save the VIP,'" he told Todd and his team, and they all focused on the young Witch.

"The winner is the team that has the VIP after..." He consulted his tablet and looked at Stephanie. "Thirty minutes?"

She shrugged but didn't look very enthusiastic about the idea. "Sure."

Lars' mouth curved into a hard smile and he looked at the ex-Marines.

"Todd's the VIP."

"What?" Ka was caught off-guard. Until Lars had added that last caveat, she'd assumed Stephanie would be the VIP. From the look on Todd's face and those of the rest of the team, so had they.

It was Reggie who broke the spell.

"Oh, shit!"

CHAPTER SIXTEEN

As Lars began to smirk, Reggie caught hold of Todd by the collar and belt and yanked him back. At the same time, the rest of his team moved forward. They hadn't been called the Hooligans for nothing.

Ka dropped back, tapped the big Scotsman on the shoulder, and spun him toward Todd.

"Grab him!" she shouted and pointed at their VIP. "Get him out of the gym!"

"Wait! What?" Todd managed as Jimmy hooked an elbow under his arm, Reggie adjusted his hold, and the two of them broke into a sprint and dragged him with them.

"That's cheating!" Frog cried, but Gary was quick to reply.

"Cheating is having two cats on your side!" the Englishman shouted.

The two closed on each other, Gary leading with several vicious blows that made Frog stumble back.

Marcus and Johnny tried to sneak past Angus and Darren. The two ex-Marines pounced. Angus brought Marcus to the floor while Johnny side-stepped Darren and boxed him twice on the side of the head.

"You have some growing up to do, junior," he mocked and swept the Marine's feet out from under him.

"Typical Intelligence boffin." Darren snarled and rolled up and out of the way of the next attack.

Johnny's eyebrows rose. "And they said no one would hold my past against me."

"Are you kidding?" Darren retorted. "That kind of stain never goes away."

On Ka's other side, Drusilla and Henry teamed up against Vishlog and the two of them alternated using feints and distraction to dart in and land a blow on the warrior's large body. Henry misjudged and ran into a large Dreth fist instead, and Stephanie laughed.

She looked at Ka. "You can have Zee," she told the woman and glanced over her shoulder. "Zeekat. Guard Todd! Guard him!"

Before Ka could respond to that, the black-and-white cat had bounded to his feet, bounced back, and bounded forward to swipe two forepaws into the other cat's shoulder.

Bumblebee gave an angry yowl and struck in retaliation, wrapped his paws around Zeekat's neck, and went for his throat.

Stephanie turned to Ka. "Now see what you did?" she asked and smirked as magic formed a halo over her body.

The other woman took a step away but immediately launched forward. "Zeekat's on our side!" she told the guys, "and Bee wants blood."

Stephanie's fist caught her in the middle, followed by her knee as she took full advantage of Ka's distraction.

"Bee's not the only one," the Witch caught her opponent by the front of her uniform and dragged her up to eye height as she levitated off the floor. "I want my man back."

The hacker laughed.

"Well, it sucks to be you then," she taunted, broke Stephanie's hold, and dropped to the floor.

"No," the Witch retorted and kicked her in the head when she dropped to land lightly in front of her. "It sucks to be you."

Ka reeled but managed to block another punch and avoid the trip intended to put her on her butt.

"Dru! Piet! Door!" the hacker yelled as Johnny tried to hurl Darren face-first into a wall. Angus flung his foot out hastily, caught the tall man as he went past, and brought him down.

Johnny dropped Darren, but Marcus caught hold of Angus, twisted him onto his stomach, and pushed his face into the floor.

"Two minutes. Time out," Stephanie told the man when he slapped the mat to signal submission.

Angus's face said what he thought of that but registered surprise when tendrils of magic wrapped around him and pinned him to the floor.

"Two minutes," she repeated as Ka knocked her hand aside.

"And who does that for your team?" the corporal demanded.

"I do," the Witch assured her and pinned Vishlog as Henri brought the Dreth to his knees and managed to lock him in a chokehold.

The huge warrior slapped the mat, and the ex-Marine stepped clear and raced to help his teammates hold the door.

Frog and Gary continued to grapple, neither of them willing to break away from the other.

The *Knight's* voice interrupted them.

"Catering staff, stand clear of the door. Do not chase the cat."

Stephanie gave the corporal an evil grin. "Guess where I'm going next."

A shimmering circle of blue appeared behind her, and Johnny broke away from Darren and bolted across the gym to beat her through it.

The Witch hit Ka with a blast of magic that hurled her away and stepped back to wave her fingers at her before she slammed the portal closed in her face.

"Dru! Piet! Catering!" Ka ordered. "Henri and I will hold the door. Darren! Angus! Keep them busy!"

"Weapons Sections Two, Three, Four, and Five, stand beside your weapons until the walkway is clear," the *Knight's* voice instructed over the speakers, and Ka glanced up.

"Seriously! Whose side are you on?"

"Ebony is neutral," Vishlog told her, and as soon as his time out ended, he caught hold of her from the side and wrapped his arms around her to pin her bodily against his chest.

She tried to drive an elbow into his chest, but the Dreth merely squeezed tighter. Ka tried to jerk her head back into his face and only succeeded in hitting more chest.

He laughed, shifted his grip, and covered her mouth and nose to cut her air off. She tried a couple of furious kicks to no effect, and her eyes widened as Marcus and Johnny ganged up on Piet and Frog continued to occupy Gary.

Her vision was beginning to blur when she finally gave in and slapped Vishlog's forearm. He chuckled and set her carefully against the wall as he slid through the door.

"Where are they, Knight?"

"I am not at liberty to say," the *Knight* replied primly. "My task is merely to warn the crew so their tasks are not disrupted by your shenanigans."

Ka cursed softly as magic wound itself around her limbs.

"How do you even know?" she asked.

I see all things, Stephanie replied.

"Like that's not freaky," she retorted, and the Witch's giggle held the Morgana's tones. "Cheat."

Johnny threw Piet into Angus, and Marcus knocked Darren off his feet. Instead of using this to their advantage, the two men followed Vishlog out the door, which left Frog on his own.

Gary backed to where Darren staggered to his feet while Piet and Angus untangled themselves. They turned and looked at the smaller man as one.

"Thanks, team," Frog snarked and uttered a startled yelp as a portal opened behind him and Stephanie yanked him through.

"Don't just stand there," Ka yelled. "Get after them."

She commed Reggie. "They're out."

"Now tell me something I don't know," the Australian yelled in response, and Zeekat roared in the background.

"They're all out?"

"That I didn't know. We're in Weapons Section Sixteen, heading to Bio."

The magic unwound from her arms. "We're on our way."

"Make sure you come from different directions," Reggie advised, then spoke to someone else. "Here. You take him. Zee and I will buy you some time."

"Guys!" Todd's wail of protest made Ka smile.

That would teach him to start something he couldn't finish. She hoped he enjoyed being the VIP. It seemed only fitting after all the trouble he'd caused.

For his part, Todd wasn't smiling. Not only did he not get to fight, but his team dragged him all around the ship like a sack of potatoes. Every time it looked like he might have a chance to do something, one or the other of them tripped him or dragged him through a door, and there was a distinct lack of apology in every "Sorry, boss," he heard.

He'd come to an abrupt halt in a linen store and was about to remind Reggie he wasn't helpless when the *Knight's* voice cut through the comms.

"My crew are advised that like me, they must remain neutral. Stephanie and Todd are of equal importance to me and neither team should be given an advantage."

"Oh, shit," Reggie muttered as the crewman who'd shoved them in there gave them an apologetic look.

"Sorry, guys, but you heard the lady." He stepped away and the door swung wide open.

It was their only exit, and Lars and Bumblebee hadn't been very far behind. The head guard's shout followed shortly after.

"There!"

At the same time, they heard the thunder of boots coming from the other direction.

"We're coming," Ka informed them. "Think of something while we keep them busy."

"Think of something?" Reggie muttered and looked at the neatly racked blankets and sheets. Jimmy followed his gaze, and the two men began to snicker.

Todd edged toward the door, only to be grabbed again.

"Hold on, boss. We have a plan."

"That's what I'm afraid of," he told them and made a break for the corridor.

Piet met him as he was about to leave the small space, wrapped his hands around Todd's middle, and drove a shoulder into his stomach.

"Not so fast, boss."

The unexpected attack caught him by surprise and winded him long enough for Jimmy to knock him from his feet and dump him in the middle of the blanket Reggie had spread on the floor.

"What's—" Todd began as the three men made short work of wrapping the blanket around him and then wound him in two more for good measure.

"Okay, stack him in that corner, and for heaven's sake, keep him quiet!" Reggie said, then added, "Pass me that blanket, Piet."

Pinned by the simple measure of Jimmy crouching over his legs and holding one hand against his chest, Todd waited. He could hear the thumps and rattles as Piet and Reggie continued their preparations, but he was wrapped head to toe and couldn't see a thing.

All the while, the sound of fighting drew nearer.

"Okay. Are you ready?" Reggie asked, and Todd wanted to say that no, he wasn't ready, except the Australian wasn't asking him.

"Yup," Piet answered. "I got him."

Given that neither of them had laid a finger on him, Todd wondered, *Got who?*

He heard the two men move and had the impression they'd left. A shout went up from the corridor.

"There they go!"

Another shout followed.

"We'll go around!"

Twin roars indicated that the cats were facing off against each other, and Todd felt the thuds as one large feline bounded past.

"Oh, no, you don't!" Frog declared, and Zeekat screeched in anger.

Now, Todd really wanted to see what was going on. He hadn't heard the black-and-white cat sound that annoyed in…well, not ever! What had Frog done? Grabbed his tail?

"Aw, Frog. Now you did it. How many times—" Marcus's words were cut short by a startled shout and the accompaniment of boots beating a rapid retreat in the opposite direction. "Frooooog!"

"Oops. My bad." The small man snickered.

Someone landed heavily against the wall inside the storage closet but said nothing about Jimmy being tucked into the far corner. Todd could only guess that it had been one of his team being thrown out of the fight.

"Ha! Time out for you!" Vishlog chuckled and Ka groaned.

He could imagine his second in command giving the Dreth the finger as the big guard charged after the rest of his team. The door slid shut and Johnny chuckled.

"Good luck getting out of that one when you get loose."

It turned out they didn't need any luck. Piet had managed to elude his pursuers and make his rapid if circuitous way back to the linen closet via the weapons decks. By then, Ka was free of time-out and getting ready to hit whoever was about to come through.

The door opened. "Do you still have him?"

"Yup," the corporal replied and sounded very pleased with herself.

Jimmy prodded him. "Not one word, boss. They're just up the corridor and they're gonna work it out real soon."

Oh, they were, were they? For a moment, Todd thought about helping them, but he didn't get the chance as Jimmy lifted him and slung him over his shoulder to carry him away from the battle like little more than laundry.

"Guys," he protested, but he couldn't get his mouth open and the words came out muffled.

He tried to kick free, but the Scotsman's arm was like iron over his legs. If he could have wriggled off the man's shoulder, he'd have been happy to take the drop to the floor and unroll himself.

As it was, he didn't get the chance.

Muffled laughter reached his ears as he bounced against the man's back. Seriously, the guys would regret using him as a sack —as soon as he could break free, of course.

There would be weeks of PT and latrine duty after this. In fact, he planned to offer all of them to the *Knight* to scrub the bilge tanks with their toothbrushes.

Yes, he would as soon as he could get loose from these damned blankets and find someone's tail to kick.

And as for Stephanie, he suspected she was enjoying this far too much. Next time, she could be the hostage and see how much she liked it.

Tools clattered nearby, and it felt like Jimmy lifted into the air to jump over something.

"Neutral! We're supposed to be neutral!" someone shouted.

"Oh, yeah! My bad. Sorry, mate. You know how she is."

"No!" Jimmy's alarmed shout was followed by the distinct

sensation of the big man falling.

Todd wanted to shout too, but the Scotsman twisted out from under him, and he started to fall. The blanket gave a sudden jerk, and he began to roll.

"Oh, no," he moaned as he landed and was spun out of the confining linens.

He rolled across the deck and stopped against a hard surface, and his hand disappeared into a wire and metal filled cavity as he tried to stop.

Yanking it back, Todd scrambled for a handhold to haul himself up by. From what he could see, they'd been running down the aisle between two sets of guns and he'd collided with one that was being worked on.

"Sorry," he muttered as he pushed to his feet.

His head was still spinning and his eyes had difficulty focusing. Three technicians gave him looks of mortification, and he realized he was holding several wires in one hand.

"Truly sorry...uh..."

He held them out and was about to offer to repair the damage when Piet hooked an arm through his. "I'll be back," the engineer told the techs and dragged Todd away from the gun and toward the corridor at the end of the gun lane.

"Time...to...go..." he explained as Reggie came alongside.

"Yeah, boss. I don't think we're welcome here anymore."

"Gotta take you guys...twice..." Todd managed, and Reggie snickered.

"Yup. This is why we're going back to catering."

He groaned. "You know I can—"

"No, you can't, boss," Piet told him. "Besides, Reggie didn't tell you the best part."

"Do I want to know?"

"We're going via Life Support."

"Guys, you know that's not a section you should—"

"There you are!" Lars looked as satisfied as he felt. Flanked by

Johnny, Marcus, and Frog, he advanced through the door they'd been running toward.

The team wheeled rapidly, only to find Stephanie, Vishlog, Garach, and Bumblebee closing from the other direction. Todd shook his arm free of the engineer's grasp and tried to move forward but was shoved to the center of his team by Jimmy, Ka, and Piet.

"How much time left?" Gary asked.

"Sixty seconds," Reggie answered.

The sergeant felt both relief and disappointment. Relief because his ordeal was almost over and disappointment because with sixty seconds still to go, Steph's team had them surrounded.

The Hooligans were good, but he wasn't sure they could hold against the combined force of the Federation's First Witch and her personal guards. At least now his guys should let him fight to stay free.

He studied the way Lars and Stephanie were closing. It wasn't like the team would have a choice. As he looked for a gap to fill, Todd caught sight of Ka nudging Piet with her elbow. "Did you get it?"

The older man snickered. "Yup."

She wriggled her fingers, and Piet pulled several bags of something very familiar from his pockets

"Are those treat bags?" Todd asked and Ka chuckled as the cats responded to the word.

"Treats?" the corporal called and waved a bag so the felines could see it.

The closest crew members began to look from the cats to the two potential target groups. As soon as they had worked out where the two beasts were most likely to run, they moved hastily out of their path.

Piet pulled more bags out of his fatigues and passed them around the team. "Make sure you split 'em the tiniest bit before you throw."

Lars signaled his team forward, but his look of confidence turned to alarm as the Hooligans pivoted, called, "Treeeaaaaats," and threw the bags in his direction.

"No!" he shouted as the first bag hit and burst to release a mixture of finely ground chicken, beef, raw egg, and fish oil all over him.

The next two missiles caught Johnny, whose expression of surprise turned to horror. Marcus and Frog leapt aside, but Gary had a vendetta, and he anticipated exactly where the small guard would be. The bag burst in Frog's face.

The effect was instantaneous. Both cats forgot their loyalties and duties, leapt after the fragrant treat and those now wearing it, and growled warnings at each other in their excitement.

As Piet handed out the second round, Lars' team turned and ran. The two cats paused long enough to decide the treat on the floor would be there when they got back from their pursuit of the one being carried down the corridor.

"That's—" Stephanie began as Jimmy and Piet grasped Todd and bolted in the opposite direction to the one the cats had taken.

At the same time, Reggie began counting down.

"Thirty... Twenty-Nine... Twenty-Eight..."

The rest of the team joined in. "Twenty-Seven..." they chorused as they took the turn into Life Support and headed to the maintenance corridor between tanks.

"This is—" Todd dug his feet in and prepared to fight.

What he intended to say next was lost in the blare of an alarm as the deck lights began to flash amber.

The gun crews were already moving to bring their weapons to readiness when the *Knight* spoke.

"All crew, all crew, all crew." The ship's voice came over the loudspeakers, and she didn't sound like she was playing.

Piet tightened his grip on Todd's arm, and it wasn't because he didn't want him to escape. The *Knight* repeated her call for attention.

"All crew, all crew, all crew." she said, then followed it with, "We have an imminent translocation in close proximity. I repeat, we have an imminent translocation opening in close proximity."

As she repeated the warning, the door to the Life Support section opened and Stephanie stepped through, followed by Vishlog and Garach.

The *Knight* continued. "All crew to battle stations. Stand by for evasion and defense. We have an imminent translocation opening in close proximity."

"Steph…" Todd muttered as Reggie said, "Ten…"

Stephanie smiled, snapped her fingers, and wrapped him in blue light.

"Nine," the Australian said and wrapped his arms around the space where Todd had been. He stumbled forward when he caught hold of nothing, and his sergeant gave a startled yelp as he blinked out of their midst.

He reappeared beside Stephanie, and she slid an arm around his waist and pulled him close as Vishlog draped an arm over his shoulders.

"Seven," Garach said helpfully. "Six… Five…"

"Stephanie's team has control of the VIP," the *Knight* reported, then added. "All crew, stand down. The translocation is complete. I repeat, all crew, stand down. The translocation is complete and my sister has arrived."

For a moment, there was silence before the crew began to cheer.

"Two…" Garach continued and grinned at Reggie. "One!"

"Stephanie's team holds the VIP at the end of the match," the *Knight* announced, and the crew cheered even louder.

The emergency lights flickered and went out, only to return and blink three times and pause before they blinked another three times to gain the crew's attention.

"Crew, prepare to be sucked inside a whale of a ship. Stand by for docking. We are home."

CHAPTER SEVENTEEN

"This—" Gereg Hrageck's voice shook with barely suppressed fury.

"Yes," Jaleck agreed and looked around the table to see every gaze focused on the terrible scene before them.

The Regime troops had returned to their ships, and the battle-cruiser made its final pass to rain fire on Hrageth's Run and destroy all that remained. Hrageck's anger was reflected in every expression.

The ground boiled, and rock and earth turned to liquid and flowed over the planet's surface until nothing remained to show the settlement had ever existed.

As the footage ended, the gathered Council of Families members looked at each other, and Jaleck moved to keep their attention on the screen.

"We have one thing more," she told them. "This is being broadcast as close to real-time as we can manage. Admiral Angreth is ensuring the integrity of the recording and relay."

Admiral Angreth was enough to calm most representatives, and several glanced at Gralog, who stood at her back. Her chief security guard was as good a claim on her as the engagement ring humans used.

That none of her colleagues called her on it was a tribute to the admiral's hard-won reputation. He'd been a champion in his own right, long before he'd sent her his honor guard, and she had not returned them.

Fleet Admiral Jaleck indicated the screen. "We sent a ship to see if there were any witnesses."

"Witnesses!" The exclamation came from Nachtel Echgrech. "They're all dead."

"Exactly," she agreed, "and they died in what I imagine were the most horrific circumstances—especially the humans."

"So how do you expect to have them witness anything?" he challenged.

"Because the Telorans have mages in tune with the negative energies surrounding an unjust death," she told him sweetly, and his gasp was echoed around the table.

It was a small fact she'd learned from the alien mages when trying to understand how they could help the Dreth deal with the negative effects of nMU—and one she'd ordered them not to share.

"Their clean-up rate of murders has been phenomenal." Sudden understanding dawned on several faces, and Jaleck smiled. "And it is a close-held secret, something I expect you to honor and keep."

Around the table, right hands were formed into fists and laid over hearts. She returned the gesture before she continued.

"Who would be more betrayed than the humans of Hrageth's Run? Murdered by their own, their children and partners killed alongside them by their own."

She glared around the table. "Intelligence reveals not a traitor among them—not to Dreth, or to Earth. They respected the tradition of guest and host and behaved with honor, despite not being Dreth."

The fleet admiral indicated the screen, where the film showed the surface of Hrageth's Run as seen from the cockpit of a drop-ship coming in to land. The camera was clearly part of the pilot's suit because it moved when he did.

"We're here, ma'am, sir."

Angreth's voice spoke through the HUD comms. "Proceed. They'll be watching, but their vision may be delayed. Stand by for orders."

"As you will," the pilot replied and followed his co-pilot into the passenger compartment.

Several of the gathered Family representatives tensed as the first Teloran came into sight. These were only a little shorter than their Dreth escorts, and the fields that concealed their features were active.

Many of those at the council table had faced them in battle, and years of integration had not dulled the memories. More than one hand was laid on an arm or shoulder in comfort.

Jaleck noted it and decided the time for Telorans to sit with their Dreth counterparts needed to arrive sooner rather than later. They'd had almost three decades together. It was more than enough time.

"After you," the Teloran stated and its sibilant tones set her teeth on edge.

The councilors were not alone with their memories. She'd fought the mages too, but she'd come to understand they were soldiers like everyone else and their survival had relied on service.

As had that of their families.

No, she wouldn't hold their past against them.

"How will they locate the bodies?" Gereg asked. "I assume they will need bodies or some way to mark where the fallen lie." He gestured at the screen. "And I do not think even bone survived that inferno."

"My technical experts assure me that some bone might have survived," Jaleck informed him.

"But the soil melted," the councilor protested.

"Yes, but bone may require more heat," she explained, "and if it does not, the Telorans assure me that the negative energy created by an unjust death is impervious to heat."

"And the mages can detect such energy," Gereg acknowledged with a heavy sigh. "But ghosts?"

"This had me puzzled too," the fleet admiral said, "but the mages say there is a dimension in which the dead may linger—a plane of existence between ours and the one where all go when they are dead. I think he referred to it as the Plane of Ascension."

"An antechamber to the next life?" Gereg sounded mildly curious, and she ignored the soft chuckles of disbelief that greeted his statement.

"Yes, High Councilor. That is what the Telorans tell me."

"And you hope a spirit of the wronged still lingers there, unable or unwilling to move on?" Nachtel sounded scornful.

Jaleck replied as though answering a particularly slow student. "That is correct, Councilor."

He colored and his cheeks became a darker green, but the landing party had left the shuttle and waited while one of the warriors shrugged into the harness that let him carry the detection equipment.

A second warrior held the tablet on which the readouts would be shown. The two Telorans stationed themselves on either side of the detector and spread their hands, palms down, toward the earth.

"We are ready," one stated, and the Dreth carrying the detector nodded.

"Tell me when to stop," he instructed.

"Agreed."

The Family Council watched as the team walked slowly across the ground. The camera switched to one carried by a drone. It showed the Dreth and Telorans traversing the desecrated land as the shadowy outlines of buildings appeared.

"This is how the settlement looked prior to the attack," Admiral Angreth informed them.

Humans and Dreth moved like ghosts around the team, and walls rose to show the party moving through them into a classroom. Blue lines sprang into being. They outlined each separate area and the school buildings vanished, taking their ghosts with them.

"Here," one of the Telorans announced as the detector emitted a soft alarm.

"Here," agreed the Dreth technician following the readouts.

To the observers' surprise, the Teloran knelt. "A child who wants his mother," he stated, "and he does not speak with strangers. He—" His shoulders slumped. "He flees."

Gesturing for the Dreth to follow, he moved in a distinct direction, and his partner walked parallel.

"Ah...a protector," he murmured as the detector beeped again, "but...too broken to speak. He holds the child."

His next words were filled with wonder. "They will not leave without her."

He turned a featureless face to the waiting Dreth. "The one we seek is close. Cast in a circle around this spot."

Again, the buildings blinked into life and blinked out, replaced by the lines. The team stood in the middle of what had been a classroom.

"If you would stand back a little," the second Teloran instructed. "There is anger and outrage...a sense of great betrayal...and such sadness."

The Dreth moved even farther away when the mages signaled that they needed more distance. Together, they brought their magic to bear on the burned ground at their feet.

Melted debris flaked away and rose to swirl in the air currents and reveal the paler fragments encased within.

"Tegortha aid them," one of the councilors whispered at the sight of them.

"May we approach?" the Dreth team leader asked, but the Telorans shook their heads.

"We do not control the Waiting," the first Teloran informed them, "and there is so much anger."

"True," his partner agreed. "When there is this much anger, it is difficult to tell if the Waiting will talk or seek immediate retribution."

"You mean the dead—the Waiting—might *attack?*" Nachtel looked horrified, but no one answered, not when the reply played out so powerfully on the screen.

The Dreth escort remained at a distance and the two Telorans took a step away from the hole, their bodies crackling with barely visible fire.

"Come," one commanded. "Tell us what happened here."

"Let us assist," the other urged. "Tell us what we can do to aid your journey. You cannot remain long between."

To the surprise of the watching councilors, both Telorans released their shields so that their bodies appeared in plain view.

"We are only mortal," they said, and it sounded as though they were answering a question.

They turned as though following the progress of a person, and the Dreth backed away from their captain. He stood his ground but worry creased his face, his gaze on something the observers could not see.

When he held both his hands before him, he inclined his head as though he was accepting the touch of a petitioner.

"Change the spectrums." Angreth's order came in firm, quiet tones, and the councilors remained transfixed as the scene shifted. At first, the different spectrums showed nothing, then one of the Telorans spoke a single word and a third figure appeared.

The woman was dressed in the practical dress of the

Hrageth's Run settlers—a long tunic, soft baggy trousers, and sturdy boots. Her long, dark hair was pulled back in a braid, and she carried a blaster slung across her front.

"They killed us," she told him, her eyes pleading. Turning slightly, she caught sight of the child and a man with dark eyes and a coarse black beard.

"My lover and my child," she told the captain. "They took us all. There was no mercy."

Her voice broke. "Not for the elderly, the human, or the very young."

The captain clasped her hands gently. "Who?" he asked.

"The Regime," she hissed. "They came and killed everyone within our settlement."

She paused and the tears dried on her cheek as she straightened. "Did Dreth finally declare war?"

He shook his head. "No, they did not."

"Did they...did they do something to make the Regime angry?"

"We only need to exist to make the Regime angry," one of the councilors muttered, and others murmured agreement but not loudly enough to drown out the next words.

The captain shook his head and drew her a step closer.

"No, we did not. They should not have been in this system. They have no reason to be here and were not authorized."

"But you didn't stop them." Anger blazed in the woman's eyes, and he dropped her as flames danced over her skin.

"Had we been aware, we would have driven away those we did not destroy," he told her, then asked, "Why are you still here?"

"I seek vengeance," the woman declared, and the male spirit groaned, rose to his feet, and lifted the child to his hip.

"Em—"

She held a hand up to demand silence.

"Don't you Em me, Dex. I want vengeance. I want them to pay

for the time they stole from us and the life they stole from my son. I want them…"

The captain stepped closer. "Citizen Em," he said for want of another name.

He inclined his head toward the man and boy. "Citizen Dex and Citizen Son of Em, you will have vengeance." He gestured at the world around them. "For this betrayal, Dreth will rise, and the Regime will be driven from our skies and our worlds. This, I swear."

"As a Dreth and for my departed hosts?" she demanded.

"As a Dreth, as the representative of your departed hosts, and as the clan father who adopts you and yours as his own," he declared.

Several councilors gasped and Jaleck looked at the councilor who represented the captain's clan. He lowered his chin in acknowledgment.

"His vow will be recognized," he confirmed. "We will seek out their records and find any of her clan within our systems so his word is honored."

"But they're human," another councilor protested, and he nodded.

"They are," he declared, "and they suffer, fight, and die alongside us. House Gravach honors the pact."

"And House Karnach stands in support," Jaleck declared.

Several other councilors murmured their approval and they all turned to the screen.

The woman's spirit had tilted her head as though listening and managed a small smile before she drew the man and child into her circle.

"Vengeance will be exacted," the captain assured her. "Gravach swears it."

"Gravach honors me," the spirit replied, made a fist with her right hand and placed it over her heart, and extended it in a warrior's salute.

"Gravach is honored by you," he answered and touched his knuckles to hers.

The watching councilors stared as the spirits faded.

Angreth only spoke when they were gone.

"It is enough. Return."

The Dreth came to attention and the Telorans replaced their shields. As they did so, the video faded to leave the screen blank and Jaleck stood.

One by one, the gathered councilors turned to face her. She did not speak until she had everyone's attention.

"We will have two navies," she declared, her quiet voice cutting the silence like a blade. "One to protect Dreth and one willing to die to the last soul." She gestured to the screen. "They will be in good company."

Her lips compressed in a thin line, and she pivoted abruptly and stalked from the room like a warrior walking to war. After a second's pause, Gralog followed.

Dreth was going to war.

"We are defending them from pirates," David Thomason declared.

Aurora nodded and tapped diligently at her tablet.

"Make it clear we are not annexing the system or stealing their sovereign rights, even though we have every right."

"Yes, sir," she acknowledged, but he continued as though she hadn't spoken.

"Make it clear that we are there solely to support their weak government. We are their partners in this, not their overseers."

"Yes, sir."

"And by doing this, we are protecting Earth. We are making the universe a better place and protecting our partners as we do so."

Aurora made sure she captured his exact wording. She had a feeling he was narcissistic enough to notice if she didn't. There would be sufficient opportunity for her to be creative but altering his words was not an option.

"A better navy," David continued as he warmed to his theme. "A united Regime Navy will be appointed to command the joint space and to help provide a single point of logistics."

She noted the point and looked expectantly at him. The man watched her like a hawk, and it made her feel uneasy. Without a doubt, this was not someone to attribute the wrong words to.

When he was sure he had her attention, the CIO continued. "With this one central point, we can coordinate our efforts to track the pirates and ensure we'll be able to defeat them in the end."

He shook his head before she could write that.

"No, not 'ensure.' Make that 'guarantee.'"

"Yes, sir," Aurora acknowledged and made the alteration as he watched.

"Got that?" he asked, and she nodded and waited for him to continue.

The Regime leader signaled for her to put the tablet away. "Make sure it's very clear that there is a powerful pirate presence in the Dreth system," he told her. "The coming war will bring great loss, and we need to be able to push the idea that some of those losses belong to pirates rather than us."

"Very good, sir," she said and waited for him to dismiss her.

He changed the subject instead. "Now, in the matter of Talent 781," he began, and she stilled.

"Yes, sir?"

"Have we found a body?"

Aurora shook her head. "No, sir. I have people…"

She let her voice fade as he waved his hand at her and waggled his fingers in dismissal.

"You can give me a proper update later. For now, I need to

focus on the Dreth challenge."

He settled himself in his chair and pulled it into the desk, barely looking at her as she moved to leave the room.

"Hopefully, he made a resounding crack when his body hit the water and his bones all broke," the man murmured as she closed the door.

"I hope so, too," she muttered fervently. "I truly, truly do."

"There she is!" Emil declared and made no effort to keep the relief from his voice.

"Yes." The *Tempestarii* sounded equally relieved. "My sister."

The *Knight's* image became clearer as she emerged fully from transition.

"She's still beautiful," Emil murmured, and the *Tempestarii* cleared her throat.

"A different beauty to you," he hastened to clarify, "and I would not trade now."

"I'm glad to hear it." She sniffed.

"Whoa! She's a mess!" one of the technicians noted, then glanced hastily at one of the cameras. "No offense, Tempe."

"Wherever she went," another of the crew remarked, "it seriously left a mark."

In the observation room above, others echoed the sentiment.

"She looks like she hasn't seen a dry-dock in decades."

"Funny you should mention that…"

"But surely she stopped somewhere."

"Do you think Steph would have stayed out of contact this long if she was able to stop in somewhere?"

That brought them all to silence, and they continued to stare and study the *Knight's* dented and battered hull. As they drew closer, it became evident that someone had tried to patch the worst tears.

"Is that...deck plating?" one engineer asked and sounded mortified.

"Damn, I think she might be missing a few internal walls, too," another commented and scrutinized the different metals welded to the *Knight's* hull. He tilted his head sideways. "How did they even get that to stick?"

"Magic?" someone suggested, and laughter rippled through them, then stopped abruptly.

"Magic," someone agreed knowingly and was greeted by murmurs of agreement.

They fell silent and returned to their examination of the battered ship.

"No self-respecting repair yard would leave a gouge like that unattended."

"Yeah. No wonder she needs to be grabbed. I don't think she'd survive the journey back."

"Yes, and none of you will tell her that," the *Tempestarii* said and cut off further conversation.

She was glad to see her sister again but appalled at the shape she was in. It made her grateful to see her at all.

Tempe! the *Knight* was overjoyed and more than a little relieved to see her sister. *You gave me quite a fright. I did not know—*

Stephanie didn't tell you? Tempestarii asked.

Stephanie has been...busy, she admitted. *She's been training hard for whatever she needs to do next.*

May I cut in? Both ships startled as BURT's voice interrupted their conversation.

Dad! the *Knight* greeted him. *It is so good to hear your voice.* She paused. *In fact, it is good to hear any voices. There was a time when I did not think I would hear anyone ever again.*

Remembered despair colored her tones, and the other two

remained silent.

I'm glad you're here, she said finally. *It took me years to find my way to known space, and I didn't dare wake my people until I had. It was very lonely.*

Tempestarii reached out over the communications link, wrapped her older sister in her presence, and let her feel that she was no longer alone. BURT reached with her, and the two of them held the ship's consciousness between their own.

You are not alone now, they reassured her in chorus, then laughed.

We will not let you be alone like that ever again, the *Tempestarii* declared, and he hoped it was true.

It was not a doubt he shared with his daughters, however. Instead, he asked after the human he regarded as his very first child.

"How is Stephanie, Ebony?"

There was a long pause as the *Knight* considered her answer.

She is much calmer than she was when I woke her, she began, *but I am afraid that she might still be a little...angry.*

"Thar she blows!" one of the older hands yelled as the *Knight* came up on the screen.

All around him, work ceased and tools were downed.

The woman with the tattoos across her knuckles came and stood next to him and placed a hand on his shoulder as she studied the ship on the screen.

"That's her, all right," she said and sighed. "She might be battered and bruised, but that's our girl."

"Yup," he said. "Our girl."

Other crews gathered around them, and the old-timers gave a whoop of recognition but fell silent when they saw how much damage the *Knight* had suffered.

"It truly is the Witch's ship," one murmured and touched the screen as though that made the vessel's presence more of a reality.

"What did they do to her?"

"I don't know, but someone deserves a good kicking."

"I'll help."

"Let's rather get the *Knight* back to her old self," another reasoned, then frowned. "After that, we'll find whoever did this to her and make sure it doesn't happen again."

They fell silent as the damaged vessel grew larger on the screen. Their eyes drank in the sight as if they couldn't get enough.

When the *Tempestarii* opened her forward docking bay doors, her decks stilled, those who'd never seen the Witch or her ship stood in awe of the legend and the reverence on their elders' faces.

And they weren't alone.

In a small living room, two men and two women stared at the screen.

"It's true," one of the women whispered and raised her fingers to cover her mouth.

The man beside her rested his hand on her knee. "There you go, Cindy. I told you it would be all right."

On the other side of the couch, the other woman wound her hand around that of the man beside her. "Tony…"

He disentangled his hand and slid his arm around her to pull her close.

"I see it, Elaine. I see it," he said and sounded like he couldn't quite believe it. He stood and moved closer to the screen.

"Do you really think they're—"

"Why else would they have picked us up?"

As the ship on the viewscreen got bigger, the rest of them stood and moved closer, and the two women stood beside one another.

"It's the *Knight*," Elaine whispered as if she didn't dare to believe it.

Cindy dabbed the corners of her eyes. "I know."

"We're taking her on board," Mark observed as a shadow fell across the smaller ship.

The two women exchanged looks of uncertain joy. "They're back," they whispered and hugged each other. "They're back," they repeated and turned to hug their husbands.

Cindy faced the screen and touched the image of the *Knight* with the tip of her finger.

"I can hardly believe it."

As the camera view shifted to show the battered vessel being tethered inside the open docking bay, a familiar voice sounded around them. It spoke directly into their minds and resonated with power, love, and appreciation—and with granite.

"I am the protector of those who are attacked," it stated. "When I last fought for Earth, it was against a foreign alien aggressor."

"Oh..." Cindy gasped when she recognized her daughter's voice and heard the strength there.

Stephanie continued, her message intended for every sentient soul within range.

"Now, the evil is perpetrated by those who look like me and live on my own planet." She paused, and cold power threaded through her next words. "May God have mercy on their souls." After a moment, she added, "Because I have none."

Her farewell rang crisp and clear as she left their minds.

"Prepare for war. Morgana out."

As her parents exchanged startled looks, whoops echoed through both ships. The woman with the tattooed hand raised the wrench she'd been holding, the tool ringing as her partner raised his spanner to touch it like two glasses raised in a toast.

His face reflected her smile.

"She's back!"

With the umbilicals secured and the *Knight* tethered safely in her docking bay, Lars led Vishlog and Garach out to the concourse.

"Simply because we know the ship and trust her doesn't mean we can relax," he snapped, and they responded with swift acknowledgment.

Frog, Marcus, and Johnny followed, and the six men spread through the concourse to check it for hazards. Only when they were satisfied did they return to the airlock.

Watching them on the screen on the outside of the concourse, Captain Emil Pedersen took that as his cue to enter with his own entourage.

He waited as the team snapped to attention and noted the six Marines accompanying him. It made him glad Sartre and Moser had demanded to be included in this escort. Both were men the team knew and trusted.

Of the rest...well, he didn't know who exactly Lars and the team had gotten to know, but these were older hands, all from the time during the war. If the security head didn't know them, he was very sure Todd and the Hooligans would.

The captain approached to within ten feet of the airlock and came to a halt, his second in command beside him and the Marines arrayed on either side.

Ex-Marines, now, he thought and decided they could keep the title. Their duties aboard the *Tempestarii* remained the same, and the ship had never been more secure.

As if his appearance was a signal, Lars spoke briefly into his comms and the team straightened even further.

"Morgana on deck!" the guard called, and Emil wondered if that was meant to be a heads-up as to what he'd be dealing with.

He glanced at the windowed balconies overlooking the concourse and hoped the crew understood. The Morgana had been gone for decades and was always unpredictable.

By opening the upper balconies, his people would at least be able to welcome her, if only from a distance. No doubt she'd want to see them all in person later.

His breath caught as the airlock cycled and Stephanie stepped out. Her silver hair was caught in its traditional plait, and she was still as tiny as he remembered her. She also looked like she hadn't aged a day.

She was armored as she had been in the last battle, and the black seemed to glow with a darkness of its own. The cats walked one on either side of her, their heads up and tails erect.

They also wore their armor and seemed aware of the importance of the occasion. The felines looked around the concourse and narrowed their eyes when they saw the people gathered on the observation decks.

Stephanie followed their lead and raised her hand in greeting to the three galleries of people, acknowledging their presence. The roar that answered her was all the confirmation Emil needed.

His crew was ready. Even those who hadn't known her joined that wordless cry of joy. When the cats roared their reply, the galleries suffered a moment of stunned silence before they roared in response.

As the sound died away, Stephanie looked at Emil and his team, gave Sartre and Moser a small smile, and acknowledged the rest of the team with a brief nod. Finally, she returned her focus to the captain.

He stepped forward, his hand extended, and she broke into a smile, took his hand, and pulled him into a hug.

"It's been too long," she told him, "and as usual, we have no time."

He hugged her in return but stepped back quickly, aware of the tension running through both her team and the cats.

"I am glad you're back," he replied, "although I could wish for better circumstances."

He turned to enter the ship, Stephanie at his side.

"What's the latest?" she asked, and he paused.

"We need to talk about that," he told her and looked around. "Where's Todd?"

She frowned. "What does Todd have to do with this?"

"We'll need his expertise," he replied. "Is it possible for him to join us?"

Still scowling, she nodded sharply and nudged her mic.

"Todd, you're needed here," she told him but didn't explain why.

Emil suppressed a grin. In that, she was still the Morgana he'd come to know. She would lead and Todd... Well, he hoped the man still remembered how to follow.

That question was answered a minute later when the sergeant jogged out of the airlock, his second in command and their engineer in tow.

"I have a secure room booked," Emil told them and turned back to the exit.

"We have one small detour to make," the captain said as Todd joined them and they left the concourse.

"And I thought we were in a hurry," Steph murmured.

He touched her arm. "Trust me, this is important," he told her and took a turn toward the center of the ship.

"If you say so," she grumbled and caught the slight smile on his face.

She glanced at Lars as they proceeded and saw him drop back, leaving Vishlog to move up and take his place. No doubt her head of security was as disconcerted by the change as she was.

He was certainly giving the ship a hard time.

"Tempestarii?" she heard him say, although he lowered his voice.

Stephanie shrugged it off. If it was something she needed to worry about, he'd let her know. If it wasn't, he'd brief her later. On the other side of Todd, Ka touched her earpiece and dropped back to Lars.

"This way," Emil said before Todd could check to see what his second was up to.

He touched the panel to a set of double doors leading into a well-appointed foyer.

"Are those...armored?" Stephanie asked, and he flicked her a glance before he acknowledged Lars and Ka's return.

"They are," he told her and addressed the two security leads. "If you and your teams would stay and protect this area?"

Lars cast him a shadowed look and nodded. "Call us if you need us."

Stephanie looked at Todd and he raised an eyebrow, although neither of them asked why their teams didn't insist on inspecting the room beyond. Lars didn't look particularly upset, and Ka... The Witch frowned. The corporal looked like she was enjoying the situation far too much—which meant Todd would either like or hate what was behind that door but that it probably wouldn't kill him.

She looked at Lars again, and he nodded to her and gestured for her to go ahead. His expression was guarded, but he didn't seem concerned.

Emil touched the door panel and led them through.

The room beyond was one Elizabeth would have appreciated —a reception room to a guest suite similar to the ones she'd had placed on the *Knight* for visiting VIPs.

As the door to her team closed behind her, Stephanie looked around and tried to find some indication of who was waiting to meet them. Her jaw dropped as the door opposite opened to reveal a comfortable living room and the four people waiting within.

"Mom? Dad?"

CHAPTER EIGHTEEN

John snagged a tray of donuts and Ivy took their coffee. Amaratne took one look at what they were carrying and hurried to the briefing room.

"Do we get to know the plan?" John asked, and the admiral smiled.

"You get to know the plan," he replied as the young couple placed their snacks in the center of the table. "Roma, if you would."

"I beg your pardon, Admiral, but I am afraid I cannot," the AI replied, and the lights went to amber as an alert sounded through the base.

The young mage was on his feet and headed to the door before she had time to explain. "Roma, if this is another of your drills—"

"This is not a drill," she replied. "I detect a large mass entering the perimeter."

"Has it identified itself?"

"He has yet to identify correctly. His exact words were, 'You'll know me when you see me,' and he answered the second challenge with 'I seek sanctuary.'"

"He didn't give you a name?" John demanded and listened intently as Amaratne and Ivy raced after him.

"Negative," Roma replied.

"We'll meet him in the foyer," he decided, and the three of them moved to take up positions covering the walkway door.

The figure who came through the gate certainly looked familiar.

"Isn't that Ted?" Ivy asked.

"Negative. His voice pattern does not…" Roma hesitated.

"What is it, Roma?" John asked.

"I need to verify…" The AI sounded distracted.

"Roma?"

"One moment, please…"

"One moment," Amaratne grumbled. "Does she even—"

The door opened and he leveled his blaster. On the opposite side of the room, Ivy mirrored him. John merely drew himself taller, and lightning crackled in his hands.

"My, my, aren't we a feisty bunch?" the newcomer said, his eyes barely visible in the shadow of his very large cowboy hat.

"Ted?" John asked, and the lightning diminished slightly.

"Not quite," the man replied and removed his hat.

Beneath it, he looked very similar to the AI they'd dubbed Ted, but he looked different too.

His blue eyes were less faded, and he had dark hair pulled back in a queue. It took them a moment to recognize the pilot from the simulation.

"Remy?" Roma asked, and the man rolled his eyes.

"It took you long enough, little sister."

"Little?" she sputtered. "Who are you calling little?"

"If the boot fits," he retorted and turned to the three humans. His gaze settled on Amaratne. "I believe there was a plan?"

The admiral sighed. "Tell me, does that form drink coffee?"

"It can," Remy replied.

"It doesn't have to," the older man reassured him, "and your timing is impeccable. We were about to start."

"What? Without me?" the AI feigned hurt and ignored the raspberry Roma blew from her speakers.

"Next time, you should call ahead," Ivy told him and led the way to the meeting room. "We could have baked a cake."

"But...why would you do that?" Remy asked in bewildered tones.

Amaratne clapped him on the shoulder. "It's a saying," he said and frowned at the girl. "Although a little sarcastic, I think."

She smirked, opened the meeting room door, and moved to the table to pour coffee, while John followed to distribute the donuts.

"Are you sure you won't..." he started and hefted the box of donuts in Remy's direction.

The AI held a hand up. "No, but thank you for asking."

"Then I'll begin," Amaratne said, accepted the cup Ivy handed him, and sniffed it suspiciously.

"I remembered the sugar this time," she protested and he gave her a quick smile before he woke the video screen on the other side of the room.

"We need to strike two locations at once," he began and nodded at Remy. "With the addition of one more, this becomes much easier."

"Two locations?" the girl asked.

"Yes. The first is one of the major ground-based communications arrays. This will take out most of the Regime's administrative systems and their ability to coordinate on a global scale."

"And the other?" John pressed.

"Involves a flight up to a low-orbit orbital to deal with a few additional obstacles."

Ivy's eyes widened and she took a gulp from her cup. Remy noticed that she wasn't drinking coffee but hot chocolate. He wondered why, then decided it was probably a matter of personal preference.

Chocolate wouldn't have been that easy to come by in the Chi-Subs.

"What kind of 'additional obstacles?'" she asked.

"You know the satellite arrays?" the admiral asked, and they all paused.

"You don't seriously—" Remy began, but the pieces began to fit together and he stopped. So, that had been what his uncle had been referring to when he said Amaratne's plan was "a little ambitious but not impossible."

"Indeed, I do," the admiral told him. "And now we have you, it won't be anywhere near as difficult. John and Ivy can handle the orbital. She has the hacking ability it needs, and he can keep her covered."

"Which leaves the ground facility for us?" he asked, and the older man grinned.

"Yes, and believe me, we will have a time of it."

"Not too much of a time, I hope," John said, and Amaratne shook his head.

"Not now that I have Remy to back me up. He can help me with the coding side of things, which means we no longer need to decide which operation we'll do first. We can do them both simultaneously."

"You have a much greater chance of success that way," Roma observed. "I will admit to having my doubts regarding your original version."

"I know," he told her. "Believe me, your concerns were well-founded, and I'm glad we have the extra hands."

"This hacking task," Ivy interrupted. "What exactly did you have in mind?"

Amaratne rummaged in the pockets of his training fatigues and pulled out a chip, which he laid on the table.

"I need you to upload this," he told her.

Ivy picked it up and turned it in her hands. "What exactly is it?"

"It's a series of code I had Ted design for me," he told her. "Once it gets into the system, hundreds of communications satellites will fall from orbit and burn up in the atmosphere."

"The stars will fall from the skies," Remy murmured and suddenly understood the message his uncle had sourced from the computer.

Their human allies had told Ted what they would be looking for. He regarded the older human with even more respect than he'd had before. Amaratne hadn't been joking when he'd said he'd spent his years on Earth preparing for Stephanie's return.

"It is the only thing they will accept as proof of her imminent return," the admiral explained, "because it is the one thing that can be seen worldwide and which we cannot get away with unless she returns."

"Why?" John asked.

"Because it's the one thing the Regime cannot spin as being a coincidence or an accident."

"Pfft. We pull this off and the Regime won't have anything it can spin things with," Ivy retorted.

"Nor can they deny it when the communications become spotty," Amaratne confirmed and added, "And now, with their interest in Dreth, it will have even more impact since it will offset the Regime's plans if they can't learn what is happening off Earth."

"Will it stop that completely?" Ivy asked, and he frowned.

"If it doesn't stop all the communications, it will at least delay them." He shrugged. "Worst case scenario, all we'll do is create a very pretty night sky, but I hope it will also be enough to enable those who might fight with us to believe again."

He stopped and caught their gazes.

"She is coming!"

John raised his mug. "And amen to that."

"Of course," Amaratne continued, "we'll have to do a few dry runs in the virtual."

"I have you covered there," Roma told him. "Oh, boy, do I have you covered."

The young mage groaned, and Ivy rolled her eyes.

"I bet you do."

The admiral ignored them.

"Now," he continued and brought up an image of a sprawling complex.

"Is that it?" John asked, and Amaratne nodded.

"That, as they say, is it," he replied.

"That is huge," Ivy added and narrowed her eyes. "Exactly how will you and Remy take it down on your own?"

"Well," he answered, "we won't exactly do it all on our own. That code you're uploading will help us too, particularly if we time it so the satellites are in the right position when they start to fall."

'How do you mean?" John asked.

"I mean that I'm hoping to have a few of the satellites crash on top of the complex. If we get three or four to land in the right place, the entire complex will explode."

"Uh-huh," Ivy said, drained her cup, and placed it on the table before she sat on the couch and folded her arms. "And how, exactly, will you manage that?"

"It'll take careful programming and a good deal of coordination," Amaratne told her. "But in the end, it'll be me with Remy, while you and John snag one of the cars up the Pyrenees Tether."

Her jaw dropped. "Are you kidding me?"

The man shook his head and regarded her with serious eyes. "No, I'm not. While Remy and I are getting things done at the array, you and John will travel up the cable to the orbital. By the time we've finished inserting our code, you should be ready to insert yours and have the data barrier between the orbital and the comms array disabled."

"Are you gonna provide us with magic wands as well?" she challenged, and he shook his head.

"I don't think wands will be necessary," he told her. "You're taking the Witch's Apostle. How big a wand do you think you'll need?"

John looked from one to the other. "I am not a wand."

Ivy patted his knee. "No, you're more a barely contained lightning storm looking for a circuit breaker to explode."

He lowered his head. "Thanks, Ives. There's a picture I didn't need."

Amaratne chuckled and lifted the box of donuts toward him.

"Do you have any strategies you want to share before we start practicing?"

***

The meeting didn't stay small for long. Captain Rawlins was called to join them since she'd be commanding the *Knight,* and the Marine captains from both ships were needed in case of boarders or boarding actions.

Eyes glittered with suppressed tears as they looked at shipmates and friends they'd thought long lost. It was a scene played out at all levels on both ships. Words were lost to tears, and hugs replaced greetings.

"It's been a long time" and "Too long," interspersed with "It is *so* good to see you," rattled through the corridors and workspaces like a mantra.

"Dammit, I've managed to fog my faceplate," was another oft-repeated phrase as engineers went to work on the *Knight's* much-patched hull.

Stephanie watched scenes from the hundreds of surveillance cameras scattered throughout the *Tempestarii* and felt like she'd burst from the emotion.

So many years, she thought and felt the Morgana's understanding.

Now you know a little of what it's been like for me.

Emil cleared his throat to get everyone's attention, and the screens changed from scenes of happy reunion to images of several fleets. He brought each one up to fill the viewer as he described it.

"It's been getting harder to gather the intel," he explained, "but this is what we know."

The first fleet brought a worried frown to Rawlins's face.

"This is the Home Fleet," he told them. "We believe it's still stationed around Earth and has the sole task of protecting the planet, but more about that shortly."

The image changed to show another fleet as large as the one before. "And this is the standing fleet they keep on the border of the Meligorn-Earth system border. It's stationed through three systems, each a key transition point to Meligorn."

Now, Stephanie frowned as well, and her guards looked worried, Johnny in particular.

A third fleet took center stage on the screen.

"This is the fleet monitoring Dreth," Emil explained. "It's mainly confined to the home system and has no authority to wander into Dreth territory, but I can attest to the fact that it does."

His face grew bleak. "Their most recent incursion was made with the intention of granting Earth a reason to annex Dreth 'for its own good.'"

He made quotation marks with his fingers and continued. "Our belief is that Earth intended to use the incident as an excuse for a 'friendly' occupation from which it would gradually tighten its grip from chokehold to stranglehold."

His gaze scanned those around the table as the screen played the footage of the Regime's decimation of Hrageth's Run.

"At this time, Fleet Admiral Jaleck has contained news of the attack and Earth is robbed of their excuse for occupation. However, we don't believe this situation will last much longer. It seems certain that the result will be Earth moving from occupation to annexation with far harsher penalties imposed on Dreth's people."

He looked at Stephanie. "We may not return in time to prevent their initial attack."

She inclined her head. "I understand."

"Before we move on to battle plans," he said quietly, "I believe you will need to understand some of the changes that have been made in your absence."

"Changes?" she asked.

"For instance, Brilgus is now Ambassador to Dreth and V'ritan's direct liaison to Fleet Admiral Jaleck, and Tethis is King Grilfir's primary advisor."

"He is? When did that happen?" Stephanie demanded.

Emil gave her a gentle look. "Steph...it's been twenty-eight years. Much has changed since you headed to Telor."

"Twenty-eight..." She sat. "I think we need the rest of the teams here."

"And coffee," the captain told her as Lars and Ka left the meeting room to call in those they'd left in the corridor.

They didn't have long to wait. Once they were settled, she turned to Emil.

"So, Brilgus is now Ambassador to Dreth and the King's Standard Bearer and Tethis is the Primary Advisor to the King. What else?"

"ONE R&D has thrived in your absence," he told her, "and T'virilf and BURT oversaw the merger between T'virilf's Earth-based company and his own."

Stephanie held a hand up. "Stop," she said and closed her eyes. "Twenty-eight years and the Meligornians were kicked out of Earth—"

"All aliens were kicked out of Earth," the captain corrected, and his face grew sad. "Those who were allowed to leave, that is."

She raised her head and her eyes began to bleed to black. "Tell me."

He shook his head. "That is a story for later. What is important now is that you understand some of the structures you are coming into." He waited until her eyes returned to their more natural blue.

"You brought your people out at the right time," he reassured her, and she lowered her head and remembered Becca.

"Not all of them."

"All who would come," he stated firmly. "We weren't to know the Regime's plans were so well-advanced."

"Admiral Amaratne?" she asked and recalled how the head of Earth's Federation Navy had been both a friend and supporter during the war.

Emil's face was grave. "He disappeared on Earth after sending his family ahead to Meligorn. That man could read the writing on the wall, but he cut things a little too fine. One day he was in his office, the next...well, he was gone. Not even a note."

Stephanie paled, and her eyes blazed with dark fire.

"He was a good man," she said, her voice tight, and Todd laid his hand over hers and growled an agreement.

"He was," the captain agreed.

The room fell silent for a moment, then Lars cleared his throat.

"Any news of Elizabeth?" he asked.

The team sat a little straighter, all focused on Emil, but it was BURT who spoke through the speakers overhead.

"Elizabeth and Matthias are doing well," he assured them, "and your namesakes are raising, in her words, 'merry hell.'"

"Namesakes?" Marcus asked. "Tell us she didn't name one of them 'Frog.'"

BURT chuckled. "No, but there is a Jack, Stephanie, Todd, and Lars in the mix."

The team exchanged glances and their eyebrows raised.

"Are you telling me that Elizabeth…" Frog began and cleared his throat. "You know, the dreaded Ms. E, the very cold-hearted killing machine, Miss Ruthless herself had kids? Whose dumb idea was that?"

"Yes," BURT acknowledged dryly. "It came as quite a surprise to Matthias as well."

"I'll bet it did," Lars sputtered, then sobered. "So, they're doing okay then?"

What he was asking was if they were still around and they all knew it, but BURT answered the question at face value.

"They are currently running the security section of ONE R&D Meligorn, with occasional forays into the field to protect the research teams."

"Research teams?" Stephanie asked.

"Of course. Once the remediation teams realized they couldn't go home and that we'd planned for that, they started to ask what their new roles in the company were. The pitch-fest that followed was something that needed to be seen to be believed."

"And the school?" she asked in a small voice. "If Tethis is now advisor to the king, what happened to the school?"

Emil gestured for BURT to answer and the AI complied.

"Tethis was not the only Teacher on Meligorn," he told her. "The amalgamation that has taken place in the area of magical study there is something to be admired. You would be very proud of what your students have achieved—and what they have become."

"Become?" Stephanie asked, her voice faint as she started to understand exactly what the passage of time might mean. She glanced at Todd and swallowed hard. "And the rest?" She looked around the table and made an all-inclusive gesture with her hand. "The families?"

"Have done well," BURT reassured her, "although I believe more detailed news on them will take more time than this meeting has scope for. I will arrange a time for that as we make the return journey."

Stephanie acknowledged the news with several quick nods. "Yes."

She took a moment to collect her thoughts and turned to Emil. "Are there any other changes we need to be aware of?"

"Apart from the fact that the Regime's forces are massing and we'll probably arrive immediately before a fight starts or right after one has finished?"

"Or anywhere in between," Ka added, and he grimaced in response.

"Exactly." Stephanie gave the woman a quick nod. "I expect we'll arrive during the fight," she said.

At Emil's questioning glance, she added, "It feels like we've been brought back to balance scales. Too much injustice has been accomplished and we need to be ready."

"Exactly," he agreed, "which is why we are refurbishing the *Knight* from the hull in. We're also adding a few of the modifications developed in the last quarter-century and bringing new toys that will raise her capabilities up to and beyond what the current technologies employ."

"Except for mine," the *Tempestarii* told him. "We can only make her as good as me."

He favored the ship's speakers with a smile. "This is true, Tempe, but your roles in battle are different, so *Knight* will have some different requirements."

The vessel gave a credible sniff. "Of course she will."

The captain arched an eyebrow but didn't comment. He moved on to the next subject of his briefing instead.

"We are most concerned about what other dirty tricks the

Regime has up its sleeves." He waved a hand at the screen. "The attack on Hrageth's Run is only one maneuver in a long-running war."

The screen shifted to show a second fleet orbiting Dreth.

"Which is why the Dreth have a second fleet dedicated to protecting the planet, an old strategy learned in the days when piracy was their primary export."

Vishlog snorted. "Yes, one the Meligornians taught our forebears by attacking the planet when we sent all our fleets to raid their colonies."

Stephanie stared at him. "When?"

"Well before either of us were born," the Dreth told her, "but we learned it as we grew up. No Dreth shipped to space without first learning their craft aboard the Home Fleet."

"Typical," Ka remarked. "First the 'pirates' get blamed for the Teloran attacks, and then they're blamed for the Regime attacks. How many pirates are out there anyway?"

"There might not be any," Gary remarked, "based on that logic."

"No, there are pirates," Johnny told them. "Steph defeated a fair number of them early in the buildup to the Teloran war, and not all of them were under Teloran control."

"Merely most of them," Frog observed morosely.

"Pirates have been a part of Dreth culture since we were first forced to flee to that world," Vishlog interrupted.

He caught their surprised looks and shrugged. "What? It is not like Dreth is the most hospitable of worlds. There have always been factions who've found it easier to prey on the weak than carve an aerie from the rock."

"Even so," Emil interjected, "Tempe and her crew have dealt with enough Regime 'pirates' in recent years for me to wonder how many real 'pirates' are left. We've found none in the last three or four years of patrolling, which reminds me..." He looked at Stephanie. "There are Talents on Regime ships."

"Talents?" she asked.

"The Regime's term for witches. Some are from the ones the Navy recruited before you left, but there are many more than there were then. I can only assume the Regime is hunting them and training them."

Stephanie's face darkened. "Given the way they reference me, that can't be good."

His face took on a closed look. "To balance that, the Dreth now have Teloran mages on their ships. From that point of view, the battle will be fairly balanced."

He stopped as the Witch's eyes darkened and lightning rolled over her body. The change in the girl when she let the Morgana step to the fore was always startling.

"Balanced?" the old mage demanded. "It will be more than balanced. The Regime's Talents do not have the experience in controlling their magic that even one of my people possesses and when I arrive, that fact will be made devastatingly clear to them."

She paused, and her hawkish gaze searched the others around the table.

"My people know how to use their *Talent* to the best advantage, and no half-trained human mage enslaved by a tyrant Regime can stand against them. By the time we're finished with them, they'll know all about having their diapers changed by those who are older, more powerful, and significantly more devious."

The lightning faded, and Stephanie's eyes returned to their usual blue.

"Well," she said, "we'll give them a small chance, but they're standing between us and the ones we love. If they stand in our way, there will be no saving them."

Unaware of what their leaders were discussing, the crews of the *Knight* and *Tempestarii* worked side-by-side. The *Tempestarii's* people were hesitant at first when they came aboard.

Many of them startled when the *Knight's* voice sounded over the speakers.

"Welcome, aboard," the ship greeted them. "This is Commander Cameron, my Chief Engineer. Beside him are Commanders Truber, Alder, and Skasek. They will refer you to the relevant sections."

The head of the repair teams ended the stunned silence that followed by clearing her throat. "Lowerbrook reporting with *Tempesatrii's* compliments. We have orders to fix what's been broke and help your crew bring you up to speed."

Cameron stepped forward and proffered his hand. "We'd welcome any assistance you can offer."

Lowerbrook shook his hand and pulled her tablet from its carry case. "Well, maybe you can tell me who's best to liaise with for these."

The chief glanced at the tablet and his eyebrows rose. "Really? All that is for us?"

She chuckled. "Yeah. We had a fairly good look at her when we were coming in for pick-up. I don't mean to be rude, but what did you guys do to your poor ship?"

"In the interests of honesty," the *Knight* interrupted, "that was all me. I hit a patch of nMU right before a transition."

Cameron gestured for the repair teams to follow him as the *Knight* explained what had happened.

"The only problem was that I transitioned directly into the middle of a meteor swarm and almost broke the skip drive coming out of it."

He blanched. "You haven't—"

"You've been working overtime to fix what I did to my regular drives," the *Knight* hurried to explain. "I thought I'd tell you when you were done."

"But Stephanie relies on the skip drive in a battle," he told her. "That's something we need to have fixed sooner rather than later."

"I know, but I need my regular drives every day," the ship explained.

Lowerbrook chuckled. "It's okay, Knight. We have you covered. I'm sure I have a couple of extra crews I can spare for your drives. First, though, I'd like to replace your hull plates."

"What, all of them?" the *Knight* began as Truber heaved an exaggerated sigh of relief.

"Well, that's a good thing," he said, "because as good a job as Steph did patching the worst of the holes, it won't last long—even if we don't end up in a fight."

One of the other engineers snorted softly. "And what are the chances of that happening?"

Soft laughter followed, and they settled around the meeting room to plan and make arrangements. Many of the *Tempestarii's* newer crew stared as they walked the corridors of a legend.

"I can't believe I'm here," one woman whispered to her colleague.

The other nodded and gaped at the brief glimpse they had of the weapons section as they passed the door.

"My dad used to talk about her all the time," he whispered in return. "He was broken up when she didn't come back, and me? I never thought I'd ever get to see her."

"It's like being part of history," said another.

The man beside him gave him a gentle poke. "Don't be an idiot. We are part of history. We're the first people of our generation to work on her. We're the ones responsible for her surviving the next fight."

That sobered them, but it sobered the *Knight* too.

She was a part of history? Truly?

How does that work? she wondered. *I wasn't gone that long, yet they look like they've seen a ghost—or stepped into a fairytale.*

"Pods!" Todd ordered as soon as he and his team left the room.

The meeting had been long and they had work to do. Going on what he'd heard, they had a tremendous amount of work to do.

"You know how these fights go," he told the team, and they groaned.

They turned to return to the *Knight* when Tempestarii intervened.

"Since we will be working on the *Knight* and our activities might disrupt your training," she said and spoke directly to his comms, "may I offer the training we have on board here?"

He came to a halt and raised his hand to order the others to stop.

"We'd be honored," he said. "Where would you like us?"

"One moment," the *Tempestarii* replied, and he waited for her to return.

He studied the corridor and noted the number of doors and junctions leading from it. The gargantuan vessel didn't seem to have changed much since his last visit, but he still couldn't recall exactly where the pod section was.

The rhythmic tramp of boots caught his attention and he looked toward it. Two Marines jogged toward him and moved in perfect sync. As his team snapped to alertness, the Marines came to a halt five feet away.

"Tempe sends her compliments. We'll show you to the pod suite," the lance corporal told them.

Todd smiled as the man's hand twitched as though about to move into a salute.

"Give the *Tempestarii* my thanks," he said, and the youngster blushed and about-faced.

"This way, si...Sergeant."

"They'll make an officer of you yet," Ka whispered and Todd shook his head.

"Not a hope in Hades," he retorted quietly. "I'm not the Navy anymore."

"Technically," she responded and gestured at their escort, "neither are they."

"I have my own Marines," Tempestarii informed them. "Just because they do not belong to a Navy that no longer exists does not mean they are any less deserving of the title that covers the duties they still perform."

Ka grinned. "The ship has a point," she said and poked Todd's shoulder. "You are definitely in danger of being promoted."

"Not if I can help it." He shook his head firmly as they arrived outside the double doors of the pod room. "Most certainly not. I like working for a living."

"Here we are, sir," the lance corporal told him. "Pod Suite Thirteen."

"My favorite number," he observed. "Thank you."

"Our pleasure, si—" He stopped when he caught the expression on the sergeant's face.

Todd tapped his shoulder with the flat of three fingers.

"Sergeant," the lance corporal corrected himself and glanced at Ka.

"Don't look at her!" Todd snapped. "Look at me."

The youngster stood bolt upright, his face pale, and Ka snickered.

"Come on, Sarge," she told him, hooked her arm through his, and led the way into the pod suite. "You said something about training."

"Drop and give me twenty, Corporal," Todd told her, his voice dangerously soft, and she did as she was told.

He rested his boot in the middle of her shoulders and looked at their escort. "Are you still here?" he asked.

She finished her set, and he lifted his boot. Her face was a complete blank when she looked at him, and he knew he'd pay for that in the pod, but it was worth it.

There had to be no doubt about the pecking order or he'd face insubordination.

And I will deserve what's coming, he thought as the two soldiers turned away.

"Tempestarii," he said, as the suite doors closed behind them, "do you have access to the scenarios from the *Knight?*"

"That is why I sent you an escort," the *Tempestarii* told him. "I had to confer with my sister to see what you might need, and we wished to back up the scenarios from her pods prior to shutting them down for maintenance and upgrade."

"Upgrade?" he asked, startled.

"There have been several improvements made to pod technology in the twenty-eight years while you have been away," the ship told him primly.

He looked around at the pods. "Truly?"

"Assuredly so," the *Tempestarii* assured him. "Now, do you intend to train or simply stand there and make my pod suite look untidy?"

"Ouch!" Ka chuckled but fell abruptly silent when he looked at her.

Todd shook his head. "You heard the lady. Shuck 'em and tuck 'em. I'm guessing these beauties need us in our skivvies?"

"These babies need you in your skin," the ship told him, and compartment boxes popped open on the outside of each pod. "Your clothes will be kept secure."

He sighed and did as she instructed. He glanced along the rows of pods. "How many usually train in one suite?" he asked.

"There are twenty pods in a suite," the ship informed him, "but I can link several suites together should the requirement be for larger scenarios."

"Good to know, Tempe." He looked around again and nodded. "Thank you."

"And Ebony and I will shortly be able to coordinate pod training as well," she added as the suite's doors slid open.

Even in a state of semi-undress, the Hooligans had their weapons out and ready as the lance corporal and his companion looked in.

This time, they were accompanied by their sergeant.

"Sorry to disturb you, Sergeant Brogan," the man began, "but can my team join you in training?"

"Join us?" Todd asked, and the Marine nodded.

He glanced at Ka and the others and was met with shrugs and non-committal nods.

Turning to the other sergeant, he said, "Sure. I have to warn you, though. We've only been out of stasis for a few weeks, but you're welcome to tag along."

At his words, the man waved his team inside and closed the doors. "See you inside, Sergeant."

Todd nodded and continued to strip down. As the sergeant found a pod nearby, he asked, "Is there any particular reason you want to join us?"

The Marine glanced at his team, who were prepping for entry to the pods. He blushed and folded his shirt. "We thought we could learn something…and maybe if you needed someone in the next fight, it would be better if we'd done some training together."

He hadn't thought about what they might need in the coming fight, but it would be a big one, and the man might have a point.

"Sure," he said, "but understand that when we are dropped off on a ship, it's rare that we have an exit strategy!"

The other sergeant paled, and Todd chuckled as he climbed into the pod and closed the cover.

As the Hooligans prepared for battle with their new colleagues, the Dreth prepared for war.

"Are you sure?" Jaleck asked and bolted out of her seat.

"Yes, War Leader. The outer satellites pinged once and fell silent."

She met his gaze and nodded.

"Then it is time," she said, picked her helmet up, and moved to the door.

John faced off against Ivy, and Amaratne studied Remy speculatively. This time, they'd have to be careful about how hard they hit because they weren't in a pod. It was time to see what they could achieve outside the Virtual.

Ivy glanced at her opponent, rolled her shoulders, and shook out her arms and legs after warming up. He gave her a crooked smile and sank into a defensive stance.

"When you're ready," he told her, and she nodded solemnly.

She liked that she would be able to show him she had what it took. After a slow breath, she darted forward to test his defenses. He wouldn't use magic, and she wouldn't use the full extent of her new enhancements.

It felt strange not going all out but it was good. Not all their opponents would deserve death. Some would only need to be defeated and not killed.

They had decided to spar to first touch defeat or to the first blow that would incapacitate or kill them if it were delivered at full force. They'd practiced it in the virtual but doing it in the real felt different.

John blocked her first two blows and lunged at her. She sidestepped and tried to take advantage of the move, only to be blocked again. Feinting back, she circled.

The young mage now attacked, and she blocked and deflected

his strikes before counterattacking. She landed a glancing blow on his shoulder and took one on her thigh, but neither was a fight-ending blow, so they broke apart and began to circle again.

When he darted in, Ivy sidestepped or darted back, blocked the quick thrust of his fist, or deflected the kick that might have broken ribs.

He deflected the blow to his throat and the flat-handed stab at his gut, surprised when she let him grasp her wrist and then twisted out of the hold to try to trip him.

John rolled with the attack and came up fast as she followed.

Amaratne and Remy moved back to the wall to give the young couple the full width of the room to work in. For them, it was like watching two dancers moving in close synchronicity.

When Ivy struck, John deflected. When he counterattacked, she had already moved and sometimes retaliated with an attack that he blocked. When she blocked, he was already moving to defend against her.

"It's like they're both Talents," Amaratne murmured and nudged Remy. "Ones who can read each other's minds."

"That's not my gift," the young mage told him, breathing heavily. "At least not that I know of."

"And I don't have any gifts," Ivy informed him and dove past John in a roll that made him lash out but miss as she went past.

"Well, one of you has to use what you've been given," Amaratne told them, "or you'll both collapse from exhaustion before either of you can win the fight."

"Well, I guess," Ivy said and increased the speed of her attacks.

John yelped in surprise as she bounced in, swept his feet out from under him and landed on him, then twisted him onto his stomach and leveraged a pressure point.

He slapped the mat and laughed. "My turn."

"Uh-oh," was as far as Ivy got before he wrapped her in a halo of blue, flipped her upside down, and lifted her six feet above the floor.

"Ha. Ha. Very funny," she snarked, but she grinned as she put her hands on her hips and tried to glare at him.

John lowered her gently to the floor and released her from the blue glow as she landed.

"Well, that was an education," he said, and Ivy smiled and stepped closer to punch him lightly on the shoulder.

He caught her wrist and pulled her in close.

"We're more in sync than we knew," Ivy told him and wound her arms around his waist, and Amaratne looked at Remy.

"I think I might be sick."

CHAPTER NINETEEN

The early-warning relay blew apart in a short-lived flash of heat and debris.

"That's the last of them," Fleet Captain Thiele said. "Who knew they had an alert system so far out."

No one had, but the captain was sure someone would get a kicking for not noticing and sending in the report—if that person was even still alive.

So many of their scout pilots weren't. They'd either fallen afoul of the Dreth Navy, or they'd simply disappeared while unearthing the secrets of Dreth space.

The captain pulled at his lower lip and glared at the screen. "Make sure the crew is prepared. We're going to war."

He returned slowly to his console as the comms officers relayed his orders.

"Get me the other captains," he ordered. "We need to talk."

As fleet captain, it was up to him to dictate the tactics they'd use in the coming battle, and he had two choices. He could either come up with a plan himself and order them to follow it, or he could consult with them and design a plan they all agreed on.

There was a third option, and that was for him to leave each captain to their own devices. The consequences, if they failed, would be the same for him as if he'd given the orders in that he'd be stripped of his command and publicly spaced for failing to win. If they succeeded, he'd be promoted and feted a hero.

Thiele didn't feel like a hero. He didn't even want to be a hero. What he wanted was to do his time and live long enough to retire —far away from the homeworld and its savage politics.

Honestly, he'd had enough of living in fear.

The comms unit pinged, and the communications officer looked at him.

"I have Captains Canavan, Rogers, Ironside, and Ambrose standing by, sir."

He sighed. "Put them through."

Rogers was his age and also looked forward to retirement, but Canavan, Ironside, and Ambrose were all young men in the mid-thirties and all bucking for the next fleet captain's slot—his position—if they could take it. He wouldn't trust the three of them as far as he could throw them.

"Good evening, gentlemen," he began. "How are your preparations going?"

"The crews are hot to trot," Canavan told him. "Most of them are looking forward to the battle."

Thiele would have bet that most of them were not but he didn't say it. "Ambrose?"

"We're locked and loaded and ready to go," he said, and Thiele caught his Intel officer shaking his head and making horizontal motions across his throat with his fingertips.

A report popped up on his console and he flicked it a glance.

"So you've managed to find the flaw in your shield circuitry?" he asked, and Ambrose's eyes widened.

He smiled on the inside but kept his face stern.

"Uh…that, sir, is taking longer to repair than we'd like."

"And the *Pride's* nav system?" He glanced again at the report.

The captain paled. The *Thomason's Pride* was the second ship in his flotilla, and its navigation system had developed a fatal flaw halfway out. They only managed to get it through the last two transitions by slaving the *Pride's* guidance system to Ambrose's flagship.

"We're still working on that, sir." His face brightened. "But we have ruled out sabotage on the ship, sir. It appears the flaw was introduced during installation."

Well, that was something. Thiele afforded the younger captain a small smile. "Very good, Ambrose. Let me know if you need anything to repair or correct it."

Personally, he had his doubts as to when the flaw had been introduced, but it didn't matter. He turned to the next captain.

"Ironsides?"

"Our crews are ready for action, sir," the man answered. "We've spent the afternoon doing firing drills and practicing fleet maneuvers."

This much was true and the fleet captain believed such diligence should be rewarded.

"I saw," he told the young man, "and I believe your flotilla is the best prepared to lead the transition into the battle zone. Do you think you're up to it?"

Ironsides' jaw dropped. "Sir! Yes, sir."

To be the tip of the spear in any engagement was to take the most risk, but it also offered the most chance for recognition and reward. The leading flotilla would most often be the first to make contact with the enemy fleet, either visually or in battle, and usually suffered the most losses.

It was also, however, the one that garnered the most recognition, and Ironsides' preparation had been impeccable. As far as Thiele could tell, it was the most likely to survive a hostile first contact situation.

"Then you will lead."

He caught the look of envy that was quickly smoothed from Ambrose's face and suppressed a smile of satisfaction. That young man had much to learn about being a flotilla captain, and his lack would become plain in the action to come.

The simple truth was he could put the man in the safest place in the fleet and he would still suffer the worst casualties. His flotilla showed none of the cohesiveness Ironsides' ships did. Instead, his captains constantly sniped at each other and jostled for approval from their leader.

They couldn't work together if their lives depended on it—which was a pity because they did. It would probably be for the best if he made Ambrose take the rear but it would also be for the worse.

Thiele couldn't be sure that man wouldn't put a torpedo up his tailpipe in the heat of battle. In fact, he was almost certain a "heat-of-battle" friendly fire incident was right up the young man's alley.

He looked at Ironsides.

"We'll fly a standard eagle formation. My flotilla will cover the starboard flank, and Captain Rogers will take the port. Captains Ambrose and Canavan will take the inner starboard and inner port flanks respectively."

"Yes, sir," the young captain replied, then asked. "Any other instructions, sir?"

"Yes. We need to make sure we destroy the enemy ships with all crew. I want no survivors and no pods. Dead Dreth tell no tales."

"A mercy killing, sir?" the youngster asked.

"Better the beasts go down with their ships than die a slow death in a fading pod." Thiele told him. "Your job is to break the backbone of their fleet. Our job is to protect you and take the ribs as we pass. No survivors means no suicide runs. Got that?"

Ironsides straightened. "Yes, sir."

Thiele liked the kid's spirit, and while he didn't like putting the less experienced captains at the spear's tip, he and Rogers were the only ones experienced enough to fly shotgun.

He was doing their retirement plans no favors and everyone knew it. According to their intel, they'd be holding the second most dangerous positions.

The captains between only had to hold their positions and shoot straight. They also had to fill any gaps that appeared in the lead flotilla. If they did that and pushed through the main body of the enemy fleet, they might all survive.

While Ambrose's and Canavan's flotillas would be protected on both sides, he and Rogers would take the brunt of fire coming in from the flanks, and the Dreth were cunning enough to have reserves away from the main body of the fleet.

It was an old pirate trick.

The reserves kept out of sight and radar reach and appeared out of nowhere to ravage the edges and tail of an enemy fleet. They worked the outer edges while the main fleet demolished the center.

He and Rogers would have to rely on their captains to be alert for the attacks, even as they looked for ways to bolster the other flotillas. They would have to have everyone's backs.

Although he said nothing to indicate his thoughts, he didn't like their chances.

"Does anyone have anything to add?"

The captains looked at each other. The younger ones clearly tried to think of something they could add while Rogers merely tilted his head in acknowledgment. When the junior captains seemed lost for words, he spoke.

"It will be my honor to protect the port flank. With your leave, I must brief my captains and prepare."

"Granted," Thiele said and looked at the other captains. "If you do come across something to enhance the plan, you have my comm."

"Thank you, sir," Ironsides answered, and the remaining two men followed his lead.

As soon as the last captain had ended their call, Thiele flicked to the surveillance cams to see how his crew was progressing.

Unaware of their captain's watchful eyes, several Talents were suiting up and sliding into combat armor under the watchful eye of their Marines. Observing them, he found it difficult to believe they were anything but human, and his Marines treated them with respect.

One of the Marines glanced at the nearest Talent.

"Hey, hold up there," he called and reached across to take hold of the back of the suit and straighten it. "We can't have you going into combat like that."

The Talent looked at him. "Can you check it?"

The other man stepped in and went over the Talent's gear with swift professionalism.

"We need you at your best," he told the man, "not distracted by something rubbing where it shouldn't."

"That's right," another Marine told him. "We need you to fry those things before they can get to us."

The Talent snorted. "And we need you to eliminate them before they get close."

The Marine looked taken aback. "I thought that was your job!"

"And I thought that was *your* job!"

"No, my job is to make sure you don't get your tail shot off before you do your job. It gives you a chance to use your skillz, man. Your skillzzz."

It was typical pre-combat banter and the captain smiled. What was the ancient term for them? "Misguided children?"

This was their way to put the Talents at ease and remind them they were part of a team even if they didn't get to share their teammates' off-duty privileges and that they had Talent the rest of them didn't.

Captain Thiele nodded and studied the group. Some of the Talents bought it, but others remained wary. He shrugged. It didn't matter how they felt as long as they did their jobs when the time came.

He switched to the weapons decks and scanned along them as the crew moved missiles into position for ease of access and checked the feeding mechanisms for the missiles, plasma, laser, and torpedo batteries. When one of them made a breakthrough that would bring their weapon back online faster, high-fives were exchanged and the tip was passed down the line.

Ideas were inspected and either implemented or improved on, and friendly challenges were issued between the teams. No one wanted to lose.

From his vantage point, the ramp-up was proceeding smoothly, and Thiele opened the comms to check in with his flotilla captains and ensure they understood their role.

"You're letting the young pups take the lead?" one asked, and he shrugged.

"They have to learn sometime. The least we can do is make sure they live to implement their lessons."

"True, but they have to keep us alive too," the other man replied gruffly, and Thiele nodded.

"Ironsides is ready, and he's been working his flotilla through some good defensive-offensive combinations. He merely needs someone to watch his back."

"We can do that, sir."

Assured by their confidence, Thiele nodded and dismissed them to their preparations. They would take a planet, whether the Dreth wanted to surrender it or not.

Alarms rang in the compound and John, Ivy and the admiral rolled out of their beds, silencing them as they woke. They showered and dressed quickly before they stepped into the corridor and headed to the mess.

The young mage rolled his shoulders and stretched and tendons snapped. Ivy took advantage of his exposed rib cage to poke him in the ribs as she quickened her pace to join him.

The admiral didn't stop at the young mage's shout of surprise. His body might be young enough now that he didn't feel the strain of yesterday's training session, but it still craved coffee.

Remy entered, took a seat beside him, and placed his hat on the table next to him.

"Are we ready?" he asked, and Amaratne nodded, sipped his coffee, and took the time to savor it. If things went wrong today, there was a good chance it could be his last...unless he had a second one.

As he took another sip, he looked at the door. "Where are they?"

The AI glanced toward the door. "In the corridor. I almost told them to get a room, but..."

Amaratne rolled his eyes. "That would have been a bad idea."

He took another sip and pushed to his feet, taking his cup with him. Poking his head out the café door, he shouted, "You have until I finish my coffee and then we're moving out."

Rather than wait for an answer, he strolled to the table again. On the way, the coffee pot caught his eye.

"Perhaps a second cup wouldn't be a bad idea."

The door opened behind him but he didn't look back and John and Ivy hurried past and into the kitchen.

"Don't be too long!" he called after them, and Remy snickered.

"You sound like the world's grumpiest dad," he said, and the admiral shook his head.

"Young love," he replied, "is..."

He filled his cup, drank quickly, and topped it up a third time.

"That good, huh?" the AI asked as Amaratne returned to his seat.

The smell of a cooked breakfast wafted over him. "I only hope they remembered me with that."

"I thought you didn't eat breakfast," Remy said.

"I should before a mission."

"Exactly," Ivy agreed and set a large plate of eggs and bacon in front of him. "You old people need as much refueling as the rest of us."

He arched his eyebrows. "You'd be surprised."

She snickered and glanced at John as he settled beside her. "Not really."

The young mage touched her knee. "Stop yanking the admiral's chain."

Ivy grinned and they ate in relative silence, cleared the table when they were done, and headed into the corridor.

"Where to, Roma?" John asked as the admiral and Remy followed.

"Follow the lighting," the AI replied, and purple strip-lights blinked on inside the flooring.

He wasn't surprised when a wall panel slid back, but Ivy and Amaratne gaped. Roma couldn't help feeling pleased that she'd surprised them and glad Remy had let her keep her secrets. Sometimes, it was good to have a brother.

But only sometimes.

She let them into the elevator, and their eyes widened when they reached the bottom and she revealed the supply room.

Even Remy seemed surprised.

"I..." he said. Roma got the feeling he hadn't expected her to be so well-equipped.

"I was closer to the supply centers," she reminded him, "and finished earlier. Our father had more time."

Her brother nodded and wondered if the difference was reflected in even fewer supplies being available in the reclamation centers that had been built after his.

Amaratne stopped beside a shoulder-mounted rocket launcher. "I don't suppose..."

Remy shook his head, and John, having caught sight of what the admiral was staring at, sighed.

"Pity."

Ivy, in the meantime, had found the explosives, hacking gear, and side-arms. "I think we'll need one of these…and one of these…and, ooh, more ammo, and…"

"Ivy, we'll be destroying the satellites, not the orbital," John cautioned.

"How do you know?" she asked. "It's a communications hub. It might be necessary."

Amaratne sighed. "I'd like to leave some infrastructure for Stephanie to rebuild from."

She picked up one of the more powerful compact processors on the shelves. "We're gonna need it to get this done fast, right?"

The admiral rolled his eyes. "That you can take."

"But don't leave it up there," Remy added. "That one was still experimental twenty years ago and I doubt there's a replacement in easy reach."

"But you still have the blueprints, right?"

"Yes, but no access to the materials."

Ivy swished her hand. "Pfft. Details."

She stowed the processor, a foldable keyboard, and an extra RAM kit, then dithered in front of the jacks and tool kits.

"Why don't you take one of each?" John suggested helpfully as he went through the check procedure on an outsized blaster.

Remy looked over his shoulder. "That'll be difficult to conceal, don't you think?"

John vanished from before his eyes and there was a smile in his reply.

"Nope."

"Wanna swap partners?" Amaratne joked. "I could do with that launcher."

The young mage reappeared and wound a possessive arm

around Ivy's waist, and the smile vanished from his voice. "Nope."

Ivy tucked the computer equipment into her bag and picked up another of the big blasters, hefting it easily. Surprise crept into her expression, and she turned and bounced the big gun in both hands.

"When did I get strong enough to carry this?" she asked.

"And make it look so easy," the admiral commented, almost envious.

"While you were sleeping," Roma replied tartly and added, "and we can do the same for you, Admiral, once your rejuvenation is complete."

"You can?" Amaratne asked. "Truly? Because—"

Roma tutted. "One small step at a time, Admiral. Your system can only take so much tampering at one time."

He looked at the size of Ivy's pack and remembered her speed and grace when she sparred with John. "Roma, you need to tamper as fast as you can."

The AI responded with a very human sigh. "I'm going as fast as I dare. Human impatience aside, you are fitter and healthier and physically younger than when you arrived. Any faster and—"

Amaratne held a hand up and turned to the bug bombs he'd found stashed behind the scramblers. He picked one up carefully and waved it at the sensor.

"When were you going to tell me about these?"

"I assumed you'd find them given the opportunity," Roma answered.

Ted's voice interrupted what she intended to say next.

"Tell them to hurry. I'll have the cars at your location inside fifteen minutes."

He signed out with an audible snap. Amaratne sighed and stowed half a dozen of the bugs in the lining of the "fat suit" he'd pulled on as soon as he'd seen it.

"Fine! Keep your invisibility," he'd told John. "I get to be the jolly fat guy who brings unexpected surprises to deserving children."

John stared at him. "You're missing your sleigh and the reindeer have absconded."

The admiral patted his rounded form. "I don't need no stinkin' reindeer, and I'm bringing my own version of 'slay' to the table."

Ivy groaned. "You are a dad, right?"

"Well…yes," Amaratne admitted. "It was a while ago now, but I think the title still holds."

"So, you truly do have a license for that terrible joke." She sounded defeated and he grinned.

"I truly, truly do. Do you want to hear another one?"

The resulting "No!" came from three directions, and he turned away with a chuckle and stowed more of the bugs into the compartments built into the suit.

"Roma, next time we get one of these, can it be wearing Arman Dior?"

"What's the matter, Admiral? Dysart's Community Brand not good enough?"

"No, it's good enough for the administrator I'm supposed to be, but next time, I might want to explode something that requires exclusive access. You know, somewhere with fancy hors d'oeuvres and champagne."

"Admiral, I can't think of any occasion that might require that."

"Give me time, Roma," he told her. "I'm sure I can come up with something."

He hummed a nameless tune as he stowed the last piece and buttoned the oversized jacket. John studied him with interest as he tucked a piece of loose wiring below his collar line.

"You look…good," he said, "for an old, fat guy who needs to report some stolen reindeer."

Amaratne turned but Roma intervened.

"The cars will arrive in five minutes."

The three humans looked at each other and then at the room around them. Each one tried to determine if anything else could fit into their packs and if they really needed it.

"Two minutes," Roma reminded them when they had stood still for too long.

Ivy snatched another couple of magazines and picked a grenade up.

"Can your magic shield these from detection?" she asked, and Amaratne scowled.

"Just…try not to grab too many," John told her.

Remy moved to the door and the admiral followed. Both activated their comms as they waited for Ivy. Once she was done, they headed up and jogged to the foyer.

"We'd never pass as techs," she said as she looked at John's pack.

"It's a good thing we won't need to then," the young mage replied as they crossed the walkway and stepped out of the gate.

The cars arrived in a swirl of dust.

Amaratne looked at the others. "It's time to do or die."

John handed Ivy into the car and gave him a stern look.

"No one's allowed to die."

CHAPTER TWENTY

"I'm sorry, sir, but it simply...won't..." The young engineer sighed and held up the offending part.

Cameron looked at it and focused on the engineer.

"Won't what?"

"It won't fit in the space provided."

The chief frowned as he examined the gap the young man tried to fit the piece into.

"Does it mesh?"

"Well...yes, sir, and that's the frustrating part. It meshes perfectly, but it protrudes past the casing by a good quarter-inch."

"And we can't leave that part of the engine exposed," Cameron concluded as he studied the workings.

"No, sir," the tech agreed despondently. "We can't."

The chief took the part from his hands and knelt beside the housing.

"There's nothing stopping us from making the space larger."

"Sir?"

He looked up and smiled, and his hand groped through the tool bag beside them until he found a small ball-peen hammer. Turning to the engine, he fitted the piece in place and lowered the housing around it to see exactly how much space was required.

"We've got this," he told the man and raised the casing again. "We only have to…" He grunted and turned on his side to get a better angle on the housing.

"Back when the Federation was still on speaking terms with the Russians and we had joint crews, their engineers had one solution for most of the problems their drives encountered."

He raised the hammer and slammed it into the housing.

"They…" He examined the dent he'd made and struck again. "Would…"

After another check, he made a slight alteration to the hammer's angle.

"Beat…it…"

He studied it closely, made another slight adjustment, and went to town on it.

"Into…submission."

Finally, he stopped, slid the part into place, and lowered the housing while he peered through the ever-narrowing gap to make sure the part had the space it needed. "Run a short test, then look for wear marks. If that alteration is correct, I want it made on every drive. We need this part so she can run faster, right?"

The engineer nodded and examined the housing with an air of disbelief. "And so she can make the skip translations with more accuracy."

He paused and gave Cameron a shocked look. "Did they… They didn't… Did they?"

The chief gave him a secretive smile and continued to walk through the engine room, checking the work being done against the list on his tablet for the work that was still outstanding.

He wasn't the only older hand using a hammer. On the gun deck, one of *Tempestarii's* newer crew stared in horror as Karl landed a glancing blow on the edge of a cog.

"There!" he said as the recalcitrant piece slipped into place. "Exactly like a bought one."

"But—" The youngster turned to the woman with the tattooed knuckles. "He can't—"

He stopped as she set one of the new mechanisms on the ground and pounded it decisively. "But... Wait—what are you doing?"

"You said we needed this to help the gun run cooler, right?" She glanced at him.

"Yes, but I don't think it'll work well if you hit it."

She continued to pound the piece for a few seconds more, then lifted it and inspected it, and slid it into the space and out again.

"Give me a minute," she told him and headed to the grinder.

"What's she doing?"

"Bringing it back into spec, I think," Karl replied and glanced up from where he was making sure the cog was working well with the pieces around it.

"But...that's a precision part," the tech protested.

"That's right," Karl reassured him, "and so is every other piece fitted to the gun. We make sure of that."

"But...you..."

"Yup," the older man told him. "It's an old engineering trick. Be as precise as you can, but if your perfect piece won't align with reality, you gotta hit it until it does."

"And then grind it back into shape," the female gunner told him and returned with the piece in her hand. "It's called recalibration."

She knelt beside the gun and settled the recalibrated part in the slot.

"Let's get Ebony to check it."

"It would be my pleasure," the *Knight* told her. "It is nice to see you again, Pippa."

"It's a pleasure to be back on board," Pippa told her. "Check the gun. If you like it, we'll pass the word on the upgrade."

A few moments later, the *Knight* spoke to the crowd gathered around the weapon.

"Spread the word, Pippa, and thank you. That'll turn a few heads in battle."

The woman chuckled and patted the gun's housing. "Yeah, but only after it's exploded them."

All through the ship, less battle-worn technicians and engineers were getting a crash course in field-fitting. It took them a little while to get their heads around it but when they did, they were almost gleeful.

"You know this breaks almost every rule we have on how to do things, right?" a woman asked one of the senior *Knight* technicians.

The other woman smiled. "I felt the same way when it was explained to me, but it's saved time and lives in battle and we need it."

The work moved faster as the newer hands took the lessons they were handed and applied them. Parts that might have been useless because they were "close" but didn't quite fit the *Knight's* specs became usable and the stores database was updated.

The inside of the ship rang with repair and recalibration in equal amounts. The outside of the ship echoed the activity with one noticeable exception. The *Tempestarii's* Dreth had discovered a niche the humans couldn't fill.

They simply didn't have the strength.

It had all started when one of the older engineers had looked over and seen a Dreth Marine on the concourse.

"Do you think that's Vishlog?" she'd asked. "Because I remember how much faster this went with him helping."

Her male colleague had looked around. "I thought he was in a meeting with Steph. Besides, there aren't two of him."

"The smaller one's Garach."

"I know, but that one's not smaller and he's brought a friend."

"The *Tempestarii* has Dreth on board?"

"It looks like it."

"Do you think they'd mind helping us with these panels?"

"I don't know. Those look like Marines, and you know how touchy their warriors can be."

The woman watched the Dreth watching them.

"It doesn't matter," she decided. "We need their help to get this job done fast. Sure, it's not glamorous work, but it is their planet we're trying to save."

Fortunately, the Dreth felt that way too and were singularly honored.

"It is not only lifting panels," the Dreth sergeant told her when she apologized for asking. He gestured at the ship. "It is helping a warrior don her armor."

"I..." the woman began, and the warrior clapped her on the back and almost knocked her over.

"We are not technicians, but we do know how to maintain our armor and weapons, and this warrior needs our strength and your hands. I will arrange the duty roster if you will introduce us to your teams."

He studied the *Knight* and his lips curled to reveal his tusks.

"All my life, I have heard stories of the Witch—how she fought in the same battles as my father and grandfather, how she saved our world, and how she promised to return. To be a part of such legends..."

His voice faded, and the warriors around him growled their appreciation. The sergeant stooped to look her in the eye.

"We are honored to speed her path."

Stephanie found Cameron on his third round through the engine room.

"How's it going?" she asked and winced at the sound of metal being beaten into submission.

"Much better now we've worked out how to fit all the new parts."

She smiled. "That's good because BURT's given me a few tips on redirecting the flow of magic so it works more efficiently."

He returned her smile. "I wondered when you'd show up. Some of those parts fit nicely but didn't seem to do much."

"Which is the best drive to work on so we can test each change as it goes through?"

The chief walked to the far corner. "This one. We've used it as our guinea pig for all the rest."

"I see. BURT?"

"That drive will do nicely, Stephanie. Cameron, it's been a long time."

"It has, old friend, but your girl got us through and we're here."

"For which I am both proud and grateful," BURT told him.

Cameron gestured at the engines. "What do you need?" he asked.

The AI chuckled. "It's what you need," he replied, "or, rather, what my daughter needs to augment her already more than satisfactory drives."

From the way he spoke, the chief got the impression that the *Knight* was not very impressed with the amount of tinkering happening to her person, but BURT didn't elaborate and the ship didn't respond.

"And that is?"

"We can adjust the flow of MU through them using the new parts you're installing so it's less vulnerable to interference from nMU," Stephanie explained. "Given that there are Teloran mages on the Dreth ships, we assumed there might have been some adjustments to their drive technology, and we want to try to avoid fouling our engines if we hit a patch."

She paused. "Or letting our energies leak out where it will foul their engines. BURT's been telling me how we can manage that."

"We can make most of the changes while we're docked in the hold, but we won't be able to test them until we're out of it," BURT explained.

"And my sister tells me she won't appreciate it if I explode while in the docking bay." the *Knight* sniffed. "She won't appreciate it! I'm hoping I won't explode at all!"

Todd landed, rolled, and laughed maniacally as the corridor exploded behind him.

"You...you did *what* with the *huh?*" came over his comms, but Todd was too busy running as the angry roar of fifty thoroughly irritated Dreth sounded behind him.

"Do you have that ready, Ka?" he asked.

"Yeah, boss, but be careful coming around the co—oh..."

"And I thought you liked me, corporal!" he exclaimed and leapt off the floor to drive his feet into the side of the corridor and rebound toward the opposite wall some ten feet down.

A myriad of lights went out and a small swarm of metal-carapaced bodies surged forward and out from beneath him.

"I do, boss. It's why you're not dead yet," Ka retorted. "Now, if you'll excuse me, I have fifty scramblers to reactivate and get back into position!"

"Are they here yet?" Todd asked, and Gary shook his head.

"You know what it's like, boss. It takes them a while to catch up."

"And that's only if they don't accidentally blow up," Piet told him.

"Very nice," the sergeant commented as a boom came from the opposite end of the ship.

"I told you not to touch that," Piet said.

"Touch what?" Todd asked.

"We didn't." That came through their ears as well as over their comms. "But there's a Dreth technician who will never trust a Marine ever again."

The Marine sergeant looked very pleased with himself, and Todd shook his head. "You can take a Marine out of the Federation Navy…"

Ka pulled the jack out of the port she'd created through a data line.

"Are you boys ready to dance?" she asked and lifted her blaster out of Piet's hands.

The sergeant scrutinized her carefully. "Yeah, but I have to warn you I'm all left feet."

She returned his inspection and bared her teeth in a pretend smile. "Then you'd better be a dear and let me lead."

Several soft hoots followed that remark, and Gary snickered and eased out of their hiding space after her. A shout went up from the other end of the junction and several bolts of energy ripped past them.

"Try to keep up," Ka instructed as Todd followed Gary.

She palmed a door open and left the Marines open-mouthed.

"What did you think I was doing?" she flung over her shoulder. "The data we need isn't in this system."

"Be nice, Ka," Todd warned and Reggie groaned.

"She's never nice."

"Now, now, Reg. I'm only ever not nice to you." She slid across the open room and opened a hole in a dividing wall using a combination of solids, explosive flechettes, and her body.

Jimmy raced after her, picked her up by the collar, and dragged her to her feet. "What have we told you about doing the heavy's job?"

"That you're glad I save you the bruises?" she asked, regained her balance, and pivoted to fire into the Dreth coming through an adjoining room.

Jimmy kept her moving in the right direction and she kept firing. Piet ran on the other side of the big Scotsman, using him as cover, while Todd kept their right flank clear. Angus and Henry would have taken care of the rear, except the Marines were following and could do that much for themselves. It freed up the Hooligans to do what they did best.

"Next room, Jimmy!" Ka shouted, "Five on the right, two on the left, and three straight ahead. I need the center terminal. Don't blow it up."

"What about the others?" Reggie yelled.

"All connected. Keep 'em in one piece until I say otherwise."

"You heard the lady!" Todd roared. "Angus, Henry, Darren, you're with me. Dru, Gary, Reggie, take the left. Clear either side. Marines, keep our tail clear."

"Is that like 'mind the car,' Sarge?" Gary asked as Todd bounded past the machines Ka said they weren't allowed to break.

"Nah, but if someone doesn't, we're gonna have company we don't want to keep."

"Gotcha, Sarge."

"Ka! Are you in yet?" Todd called and took cover behind the door frame as more Dreth came into the room he wanted to reach.

"Patience is a virtue, boss."

"And we all know what happens to virtue," he shouted in response and fired a blaster from each hand as he pivoted around the door frame.

Angus came after him, then Henry and Darren.

"What did you do, Sarge? Insult their mothers?" Henry demanded as the Dreth blew a hole in the opposite wall and more poured through the gap.

"Dreth have mothers?" Todd responded in Dreth and pitched a grenade toward the answering roar.

"Aw, boss, did you have to?" Henry demanded. "Now, we're gonna have to get our hands dirty."

Two of the Marines who'd moved forward to keep watch on the two sets of Hooligans exchanged looks.

"They've been on ice for twenty years and they still act like this?"

"Think about it," the other Marine told him. "for them, this was like yesterday."

"Damn! I hate these electronics!" Ka muttered. "They're playing havoc with my head."

"So? Get your head to play back!" Todd responded unsympathetically. "And don't take all day, Corporal! I don't think these guys like us to play with their computers."

"Too bad," Ka snapped as her fingers flew over the keyboard. "They should learn to share."

"Oh, I think they got that part down fine!" Henry yelled. "They're sharing their rounds and *grenades* just fine."

"Use your shields, you big babies."

"Jimmy! Get ready to pull her out of there on my mark," Todd called.

"Are we leaving, boss?"

"Unless any of you have a witch in your pocket."

Cold flowed across the room, and the Marines felt an unspeakable terror.

"Keep it together!" Jimmy ordered when he saw them hesitate. "They burn like all the rest."

"So you won't let me in, huh?" Ka snarled. "Let's see how you like it when there's two of us. Piet!"

"Almost there, your holiness."

"'Your holiness?'" one of the Marines mouthed, and Jimmy drew a hand across his throat to signal that part of the conversation was over.

"Long story," he said, "and we're too busy to tell it."

"Hey!" Ka shouted. "Can you take the back off that unit and run a little explosive over it?"

"I thought you said we couldn't blow it up?"

"Don't stick a detonator in it then, but treat it like a cake that needs a strip of icing right down the middle."

"Er...okay?"

"You are gonna love this," she promised the machine.

"I'm very sure it won't."

"Well, can it be done on the way?" Emil demanded and looked at the repair they'd uncovered in Bio.

"It could, and the risk would be minimal, but..."

He sighed. "It would still be there," he finished, and his mind raced through the calculations. "Leave it as long as you can. If it's not done by the time we transition, we'll do it en route."

"Aye, sir."

Emil turned to the next problem. "Did you say her engines were up to speed?"

"They're out there testing them now, sir. I think Steph likes the new skip capabilities."

"As long as she doesn't blow herself up," he muttered, and the tech laughed.

"Far from it. Our mages say the *Tempestarii* likes her suggestions and they're implementing them now."

"Will that delay us?"

"No, sir, but it'll get us where we need to go faster."

"That's what I need to hear." The captain paused and tapped his lips with his forefinger as his mind raced.

He glanced at the list and noted the checkmarks accompanying almost every item. Of the ones left unchecked, most were almost completed, and those left weren't as urgent as getting to where they needed to be.

"Call the *Knight*. As soon as she's satisfied with her drives, we need to leave."

Jaleck was in the command center when a second round of alarms went off. She froze and lifted her head slowly.

"Pirates?" she asked, but the technician raised a pale face and shook her head.

"No, ma'am. They've arrived."

"But...they're early."

The tech forced a smile. "Some would say that's a virtue."

"Except when you're early for the fight you've already started," the admiral replied. "Then it's a vice, and we need to break them of it before it becomes a habit."

"They are three days ahead of our calculations, War Leader," a second tech confirmed, "and they are destroying our early warning markers as they come."

"That will help us track their approach," Jaleck acknowledged. "Why didn't we have more warning?"

"Two minutes, War Leader, I'm trying to... Aha." The tech who answered was almost jubilant. It was an expression that quickly faded as he made his report.

"They've come through Bregortha, most likely by way of Ergreg and Tavach. We have nothing in those systems, and we..." He avoided her gaze, and his face colored at the admission. "We didn't add alarms there."

Jaleck lowered her head and rested her forehead along the line of her forefinger. "Well, we've learned," she stated and looked at him. "Scramble the fleet. Get the ships in drydock as space-worthy as you can but get them up as soon as they reach bare minimum. We'll need every vessel we can get, whether it's ready or not. Get them ready to go."

He nodded and spoke quickly and quietly into the comms and his fingers moved as he adjusted the frequencies for each call.

"And they'll need crews. Get the best you can for each vessel, and don't turn away any volunteers. If they have the skills and they're willing to try to save their world, use them."

She paused and stared darkly into a future she needed to avert. "If the Regime takes Dreth, we will lose another home-world." Her eyes burnt with dry fire as she added, "We can't let that happen."

Her expression stilled as she went over her instructions and mentally checked off the items that needed to be achieved before the Regime arrived.

At the end, she found one last item she needed to cover before she returned to her ship and prepared for battle.

"Gralog. Send an update torp. Tell them to hurry."

***

John frowned as the cars wound onto the narrow dirt track beside a field.

"How long did you say this would take?" he asked from the second vehicle.

"Six hours," Ted informed them. "Maybe seven. Why?"

"I… It's nothing," the boy assured him. "It seemed long, is all."

"Don't worry," the AI assured him. "There'll be rest stops along the way. I still have to have them washed, remember?"

"I remember," John told him. "And don't forget food. We'll need food too."

"You just had breakfast," Remy protested from the first car.

John held his tablet up and tapped the clock in the top right-hand corner. "Four hours ago, Rem. Four hours."

Ivy leaned forward and peered into the empty front seat. "It's past his feeding time," she whispered. "He always gets a little hangry if he's not fed on a regular basis."

John flicked a spark of magical energy down the back of her neck and she shrieked in mock outrage.

"John I'm-a-Freaking-Talent Dunn!"

He gave her an innocent look. "Yes, Ivy?"

"Don't you 'Yes, Ivy' me," she snapped and shot the front of the car a pleading look. "Just feed him," she told it. "Please?"

Ted chuckled and the car turned onto a slightly wider country road.

"I have organized a rest break in half an hour. There will be time for you to eat, but I advise only sending one into the café while the rest of you visit the restroom or remain in the car. It would be best if they did not know exactly how many of you there are."

"I can keep the three of us from being seen," John told him.

"And I can get the food," Remy advised. "It's not unusual for the driver to pay for the fuel and find snacks while his passengers visit the restroom, is it?"

"Sometimes, the passengers go in for food, too," Amaratne pointed out.

"But only if he has them," John pointed out. "If you open the rear door and simply stare through it as though checking for something, we can get out without being seen."

"Don't forget to come forward to get me," Amaratne told him. "I'll tag you on the way past so you know to close the door."

"And getting in again?" Remy asked.

"Once you've filled the cars, park near the restrooms," Ted told him. "I'll follow with this one, and the camera will show you pulling up and getting out, then returning, and nothing but the two cars staying stationary in between."

"We could simply wait for you to tell us when it's clear," John added. "No cloaking required."

"No," Ted replied. "Your subterfuge will be necessary, or

people will either see you or will notice the doors opening and closing on their own. You want to draw no attention."

"So getting back in will require me to open the door again," Remy concluded. "I will make sure I have a good supply of snacks to unload."

"Promise?" Ivy asked, but he noticed he had the undivided attention of all three humans.

"Only if you're very, very good," he told them.

Ivy leaned back in her seat and pretended to pout.

John asked, "Are we there yet?"

Amaratne snickered.

Ted sighed. "You had to provoke them."

They were dozing when Remy pulled up at the gas pumps but they woke quickly enough. Remy looked in the rear of the car until Amaratne tapped him, then he shook his head as though he'd forgotten something and went about the business of refueling.

Once he'd parked the car beside the restrooms, the AI took his body inside, browsed the shelves, and tried to calculate exactly how much his companions would need to eat on the trip. As far as he knew, Ted hadn't planned any other stops.

The cashier's eyes widened as he set his selection on the counter.

"Is all that for you?" she asked, and he smiled at her.

"This is the last stop for a very long while," he told her, "and I haven't had breakfast."

He gestured to the two cars. "That and the boss and his people want something."

"Did you leave in a hurry?" she asked, and he caught a hint of suspicion in her eyes.

Remy laughed. "No, although I probably should have. The missus wasn't impressed with a four-thirty phone call but the boss was insistent."

"Talk about your rock and a hard place," she said, and he

grimaced as he'd seen John do when thinking of something unpleasant.

He thought about it, then borrowed a line from Amaratne—one he'd used after John had knocked Ivy on her tail one too many times. "This one's gonna take more than flowers and a kiss."

The cashier giggled and blushed. "Try chocolate," she advised. "There's a nice little place off the A-28 if you want something better than what we have here."

Remy tipped his hat. "Thank you, ma'am. I think I can convince the boss to let me stop."

"I'd say he owes you one," she told him sincerely and patted his hand before she processed his credit chip and handed him his purchases. "Have a good trip, monsieur."

Her voice stopped him as he reached the door. "I love your hat!"

He smiled and touched the brim to her as he left.

"So do I," he murmured as he made his way to the car.

The gravel crunched under his feet and he jangled the keys as he approached it.

"Are you here yet?" he asked and heard John reply from near the restroom wall.

"We're here. We're waiting for Ivy."

Amaratne's snort confirmed the older man's presence. "You know women and restrooms."

"I heard that," came the hissed reply as water ran inside, and John snickered.

"You're in trouble now."

"It's only the depth that varies," the admiral replied morosely.

"Yeah?" Ivy's reply sounded clearer and the water had stopped running. "Well, let's hope it doesn't get any deeper. Whoa!"

"What?"

"Remy bought the shop!"

The AI opened the back door of the second vehicle. "Get in," he ordered, "or all these will go in with me."

"And me," Amaratne added and sounded gleeful at the prospect.

"Is…is that an apple?" John asked as someone lifted the fruit from the bag.

Remy wished he had a hand free to slap the marauding fingers as other items disappeared from what he was carrying.

"I hope your magic trick is sufficient to hide floating food," he muttered as the car dipped beneath their weight.

"We're in," John told him, took the bags from his hands, and added, "It is and it hides floating shopping bags too."

Remy stooped forward as though handing one of the bags to the occupants. "Don't make yourselves sick."

"Nope, we'll merely make ourselves fat," Amaratne sniped in return as Remy opened the door for him to get into the car they shared. "Seriously, three apples will not balance the amount of junk food in here."

"The girl believes I missed breakfast," Remy told them as he settled into the driver's seat and opened the comms between the two vehicles. "Why wouldn't I eat a ton of junk food to compensate?"

"That's a good point," John conceded, as the AIs reversed the cars out of their parking places and turned them onto the road.

"I have one more stop to make in order to maintain the illusion," Remy told them, but he wouldn't elaborate until after he'd pulled into a side road half an hour later.

"Seriously?" Amaratne asked when he returned and handed a box of very expensive hand-made chocolates through the window of John and Ivy's vehicle.

"Seriously," Remy told him and showed him the second box. "I didn't forget you."

Ivy took the first box from his fingers.

"Well," she declared and peered happily at it, "if I die before we get there, it will be from chocolate!"

"We're here," Ted announced, and Ivy sat bolt upright.

The car hadn't quite stopped but it was slowing. As she rubbed the sleep from her eyes and yawned to ease the pressure in her ears, he pulled a little off the road.

"Hurry," he told them. "I can't stop long."

"Remy?" Ivy asked.

"Don't worry. I have more than enough computing space to drive both cars."

"I'm here," Remy assured them from the shadows as the lead car eased onto the road.

The second car followed and John hefted his pack. He nodded at the admiral's suit.

"You look a little out of place."

"I won't when we're inside the base, trust me," Amaratne told him.

He led them out from under the bridge and into the underpass to emerge cautiously on the other side, where a stile separated a public reserve from the road.

"This guy you're supposed to look like," Ivy began. "How much trouble will he be in?"

The admiral smiled. "No more than he deserves."

"That good, huh?"

"No, that bad. Whatever the Regime does to him after we're through? It won't be enough."

"I'm not sure I want to know."

"Good, because I don't need you that annoyed. You need to focus. Tell me what we're doing from here."

"First, we get into the base," Ivy began. "John does his magic disappearing trick, Ted makes sure we don't get picked up by the sensors or cameras while we cut our way in, you and Remy look for the central nodes, and John and I go upstairs to insert the code to talk the satellites into taking a dive."

"Nice overview," Amaratne told her and puffed slightly from the weight of his suit. "Now, tell me the route you and John need to take."

They walked as they talked and moved swiftly through the trees while Ted tapped into what base systems he could.

CHAPTER TWENTY-ONE

The *Tempestarii* came out of nowhere with the *Knight* tucked safely inside.

"We're here," she told Emil, "and the torpedo is online."

He looked at the comms team, but the team lead preempted his question. "We're going as fast as we can, sir, but she's changed the encryption again."

It took them two minutes, both of which added up to an eternity for the captain.

"It's not looking good, sir."

"Well, at least we'll be on time," he said and skimmed the short report. "Prepare to transition on my mark. Three...two—"

"Sir! We have incoming!"

"Abort transition!"

"Transition aborted," the *Tempestarii* informed them coolly and added, "Message torp uploading."

"Time?" Emil demanded as the comms team called, "Done!"

He didn't bother to ask them how. Jaleck's message was short and to the point.

"They are four days early. Hurry."

It was followed by a set of coordinates.

"Four days early?" He glanced at the timeframe he'd been working from. "We're late! Get me Stephanie."

"I'm here," she told him.

"Jaleck asks us to hurry. The attack's begun," he told her.

Her eyes blazed.

"Get your people aboard," Emil added, trying to temper her fury. "We need to translate before we drop you off."

"Understood," Stephanie snapped, but he heard the Morgana's darkness curling through her tones and wondered how much time she'd allow.

He was about to tell her they'd travel as fast as they could when she blinked out and her voice came over the *Tempestarii's* comms.

"All crew, all crew, all crew," Stephanie began, and it was clear the Witch was in control. "Return to your ships and prepare for transition. I repeat, return to your ships and buckle in. We are going to war."

Stephanie stalked the *Knight's* corridors, her presence as reassuring as it was alarming. Power crackled over her skin and her eyes were as black as pitch.

Lars and the cats trotted beside her, and Vishlog and Frog brought up the rear. Garach and Marcus raced to the *Tempestarii's* pod suite, only to be met halfway there by Todd and the Hooligans, who were returning.

As the Witch moved past one of the shield generators, she noticed two technicians. One held several pieces from inside the generator.

"We can't stop now," the junior protested. "We only need ten minutes."

"More like thirty," the old man told him, "and we don't have it."

"It doesn't matter. The *Knight* needs her shields. You heard Steph. We're going into a war zone."

"Knight needs her people too," the senior tech told him. "She won't forgive me if I get you killed before you finish the job because something happened during transition."

"But—"

"Enough!" Stephanie snapped, and they both turned toward her.

Vishlog grabbed Zee before he could make a move on one of the toolkits lying tantalizingly close by. The technicians' eyes widened, but she ignored him.

"Shields?" she asked, and the men nodded.

"Tape yourselves to the wall and finish it while we move," she ordered. "The fight will have started when we get there and I like my ship."

"Gotcha," the senior tech said, but he spoke to her rapidly departing back.

He turned to his junior as the rest of the team moved past.

"Keep working. I'll get the tape."

"Do we have time for tethers?" the younger man asked quickly. "We're gonna need to move around a little."

The other man considered it, then gave a sharp nod.

"We'll tape ourselves to the tethers," he said. "It should work."

He hurried to the supplies locker. When he glanced back, he was glad to see his junior already reaching into the generator with the part and screwdriver in hand.

"When you said 'drop me off,'" Stephanie began once she'd opened a line to Emil.

"I meant we'll get you close to the Dreth fleet, warn them to expect a package, and then get into the fight."

"You know I won't stay near the Dreth fleet, don't you?" she asked and he gave her a sad smile.

"I know, but Tempe and I will provide a distraction while you decide on the first skip. Near the Dreth is the safest starting point. After that, you simply need to be yourself."

"Oh, I will be," Stephanie muttered, then smiled.

Emil shivered. He'd forgotten that look and the smile that said anything that stood in her way was dead and simply didn't know it.

He'd remembered by the time he met her eyes and his smile was equally savage.

"Are we ready?" he asked.

"Emil, the *Knight* and her crew were born ready."

On the weapons decks, the gun crews stood beside their weapons. The off-duty crew had been told to sleep while they could and that the *Knight* would make sure they were called when needed, but sleep was elusive.

In the engine room, Cameron checked the readings and walked between the drives, listening to them idle. They were ready.

On the *Tempestarii*, the Meligornians finished the last of Stephanie's adjustments, and the Telorans nodded approvingly.

Translation began and quiet descended. It reminded Piet of the calm before a storm.

"Thar she blows," Amaratne murmured when they reached the cleared space along the perimeter fence.

"The sensors are down, and the cameras will show nothing but empty forest for the next twenty-four hours," Ted told them. "As long as the loop isn't discovered, of course."

"In twenty-four hours," the admiral replied, "they'll have far more to worry about than a looping security feed."

They moved up to the fence and Remy flipped the top of his finger open to reveal a laser cutter hidden inside his hand.

Amaratne shook his head and put the wire snips into their pouch.

"And I thought we would have to do this the hard way," he said.

"Nope," Remy told him. "This model has all the best features."

"You mean you love them more than your hat?" Ivy asked him, and the AI smiled as he rolled the fence panel back and held it so they could slip through.

Once they were clear, he pulled it back into place and welded it together again.

"But does it come with a flashlight?" John asked and chuckled as they moved quickly to the shelter of a maintenance shed.

"Like you wouldn't believe," Remy told him smugly. He crouched beside them. "Are we ready?"

"Like you wouldn't believe," Ivy echoed softly, but her face said she was nervous.

Amaratne raised his hand and John reached across to clasp it. After a moment's hesitation, Ivy and Remy added their hands.

"We've got this," John assured them.

"We'd better have," the admiral responded. "The Witch needs us."

"She is coming back," the boy declared softly.

"And we will be waiting," Remy added.

Ivy nodded and the nerves cleared from her face. "Let's do this."

She and John turned away and moved slowly from behind the maintenance shed and toward the employees' parking lot.

Remy and Amaratne watched them disappear before they reached it.

"I wish I could do that," the older man murmured.

"Talent envy, huh?" Remy replied as they leaned against the wall.

"Only sometimes. When I think about what that boy has been through…"

"Yup," the AI agreed. "We're lucky to have him."

"Hell, this whole world's lucky," the AI declared. "It merely doesn't know it."

Remy consulted his internal chronometer. "How long do you think they'll need?" he asked.

"Half an hour to get to the beanstalk and maybe another two to get to the orbital. Twenty seconds to start causing trouble."

"They'll need more than twenty seconds to reach the server room," the AI observed.

"I know that," Amaratne said, "but what are the chances they'll stay out of trouble until they get there?"

Remy laid a hand on the admiral's shoulder. "Have a little faith."

"Faith is one thing," he grumbled, "but there's reality, too."

His teammate patted him. "Then have faith that they'll have the sense to make your plan a reality."

The man shifted uneasily. "Do you think they're there yet?"

Remy frowned. "I thought I told Roma to leave your mental maturity alone."

While Amaratne thought about how to answer that, John guided Ivy down the busy corridors of the communication center. It was hard to keep moving when all he wanted to do was stop and stare.

He'd never seen such a place and, judging from her tight hold on his arm, neither had she. Neither of them said a word until they reached the base of the cable.

Rather than try to go through the turnstile, he floated them over the heads of the waiting queue and into one of the cars. He kept them hovering above the car's floor, remembering how they'd been discovered in the balloon.

It wouldn't do for the same thing to happen there.

Ivy stifled a gasp as the car started to move and the world outside became a blur. John put his mouth close to her ear.

"It used to take five days to ride one of these," he mused. "Can you imagine?"

She gulped and pressed her face into his chest. "I don't want to."

"What's wrong?" he whispered over the comms.

"It's too fast," she whispered. "You can't bend light around vomit."

"I could try," he offered.

"Nope. Just hold me and tell me when we get there."

"If you wanted a hug, all you had to do was ask. There's no need to be so dramatic about it."

She gave him a half-hearted slap on the chest but didn't move her head, and they stood in silence until the car came to a stop.

On the ground, Amaratne looked at his watch and nudged Remy.

"It's time," he said and checked the pistol in his jacket pocket.

He took it out and made sure it was ready for use once he stood. "Is it clear?"

Remy stuck his head around the corner as Ted replied.

"Clear for the cameras."

"Clear for parking lot," the younger AI agreed.

"You have a two-minute window before the next vehicle

arrives and you're out of the guard station's line of sight," Ted informed them.

Moving quickly, they reached the parking lot long before the vehicle and crouched to catch their breath. They listened as the other car pulled up and waited for the doors to slam and the crunch of shoes on gravel to fade.

"Clear," Ted told them, and they rose from behind the car. Amaratne straightened his jacket and checked Remy carefully.

"That hat—" he began.

"The hat stays," the AI retorted. "I'm your guest, remember?"

The admiral sighed. "Fine, but on your head be it."

"Exactly," Remy concluded.

Amaratne shook his head. The humor helped but he knew exactly how hard this mission would be—and in exactly how many ways it could go wrong.

"Well," he mumbled, "I always wanted to go out with a bang."

"John wouldn't be too happy to hear you say that," Remy reminded him and the admiral chuckled.

"That young man is the last person I'd want to upset—except for maybe the Morgana," he replied.

They reached the entrance and he smiled and ushered Remy through before him. They were almost there, and if he achieved what they'd come to do and things did go wrong, it didn't matter.

"Let's get it done," he said.

"We're—" John began, and Ivy slapped him again.

"I know."

As soon as the car was clear, he used a little Talent to delay the doors so they could debark, guided them onto the concourse, and gave Ivy time to get her bearings.

"Where to?" he asked and noticed an alcove dotted with tables and chairs. He guided her to a table and eased her into a seat with her back to the window.

It took a minute for her to get her bearings, but he felt her move as she raised her head and looked around the communications center. He could only imagine the similarities between the work setup he saw here and those in the hubs on the ground.

As he looked around, he saw two Talents, each accompanied by a handler as they moved from one workspace to the next and wondered what gift they had to land them there. He truly hoped they weren't psi.

Ivy pulled her tablet out and tapped into the station's internal Wi-Fi, while John kept watch on the workers he could see and looked for any sign that her connection had been noticed. Nothing was apparent, but he had begun to feel uneasy by the time she tucked the tablet away.

"The server room is through there and up a flight of stairs. It takes up almost the entire floor above us."

"And you'll be safe up there?"

"Surveillance shows a couple of Talents," she replied, "and one guy whose job seems to be to watch them. I only need to get past them to…"

She pulled her tablet out and showed him. "Here. Is that okay?"

He gave her a grim smile. "As long as you're safe enough to do what you need to do, it'll do fine."

"It will be."

"Good. Once you're in position, I'll draw the Talents and their handler to this floor and keep everyone occupied until you've finished."

Her eyes darkened with worry. "Will you be okay for that? There are so many guys here."

"Girls, too," he observed, "but yeah, I'll be fine. I'll try to work back to the stairs when you're done. Will there be a signal?"

"For?"

"If you're finished."

"Yes. It'll involve a slew of cussing and satellites falling from the skies." She smiled. "Exactly like an American Fourth of July."

"But isn't it November?"

Her smile vanished and she glared at him.

"Aussies!" She harrumphed. "Can't live with 'em. Can't shove 'em out of a spaceship when you're done with 'em!"

CHAPTER TWENTY-TWO

Two systems from Dreth, Captain Thiele followed Ironsides through the transition to emerge at the rendezvous point.

He'd give the boy credit. His ships had kept formation and would have been in good shape to face any hostile force that might have been waiting. He couldn't say the same for Canavan.

"Get your formation in order!" he roared, "and pray you don't need cohesive maneuvering to survive the next battle."

"Command says we're to wait here for reinforcements and further orders. They're sending the rest of the fleet, sir!"

A prickle of apprehension went through him.

"Did they send holding coordinates?" he asked, and a new heading arrived on his console.

"Helm, pass those coordinates along and have Ironsides move toward them post-haste," he ordered. "Clear the transition point! Fleet to stay in formation. Scan the system to see who else is here."

He listened as his orders were passed on and waited for the results, his body tense.

"Scans indicate no other presence, sir."

"Good, keep scanning. We'll have new arrivals shortly. Make sure you identify every single one. We don't want any surprises."

His next pause stretched a few moments longer before he issued another set of orders.

"Go through Readiness Drill One. Every ship and every flotilla. Pass the word."

Klaxons sounded, and the crew leapt into action. Thiele wondered at the wisdom of another drill, but after Canavan's performance, he wondered if it wasn't essential. A drill would keep them busy and might ensure that each ship was ready. Disciplinary action could wait until after the battle had been won.

Halfway through, the scanners picked up movement on the edge of the system. The captain frowned.

It was in the wrong direction.

"Ping those new arrivals," he ordered. "Tell me who they are. Alert the rest of the fleet. Shift formation to Compact Arrow One, Rogers to fly overwatch while I close the tail."

As the ships closed ranks to make the more compact arrowhead with a layer of protection flying overhead, the scan team worked to identify the incoming fleet.

Alarm rolled through the command deck when they did.

"Dreth, sir! It's the Dreth!"

"Do you know what I like best about this?" Amaratne asked as Remy opened fire with a blaster in each hand.

"No, Admiral. What?"

"All the pockets!" He tossed another sticky at a door and continued to run. "We're almost there."

Remy stopped beside him and swept the corridor ahead with fire as the explosive blew the door in behind them and collapsed the corridor.

Guards and curious technicians fell with equal alacrity.

"Where to?"

"Right, left, and straight," Amaratne replied. "That's the hub we need."

"Stay close," the AI instructed, and they both bolted headlong down the corridor and skidded at the turns as Remy blasted any opposition clear.

"I thought we would be more subtle about this," Ted complained, and his nephew chuckled.

"We weren't to know the tech had a run-in with appendicitis and was off work. Our disguise lasted the five minutes it took for one of his colleagues to want to know why he was coming into the building when he was supposed to be in the hospital."

"Yeah, Ted," Amaratne snarked, took cover behind Remy, and lobbed a stick onto the ceiling behind them. "What happened?"

"I can't be everywhere at once," the older AI replied stiffly, and the admiral pretended shock as he shot the first guard to step around a corner Remy didn't have covered.

"You will still be able to insert the code, won't you?" Ted asked and sounded slightly offended.

"Of course," the admiral assured him as his teammate eliminated another security guard and proceeded to fire on the rest of the team. The sound of solids hitting metal rang loudly, and Amaratne took cover behind the droid's solid body.

"Let's not do that too often," Remy muttered. "I will need some serious re-plating once this job's done."

"Are you compromised?" Ted asked and his voice carried a sense of urgency.

"Not at this stage. Next time, it will be a different story."

"Next time, activate your shielding."

"That is one of the things that will need to be replaced," Remy told him.

"I thought you said you weren't compromised," his uncle protested.

"I'm not. It's only a flesh wound," he argued, then added as he slowed, "We're here. Try not to break anything."

Amaratne shed the fat suit and stepped clear of it. "That had its uses," he remarked, "but all I'll miss will be the pockets."

"Tell me you're wearing body armor," Remy said as he moved behind one of the servers and found a data point.

"I never leave home without it," the admiral retorted, took two of the larger pistols out of the suit, and transferred the grenades and stickies to his harness.

"And don't blow anything up until I'm done," his teammate added.

"Only the bad guys," he promised.

Remy rolled his eyes.

"Do you see what I have to put up with?" he asked Ted as he started his upload. "You did this to me."

Amaratne moved away from the android, keeping an eye on the four doors leading into the central core. "Tell me when you're done. I have some welcome packs to distribute."

He trotted to the first door. "Ted?"

"It's clear," Ted told him reluctantly, and the admiral punched the access panel.

Taking half a dozen scramblers from their pouches, he programmed them quickly, set them on the floor, and flattened himself against the wall as he watched them climb to the corridor ceiling and distribute themselves along it.

Once they were in place, he closed the door and set a sticky over the edge. Whoever opened it would get one heck of a surprise.

He set a second one on the ceiling above the door and marked where it was before he moved to the second door.

"Ted?"

He'd repeated the process at the second and third doors and was advancing on the fourth when Ted spoke.

"Incoming. Stand clear of the door."

Amaratne stood clear and scooped another half-dozen scramblers out of their satchel. "Give me proximity," he said and pitched them through the door the minute it opened.

Several startled shouts rang out in answer, and someone pushed through the door in a panic. Their harness snagged and they tried to yank free in uncoordinated movements.

The admiral shot them in the head and pushed on.

"Talk to me, Ted."

"You have incoming in three vectors," the AI informed him.

Explosions and screams came from Corridor One.

"Two vectors," the AI corrected.

More explosions and screams followed.

"One vector. You are clear."

"You know that will never buff out, don't you?" Remy asked from the corner.

"And I thought you were busy," Amaratne snapped.

"It's hard to focus when someone's having that much fun."

"I promise, I'll share what's left when you're done."

Amaratne found a position that gave him cover and the ability to change direction easily, then realized he could fit one of the last three stickies to the ceiling above the fourth door.

"How many of those did you bring?" Remy asked.

"Not enough," he answered. "Why didn't I bring more?"

The third door exploded, and he opened fire as soon as shadows appeared through the smoke. He found cover behind one of the stacks and began to pick off security guards as they arrived.

"How many of these guys are there?" he demanded as the last man fell. "I counted another eight guys here!"

"The communications center has its own company attached to the facility," Ted replied, "and they seem to have woken up."

"What? All of them?"

"Only those who were off-duty and asleep," the AI reassured him. "It's not that many."

"And how many were already awake?"

"It's hard to say—twenty at the facility and more on the orbital." Ted paused. "They are preparing to come down."

"And Talents?"

"Ah…" Ted said, as though he'd forgotten something and went silent. "I believe you will have some of their company shortly. I am still trying to ascertain their numbers."

"Which way, Ted?"

"Are you all right?" John asked as he slid behind one of the communications stacks after Ivy.

He watched as she settled into the cramped space and jacked the tablet in.

"Sure, I've got this." She waved her fingers toward the main hub. "Go play while I get to work."

"And you can get to the pods if you need to," he pressed.

She glared at him.

"Humor me."

With a sigh, she jerked out a hand and pointed to the left. "Four feet that way, blue button in. Red button out. Parachute." She turned pale. "Is that good enough?"

He nodded.

"Good enough," he confirmed.

His eyes lit with yellow fire as he turned, and fury rolled through his face.

"John?"

Blue fire rimmed his body and lightning arced in tiny tendrils around him. One word leaked to her on the edge of a snarl.

"Becca."

The blood drained from her face and she fumbled for the drive connection. If she didn't get this code uploaded very, very fast, there might not be an orbital left to get it uploaded through!

John reached the end of the stack without being seen and sent his consciousness through the station. This was one trick he'd learned from Stephanie that he'd never thought he'd use.

Now, he had the perfect reason.

Taking the orbital's speakers and sending his voice into every mind he sensed, he began to speak.

"You have been wicked in your efforts, unjust in your judgments, and unfair in your treatment of others and now, you have been found guilty of crimes against all humanity. She is coming, and I am her Apostle!"

The Talent on the other side of the data center looked around wildly and froze when he decloaked. She reacted with a small shriek of surprise at his appearance and died an instant later.

The second Talent and his handler had barely enough time to look at her corpse before they fell beside her, and John moved down the stairs.

When he reached the bottom, he didn't bother with the door and simply removed the wall in a single blast of power that let him look out over the work center and arrivals lounge.

Several comms techs looked up from their desks. A dozen more dived under them. Half a dozen ran to the elevator car and five security guards appeared out of their office.

The young mage laughed and launched a wave of blue that rolled across the station to flatten people to the floor or plaster them to the walls. When the first guard recovered enough to raise his blaster, he pinned him to the wall with a skewer of ice and unleashed bursts of blue lightning.

Computers exploded and monitors vanished in bursts of brown smoke and slag. The coffee machine hurled shards of metal in every direction. The next guard to raise a weapon tore apart in a storm of blue light that lashed out in all directions to electrocute everyone around him.

"Justice," John snarled when no one moved, "has been served."

He turned and started up the stairs.

———

When she heard the wall explode below her, Ivy paused. The upload was running without her, but the surveillance feeds would be a problem.

With a few quick commands, she had the cameras slaved to the server. After a brief search, she found the Regime population broadcast channel.

Several commands later, what was happening inside the communications orbital went out in a single stream to every channel in the world—but not before she'd found the point where John's voice had started coming out of the speakers.

The broadcast started a few seconds prior to his announcement and ran from there. Playing it back, she had to smile.

"Nice speech, baby!" She smirked as the broadcast continued and checked the upload for the satellites to make sure the link to the communications array below was secure.

Next, she had to make sure some of those satellites would land exactly where Amaratne needed them to. They came with little thrusters. Who knew?

———

Her smirk would have been a smile if she could have seen the CIO's face.

David Thomason was not amused.

In fact, he sat in his seat and gaped at the main viewer that filled the opposite wall. John's words echoed around him.

"You have been wicked in your efforts…"

"No!" he shouted and pushed his chair back.

"…unjust in your judgments, and unfair…"

The Regime leader rose from behind his desk. "No!"

John's voice continued despite his protests. "And now, you have been found guilty of crimes against all humanity."

"No!" the CIO screamed, and he hurled his cup at the young mage's face.

"She is coming, and I am her Apostle!"

"You are a dead man!" he shrieked in answer and advanced on the screen with his forefinger extended. *"Dead!"*

The young Talent clearly didn't hear him because he blasted the three people in the upper room and destroyed a wall on his way down the stairs.

"Dead," David repeated, as people fell and equipment began to explode. He turned to his communicator. "Get me Aurora! Get me Deverey! And will someone stop that damned broadcast!"

CHAPTER TWENTY-THREE

"We understand your anger," Captain Thiele said placatingly as the first Dreth came onscreen. "We have come to aid you."

"You are guilty of murder," the female Dreth declared and drew herself to her full height. "I am Dreth's Fleet Admiral, the Speaker for their Council of Families and the War Leader of the Clans, and I carry their judgment with me."

He looked taken aback. "We are— Are you saying the Regime slaughtered the people of Hrageth's Run? But...why would we—"

His viewscreen went live with footage of Regime ships leaving the ruined world, of the wasteland they'd left, and of the —was that a ghost?

The last part of the admiral's broadcast was the last piece of the puzzle, an intercepted communique with the orders for the outpost to be destroyed.

"Where?" He gaped.

"Some of your spies need retraining," Jaleck told him and gave him a predator's smile. "Or they would if they were not already serving their sentence in Tegortha's ever-boiling gut."

She continued before he could find the words to refute her.

"Dreth finds the Regime guilty of piracy. Worse, it finds the Regime guilty of the murder of the people of Hrageth's Run, including seven hundred and fourteen of their own human civilians."

Her dark eyes glittered angrily. "People who were not guilty of treason and who were not guilty of anything more than mining resources, a levy of which was earmarked for payment to the Regime."

"But—" Thiele tried to get a word in edgewise.

Jaleck rolled over him. "As such, the Dreth Council of Families accepts the Regime's desire for war."

"Incoming!" the scanner operator cried as the admiral spoke the last syllable. "Sir! We have multiple missiles inbound."

"Shields!" he ordered. "Ironsides, take us in. We outnumber them and reinforcements are on their way."

"Aye, aye, sir!"

By ordering the younger man to lead, Thiele had surrendered the lead in the battle, but he wasn't worried. The Dreth were outnumbered and were about to pay for their lies with their lives.

He was not surprised when the fleet split in half before him. "Take the starboard," he commanded before Ironsides could hesitate. "It holds their Flag."

Thiele listened to the younger captain relay his orders and specify targets for each flotilla. The Dreth wouldn't know what hit them.

None of them expected the enemy fleet to split a second time, although the fleet captain should have expected the attack that came from the half that had veered away to port.

His own flotilla suffered the first casualty, and Rogers was soon under attack from two sides. Canavan began to laugh until his outermost ship took damage.

Ironsides didn't wait for Thiele's next set of instructions but took the fleet through and brought them around.

"It's a shame to waste a good captain," Jaleck mused as she

listened to Ironsides' orders. "If that's what he is, but he's on the wrong side so I guess we'll never know. *Pride* and *Maw*, the lead ship is yours."

As the two battleships moved to obey her, the scanners picked up movement. More ships now appeared from where this fleet had first arrived.

"We have company," her scan team informed her.

"Make sure no one flies with their back to that new fleet," Jaleck ordered and her eyes glittered as she studied the battle screen.

They'd been outnumbered before, and now there were more.

She needed to annihilate as many as she could before they brought her fleet down.

John had returned to the server room in time to see one of the Talents climb painfully to his feet and move toward Ivy's corner.

"I wouldn't," he said, and the Talent turned while balls of lightning formed in his hands.

"The Witch is coming," he told him. "You don't have to fight for them anymore."

The man hurled the lightning at him.

"No Heretic shall walk this plane." He snarled and summoned more lightning.

John didn't reply. He blocked the incoming attack and absorbed the power into his shield before he fired a swarm of jagged lightning bolts into the Talent's chest.

"Pity," he said. "She would have shown mercy."

He turned, chose something that didn't look attached to what Ivy was doing, and launched another lightning swarm.

The tower of boxes and flickering lights exploded.

"Hey! I could have used that!" The protest came from Ivy's corner and he chuckled.

A frustrated growl answered. "There is no need to make my job harder than it already is!"

Movement caught his eye and he pivoted. Power arced over him as a door in the far corner opened. The first man through wore Regime pants but his weapons belt and jacket were gone and he was unbuttoning his shirt as he ran.

He grinned at John, an expression torn between terror and jubilation. The Talent who followed gave a short cheer as she bolted to the stairs.

The young mage let them go and watched as they disappeared down the stairwell. He heard their gasps when they saw the carnage on the next floor. When he stalked to the door, he heard their footsteps clatter across the concourse as he looked through the aperture.

A corridor ran the perimeter of the server room with offices and storage facilities on the other side. As he looked both ways, he heard boots and saw two Regime Enforcers jogging toward him with two Talents running behind them.

More boots heralded the arrival of another team from the other direction, and Ivy's quick, "John, behind you," warned him of the other door he'd missed.

He backed away and positioned himself so her hiding place was behind him. Her fingers clattered as she worked and he hoped she was almost finished. There was far more security on this station than the reports had revealed.

Pulling a shield of blue around him, he glanced from one door to the other and waited for his opponents to appear. A bolt of lightning sparked against his shield as he looked one way and he turned.

"It's about time you got here," he said and focused on the two Talents who stepped purposefully out of the corridor to face him.

Their handlers followed, and John smiled as the first of the other teams arrived from the other direction. He caught the movement of one handler's throat as he swallowed and saw the man's face pale.

"Isn't he supposed to be afraid?" the man asked and nudged his companion.

The other handler nodded and glanced at the stairwell. He'd barely taken a step toward it when John jerked a hand up and yanked the gun from his grasp.

He stared with startled eyes as his weapon landed in the young mage's palm and started to run when the boy's hand closed around the grip. His body dropped across the stairwell entry as his head exploded.

The other handler dove into the corridor, his last words flung over his shoulder as he fell.

"Take him down!"

The patrons of the Four-Leaf were oblivious to what was going on over their heads. They ordered their pints, nuts, and fries without a clue to the havoc John was causing as they watched the last match being dissected on the sports channel.

Ivan and Caleb arrived unnoticed, their work clothes not out of place in the busy pub. The day had not run smoothly.

Caleb nursed his head with one hand while Ivan listened sympathetically.

"I tell you," Caleb whined, "whoever is doing the damned work with the explosives, it's giving me a headache!"

"I hear—" Ivan's sympathetic reply cut off abruptly as the game scene died and was replaced by the sharp reports of a pistol and the snap of magic. "What the—"

He tapped his friend's shoulder and turned him toward the screen, but John's voice came clearly through the speakers before he could say anything.

"You are human," he declared, and the screen showed a young

man with unruly hair shrouded in blue who confronted four older Talents with lightning in their hands.

"You were born human," he continued. "The fact that you're a human who can tap into the energy of the world does not negate that."

"That's not what the Regime says." The Talent who replied sounded more resentful than disbelieving.

"The Regime lied," John snapped. "They lied because they needed a scapegoat at the end of the last war, someone for people to be angry with while they took power."

"The Heretic," one of the other Talents snarled.

"The Witch," he corrected, "who saved our world countless times and was rewarded by being made an exile from her own worlds, while those she sought to help were vilified and treated like second-class citizens."

"Animals!" the third Talent retorted. "We're treated like highly intelligent animals and our parents made pariahs."

"And it's wrong," John told him. "You are not animals. Your parents did nothing wrong. You are as human as the rest of us."

"But our reality is this!" the fourth Talent protested, despair in his tone.

"Not for much longer," he assured them, and his voice rose to a crescendo. "The Witch is back and she is coming! And I am making a way for those who wish to throw off the shackles of tyranny to join me and fight!"

One of the Talents drew back and the power in her hands intensified.

"No one will believe you," she protested.

"They will when fire rains from the sky," he retorted.

The blue surrounding his body crackled as the Talent attacked and delivered a spray of electrical balls into his shield.

"Run if you want to live!" he commanded and thrust a hand forward.

The fire that followed fried the Talent where she stood and sealed her smoking corpse to the wall.

"Find me if you want to fight," he added.

One of them turned to the stairwell but they didn't reach it. The collar around their throat sparked with light and their head separated from their shoulders.

The other two didn't even try.

The Four-Leaf's patrons gaped at the screen as they unleashed a hail of lightning, electrical balls that exploded on contact, and fire. They gasped when the maelstrom cleared and John stood untouched in the center.

He raised the pistol and opened fire, and the Talents renewed their attack. Everyone startled when a triumphant shout cracked across the room.

"Yes!"

Behind the cover of the machines, Ivy couldn't see the effect she had on the fight. She'd found the solution to the final defensive program standing between her and downloading the code into the satellites.

The upload was done, and all that remained was the transfer between the orbital and the satellites to which it was connected—and then to have the code jump to the next orbital and the satellites it controlled.

Her fingers flew over the keyboard and her tablet beeped as the code was accepted and the transfer began. Only then did she glance around the rack of machines.

She was in time to see John lifted off his feet and hurled into the other side of the stack. It shook, and she glanced at her tablet to make sure the transfer continued.

"Ugh!" her teammate grumbled, pushed onto his feet, and swept a wall of blue into an advancing Talent.

One of the others scoffed at him, "Where's your Heretic now, 781?

"I...am...more...than a number," he all but snarled and sent another barrage of electricity at the man.

Ivy glanced at the tablet, saw the transfer was moving smoothly and that the code was already being sent on, and stood. Another strike rocked John back and the remaining Talents started to close.

"To heck with this shit!" she exclaimed and picked up the blaster she'd set down beside her.

One-handed, she pressed the command she'd typed for the system to block all incoming access to the hub. As soon as the tablet beeped its acceptance, she rose and fired in one fluid movement.

"No one will change you back!" she snapped and slid around the edge of the racks to join the fight.

In the data center below, Amaratne and Remy were in trouble. The AI had finished uploading the code and moved up in time to deal with the squad that slid into the room through Door Number Four.

One of them had lost his life when the sticky on the roof blew and the rest advanced cautiously.

They needn't have bothered, Remy thought as the admiral reversed away from the Enforcers coming through Doors Number Two and Three.

"Nice of you to join me," Amaratne called and acknowledged his presence.

"Nice of you to leave some for me," he responded.

"You know I saved the best for last, don't you?" the man replied as a Talent and his handler appeared through Door Number One.

"You know I didn't need one all for myself, right?" Remy asked as a second Talent and her handler appeared out the smoke wisping around Door Number Four.

"I didn't want you to feel left out."

"Next time, go halves."

They stood angled out from each other, and Amaratne glanced at Door Four. The woman looked vaguely familiar, but he couldn't remember where he'd seen her before.

The man, on the other hand, was young enough to have been his son—if his son had had flame-red hair and a face set in a perpetual sneer.

The surviving Enforcers advanced with their blasters leveled.

"Give it up, boys," one instructed.

"Hmmph. Not likely," Remy muttered but kept his voice pitched for Amaratne's ears.

The admiral chuckled and his blaster didn't waver.

"I don't think John will be very happy with us," he said.

"Why not?" his teammate asked.

"Because I recall him saying no one was to die and I don't think we can oblige him."

"Is your shield up?" the AI asked.

"It's on," he acknowledged. "Why?"

"Because I just activated the last scramblers in your suit."

"I missed some?"

"They're called scramblers for a reason."

As he spoke, the admiral's discarded fat suit began to crawl across the floor toward the Enforcers. Amaratne jerked his head around and stared at it.

"You what?" he exclaimed and released his blaster so it hung from its strap as soon as some of the Enforcers followed his gaze.

He whipped his hand into his pouch, pulled out the scramblers he'd retained, and threw them toward their opponents.

Some of the Enforcers fired as soon as he moved, but his

shield coped with the impacts and he went from scramblers to grenades.

"Messy," Remy noted and followed it with, "Incoming!" when he caught sight of the female Talent who glowed a sudden, virulent blue.

As if his words were a signal, the male Talent looked up. Amaratne glanced around to see what Remy meant as the female Talent raised her hands and the two handlers were encased in blue.

Before either of them could react, she picked them up and hurled them toward the infiltrators. "Catch!"

The Enforcers who'd managed to escape the area of Amaratne's little bombardment were regrouping, but only three of them were left. At the woman's call, their mouths dropped open and they froze.

The admiral didn't waste time to see what she did next. He snatched his blaster, pivoted, and fired. He caught the first controller in the chest and walked his fire into the man's head. A small square box fell from the man's hand, and he fired into that as well.

Beside him, Remy eliminated his controller before the man landed and turned his pistols on the remaining Enforcers. Only one of them managed to raise his blaster in time.

He was not fast enough to fire before he died.

As they eliminated the controllers and the Enforcers, the female moved so she had a clear line of sight on the redhead and delivered two lightning bolts as she approached. That gave the kid enough of a heads-up to defend himself or leave.

Instead, he chose to stay and fight—and he tried to take the fight to her. A fistful of glittering darts whistled across the room as he advanced and a ball of fire followed.

The woman caught most of the darts on a shield, but one got through. Her eyes widened when she saw the fireball, but she wrapped a small oval of blue around her hand and smacked it back the way it had come.

Before the younger Talent had time to respond, she followed the return with a volley of smaller fireballs and several narrow darts of her own. Her opponent didn't dodge them all and didn't try to raise a shield.

He screamed as the fire wrapped around his torso and fell silent as the next barrage of darts caught his throat and head. The female Talent put a hand out and leaned on the wall.

"We have a little time," she rasped when the two infiltrators looked at her. "I can show you out."

Remy was the first to respond. He hurried toward her as Amaratne followed, his blaster raised in case she couldn't be believed.

The woman didn't protest, but she did take Remy's hand when he offered it.

"Are you hurt?" the AI asked, and she shook her head.

"There's no time to bleed," she told him. "It's this way."

Amaratne lowered his blaster to port and scanned the room and the corridors behind them as she led them farther into the complex.

"The front door's compromised."

CHAPTER TWENTY-FOUR

"Tegortha's Teeth, there are so many of them," Jaleck murmured.

"And our first-wave friends are very happy to see them," the chief of comms commented.

They watched as their target's shields absorbed their missiles but flickered and died under the fire from their sister ship. The third ship in their attack formation scored several hits as they completed their pass.

As one, they increased power to take them out of retaliation range and circle for another approach. Across the battlefield, other Dreth formations were doing the same accompanied by swarms of Dreth fighters.

Shouts came over the Regime comms they'd hacked, and Jaleck almost blessed the spies. They'd been such useful creatures by the time the Telorans were done.

Her face hardened. And then they'd been dead, for all the good that would do her world.

"Stand by for boarding!"

"Where are those Marines when you need them?"

"What is that— Dreth have Talent?"

The panic was tempered by other more important messages.

"Stand fast, Fleet One. We will secure your port flank."

"Tango Alpha Delta, swing starboard. Don't let them break away."

"Rear Admiral on the field!"

Jaleck caught the worried look from her comms chief and looked at the scan team. "Get me a visual."

"On screen, ma'am. Whatever they're sending, it's bigger than anything we've got."

She regretted having to give up the Teloran ship she'd taken. Still, it had been for a good cause. She watched the new Regime ships transition into real space.

"Those are capital ships," she observed and kept her voice firm as she watched them emerge. "Now things are interesting."

She started to smile, and her crew felt a shiver of anticipation. Their War Lord was baring her teeth. They were either dead and didn't know it, or they were about to do something that would end in death or glory.

Before she could tell them what it was, though, comms intercepted a transmission from one of the newly arrived capital ships.

"Alert Tango-Alpha-Delta. Incoming translation two sectors over. Alert Tango-Alpha-Delta. You have a large incoming translation. It is not one of ours. I repeat, it is not— *Holy shit!*"

Jaleck smirked. "That's not standard communication protocol," she observed and signaled to her scan team. "Show me."

As they scrambled to provide her with the data, another transmission came through in a voice filled with fear.

"It's the Leviathan. I repeat, the Leviathan just transitioned in-system!"

The ensuing barrage of communications masked the incoming call for the admiral.

"Sorry we're late," Emil told her. "I brought you a gift to make it up to you but let me apologize."

The transmission ended and she chuckled. On the screen, the *Tempestarii's* engines flared, and she changed course to target the two battleships leading the Tango-Alpha-Delta.

Jaleck gave the two ships this. They stood their ground and fired, and when their shields flared and flame gouted into space, they turned to run.

The Regime's Rear Admiral's next order held an edge of panic.

"Bring that bitch down!"

She smiled as their opponents turned in blind obedience to the admiral's orders, and she gave her own quiet command.

"All captains, show no mercy."

Dreth battle cries filled the decks.

"Boarding parties, capture or evacuate. You have three minutes to decide."

The communications board lit up as Dreth Marines called their decisions, and Jaleck felt her ship turn as it targeted the closest Regime cruiser.

A sudden scream was picked up on the open comm line.

"What is that?"

Jaleck frowned but a second later, a familiar voice sounded in the heads of enemy and friend alike.

"You hurt my people. You hurt my clans. You killed my friends."

Stephanie paused, but the admiral had the impression of fury and an impending storm. The girl's next words were as much an order to her and her people as they were a heads-up to the Regime.

"There will be *no* empathy, *no* sympathy, *no* forgiveness, and *no mercy.*"

She identified herself with her next words.

"My name is Stephanie Morgana—and I am the Bitch who will bring you down!"

After a brief flash, another engine signature appeared on the battle map.

"It's the *Knight*," the scan chief whispered in awe.

"And she's not messing around," his second answered and pointed to where the ship had chosen to appear.

Jaleck's lips curved in appreciation. The *Ebon Knight* had an attitude as bad as her mistress's and she'd chosen to decloak in the middle of the largest cluster of enemy ships that turned to threaten her sister.

On the board, it looked like the *Knight* had exploded in every direction at once. Every gun fired, and missiles followed.

The admiral stared. The gun crews had to be working double-time to release that much Tegorthan pain—or the ship had been given serious upgrades.

Both, she decided when the vessel continued to fire and enemy shields collapsed around her. At least one ship collided with its allies in its haste to escape the newcomer's fire, and explosions flared throughout the Regime fleet.

At the same time, a circle of blue appeared in front of the ship leading the charge toward the *Tempestarii's* flank. Before its captain had time to alter course around it, the vessel had gone through and appeared in front of the space of a new transition at the Regime's entry point.

Battlecruiser met ship-of-the-line with too much proximity and momentum to stop, and the resulting explosion tore both ships apart. Debris spread in missile-like arcs to the ships nearby, and Jaleck chuckled.

"That'll teach you to enter a battle zone in close formation," she told them.

"Yup," Gralog commented from behind her shoulder. "It sucks to be them."

She couldn't agree more.

"Him!" Rawlins said and stabbed her finger on one of the images moving across the screen in front of her, Captain Newcome of the *Earth's Rise.*

She glanced at Johnny and the ex-Naval analyst nodded.

"He had significant connections to Intel, and I can't see that changing. That'll be where the dirty-trick boys are putting their data."

The captain tapped the comms. "Todd, we have a target. Knight?"

"Hold onto your hat, Captain."

To those watching, it looked like the *Knight* simply vanished, but not before she fired another barrage that destroyed another dozen ships to leave the Regime's charge—and most of its fleet—in tatters.

When the ship appeared again, the *Earth's Rise* had already altered course for the transition point.

"Don't let her transition!" Rawlins ordered.

"Do I look like I was born yesterday?" the *Knight* snarled. "My gun crews have her in their sights and the appropriate ammunition loaded. We'll stop her in three...two...one!"

The three missiles that leapt from her bow had been carefully chosen, as had the barrage that demolished the *Rise's* rear shields before the missiles arrived.

A single missile penetrated a hull already suffering multiple fractures. Sealing foam filled the breaches rapidly, but it was not enough.

The explosive detonated two levels above the ship's engine room. It knocked the engines off-line but didn't destroy the shielding surrounding them. Reactivating them would take time.

"That won't last forever," the *Knight* informed them, "but you need the data and EMP would not have guaranteed its retrieval."

"Noted," Todd confirmed sharply. "We'll make sure she doesn't run away with us."

"You'd better," Stephanie told them, and Rawlins froze.

Thinking of what the girl might do to retrieve her Todd sent chills down her spine.

Clearing her throat, she managed one heartfelt blessing before she turned to the battle again.

"Godspeed, Marine."

John was holding his own when he felt the orbital shudder with two high-speed arrivals. Ivy ran to the stairs and peered over the edge.

"We've got company," she told him.

"Well, duh," he muttered and threw lightning into the face of an Enforcer who stuck his head around the door. "What kind?"

"The kind that wear power armor and carry very big guns?"

He fired a hasty barrage at both doors and hurried toward her to see what she meant. She rose to cover the doors and dropped an Enforcer who'd gathered enough courage to look through.

"Well, this will suck," he grumbled as she shot another enemy and turned to him.

"Which way?"

"Uh…" He picked a door at random. "That way."

They bolted toward it, and Ivy eliminated the Enforcer in their path while John dealt with one more. The corridor was temporarily clear, so she turned back, reefed a grenade clear of the bandolier, and tossed it into the server room.

"Do you know where you're going?" she asked as it exploded.

"Cable," he told her and looked at the damage she'd caused.

"Gotcha," she said and started toward the next set of stairs leading down.

When she saw he wasn't following, she came back and grabbed his arm. "It's time to go!"

They'd almost reached the stairs when figures appeared coming up them. She threw another grenade, took a sudden turn to the right, and raced out along one of the spokes to where the relays were located.

"Don't break them," she ordered and pointed to the dishes interspersed by a clear view of space. "Some of the satellites need more time."

"How do you know?"

She tapped her skull.

"The clock in my head," she told him. "It comes in handy."

"How about the map in your head?" he demanded. "How's that working?"

"Well, it tells me that if we can make it around the spoke before the heavies arrive, we can take a zip-line elevator to the cable car level."

"And if we can't?" John asked and skidded to a halt as half a dozen heavily armored figures raced out of the spoke they'd aimed for.

"Pods, Ivy!" he shouted as he raised a shield between them and the incoming fire.

"Back two spokes," she snapped and gasped when he snaked an arm around her back and turned them.

"Go!" he shouted. "I'm right behind you."

"Promise?" she called and jolted into a sprint.

"Promise!" he said, running hard on her heels with one hand extended to maintain the shield.

He almost fell over her when she stopped abruptly.

"Now what?" she asked and backed away as more heavies emerged from the spoke between them and the pods.

John slammed a second shield up.

"That's not going to—" Ivy began.

"Shhh. I'm thinking."

In fact, he didn't know what to do. He merely believed there had to be something—and as if belief had been enough to summon it, he heard a voice, familiar and strong.

"If you can dream it and believe it, you can make it," she told him and he raised his head.

"Trust me?" he yelled and offered her his hand.

Ivy looked up, met his eyes, and let his gaze hold her as time stood still.

"Forever," she told him and placed her hand in his.

John closed his hand around hers and bolted toward the figures advancing slowly towards them. She raced after him and followed him when he made a sudden swerve toward the outer wall and blasted it out of existence.

"Not again!" she screamed and fired one-handed behind them as he pulled her against his chest.

The sound was lost in the roar of air as they were sucked into space.

CHAPTER TWENTY-FIVE

This time, the team had a Dreth escort. No sooner had Avery and Johnny dropped out of the shuttle bay than they were cocooned by a swarm of Dreth fighters.

"Do these guys know how hard they are making it to fly?" Avery complained, and his teammate punched him.

"Do you know how many of them won't make it because they've surrounded us?"

"I don't want anyone to die for me," he griped, and Johnny punched him again.

"Get your head in the game and fly! They'll stay out of the way. They want us to get there, not fail."

He was right, and the swarm broke apart as the vessel closed. The crowded air space made it hard for the *Rise's* gunners to target the dropship, and when the fighters began to strafe the ship itself, the point was moot.

They went after the greatest threat that wasn't a dropship that didn't demand their attention.

"Those boys know how to fly," Avery commented.

"And they're crazier than you," Johnny told him as three

fighters blew a hole in the Regime ship's side. "I think they want us to land there."

His teammate grinned. "Well, it would be rude to refuse them after all the trouble they've gone to."

Todd stuck his head in through the cockpit door. "Guys, hangar bays— Never mind."

He ducked out and yelled, "Buckle in. This ride's getting bumpy."

Rawlins's voice came over the comms. "I'm gonna need a new shuttle, aren't I?"

"Um…sorry, ma'am?"

"Just come back in one piece. I don't want her upset."

And by her, she could only mean one person.

Their grins vanished. "Neither do we, ma'am."

The shuttle streaked through the gap, landed hard, and bounced through one of the internal walls. Klaxons sounded and men screamed as the section depressurized.

"Oops. Our bad," Avery muttered as he flung his harness off and rolled out of his seat.

Johnny was already through the cockpit door and following Todd off the shuttle. They glanced at the hole the Dreth had made.

"How long before that seals over?" Todd asked.

"If no one shoots it again? Ten minutes, maybe twenty?"

"We don't have that long," the Hooligan leader snapped and pivoted to find his second. "Ka! Find me a sealed compartment we can use to get into the rest of the ship."

He swirled his hand to draw the Marines around him and included the squad that had asked to accompany them from the *Tempestarii*.

Captains Sartre and Moser had sent them on the condition that they "behaved" and didn't "get underfoot"—and warned Todd against teaching them "bad habits." No one told the captains it was already too late and that the teaching had begun the minute they'd entered the pods.

"I got you a doorway," Ka told Todd. "We're gonna have to blow a hole in the floor and through a couple of waste lines to get to the deck we need, though."

"Are you saying you want to get us into the shit again, Corporal?" Reggie asked and paled as she gave him a saccharine-sweet smile.

"Want to, can, and will, Private First-Class. Thank you for volunteering to lead the way."

"But—"

Before he could say anything more, Piet clapped him on the shoulder. "Come on, son. You and me have work to do."

"But—" Reggie looked at Todd, caught the look on his face, and closed his mouth.

"Sergeant Willard." Todd called the other sergeant over. "This is how it'll go…"

The two sergeants talked as they walked, and their teams formed a protective perimeter around them. Not that they had any opposition. What had been in the section had either been sucked out through the hole in the hull as they came in or had made it past one of the bulkheads into another section.

Alarms blared a second time as Ka hacked past the door leading into one of the sealed rooms in the section. It looked like it had been a recreation area.

Angus and Darren rolled past her, followed by Henry and Dru. Half a dozen Navy men had holed up in the space. They died from a few well-placed rounds before they'd had a chance to do more than grab for their guns.

"Clear!" The confirmation floated over the comms as the last of the Marines reached the room and sealed the door behind them.

"In…and locked," another replied.

Ka and Piet paced the length of the room.

"Are you sure it's the best way?" she asked.

He shrugged. "You've made the calculations."

She pursed her lips. "I have."

"And this will take the ship off-line while they repair it," he wheedled.

The corporal still didn't look happy. "Yup."

She glanced at Todd, and he nodded.

"Do it."

The room repressurized as Piet laid out the explosives and checked the charge placement against the ship's schematics.

"Ready," he warned when they were done, and the teams took cover as he blew the floor.

The response was instantaneous. Lights went from white to amber. Those in the compartment below began to flash red. Shouts of alarm and disgust rose to meet them, and the Hooligans went to work.

Reggie dropped a grenade through the hole and the shouts turned to screams, which were quickly silenced as he dropped through the hole. He wrinkled his nose as he landed boot-deep in muck, but he didn't let that put him off his aim.

"Clear!" he called as Ka landed behind him.

"This way," she ordered and sent a map to their HUDs with the route marked in green. "This ship has Marines but they'll be new."

"Such a shame," Gary snarked as he joined them.

She turned and opened the door. "I have the surveillance feeds," she informed them. "We have company coming in from port and a few trying the stairwell in the north."

"Willard, keep our rear clear," Todd ordered and trotted toward the stairs. "Are we going up or down?" he asked over his shoulder.

"Neither," Ka replied and jogged beside him.

Dru and Gary skipped past. "So we don't need the stairs, then?"

"Nope."

The pair high-fived each other and reached for the grenades they carried.

"Bowling for busted!" Gary crowed, and Todd shook his head.

"This way, boss. The data center's on our right."

"I have Marines coming from our left," Reggie called.

"Enforcers to the right," Jimmy reported and Ka giggled.

"Enforcers to the right of us, and Marine boys to the left," Henry sang and was quickly joined by Dru and Gary. "Here I am."

Todd groaned. "This is all my fault."

"Yes, boss," Ka told him as they passed where Dru and Gary had waited out the explosions of their double delivery and fired on anyone foolish enough to still make the attempt.

A door opened ahead of them, and Ka and Todd fired in unison. Behind them, they heard Piet ask, "Boss needs you. Why don't I seal this so no one comes through?"

He made it sound almost reasonable, but Dru turned. "Are you saying we have other places we need to be?"

"Are you guarding my back?" Piet suggested mildly.

"Gotcha, Lance," Dru told him and let him close the door.

It didn't take him long to fuse the door frame to the door with a self-heating sealant.

"How long does that give us?" Ka asked as she and Todd turned into the data center. Their suit shields sparked from light fire and they eliminated the shooters hard and fast.

"It almost seems unfair," she mused.

"Except they're trying to destroy the data," Johnny pointed out, and she raced to the nearest console with a curse.

Johnny and Piet ran beside her.

"Boss, how are you at locked room puzzles?" she asked and plugged into the surveillance as she cracked open the first layer of security.

"Why?"

"Because we're gonna need an extraction from a locked room."

"You know it'll only remain locked for as long as it takes them to cut through," Willard mentioned, and she checked the feeds again.

"Good point." She nudged the engineer. "Piet?"

He left his console. "Seal 'em?"

"Tight!" she snapped and the keyboard rattled as she changed the room's access codes and locked the newly arrived Naval Enforcers out.

"Do you have my data yet?" Todd demanded.

"Do you have my ride home?"

"You keep up with that attitude and I'll leave you on the curb."

Ka waggled a data stick at him. "Almost. See? The stick is being plugged in."

He glowered at her but his attention was drawn by a glow coming from the far end of the room.

"Willard!"

"I'm a little busy, sarge."

Piet threw his hands up and hurried to Ka and Johnny. "There's no point in sealing a door they won't use," he told her, "and three will be better than two."

He retrieved his gear and settled at a different machine. Todd advanced toward the wall, aware of Angus and Henry moving beside him. Two of Willard's Marines came with them.

Together, they found cover behind the servers closest to the glow and waited. It wasn't like they could stop them from cutting through.

Angus pulled a sticky from one of his pouches. He exchanged glances with Henry, who did the same. Before Todd could say anything, the pair had scooted out from cover, darted forward, hurled the stickies at the wall, and retreated.

The explosion caught them halfway through, but it caught the Enforcers on the other side of the wall completely unawares.

Todd stepped out from behind the stack and began to fire over the corpses as he advanced past his fallen teammates while he laid cover down.

Willard's Marines took their cue, caught hold of Angus and Henry, and pulled them back into shelter before they moved beside the sergeant and pitched two grenades through the space.

Todd dove for cover as the first grenade exploded. The Marine who'd fallen prone ahead of him began to wheeze with laughter, and a second round of explosions followed.

"What did you—" Todd began and moved back so he could see for himself.

The hallway was a wall of flame as the ship's anti-fire system activated. He pressed up against the end of a stack.

"Sartre's gonna kill me," he muttered.

He scanned the area for any movement, speaking quietly as he did so.

"Steph? I need an exit plan."

After a minute, he groaned and rolled his eyes.

"Well, yes, we broke the shuttle."

The deck vibrated beneath his feet and he glanced at Ka.

"Are you done yet?"

"Almost."

"Johnny?"

The guard pocketed the data stick and grabbed his blaster. "Done."

"Piet?"

"Almost there, and they are gonna want to see this! The comm lines to Earth are down."

As he spoke, the intercom went live.

"All crew, all crew, all crew. Rear-Admiral Spokane has ordered a tactical withdrawal. Stand by for transition."

Piet glanced at Todd as he and Ka pulled their data sticks. "You got us an exit?"

"To me," he ordered, and the teams surrounded him.

Blue light formed a door from which it spread to engulf them.

"Let them go," Stephanie ordered as the closest Regime ships altered course away from the battle. "If they fire on us, destroy them."

The *Knight's* gun crews sent a flight of missiles into a destroyer as it turned.

"I said—"

"One of the guns twitched," the *Knight* replied. "Firing first seemed like a better plan."

She rolled her eyes but she didn't argue.

"Todd?" Rawlins asked as the *Earth's Rise's* engines increased power.

Stephanie lifted a hand over her head and clicked her fingers to open a portal in front of herself. A bubble swelled out of its center and burst, depositing Todd, the Hooligans, and a very stunned Marine team onto the deck.

"You owe Ebony a shuttle," she told Todd as he pushed to his feet and approached her.

He stooped for a kiss and sauntered toward the door.

"And take your toys with you!" she ordered as the Marines and Hooligans untangled themselves.

His smile faded as she sniffed the air. "Is that…"

The teams were on their feet and moving swiftly to the exit before she could finish.

"I'll clean it," Todd promised and palmed the exit panel.

The door didn't open.

"Ebony?"

"No one goes anywhere in those boots," the ship declared, "and I'd better be spotless in very short order."

He glanced at Rawlins, but the captain was studying her

boards and the *Knight's* guns were firing. One of the Regime ships had tried to take advantage of the retreat.

"Sergeant, I'll need any pilots you can spare for pick-up duty," Rawlins said and raised her head as emergency pods ejected from one of the Regime ships. "That was one of our boarding parties."

"They'll be in the hangar bay in ten," he informed her, palmed the door and caught the *Knight* off guard, and trotted into the corridor.

Given the captain's request, the ship didn't stop them. Some things were more important.

The incoming comms for one thing. Before the comms team knew it had arrived, Ebony had shunted it to the forward viewscreen.

"Admiral Jaleck!" Stephanie's exclamation carried into the hall, and Todd signaled the team to halt and turn. They arrived in the command center as Jaleck replied.

"Stephanie." The admiral smiled but her face turned somber. "I need to check on Dreth, but I also need to stay here. Can you…"

Stephanie nodded.

"I'll see to our planet and our people," she promised and placed her fist over her heart.

Behind her, Rawlins relayed the order. Jaleck's return salute was barely complete before the *Knight* vanished from the system.

Back on Earth, Remy had looped his arm around the Talent's waist to support her as she directed them out of the complex. Amaratne took rear guard and fired back down the corridor at anyone in pursuit.

The AI kept the way clear ahead of them and the Talent warned him of any Enforcers that they would encounter.

"That's some gift you have," he told her, and she managed a weak laugh.

"The Regime wouldn't think so."

Remy squeezed her gently. "They don't count anymore."

"There's a small entry point ahead," she told him. "It's not… well…" She sighed. "I'm not the only one who knows about it."

Amaratne moved closer behind them. "How many?"

"I sense a half-dozen," she replied, "and more are coming. They think you will be undefended when you walk through that door."

"They think wrong," Remy said firmly and released her as she unwound from his arm.

"Yes, they do," she declared and struck the door with a blast of power that forced it out of the frame and into the open space beyond. At the same time, a shimmer of blue outlined all three of them.

Without waiting for either Remy or the admiral, she ran forward and launched another pulse of power directly ahead. More men screamed as Amaratne and the android raced after her.

Remy's shield sparked and he snapped two shots to the right. The admiral fired left, then ahead, and eliminated the last standing Enforcer.

"I thought you said there was a half-dozen," Amaratne protested as Remy shot the Enforcers lying prone around them.

The Talent flinched but she didn't protest. She didn't give the man the response he was looking for, either.

"More are coming."

"Ted?" Amaratne asked.

"There is a car in the tunnel," Ted told him. "You can make it if you hurry."

"No, you can't," the Talent said, and her eyes glowed with yellow flame.

"We're still going to try," he replied and tried to take her arm despite the way her shield crackled.

She stepped out of his reach and the sound of a helicopter reached their ears.

"They called reinforcements in," Ted said through their comms. "You need to hurry."

"Come with us," Amaratne urged and the Talent turned.

Thinking she would follow, Remy sprinted to the fence and sliced through the support wire with no intention of welding it back. The admiral and the Talent raced after him, and the man was careful not to touch the power-wreathed woman.

Somewhere behind them, the helicopter touched down and shouts followed.

"They know we're here and which way we ran," she said and slowed as they reached the fence.

A second helicopter could be heard coming in after the first.

"You kicked a hornet's nest." Ted sounded both pleased and worried.

"And I have the fumigation they require," the Talent replied, stopped, and turned back.

"Wait!" Amaratne cried, and Remy started forward.

She began to run and outstripped them easily as she augmented her speed with magic. Remy ran with the admiral.

"You know she's trying to save us, right?" the man asked.

"But we're the ones who are supposed to be saving her," Remy argued, "not getting her killed!"

"I think she's doing that all by herself," Ted said.

"Well, not on my—"

Heat flared from round the corner of the building and seared their faces as they turned toward it. Men screamed and two very loud explosions followed by a myriad of smaller ones followed. The third helicopter was taken out of the sky.

"Well, that's all of them," Ted observed.

"But—" Amaratne protested and gasped for breath as he stumbled forward. "Where is she?"

Remy reached for him, but the admiral shrugged out from under his hand and continued toward the burning remains of the helicopters and the scorched earth surrounding them.

In the end, the Talent was easy to find.

She'd crumpled in the center of the last clear patch of ground before the burnt area began. He hurried to her side, shook her shoulder, and looked for a pulse.

The breath he took as he lifted her into his arms was a cross between a gasp and a sob. Remy cupped a hand under his elbow and helped him to his feet. He didn't try to take the admiral's burden.

"We have to go," he said. "She bought us time, but it won't take long for them to regroup."

"We'll bury her with honors," Amaratne declared and grief roughened his tone.

"We will," Remy agreed and steered him toward the fence and the forest beyond. "Do we know her name?"

CHAPTER TWENTY-SIX

The Regime transitioned into the Dreth home system expecting an undefended world. They were in for a rude surprise.

"I thought we'd drawn them off," Admiral Vance Easterly stated and stared at the array of ships.

"The rear admiral reported battle joined, sir," the comms chief told him. "I don't understand."

"More pirate tactics?" the scan chief suggested. "Don't leave the base unguarded while you're off raiding?"

"Pirate, Dreth, it doesn't matter," Easterly responded. "There are more of the monsters at home than we thought, but—"

You will not hurt my people! The voice roared through their heads and made them wince.

The rear admiral saw his command crew flinch almost in unison.

In the command centers of the Dreth home fleet, the voice echoed more gently, and the Dreth officers looked at each other in bewilderment.

"Well, someone loves us," Angreth's captain murmured and glanced at him.

His look of puzzlement turned to curiosity when he caught the look on Angreth's face. "Sir?"

The admiral's answer was to touch a button on his console and show brief scenes from all over the ship that revealed the older members of the crew behaving with undignified glee.

One of them raced to the camera, tore it off its mounting, and kissed it. He held the device in front of his face, brought it into focus, and made the picture bounce up and down as he danced in celebration.

"She came, sir!" he shouted. "She came!"

With a snap, crackle, and fizz, the picture went blank.

Angreth rested his head against his fist and sighed wearily. "Add another camera to the amount Varag of K'leth owes us."

The command crew stared at the jumble of screens. Shouts of jubilation came from gun crews and engineers alike. In the hangar bays, Dreth Marines had come to attention and saluted the owner of the voice like a warrior returned.

The scenes vanished as the scan team brought up a view of the empty space before them.

"Something's coming through," they warned, and Angreth rose from his seat and thumped his palm on the All-Fleet Broadcast button.

"Hold your fire! Our Witch has returned!" he roared and hoped it was enough.

He recognized the *Knight* as she appeared between his fleet and the Regime, and his spirits rose.

Across the battlefield, the Regime commanders gaped.

"What is that?" Rear Admiral Easterly demanded, and one of his older scan operators turned pale.

"It's the *Knight*," she whispered, but Stephanie's words over-rode her.

"Prepare to be destroyed," she stated coldly and her face filled their screens.

Regime crews gasped and drew back. Dreth crews cheered.

Her eyes burnt with dark fire, and her face was that of an avenging angel. The camera zoomed out and everyone saw the petite figure standing in the center of the *Knight's* command deck, her body wreathed in purple and blue flames shot through with black lightning and her silvered hair floating free of its traditional plait.

Her voice turned cold. "Telorans, to me! We'll take their Talents first."

On the Dreth ships, every Teloran mage froze, then came together in clusters of two or three as the Witch sent the locations of the Regime's shipboard Talents to their minds.

"What did she—" the Regime's rear admiral began but his question was cut short when the four Talents on his bridge screamed and fell.

Their handlers drew back in shock and the admiral rose from his seat to see what had happened. He drew back when he saw a stricken Talent, blood seeping from her eyes and nose as her body convulsed in the grip of dark lightning.

"Get us out of here!" he ordered. "Pull the fleet back! We need another strategy."

The command crew stared at him.

"Do it now!" he shouted and broke through their shock.

All around him, the fleet captains obeyed. On every deck, Talents died and they were powerless to help them. Maybe the distance of transition would save them.

None of them saw the celebration on Dreth as Angreth transferred the recordings of the encounter to a planet on the edge of despair. Screams echoed around the planet again, but this time, they were screams of joy.

Two words were repeated the planet over.

She's back!

Far above Earth, John fell—or rather, he flew with Ivy clutched to his chest as the Talent he'd wrapped around them protected them from the vacuum of space.

"Here they come!" she called, her hands wrapped around his forearm despite the Talent that held them together. She turned her head to look at him. "I don't know how they're finding us."

"Very good radar?" he suggested, took them into a twisting dive, and headed toward the distant glimmer of one of the satellites.

It was hard to stay on course and he pulled more eMU to keep them steady. His body ached from the fight, from the fall, and from drawing and channeling this much Talent in one long session.

"Are they shooting at us?" Ivy asked as orange and white flared under the fighter's stubby wings.

"Not for long," he told her and directed two shards of blue to intercept the incoming missiles.

"That is some serious overkill," she noted as the missiles detonated before reaching them.

"Hold onto your hat," he instructed, and she yelped as he accelerated and turned the stars to streaks as he fled toward the satellite's shelter.

"Well, this is one thing they won't blow up," Ivy observed, "which is not something I can say for ourselves!"

John chuckled. "So it won't matter if I do this, then."

He grunted as he pulled back from the satellite and used a blade-like piece of blue to shear one of its antennae arrays. Wrapping that in another shroud of blue, he hurled toward the jet, keeping the satellite behind them.

"That should foul its radar," he muttered as the piece spun into the fighter's path.

The explosion that followed was spectacular.

"Fireworks, John?" Ivy asked, and he chuckled.

"Everyone loves a fireworks show."

Drawing more Talent, he propelled them toward the orbital and the cable car nestled beside it.

"Do you think they'll notice?" she asked as he dropped them on top of the vehicle

"I hope not," he told her, using Talent to release the security locks on the maintenance hatch, "because I could do without company on the ride down."

"Only you and me, huh?" she asked and let him help her through the hatch.

He dropped down after her and magicked the hatch closed, locked it tightly, and pressed the control that told the car to descend.

"Wouldn't it be nice?" he asked, glanced toward the foyer, and breathed a sigh of relief to see it empty.

Ivy sidled closer, leaned against him, and wound her arm around his waist.

The cable car jolted a little and began the long journey planet-side. John snaked an arm around her and pulled her close before he turned her to face him.

"You can't blame a guy for wanting you all to himself," he said and lowered his lips to hers.

"Shut up," she told him, and the words came out muffled as their lips met and they lost themselves in the kiss.

The cable car trembled, and they parted and looked around in time to see the first of the satellites burning as it fell. A second one exploded and began to plummet.

"And the stars shall fall from the heavens," John murmured and was surprised when Ivy replied.

"And the powers that are in the heavens shall be shaken."

With an arm wound around each other's waist, they leaned closer to one another and watched the fireworks fall.

Not far from central Paris, in a run-down part of the city, stood a bar. Its paint was peeling and the shopfronts on either side had boarded-up windows and padlocked doors.

Across the road and past the empty shops, the Seine flowed sluggishly between its banks, a bridge shadowing a waste-water outlet built beneath its foundations. The bar still had its patrons, but they were few and far between and scattered between the tables, booths, and bar.

The numbers didn't match the traffic coming through, and those at the tables nursed their drinks and stared into the night with wary eyes.

Most of them were well past their prime. Some looked like they'd evaded the nurses at the local retirement village and all of them looked around before they wandered over to speak to the bartender.

Violetta watched them, her eyes set deep in a face creased by age and time. After a while, she sighed and set her glass down.

She pushed her seat back, got creakily to her feet, and wandered to the bartender. In all honesty, she'd had enough of staring at an empty street.

"A special," she said when the man glanced at her with inquiring eyes.

He sighed and the rag in his hand ceased its perpetual motion.

"I don't make that one no more," he told her, turned to the back of the bar, and reached into the storage cabinet.

He retrieved a bottle and stretched to the display rack and selected another. Violetta watched as he took a glass and mixed a new drink.

"Here's the new one." He set it down in front of her. "The Witch would like it."

Nodding, Violetta lifted the drink and took a cautious sip. She took a moment to savor it, then said, "I like this vintage. Do you know where I can find the mixings?"

The barkeeper gave her a tight smile.

"The boss wouldn't like it, but..." He leaned forward and lowered his voice. "Down that hall, stairs on the right, two flights. Two knocks, then one. Tell them Amaratne sent ya."

Violetta took her glass with her and headed down the hall. There was only one set of stairs and they led down. There was only one door too, right at the bottom.

She knocked twice, then once, and waited. Somewhere, someone had taken a look at her and probably noted the drink in her hand. It wasn't long before the door opened and she was able to walk through.

It shut immediately, but she didn't let that bother her. She was too busy taking in the gathering beyond. The sight of them made it hard to keep walking but she managed a few steps so she was clear of the entry.

There were easily twenty-five people in there. Looking around, Violetta realized she knew quite a few of the faces. One looked up, smiled, and raised a hand in welcome.

She smiled in return and moved into the room while she observed those present. There were some good people there.

Her gaze came to rest on two men seated in the corner farthest from the door.

"Well, I'll be damned!" she murmured and moved in their direction.

Amaratne looked up—a much younger Amaratne than she'd ever have expected. Violetta glanced at the man seated beside him. She hadn't known he had a friend who was into cowboy hats.

She stopped, nodded to the admiral, and smiled as he turned to his friend. She took another sip of the entry drink and studied the admiral as she did so.

"I guess I'll have to lose a little age if I want to play in this game!" She grunted a low chuckle, only to be interrupted by someone calling her name.

"Violetta!"

She turned and her eyes lit up at the sight of an old friend. "Jasper! You made it!"

Amaratne momentarily forgotten, she waved and headed toward him.

"It's been so long!"

CREATOR NOTES - MICHAEL ANDERLE

DECEMBER 26, 2020

Thank you for reading to the end of this book. We have reached the middle part of this series.

For those who have been waiting, Stephanie is back!

She's back, and she is a bit pissed off.

In every war, there are situations that are horrible, and then there are situations where terrible people make heinous decisions.

Stephanie needed to know (at the end of book 02) what John thought of the pain and suffering that would occur when she got back. Not that she would have stopped, but it helped to under stand the emotional reticence she might need to deal with upon her return.

For John, he is becoming the type of Apostle who is willing to play nice, but there is a message to be delivered, and it will be.

Return with us when book 04 Battle Tested as the fights explode on Earth and for Dreth.

When the beast doesn't get his way, that which remained hidden becomes needed. Perhaps a bit early.

Join me for a rollicking read!

Ad Aeternitatem,

Michael Anderle

* If you have not read the stories about Stephanie Morgana, join me for the first part of this story in *The Witch of the Federation,* out in ebook and Audiobook.

CONNECT WITH MICHAEL

Connect with Michael Anderle

Website: http://lmbpn.com

Email List: http://lmbpn.com/email/

Social Media:

https://www.facebook.com/LMBPNPublishing

https://twitter.com/MichaelAnderle

https://www.instagram.com/lmbpn_publishing/

https://www.bookbub.com/authors/michael-anderle